MW00527015

BETRAYAL
AT
BLACKTHORN PARK

ALSO BY JULIA KELLY

BETRAYAL
AT
BLACKTHORN PARK

An Evelyne Redfern Mystery

Julia Kelly

MINOTAUR BOOKS
NEW YORK

This is a work of fiction. All of the characters, organizations, and events portrayed in this novel are either products of the author's imagination or are used fictitiously.

First published in the United States by Minotaur Books, an imprint of St. Martin's Publishing Group

BETRAYAL AT BLACKTHORN PARK. Copyright © 2024 by Julia Kelly. All rights reserved. Printed in the United States of America. For information, address St. Martin's Publishing Group, 120 Broadway, New York, NY 10271.

www.minotaurbooks.com

Designed by Gabriel Guma

Library of Congress Cataloging-in-Publication Data

Names: Kelly, Julia, 1986– author.
Title: Betrayal at Blackthorn Park : a mystery / Julia Kelly.
Description: First Edition. I New York : Minotaur Books, 2024. I Series:
    Evelyne Redfern ; 2
Identifiers: LCCN 2024019598 I ISBN 9781250865519 (hardcover) I
    ISBN 9781250865533 (ebook)
Subjects: LCGFT: Detective and mystery fiction. I Romance fiction. I
    Novels.
Classification: LCC PS3611.E449245 B48 2024 I DDC 813/.6—dc23/
    eng/20240426
LC record available at https://lccn.loc.gov/2024019598

Our books may be purchased in bulk for promotional, educational, or business use. Please contact your local bookseller or the Macmillan Corporate and Premium Sales Department at 1-800-221-7945, extension 5442, or by email at MacmillanSpecialMarkets@macmillan.com.

First Edition: 2024

10 9 8 7 6 5 4 3 2 1

For Mum and Dad. Look at what all of those Thursday nights spent watching *Mystery!* on PBS led to!

Saturday
November 2, 1940

ONE

The cold autumn air hit me the moment I stepped off the bus just past seven o'clock in the morning, but that didn't matter.

After six weeks away, I was home.

I strode through the faint light of dawn, my case slapping against my thigh as I rounded the corner of Bina Gardens. The moment the black door of Mrs. Jenkins's boardinghouse came into view, I broke into a sprint, an involuntary grin spreading across my face.

At the door, I dropped my case, dug into my handbag, pulled out my key, and let myself in. As I crossed the threshold, I breathed in the reassuringly familiar scent of baking bread, laundry, and a dozen different perfumes. Setting my bags aside, I shucked off my camel coat and managed to find a home for it on the rack piled high with things that Mrs. Jenkins was constantly pleading with us to keep in our rooms. From somewhere up the polished wood staircase, I could hear the faint sounds of shuffling slippers and early-morning conversation as my fellow boarders queued up for the loo, negotiating who should have the next bath. From the direction of the kitchen at the back of the house, I could hear the clank of a metal pot being placed on the hob, no doubt Mrs. Jenkins beginning the monumental task of producing one of the fortifying breakfasts she managed to turn out each morning no matter what had recently gone on the ration.

After a long train journey from Yorkshire that had been delayed several times, I was ravenous, but food would have to wait. There was one person I wanted to see more than anyone else in the world.

I mounted the stairs, grateful that the new muscle I'd acquired during my time away let me move more swiftly than ever before. As I reached my floor's landing, I spotted Cynthia, a secretary who worked in one of the government buildings in Whitehall, emerging from the room across from mine.

"Good morning," my fellow boarder said, as though I hadn't been gone for weeks. Since joining the secretive world of the Special Investigations Unit, a shadowy operation that investigated leaks, rooted out moles, and generally kept an eye on all branches of our wartime government, I'd come to appreciate Cynthia's quiet discretion. Although we lived under the same roof, she never pressed me about my job. In exchange, I never asked what department she worked for or what that work entailed.

"Hello. Have you seen her this morning?" I asked, jerking my head in the direction of my door.

Cynthia shook her head. "She's been coming home late from rehearsals, so I wouldn't be surprised if she's still asleep. Shall I tell the others you're home?"

"Thank you." My stomach growled. "And would you let Mrs. Jenkins know I'll be needing breakfast?"

Cynthia nodded and began to make her way down the stairs.

I opened the door to my room and found it dark save for a spot where the blackout curtain had folded back on itself, letting in a weak stream of morning light that illuminated the angelic face of Moira Mangan, my roommate and best friend. From Moira's twin bed came a soft, ladylike snore that made me smile. If she had late rehearsals, I should let her sleep, but I had no idea what my first assignment as a new SIU agent might be or when it might come, and I wasn't going to squander the chance to catch up with her after so much time apart.

I switched on our room's overhead light and almost immediately a rather pathetic groan came from under the bedclothes on Moira's side.

"Turn off that horrid thing or I swear on everything I hold dear that I'll despise you forever," came Moira's muffled voice.

"Well, if that's the way you greet your best friend . . ."

The duvet flew back, and Moira shot out of bed. "Evie! You're here!"

I laughed. "I am."

"But you didn't say you were coming home."

"There wasn't enough time," I said honestly. "I didn't even know I'd be on a train until a few hours ago."

Since September, my life had been focused on one thing: transforming me from an ordinary young woman into a highly trained SIU agent. At the Special Operations Executive's "finishing school" at Beaulieu in Hampshire, I'd been schooled in surveillance, weapons training, hand-to-hand combat, parachute training, wireless radio operation, evasive action, explosives—all manner of nasty things to make sure that nasty people didn't do them to me first.

For the culmination of my training, I'd been shipped up to Yorkshire, where I had been expected to plan and execute an operation meant to simulate a field mission. I must have passed because as soon as I'd broken into a requisitioned house held by the army and stolen a file from a locked safe as instructed, I had been bundled onto a special train and shipped back to London to await instructions from my handler, Mrs. White.

"I was beginning to worry that you might never return," said Moira.

I tilted my head at the slight edge to her voice. "I said I would be back."

"But you didn't telephone. You didn't write. I know you warned me that I might not hear much from you, but I didn't expect six weeks of *nothing*."

I dropped onto my little bed, the mattress sagging under my weight. When Mr. Fletcher, the head of the SIU, recruited me to unknowingly work on my first mission—being his eyes and ears in Prime Minister Winston Churchill's cabinet war rooms—I had been required to sign the Official Secrets Act. The document compelled me to remain silent about everything related to my war work. That had been hard enough when I'd been shuttling between my room with Moira in Bina Gardens and my shifts as a typist in Churchill's secret underground bunker—even more so when I stumbled across the body of one of my fellow typists. However, I hadn't anticipated how strong the urge would be to pore over all my triumphs and frustrations at Beaulieu with Moira.

Still, I'd signed the document, and I took that promise seriously.

"I'm sorry, Moira. Please believe me that if I could have written or telephoned, I would have," I said.

"Why does training to be in a typing pool require six weeks of no contact with your best friend?" she pushed.

"You know I can't answer that."

I was well aware that my lie about having to go away for specialized training as a government typist was so thin Moira could see straight through it, but London was full of young women and men with vague jobs that one wasn't supposed to ask further questions about because we *all* knew that "careless talk costs lives" and all that.

"I know, I know," said Moira with a shake of her head. "It's just that I worried about you."

I swallowed. I wanted to reassure her, but she was right to worry. What I had been doing . . . well, let's just say that graduating training—or even surviving it—wasn't guaranteed.

"I'm sorry," I repeated.

Moira held my gaze for a moment longer but then slowly a little smile touched her lips. "Was it a long train journey back from your . . . typing pool training?"

"It shouldn't have been, but there were delays all along the line. I left just before midnight and only made it into London a half hour ago," I said.

"Oh, darling, you must be simply *exhausted*," said Moira.

"Mostly, I'm hungry. Hopefully Mrs. Jenkins won't mind an extra mouth to feed at breakfast."

"She'll be delighted. We all will. It hasn't been the same around here without you. Now come give me a hug," she said.

I popped up from my bed and crossed the room to let Moira pull me into a warm hug. Goodness, I'd missed my best friend's company—and the company of anyone who hadn't been learning the many varied ways there were to kill other people.

It felt wonderful to be just a little bit . . . normal again.

"I've missed you so much," said Moira, giving me an extra squeeze and accidentally hitting one of the bruises I'd sustained while sparring with a wiry but strong former professor from Durham during hand-to-hand-combat training. I winced, and immediately Moira asked, "What's the matter?"

"I bumped into a doorknob." The lie slipped off my tongue a little too easily for my own liking.

She raised a brow. "It must have been quite the rap."

"It was." At least that much was true.

Moira set me at arm's length and gave me a look-over. I worried for a moment that she might press me further, but instead, she asked, "Did they feed you wherever you've been? And what's happened to your hair?"

I touched the ends of my hair, which was a good four inches shorter than when I'd left London. "It's awful, isn't it?"

She shook her head. "Not awful. Just different."

I couldn't tell her that it had become so entangled with a bramble while on a nighttime escape-and-evasion drill that I'd been forced to saw a hunk of it off and had to ask a Geordie woman to even it out for me the next morning. That and the fact that I hadn't had the energy to pin-curl my hair while training meant that it was currently in its naturally wavy state, and I was beginning to look like one of the poodles my aunt Amelia had kept for a time in the early thirties.

"Well, I think the shorter length suits you. It brings out your cheekbones," she said loyally.

"Thank you, darling," I said. "Now, tell me what you've been up to. Cynthia said something about rehearsals?"

Moira stretched into a yawn. "Yes, I've been cast in a rather thin comedy of manners called *Whoever Could Say?* I doubt anyone will win any awards for it, but it's work. We open on Friday."

"If I can be there, I will be in the front row," I said.

Moira smiled. "Thank you, darling. It would mean so much to have you there."

"How is Jocelyn?" I asked. Cynthia's roommate had moved in across the hall from us when Moira had brought her into the boardinghouse ages ago, but recently I'd found myself growing closer to the model-turned-journalist since she'd helped me track down some vital information for solving my first case.

"She's on assignment. Her editor had the bright idea that she should embed with each of the women's auxiliary services, so she's been shipped off to a base in Osterley for a week with ATS trainees to learn the ways of the army," said Moira.

"I'm sorry I've missed her," I said.

"She'll be home soon," said Moira. "Now, tell me. Did you see the delicious Mr. Poole while you were away?"

I scoffed. Despite a rocky start, David Poole and I had managed well enough as partners on the cabinet war rooms case, catching the killer and uncovering a dangerous mole in the process, but our final meeting hadn't been all sunshine and roses.

"'Delicious'? David? That's going a bit far, isn't it?" I asked.

Moira arched a pencil-thin blond brow. "What would you prefer? Handsome? Dashing? Debonair?"

"Irritating is more like it. Did you know the man actually believes that those awful American pulp authors are superior to our British detective fiction writers?"

"Perish the thought," Moira teased.

"He has abominable taste in reading," I sniffed even though I knew I was being slightly ridiculous.

"You may protest as often as you like, but any red-blooded woman with a taste for tall, handsome men would tell you you're wrong about Mr. Poole," said Moira.

I shot her a look, but she ignored me and rolled over to pull a package wrapped in brown paper out of her bedside table.

"Well, speaking of reading material, I have something for you," she said, closing the drawer.

I took the parcel and tore open the paper, revealing a book inside. "*Death in the Stocks* by Georgette Heyer," I said, opening the cover to examine the title page. "I've been meaning to read her detective novels."

"I'd hoped as much. You'll never believe how long it took to search through all of your books to try to figure out whether you had any of hers."

"Thank you, Moira," I said, giving her another hug. "There is nothing like a new book to make everything right."

"Now," said Moira, "let's find you some breakfast while the queue for the bath dies down. Then we're going out because we have a very important morning ahead of us."

"Do we?" I asked.

She nodded. "We do indeed."

TWO

A very important morning, it turned out, centered around a trip to the hairdresser's.

"What have you done?" my regular hairdresser, Mrs. Partridge, asked with horror as soon as I sat down in her chair. "Cut it with the kitchen scissors?"

"Chewing gum," Moira called from the sinks behind me, saving me from fumbling for an explanation.

Mrs. Partridge clicked her tongue. "A nasty habit. Well, I will do my very best, but I don't know if I can save it, dear."

"Thank you, Mrs. Partridge," I said before allowing myself to be subjected to a shampoo, cut, and set all while having my nails varnished, my face moisturized, and my shoulders, arms, and hands massaged at Moira's insistence.

"In order to make you feel like your usual self," she explained, yelling over the sound of our dueling hood dryers.

When Mrs. Partridge finally turned me around to reveal my set-and-brushed curls, I did, in fact, feel like an entirely new woman. Thanks to my hairdresser's ministrations, my dark hair now gracefully kissed my shoulders. My skin glowed from the treatments. My cheeks, thinned out from weeks of exercise that left me and my fellow trainees ravenous at all hours of the day, were hollower than I would have liked, but the makeup girl had done a good job of trying to round them out with rouge.

While I pulled on my coat, Moira paid what was likely an eye-watering bill with a flip of her hand and a simple "I will not think of you paying a shilling for any of it." Once everything was settled, we stepped out into the clear midday sun.

"Do you fancy a bite to eat?" asked Moira.

I was just about to answer an emphatic yes when a boy who couldn't have been more than ten ran up to me and asked, "Are you Miss Redfern?"

"That depends on who is asking," I said.

He stuck his hand in the pocket of his trousers, producing the sort of small envelope ladies use to send short notes. "This is for you."

"What on earth . . . ?" Moira muttered next to me as the boy ran off again.

I tore open the envelope and pulled out a single sheet of writing paper.

You are needed. Report to HQ at 14:00. Do not be late.

—E. White

I looked up and scanned the road for a sign of Mrs. White. I saw nothing.

"What is it?" asked Moira.

"Work," I said, stuffing my handler's note back into its envelope before Moira could see anything.

"Work? But how would they know where to find you?" she asked.

I suspected that Mrs. White had ways of finding anyone she wanted to in short order, but instead of explaining, I looped my hand into the crook of Moira's elbow and nudged her with my shoulder. "Come along. Lunch is my treat."

Moira started to protest but then snapped her mouth shut and let me lead her away.

M oira and I made the most of our early lunch at a little café, gossiping about what had happened with our fellow boarders while I was gone. She told me more about her play—"It's set twenty years ago. I'm meant to be a debutante who really wants to be a flapper. The part isn't very good, but at least it's a bit more interesting than those Ministry of Information films my agent has been sending me on recently"—and I told her about all of the things I was looking forward to doing now that I was back in London. However, throughout all of it I couldn't shake my curiosity over Mrs. White's note.

I was needed, but for what? Rooting out another mole in an intelligence unit in London? Taking down a bribery ring at a base in Scotland? Or perhaps Mrs. White would see fit to make use of my native French and parachute me into occupied France so that I could help set up communications with local resistance groups.

A mix of fear and excitement filled me at the prospect of that last possibility, and I crossed my fingers, hoping that was where I would be sent.

Finally, Moira and I made our way back to Mrs. Jenkins's, where I changed into my burgundy suit, white shirt, and best shoes. On top of it all went my camel coat and a navy beret. I added the gold watch and pearl earrings I'd inherited when *Maman* died. Picking up my good black handbag and gas mask case, I wished Moira the best for that evening's rehearsal and then let myself out of the boardinghouse feeling more like myself than I had in weeks.

What people had taken to calling the Blitz had started back in September, but even though it was now November, the Luftwaffe still seemed intent on blowing London to bits. The bombing had destroyed entire roads, making bus service patchy at best, so I walked.

It was sobering crossing the city and seeing all of the destruction that had happened while I'd been away. A road could be untouched until, suddenly, I came across a pile of rubble where a house or a block of flats had once stood. On some roads, there wasn't a pane of glass in any of the shopfront windows, while others were streaked black and charred by the fires from incendiary bombs.

The farther I walked, the more determined I became to do whatever I could to end the horrible war.

A little more than an hour after leaving home, I followed the curve of Langham Street and spotted the corner of Gosfield Street. And standing on that corner was David Poole.

I pulled my shoulders back as I approached my erstwhile partner. "Hello, David."

"Evelyne." He nodded. "How was your time at finishing school?"

"Very instructive," I said, holding back a little after our last encounter.

"I'm glad to hear you enjoyed your stay at the 'Stately 'Omes of England.'"

I didn't smile at the play on the Special Operations Executive's nickname. Firstly, the secret organization charged with all things espionage, sabotage, and reconnaissance had so many—the SOE, Baker Street, the Ministry of Ungentlemanly Warfare—it could be difficult to keep track of them all, and secondly, to know of the Special Operations Executive was to never speak of the Special Operations Executive.

"I take it that you've been called in as well," I said.

He nodded. "How did your message come?"

"Delivered by a boy outside of my hairdresser's. It was almost like something out of a Dickens novel."

He huffed a small laugh at that. "Mrs. White has always had a flair for the dramatic."

Or the formidable handler wanted to make sure we understood that she could find her agents at any time.

"What about you?" I asked.

"Folded up in my morning newspaper," he said. "I was a little disappointed. I thought it lacked her usual creativity."

"Usual creativity?"

"I once had a message dropped into my lap at the cinema. The messenger hooked it onto a fishing line and cast it over the balcony during the newsreel," said David. "I missed the film because I found myself shipped off to the Highlands. I think it was all Mrs. White's idea of a little joke."

"I can't imagine Mrs. White ever having a sense of humor," I said.

"You would be surprised."

I turned to face the modest headquarters of the Special Investigations Unit at 54 Gosfield Street. I had been to this building three times before. The first time, curiosity and the offer of a potential job from Mr. Fletcher, a long-ago friend of my parents', had carried me to its unassuming front door. I had been naïve, eager, and utterly unprepared for what was about to happen to me. I returned the last time a changed woman, weighed down with the responsibility of giving her first briefing after catching a killer. Now I was a fully trained SIU agent.

I inhaled deeply. "Shall we?"

David leaned heavily on the bell for number 4 and a mercifully short moment later, Miss Summers, Mr. Fletcher's always efficient secretary, opened the front door to us with a smile. "Good afternoon, Miss Redfern. Mr. Poole."

"Good afternoon, Miss Summers," I said. "I hope you're well?"

"Very well, thank you," she said. "If you'll please follow me. They're expecting you."

We followed her up the creaking stairs, past her tidy desk with its in and out trays bracketing a typewriter, and through the heavy white painted door to Mr. Fletcher's office.

"Miss Redfern," said the head of the SIU, standing up from behind his desk to greet me. "Or should I say Ensign Redfern?"

It was so strange hearing Mr. Fletcher, whom I'd first met at a party in my parents' Parisian home all those years ago, call me by my newly acquired rank that I almost laughed.

"Don't expect us to use your rank, Miss Redfern," said willowy Mrs. White from her perch in an armchair before the coal fire, bringing me back down to earth. "We don't go in for that much in the SIU."

"Still, we should celebrate these things," said Mr. Fletcher with an avuncular smile. "We heard excellent reports from your exploits in both Hampshire and Yorkshire. Isn't that right, Mrs. White?"

Mrs. White sniffed and rearranged the file folders on her lap.

"Thank you, Mr. Fletcher," I said.

"And Mr. Poole," said Mr. Fletcher, turning to David. "You're looking well after your own retreat."

I glanced at my once-partner, wishing I could ask what he had been up to when I was crossing rough country in the dark of night on moonless reconnaissance training operations.

"Thank you, sir," said David.

"Please sit, please sit," said Mr. Fletcher, gesturing to the empty sofa as he joined Mrs. White in the pair of armchairs across from it.

David and I retreated to opposite ends of the sofa, a gulf of cushion separating us. I started to spread my hands over my skirt to smooth it before I realized that the gesture might be mistaken for nerves and deliberately folded my hands in my lap.

"Right, I'm afraid that's all the time we have for niceties," our boss continued, adjusting his rimless spectacles. "We have an assignment that we believe is uniquely suited to take advantage of both of your recent training efforts. Mrs. White, if you will?"

Mrs. White handed first David then me a file each. "We've had a request from the Special Operations Executive fellows at their Baker Street HQ to investigate some goings-on at an estate called Blackthorn Park located just outside the village of Benstead in Sussex. The house was requisitioned by the SOE for use as a research and development facility run by an engineer called Sir Nigel Balram. He had a reputation as being a genius inventor before the war, and Baker Street managed to persuade him to work for them.

"The facility has been operational for just over a year, and it now faces additional scrutiny because of Sir Nigel's ambitions to expand its remit into the production of his inventions as well as their development. Very recently one of the barns on the estate was converted into a manufacturing facility, which shows Baker Street's commitment to Sir Nigel's work."

"A manufacturing facility meant to produce what?" asked David with a frown.

"Clandestine weapons," said Mrs. White.

"What makes them clandestine?" asked David.

"They're small, disguised, or generally very difficult to detect— much more so than anything the army or Royal Navy are currently using—which makes them uniquely suited for use in the field, often for acts of sabotage." I realized everyone was staring at me, so I added, "We had an instructor at Beaulieu who took great delight in intriguing, wicked-looking objects of destruction. I think he would have happily taught nothing but explosives for the full six weeks if he'd been allowed."

"It sounds as though my training is out-of-date already," said David, hitching an ankle over his knee.

"Something I'm certain Mrs. White will remedy between future missions," said Mr. Fletcher. "A great deal has changed since our organization was founded. War necessitates both evolution and invention."

"If I may," said Mrs. White, pulling our attention back to the matter at hand. "Recently Baker Street received word from an anonymous source that some things have gone missing from Blackthorn Park."

"What sorts of things?" I asked.

Mrs. White slipped on a pair of horn-rimmed reading glasses and opened the remaining file on her lap. "It looks like metals mostly. Some wire and chemicals too. Baker Street is worried they might have a thief on their hands. Probably someone looking to sell materials restricted for war use on the black market.

"Apparently security measures have already been tightened at the site, but the higher-ups at Baker Street are concerned that this may not have been enough, especially if the thief is a member of the Blackthorn staff. However, they can't figure out how it's being done.

"Miss Redfern." Mrs. White peered over the rim of her glasses at me, looking for all the world like a harmless village librarian and not the ruthless spymaster I knew her to be. "You will travel to Benstead with an eye to covertly infiltrating the house and buildings on the estate at Blackthorn Park. You are to attempt to gain access to areas where supplies might be stored. You will then file a security assessment, highlighting what improvements may continue to be made as well as your assessment of how someone might be ferrying equipment off the estate—if that is indeed what is happening."

I waited, expecting her to continue. When she simply stared at me, unspeaking, I asked, "Is that the entire mission?"

Mrs. White's lips thinned. "Yes."

"You don't want me to interview staff or try to figure out who the thief is if Blackthorn Park does in fact have one?" I asked.

"Baker Street believes that it would be best if this was handled internally for the time being," said Mrs. White.

"Why?" David asked, and I felt more grateful than I probably should have that he'd decided to join the conversation.

"Because of the sensitive nature of the work being done there," said Mrs. White. "There are concerns that, if an outsider begins poking around, it may be too much of a distraction."

The excuse felt weak, and I couldn't understand why she was so reluctant to let me engage unless she didn't trust me.

"Mrs. White," I started, "with all due respect, I've been fully trained as an agent. I'm ready to take on real fieldwork."

"This is 'real' fieldwork, Miss Redfern," she said.

"It's just, I thought after solving a murder—"

"Don't think that because you caught one murderer, you know what you are doing," Mrs. White cut across me.

It was actually one murderer who had also turned out to be selling secrets to the Germans, but I recognized that this probably wasn't the best time to correct my handler.

"Working as an agent is very different than training to become one," said Mr. Fletcher gently. "This is an ideal first assignment for you."

I wanted to sit back and cross my arms like an upset child, but I had too much dignity for that. Instead, I shot David a look. "Then I suppose Mr. Poole and I should begin to make arrangements to travel to Blackthorn Park."

"Mr. Poole will not be going with you," said Mrs. White.

"I'm not?" he asked at the same time I asked, "He isn't?"

"Mr. Poole has recently undergone training to become a handler of field agents," Mr. Fletcher explained.

Mrs. White turned her attention to David. "You will remain in London where you will run Miss Redfern. A simple operation like this should be a good test of how suited you are to the role."

"Madam," he said, "I have been an agent since before the war. I have worked on multiple complex cases. Surely I should be the one who attempts to breach Blackthorn's security protocols or at the very least shows Evelyne how a real mission is meant to run."

I raised a brow as I watched him try to prize my first official

assignment from me. "Isn't that why I've just spent six weeks in training just like all of our agents?"

"It is," said Mr. Fletcher, his expression neutral as he watched
David and me.

"Mr. Poole," said Mrs. White, her tone warning, "I should not have
to remind you again that you were sent on a training course for a
reason and, just like Miss Redfern, it is imperative that you put those
newly learned skills to use."

"But shouldn't I go with her?" he asked.

"The village of Benstead is too small to reasonably provide you
both with cover stories about what you are doing there," said Mrs.
White. "It was difficult enough securing one for Miss Redfern."

"What is my story?" I asked.

"You are visiting your cousin, a Mrs. Smythe, while waiting to be
called up to one of the women's auxiliary services. You will stay with
her at her home, Russet Cottage. One of the maids from Blackthorn
Park is boarding there, and she may prove to have useful information."

So I would have the chance to interview a member of staff after
all, even if it was part of a cover story.

"You are to speak to the maid *only* to ascertain the working pat-
terns of Blackthorn Park so that you may assess what times of day the
site might be most vulnerable," said Mrs. White as though reading my
thoughts.

"Yes, Madam," I said reluctantly.

"Now, you have your assignment. Complete it and file your report.
Then I will consider putting you two on a mission you deem more
worthy of your skills," Mrs. White finished.

Although I thought the sarcasm with which she delivered that last
sentence was uncalled for, what else could I do but take my orders
and go?

I made to stand when Mr. Fletcher cleared his throat.

"There is one additional small matter that you should both be
made aware of," he said, casually crossing his hands on his knees as
though we were chatting at a cocktail party rather than in the office
of the head of a secret branch of government. "The prime minister

has put a great deal of faith in what he is calling 'ungentlemanly warfare.' That sometimes means backing Baker Street and facilities like Blackthorn Park against that advice of some of his generals and ministers.

"As a show of support, he will be traveling there this Thursday for a series of demonstrations of Blackthorn Park's latest designs. I will be one of those accompanying him along with several Baker Street higher-ups. At the moment, manufacturing on the site is dedicated to producing prototypes and test weapons. However, the engineers there have struck on something called a barnacle bomb, which shows a great deal of promise.

"The barnacle bomb is currently being tested at training grounds and even as part of a field mission. Mr. Churchill is eager to see the device and other inventions demonstrated in person and, if it goes well, I believe he will immediately order the barnacle bomb into wider production for all SOE field operatives. Every single agent could be sent on missions with one of these devices on their person. It could help us win the war of sabotage."

"This interest from Mr. Churchill wouldn't be the reason that Baker Street would like the potential theft to be dealt with quickly and quietly, would it?" I asked.

Mr. Fletcher rewarded me with a broad smile. "Very astute, Miss Redfern. There are some who are concerned that the more people involved with rooting out the thief, the higher chance that word of his existence could make its way to Mr. Churchill. It is imperative that this matter be resolved discreetly and before his visit."

"As you can see, Miss Redfern, every mission is important for its own reason," said Mrs. White in that superior way of hers.

I gave a somewhat begrudging nod.

"Miss Summers has blueprints of the house and other materials for both of you. You will have tomorrow to study them and formulate a plan. Miss Redfern will then travel to Benstead on the 8:11 train out of Waterloo on Monday morning. We expect a full report by Tuesday evening," said Mrs. White.

One night. My first mission would be one night long. At least, I reasoned, Moira would be happy to have me back so quickly.

"That doesn't give Evelyne much time to prepare," said David, already stepping into his role as handler.

"No one ever claimed that what we do is easy, Mr. Poole," said Mrs. White.

"Good luck to you both. We look forward to hearing from you Tuesday evening," said Mr. Fletcher as David and I both rose to our feet.

———

As soon as we'd collected the blueprints of Blackthorn Park, a dossier on the facility, and my train ticket from Miss Summers, I made for the stairs. I was already on the landing when David stopped me with a light touch on the elbow.

"Are you all right?" he asked in a low voice.

"Why wouldn't I be all right?" I asked.

"I can imagine you probably wanted something a bit more exciting as your first mission."

Even though that was precisely what I had been thinking in our briefing, I held my hand up to stop him. "I am willing to do whatever it takes to prove that I can do this job to you and," I nodded in the direction of Mr. Fletcher's office, "to them."

"You don't have to prove yourself to me," he said.

"Don't I though?" I asked. "Or did I just imagine that you tried to take my first mission away from me?"

"Take it away? Are you angry because I said I should go with you?" he asked.

"I can do this on my own, David. I do not need you there holding my hand."

"I never said that," he said.

"No?" I asked, my annoyance bubbling up. "And what about the last time we met with Mrs. White and Mr. Fletcher?"

"What do you mean?" he asked.

"You told them you didn't think I was suited to become an agent because of my tendency to go—what did you tell Mr. Fletcher exactly? Oh yes. 'Haring off with an alarming disregard for my own personal safety'?"

To his credit, rather than argue with me, he dipped his head. "I apologize."

"Oh," I said, some of my bluster deflating. "I didn't think that you would apologize."

"I know when I've done something wrong, and I am more than capable of showing contrition. I never meant to imply that you wouldn't make an excellent agent."

"You called me a novice," I said, clinging to my resentment a little longer. After all, I'd had six weeks to stew on it.

"You *were* a novice. Now you've been trained. However, I shouldn't have cast doubt on your potential abilities."

My expression must have remained skeptical because he sighed and added, "Please understand, my reservations weren't about you per se."

"Then what were they about?" I asked.

"Your life."

"My life?"

He shook his head. "You have one. I know because I've seen it. You have friends who love you. You go out dancing. You're personable. You live in a boardinghouse, for goodness' sake."

"Just because I go dancing and live in a boardinghouse does not mean—"

"An agent's life is lonely, Evelyne. It has to be. You have to keep secrets. Constantly. You have to lie to the people you love most and push away the thought of how hurt they'd be if they ever found out about your double life."

My stomach twisted as I recalled the disappointment in Moira's voice when she told me she'd expected to hear from me during my time away. I couldn't help but feel that I had failed her as a friend, and my worry only deepened when I thought about what would happen if she ever found out I was an SIU agent. Would she be capable of forgiving me for keeping something so important from her?

"I thought Mr. Fletcher should be honest with you about what this life is like before you agreed to join up. It's isolating and dangerous, and all of us live with a crushing sense of responsibility because if we make one mistake, people could die. However, before I could say anything, you'd made your choice."

"David, you have to understand, solving that murder was the first time I've ever felt as though something I was doing actually *mattered*." I couldn't give that up.

He inhaled sharply and then exhaled slowly. "I know exactly what you mean."

"You do?" I asked, surprised.

"I do. Now, let's finish your first mission, and then maybe Fletcher and White will put us on something a bit more diverting.

"Study those," he said with a nod to the file Mrs. White had given me and Miss Summers's plans, refocusing us on the job at hand. "Tomorrow we'll meet and go over plans."

"On a Sunday?" I asked, doing my best to give him a wry smile. "Whatever would the archbishop of Canterbury say?"

"I'd expect he'd tell us that war calls for extraordinary sacrifices, including working on the Lord's Day," he said. "I'll ring you tonight and let you know a time and a place."

"Right. I suppose I'll see you then."

I started down the stairs again when he called out, "Evelyne?"

I glanced back up at him.

"You have every right to be annoyed with me for expressing my hesitation with Mrs. White and Mr. Fletcher, but I also seem to recall telling them that you'd be an asset to this department," he said. "If that counts for anything."

I opened my mouth to protest but then shut it again because, in fact, it did matter. He was asking me to trust him, just as I wanted him to trust me. We hardly knew one another, thrown together as we had been on our first case, but some baser instinct had told me that he was a man I could rely upon to catch a murderer and a mole. Now that he was my handler and I was his field agent, that trust was even more vital than ever.

"You told Mrs. White and Mr. Fletcher that we worked together perfectly well on our first case," he continued. "Give me the chance to prove to you that I believe you were right."

I gave him a nod and retreated down the stairs to the road, hoping very much that he would be a man of his word.

Monday
November 4, 1940

THREE DAYS UNTIL CHURCHILL'S VISIT

THREE

D espite the seemingly ever-present wail of the air-raid siren, I managed some sleep Sunday evening and awoke early Monday morning fresh and ready for my trip to Benstead.

I had spent the previous day with David, returning to Gosfield Street and the SIU HQ to pore over blueprints of Blackthorn Park. When we finally identified all of the suspected points of vulnerability and David was satisfied that I had memorized the floor plan of the manor house, he released me to pack a suitcase that would be a useful part of my cover story of staying with a cousin while I waited to be called up to serve.

Moira had found me picking up the copy of *The Unpleasantness at the Bellona Club*—Lord Peter Wimsey is always a source of comfort—having just finished my packing.

"You're going away again?" she asked, her gaze landing on the smaller of my two pieces of luggage standing at the foot of my bed.

"I'm afraid so."

There was a pause before she asked with a sigh, "How long will you be gone?"

"Only a night. I'll be back in time for your opening," I said, even though a little part of me knew that it was foolish to promise such a thing. "I'll take you to supper. Wherever you like."

She gave me a little smile. "You don't have to do that."

Oh, but I did. I had to do something to make up for all of my absences and evasions.

"Good luck with whatever it is," said Moira.

"Thank you," I said.

Now, standing under the hanging clock in the middle of Waterloo Station on Monday morning with the acrid mixture of smoke and steam from the trains wrapping itself around me, I hoped very much that I wouldn't have any need for luck at Blackthorn Park.

I'd dressed carefully that morning, pulling on an unassuming navy suit and a white shirt. My camel coat was pulled tightly around me and my usual black handbag hung from my left hand. At my ears I wore *Maman*'s earrings and at my wrist her watch. I knew I would have to take the jewelry off when I donned the black jumper and trousers that would make it easier to sneak around Blackthorn Park undetected, but I couldn't leave the things behind. They were all I had left of my beloved late mother, and I'd come to think of them as talismans.

I scanned for David in the growing number of people hurrying through the station, spotting the crown of his usual gray hat weaving through the crowd from the direction of the Waterloo Road entrance.

"Good morning," I said as he joined me under the station clock.

"Are you ready?" he asked.

"As I'll ever be." It wasn't that I was nervous exactly, but I was beginning to feel the weight of my first assignment pressing down on me. I wanted to do well, to prove that I had what it took to be an agent, not because Mr. Fletcher had remembered me as the daughter of old friends from Paris, but because I had the intelligence and resourcefulness this job required.

"You'll be fine," said David.

I took a deep breath. "Thank you."

"Tell me what you'll do when you arrive," he said.

"Leave the station and go to Russet Cottage," I said, reciting the plan we'd come up with. "I'll drop my bag and then go for a walk to stretch my legs, which will conveniently take me along the perimeter of the Blackthorn Park grounds, past the gatehouse, and by the estate's access road."

He nodded and held out a slip of paper he'd produced from his pocket. "When you are ready to report this evening, ring this exchange from the telephone booth on the village high street between seven and quarter past seven and then hang up. I will ring you back straight away from a secured line."

I took the piece of paper, which had "Dreadnought 1804" written on it in pencil. "Isn't that an Earl's Court exchange?"

David merely grunted.

"Shouldn't I use the telephone at Russet Cottage rather than the one on the village high street?" I asked.

He shook his head. "A Blackthorn maid is a lodger in the house, remember? The telephone booth is safer. If something happens and you need to reach me outside of the usual quarter hour window, ring that exchange and tell whoever answers, 'The apple crumble has gone cold.'"

"'The apple crumble has gone cold'?" I repeated skeptically. "Really?"

"Just promise me that you'll remember it."

I held my hands up. "I will."

There was a pause, and I began to fiddle with the handle of my handbag.

"Don't be nervous," said David.

"I'm not."

He pointed to the spot between his brows. "A line appears right here when you worry about something."

I folded my hands to keep from scrubbing at my forehead and made a mental note to redouble my efforts with my cold cream when I returned from my mission.

David stepped forward and placed a hand on my elbow. "Do the day surveillance and then the night mission just as we discussed and you'll be back in London by lunch tomorrow to write up your report. Then we can move on to a proper assignment."

A whistle reverberated through the railway station, and I stepped back. "I should find my platform."

"Right," said David, letting his hand fall to his side. "I'll speak to you tonight."

I picked up my case and set my shoulders. Nerves jittered in my stomach as I walked away from him, but I forced myself to breathe and, with every step, I shed Evelyne Redfern, the SIU agent, and pulled on the guise of Evelyne Redfern, young woman off on a jolly to see her cousin in rural Sussex.

———

Traveling to Benstead, it turned out, was not quite as simple as I had anticipated. I boarded the train only to find that it would be delayed to give priority to several trains carrying troops. Once we were finally underway, we seemed to linger at every station between London and Sussex before grinding to a halt for no apparent reason on a bit of track surrounded by nothing but fields in either direction. We sat there, unmoving, for nearly an hour.

At least Miss Summers had booked me a first-class ticket. For much of the journey, I had a compartment to myself, and I contented myself by finishing *The Unpleasantness at the Bellona Club* and then moving on to *Death in the Stocks*. I read with the books open on the seat next to me so I could also work on the burgundy jumper I was knitting up using the yarn from an old skirt I'd unpicked before leaving for training at Beaulieu.

I sat like this, very content, until two men entered my carriage around Woking and an elderly woman joined us from the next station down the line. Then I packed my knitting away to make space and contented myself with just my book for the rest of my trip.

When the train finally pulled into Benstead Station, I stood to retrieve my case from the luggage rack, remembering just in time that most people would assume a young woman would struggle under the weight of a packed bag, even if my newly honed muscles courtesy of my training meant my arm hardly protested as I walked.

On the platform, I set my case down and made a show of shaking out my hand while looking about me. The station was small, as fitted a rural stop, with a single platform on either side of the tracks. However, there was a ticket hall to my right to greet passengers from London. As I studied the building, a stationmaster emerged, distinctive in his navy coat with shining brass buttons. He took one look at me, crossed his hands behind his back, and strode over.

"Good afternoon, Miss. Are you in need of assistance?" he asked in a gruff tone.

"Oh, thank you," I said, hoping I sounded remotely innocent and a little bit lost. "I'm meant to be going to Russet Cottage. Would you happen to know the way?"

"Why are you wanting the Smythes?" he said, rocking back on his heels as he seemed to assess me.

A little taken aback by the direct nature of his question, I stammered, "I—I'm visiting. Mrs. Smythe is my cousin."

"I see," he said, relaxing a little. "You'll forgive me for asking, but I keep an eye on all of the comings and goings here. Captain Christopher Sherman of the Benstead Home Guard at your service." He gave a little half bow. "An old wound from the last war kept me from joining up with the army again, but there's important work to be done here too."

I suspected that a man who appeared to be approaching sixty was too old to be called up by the army whether he carried an old war wound or not, but I would never say anything to diffuse his enthusiasm.

"I'm certain the people of Benstead feel much better knowing that you and your men are looking out for them, Captain," I said.

He nodded in a rather self-serious manner. "Now, you'll want to turn right out of the station and follow the village road. When you see the sign for Brook Road, make a right again. You'll see Russet Cottage soon enough."

"Thank you," I said, picking up my case again.

I dutifully made my way to the entrance before turning back to give him a little wave.

FOUR

With the help of Captain Sherman's directions, I found Brook Road. Russet Cottage proved to be a sweet little timber-framed house with the skeleton of a climbing rose reaching up the front of it and a hand-carved wooden sign bearing the house's name next to the front door. I knocked using the large iron knocker, and a moment later a small woman who looked to be in her late thirties, dressed in a blush calico dress with a dusty rose cardigan, opened the front door with a smile.

"Cousin Evelyne," she said.

"Cousin Caroline," I said, remembering her Christian name from my briefing folder.

She stepped back. "Come in, come in. You must tell me how your family is."

I bit my lip and imagined myself saying, *Well, Cousin Caroline. Where do I even start? Maman, whom I loved more than anything in the world, died of what a Parisian detective called a careless accidental overdose of laudanum in the hotel suite we shared after my father tried to fight her tooth and nail for custody of me in the French courts because he knew that being separated from me was the one thing that would hurt her most. As far as I can tell, my father, famous adventurer and somehow a knight of the realm, is still the same bounder who dumped me in a boarding school and whom I haven't seen since I was eighteen. Aunt Amelia, his sister and the only remaining member of my family, seems to tolerate me as well as she tolerates anyone—which is to say barely and only when it suits her.*

Of course there's always my best friend Moira, whom I'm currently lying to by omission, and David, my partner, who sometimes feels utterly unreadable to me, but he's a man, so perhaps that should be expected.

Instead, I settled for "Thank you for inviting me to stay."

I thought I caught a twinkle in her pale blue eyes as she closed the door behind us. "Oh, it's our pleasure." She held up a finger and lowered her voice. "We've had all sorts stay with us since the war started. The kind who work up at the big house. None of them talk about what they do, of course, but you can always tell when those professorial types turn up.

"I shan't say more than that. Mr. Smythe and I are relied upon for our discretion, and we have a lodger with us."

"A maid who works at Blackthorn Park," I said.

"That's right. Miss Daniels is a sweet girl, but she gossips like a fishwife. I doubt she'll last, but it's difficult to find good help in the country, isn't it?" asked Mrs. Smythe.

I almost laughed at the platitude so many country ladies bemoaned before the war when their greatest concern had been whether they would ever have both a cook and a maid on staff at the same time. However, I realized from her earnest expression that Mrs. Smythe, despite living in a modest cottage, really meant it.

Fortunately, a short man with perfectly combed dark blond hair stuck his head out of the door to what I assume was the front room and saved me from any response.

"Hello," he chirped. "I'm Mr. Smythe. Or rather Carl, if we have company listening. Why don't I help you with that?"

He reached a hand for my case, which I allowed him to take.

"If you'll just follow Mr. Smythe," said his wife.

Rather than climbing the stairs as I might have expected, we shuffled down the corridor leading to the back of the cottage in a single file.

"Your sister mentioned that you can have trouble sleeping some-times and that it was best to put you somewhere quiet and rather private," said Mrs. Smythe as we entered the kitchen.

Assuming that my "sister" was meant to be Miss Summers, I nodded.

"It's good luck then that we have just the thing for you," she said, opening a door next to a set of cabinets. "This room has its own en-trance via the boot room. I'll give you a key to the back door, and you'll be able to keep the kitchen door that opens to the boot room closed so no one disturbs you. You'll be able to come and go as you please."

I followed the Smythes up a small set of stairs, stopping on a land-ing with two plain doors set into the wall across from the stairs.

"When the previous owners extended the kitchen, they built this little part on for their cook to live in," Mrs. Smythe explained. "It's small, but I hope it suits."

She opened the door, and I was pleased to find a tiny but comfort-able sitting room with a rose-patterned chair and a small table topped by a white lamp. Across from it was a chest of drawers with an oval mirror on top that, I guessed, served as a vanity as well. There was a recess differentiated by a squared-off arch, through which I could just make out the edge of a brass bed covered in a white duvet.

"It's perfect," I said. "Where does your lodger sleep?"

"Miss Daniels took the room in the attic. It was her choice, mind you," said Mrs. Smythe.

"You'll meet her at supper, won't she, my dear?" asked Mr. Smythe, setting down my case.

"That you will. We can give you breakfast and supper as well, so long as you let me know the day before," said Mrs. Smythe. "Breakfast is at seven o'clock, and supper is at half past six."

Downstairs, Mrs. Smythe showed me the quirk of the back door—you had to pull the key toward you while also pressing the door away about three-quarters of the way up—and handed me the back door key and the key to my room.

"Well, I think that's everything. I'll leave you to it," said Mrs. Smythe.

After the Smythes retreated, I waited a few moments before slipping down the stairs and letting myself out the back door.

Recalling the map of Benstead I'd memorized the day before, I quickly made my way out of the village. Cottages gave way to hedgerows punctuated by trees that had long since shed their leaves. In one of the fields on my right, an unkindness of ravens pecked at the plowed ground.

After about ten minutes of walking, I spotted the tops of brick chimneys and, soon enough, the pitch of an expansive red roof came into view. At a gap in the hedgerow, I stopped to take in a white manor house framed in dark brown timbers on a much grander scale than anything in the village of Benstead. This, I reasoned, must be Blackthorn Park.

I kept the house in my sights between gaps in the hedgerow until the tangle of hawthorn gave way to a tall brick wall. This, in turn, became an iron gate, remarkable in that it was still standing while so many others had been hauled away for scrap to be used in the war effort. Without slowing, I walked by the gate, turning my head slightly to take in a gatehouse that looked as though it was built a good two hundred years after the main house. It was guarded by a bored-looking man sitting on a stool, who leaned against the brick structure as he read a newspaper.

I continued on, noting where the brick wall gave way to hedgerow again. Then I stopped, a smile spreading over my lips. I'd come to what I remembered from the map was an access road for the farm that had once served Blackthorn Park. It was outfitted with a new metal gate with barbed wire on top. However, between the hedgerow and the gate post was a gap wide enough for a person to slip through.

The day before, David had urged me not to enter the estate's grounds until I had the cover of darkness working in my favor. However, I wanted a little look around at the outbuildings because we had noticed that the new manufacturing barn was not present on the map, rendering it already out of date.

Turning sideways, I slipped through the gap, not even a branch of hawthorn grabbing at me as I went.

A little way beyond the gate, trees rose up on either side of the access road. It was nothing to step onto the verge and melt into the wood. I followed the line of the road, careful to keep to the shadows so that the light color of my coat wouldn't give me away. When I reached a three-pronged fork in the road, I hesitated. If my memory served, the far left should wind back to the manor house, but the other two looked more recently laid. Neither had appeared on the plans David and I had pored over, and I didn't know where either would lead.

After a moment's contemplation, I chose the middle one.

I wove my way through the trees along the road until I spotted a clearing up ahead. There was a vast single-story building set in the middle of it. Outside of the building, I saw several women in blue boiler-suits with their hair caught up in the same sort of handkerchief that I'd once used when I worked on the line in an ordnance factory and was banned from wearing hairpins for fear of sparking an explosion. A couple of the women smoked cigarettes, while another reapplied her lipstick using a slim compact.

I had, I surmised, found the manufacturing barn.

After a moment, a tall woman, who even from a distance managed the very great feat of making her boilersuit look elegant, emerged, said a few things to the idling women, and gestured to the door before heading back inside. The smoking women ground out their cigarettes under their work boots while the woman with the lipstick snapped her compact shut. A few moments later, I heard the great racket of machinery starting up.

I crept back to the fork and was about to run across the road to follow the right branch when a man with a handcart appeared from the direction of the big house. He was pushing it with his right hand, and when he shifted I saw the sleeve of his left arm pinned up at the elbow. He whistled as he went, his cart clattering away across the rougher surface of the service road. He passed so close to me I could see that his ginger whiskers were already coming in salt and pepper on his cheeks.

I waited until he was far enough ahead of me that I could no longer hear the rattle of the cart, and then I followed.

I was rewarded a few minutes later when the trees and shrubs parted and I found myself standing on the edge of a wide clearing in front of three wooden buildings painted dark green. One of the buildings was open, a large padlock hanging off the door's hook, and the man's handcart was parked just outside of it.

From where I stood, I could just see metal racks stacked with boxes, tools hanging on pegboards on the walls, and metal barrels lined up under them. These must be where Blackthorn Park stored its extra supplies and equipment and, isolated as these sheds were, the most likely place for a thief to be operating.

I decided I would give the sheds a closer look later that evening when I returned for my proper poke around.

I was just about to melt back into the trees when, from somewhere to my left, a man shouted, "Wait!" and I froze on the spot.

FIVE

M y heart hammered in my chest, my entire body tensing for the moment when I'd be roughly pulled from the under-growth. I silently cursed myself for failing my first opera-tion. I could just see it, Mrs. White looming over me in one of the Gosfield Street interrogation rooms, a smug smile on her face as she informed me that my career as an SIU agent was over before it even properly started.

"Wait!" the man shouted again. "Hold the door!"

My muscles unclenched. He wasn't speaking to me.

The man strode past my hiding place. I couldn't catch a glimpse of his face from where I was standing, but I did see the back of a natty navy suit and a beautiful pair of handmade leather shoes.

The man stopped in front of the open door, hands crossed over his chest. I couldn't quite make out what he was saying so I carefully crept closer.

". . . don't understand what is the matter," I caught him finish.

"It's Sir Nigel's rule, Mr. Hartley," said the muffled voice from in-side the shed.

Sir Nigel Balram. I remembered the name from Mrs. White's briefing file. A celebrated scientist and inventor before the war, he'd been handpicked by the head of the SOE to lead the engineering team at Blackthorn to, as far as I could see, great success.

"Hang his rules. You more than anyone else should know what a bother all of these log sheets and key sign-outs are. It's hardly worth it," grumbled Mr. Hartley. I could see him better now. He had a sharp, proud nose, thick dark hair brushed back from his forehead, and a slight scowl on his lips.

"Nevertheless," said the other man.

"It used to be that Sir Nigel would blow hot and cold, but he would usually leave you alone to do your work. But now—well, Jamison's at the end of his rope and I'm one more argument away from blowing the entire place up."

"You shouldn't joke about things like that, Mr. Hartley," said the man with the handcart, a distinct chill entering into his voice.

"Don't worry. I would never put Clarissa at risk."

"Find what you need but be certain you sign it out properly," said the man with the handcart.

Mr. Hartley disappeared into the shed, and I took my opportunity while the two men were occupied to slip away and head straight for the access road.

———

I returned to Russet Cottage in time to wash away the dust of the afternoon's preliminary investigation, read a few chapters of my book, and make it downstairs for supper at half past six.

I went through the door connecting the boot room and the kitchen and found Mrs. Smythe standing over the hob stirring a metal pot out of which wafted the most delicious smells.

"Supper won't be a moment," she said cheerfully. "Miss Daniels, our lodger, is just through in the dining room if you don't mind making your own introductions. Second door on the left."

I thanked her and poked my head into the dining room. The table was laid for four, and across from the door sat a petite young woman with auburn hair and rosy cheeks. She popped up the moment she saw me.

"Hello, are you Evelyne? I'm Jane Daniels, but you can just call me Jane. Everyone except the Smythes do. Mrs. Smythe just told me all about you. I didn't even know she had a cousin. Fancy that!"

She spoke like a machine gun, firing sentences at me so quickly I hardly knew where to start.

"You can have that seat," she said, pointing at the one across from her. "Mr. and Mrs. Smythe sit at the head and foot of the table, naturally."

"Naturally," I repeated, sliding into my chair.

"Mrs. Smythe tells me that you've come all the way from London," she said. "I should love to live in London one day. Is it simply marvelous?"

I almost laughed at the way she said "simply marvelous" as though she were starring in a holiday film but checked myself when I saw the eagerness of her expression. "It's a wonderful place if you can find work and a good place to live."

Jane nodded her head vigorously. "That's what I'm doing here in Benstead, working hard enough to earn a good reference. I'm a house-maid, you see. At the big house."

"Would that be Blackthorn Park?" I asked, affecting a casualness.

She began nodding again. "It's beautiful. Or at least it once was. That's what Mrs. Sherman tells me. She's the housekeeper. She's been at Blackthorn for years, and the Mountcastles—they're the family that owns Blackthorn—trust her enough that they asked her to stay on specially after the house was—"

Jane clamped a hand over her mouth.

"What's the matter?" I asked.

Jane looked guiltily down at her place. "Nothing. It's only, no. I really can't say."

I shrugged as though telling me everything wasn't precisely what I wanted her to do. "Do you like being a housemaid?"

Her face brightened a little. "It's all right. What I really want to do is become a housekeeper in one of those grand houses in Mayfair. Can you imagine? Mum was a lady's maid to a countess when she was my age. She tells me that if I do my job well and I mind myself, I might have a chance. If I get a good reference, that is."

I tilted my head. "You said that your boss is Mrs. Sherman? Is she any relation to Captain Sherman, the stationmaster?"

"She's his wife," Jane said. "She's ever so strict, but she isn't too bad really. It's just that she remembers the way things used to be at

Blackthorn when there were great parties for the hunt and Christmas. Can you imagine? All of those women in beautiful gowns? And the jewels! It must have been like something out of a film."

"It must have been a sight to see," I agreed. "Is there no one from the family still there?"

"It's mostly engine—men. Mostly men."

I gave her a conspiratorial smile. "Men who aren't in uniform are in short supply these days, even in London."

Jane pulled a face. "Yes, but I don't have to clean up after those ones. They can be awful. Especially Sir Nigel."

My ears perked up at hearing the head of engineering's name for the second time that day.

"He's a beast," continued Jane bitterly. "Just the other day he shouted at me for nearly a quarter of an hour because I cleaned his desk."

I blinked. "But isn't that what you're meant to do?"

Jane nodded vigorously. "That's what I told Mrs. Sherman, but she said that I should know the rules by now."

"The rules?"

"Oh, rules are ten a penny at Blackthorn Park," said Jane, beginning to count off on her fingers. "I can't clean any of the offices without express instruction from Mrs. Sherman. I'm never allowed into the east drawing room alone. I'm not allowed to leave the house, not even for a walk in the gardens while I'm meant to be having my lunch, even though other people can walk about. Can you imagine that?"

"It sounds positively draconian," I said.

She laughed. "Draconian? I'll have to remember that next time she yells at me. Like today. You'd think the world was ending just for breaking a silly little pane of glass in the orangery. There aren't even any orange trees in it these days."

"What happened?" I asked.

"One of the men set off an explosion and—"

"An explosion?" I asked.

"There's *always* something exploding at Blackthorn, but it doesn't make it any easier to become used to it," said Jane.

Having lived through the start of the Blitz in London, I could sympathize.

"Well, in that case, that feels doubly unfair on Mrs. Sherman's part. And I'm very sorry to hear that this Sir Nigel has caused you so many problems too," I said.

A sly smile slipped over Jane's lips. "Don't worry yourself about Sir Nigel. The thing these men always forget is that if someone cleans your space, they learn things. In fact," she said, leaning across the table, "I overheard Sir Nigel—"

"Good evening, ladies," said Mr. Smythe in a rather jolly tone as he opened the dining room door.

Immediately, Jane snapped her mouth shut and sat bolt upright.

"Ah, I see you've made Miss Daniels's acquaintance, Evelyne," said Mr. Smythe, adopting my Christian name now that we were in the presence of someone other than his wife. I admired the ease with which he moved between the formality of strangers—which we were—to the familiarity of family, as we were pretending to be.

"Yes, we were having a nice little chat," I said.

"Not too much, I hope," said Mr. Smythe, shooting a look at Jane.

"No, Mr. Smythe," said Jane.

"Here it is, here it is," sang out Mrs. Smythe as she carried a steaming dish to the table.

As my hostess served supper, I sat back, thinking about what Jane had told me, what I'd overheard at the equipment sheds, and all of the questions I now had about Sir Nigel.

SIX

More than two hours later, when I finally reached the telephone booth on Benstead's tiny high street, I pushed the door open and hazarded a glance at *Maman*'s watch. I was late, and I suspected that David would have something to say about it.

I picked up the receiver and asked the switchboard operator to put a call through to London for me before giving the Dreadnought 1804 exchange David had made me memorize. I let the telephone ring and then hung up to wait. I was rewarded a few moments later when the receiver in front of me jangled.

"You're late," David said by way of a greeting.

"Yes, well, you try to extract yourself from the dinner table when your landlady is describing the history of cross-stitch in extraordinary detail," I said sourly.

"That sounds . . . diverting," he said.

I rubbed the spot on my forehead behind which a headache was threatening. "I can reassure you, it is not."

"How did you get on after you boarded the train?" he asked.

"My train was delayed, but I managed the journey well enough. The Smythes are just the right combination of welcoming and discreet. After settling into my room, I went for a wander up to the big house to see it in the light." I hesitated. "I may also have taken the opportunity to slip in and have a quick look around the grounds."

"In daylight?" he asked. "That wasn't part of the plan we discussed."

"I was careful," I reassured him.

I thought for a moment that he might chastise me, but instead he asked, "What did you find?"

"Modifications have clearly been made to the estate since the plans we were given were drawn. There's new fencing topped with barbed wire at the access road, but there are obvious weaknesses too. Most of the estate is lined by hedgerow," I said.

"Making it easy to push through if someone was very determined and didn't mind a few scratches," he said.

"It also looks as though the new gate at the access road was put up hastily. There's a gap between it and the hedgerow that was wide enough for me to easily slip through."

He cursed. "That's sloppy."

"It is," I said.

I quickly told him about my survey of the manufacturing barn and the equipment sheds from a distance, relaying the conversation I'd overheard between the man with the handcart and Mr. Hartley.

"Do you think an embittered employee would be angry enough to steal from his employer?" he asked.

"Maybe. It sounds as though Sir Nigel is a bit of a nightmare in all aspects. Jane Daniels, the Smythes' lodger and Blackthorn Park housemaid, had some choice words to say about him. Apparently he shouted at her for cleaning his desk."

"A bit unkind," said David.

"Or paranoid. She also implied that she knew something about Sir Nigel that he might well want to keep quiet," I said.

"Perhaps that's why he's so particular about his desk," said David.

"Hopefully I will find out more when I take a look around tonight."

"I've been thinking about that. Perhaps you should stay to the grounds. You've already found the equipment sheds and—"

"Why would I stay to the grounds?"

When he didn't respond, I pushed, saying, "You and I have been through the blueprints. We've reviewed the previous security reports. The next logical step is to examine things up close. That includes the manor house, unless you can think of a reason why I shouldn't."

The pause on the other end told me that he was grasping for an answer.

"David, do you doubt my training?" I asked.

"No," he said. "I just think that this is your first reconnaissance job. Maybe you should take some more time—"

"We don't have time. The report is due on Mrs. White's desk tomorrow evening, so unless you can give me one good reason why I should not go ahead with the plans we agreed upon, I will go to Blackthorn Park tonight and have a proper look around."

His sigh filled the line. "Fine."

"Don't worry," I said.

"That's easy for you to say when you're there and I'm here," he grumbled.

"Do you intend to be a mother hen every time we work together?" I asked.

"I'm not a mother hen." I could practically hear him puffing out his chest in indignation.

I waited.

"Fine," he said. "I'm worried about you."

"Well, isn't that sweet?" I asked, my tone dry as good champagne.

"I'm serious, Evelyne. This is your first full operation. Less than two months ago you were in a typing pool, and now you're working in the field. Alone."

"Being a typist served me well enough in the cabinet war rooms," I reminded him.

"It did, but being an agent . . . It's different. Dangerous."

I was very aware of that. My instructors at Beaulieu had made it clear enough that we were entering an area of the service where the usual rules did not apply, and I had to confront the horrible truth that there would be no cheerful reunion for all of us when the war ended. Some of us would work in intelligence or signals, but many would be sent into enemy territory to organize resistance cells or sabotage key locations and supply lines. The risk of being captured, tortured, and killed was almost too high to comprehend because if any of us dwelled on it for too long, we would never do what needed to be done.

I knew that I was, in my strange way, in a privileged position. Although I was now trained just like everyone else in the SOE, I had a different objective. The Special Investigations Unit was tasked with figuring out what happened when things went wrong in all branches of government, all areas of the service. Our remit was infinitely flexible, catching killers, plugging leaks, stopping people from doing the very things that would hurt Britain the most. However, I knew that my job was not without its own risks. Desperate people could be unpredictable and, if pushed far enough, deadly.

Still, this was the life that I'd chosen and I was going to do my level best to do the job well.

"You had a first operation, didn't you?" I asked quietly, trying to appeal to David's reason.

"We weren't at war."

"The sooner that I test the security measures and write up my report, the sooner you and I can move on and tackle another mission. One that uses both of our skills properly."

The crackle of the telephone line filled the silence until, finally, he said, "You're right."

Even though he couldn't see me, I beamed. "I knew you'd eventually see logic."

He huffed out a laugh.

"Don't worry so much, David. I will be fine."

"You might be, but will I?" he asked.

"What do you mean?"

He sighed, and I could imagine him dropping his head back for a moment and letting his concern carry him away.

"This might be your first mission as an agent, but it's also my first as a handler and it's taking some adjustment not being out in the field with you. I'm not entirely certain I like it," he admitted.

I smiled. "I will take care of myself."

"Promise it," he said, his voice soft but intense.

I parted my lips, not entirely sure what to think of his tone. It was too intimate for our roles of agent and handler, and I had become so very good at ignoring anything approaching what Moira might call a "frisson." It wasn't because David wasn't appealing to look at—even I had to admit that he was—but I couldn't see him that way. Not when I had worked so hard to convince him to take me seriously, first as his partner and then as an agent.

"I promise," I said.

"Right." He cleared his throat. "Take care of yourself, Evelyne."

"I will. I promise," I repeated.

I hung up, hesitated, and then picked up the telephone again. I knew there was a risk that I wouldn't reach her, but I felt as though, after weeks of being unreachable, I should telephone Moira even if I was only due to be away for a night.

I gave the operator Mrs. Jenkins's telephone exchange. While I waited for the call to connect, I watched an older man with a dog on a lead walk by the booth. Like so many places in Britain, the village of Benstead was a world of women, children, and older men. The military had claimed so many young men to fight, and more and more advertisements were appearing in magazines, newspapers, and even on railway station platforms imploring women to join the war effort too. I thought of Moira, who was desperate to finally receive top billing in film or on the West End stage. Or Jocelyn, who had told me over a glass of scotch that her ambitions at her newspaper far outstripped what her editors deemed suitable for a woman. What would happen to them if the government finally decided to conscript women as well?

I supposed they would get on with it like so many women across the country did every single day.

Mrs. Jenkins's voice filled the line with her usual "Jenkins's residence; lady of the house speaking."

"Mrs. Jenkins, it's Evelyne."

"Oh, Evelyne, Moira said that you've left us again," said Mrs. Jenkins.

"That's right. I did leave a note for you," I said with a frown.

"Where?" she asked.

"On the kitchen table."

"When was this?" asked my landlady.

"This morning, before the regular breakfast service."

"That would explain it then. Marjorie knocked over an entire pot of real coffee this morning and ruined everything on the table. Can you imagine the waste?"

I cringed in sympathy. Real coffee was becoming more and more of a luxury these days. It was incredible Mrs. Jenkins hadn't taken to her bed to mourn its loss.

"I suppose you'll be wanting to speak to Moira," said Mrs. Jenkins.

"If she's there."

"I'm afraid she's not," said Mrs. Jenkins. "She's out late with rehearsals most nights. I worry about her making it back safely in the blackout."

Disappointed, I asked, "Will you let her know that I rang?"

"Of course I will, dear. Come home soon," said Mrs. Jenkins.

I thanked her and said goodbye.

Pushing out of the telephone booth, I hurried across the cobblestone street and back in the direction of Russet Cottage. However, as I rounded the corner of Brook Road, I walked straight into a short man moving at quite the clip. The leather attaché case he had jammed under his arm fell to the ground. The flap must not have been properly buckled, because it flopped open and a few papers spilled out.

"Oh, I beg your pardon," I said hurriedly, stooping to pick up the papers.

"Don't touch those!"

I froze, my hand stretching toward them.

"Those papers are delicate," he said sharply, his gray overcoat gaping open to reveal a tweed suit. "It's best if I collect them myself."

"Of course," I said, taking a step back, all while trying my best to surreptitiously steal a glance at what he had been carrying. However, all I could see was the top paper, a letter, which began:

```
30 October 1940


Dear Dr. Jamison,
     We are sorry to inform you that circumstances
have arisen that necessitate retracting our previous
offer. I'm certain that you will understand . . .
```

The man I presumed to be Dr. Jamison covered the letter, cutting short my chance to snoop.

I studied his pinched expression. So this was the man I had overheard Mr. Hartley gossiping about to his rather reluctant companion at the equipment sheds earlier that day. Mr. Hartley had said that Dr. Jamison seemed on his last nerve with Sir Nigel, but if I was to judge by the letter of rejection I had just spotted, Dr. Jamison wouldn't be leaving the research facility anytime soon.

As Dr. Jamison finished buckling his briefcase, I said, "I apologize again. I should have looked where I was going."

"Yes, Miss, you should have. Good evening," said Dr. Jamison in a brusque tone before clamping his pipe between his teeth and then adjusting the cuffs of his shirt where they poked out from under his tweed jacket.

"What a charming man," I muttered, watching him hurry off. Every instinct screamed at me to chase him down and ask him everything he knew about Blackthorn Park that might point to who was stealing from the facility. However, I had my orders, and Mrs. White had emphatically said I wasn't to approach members of staff.

Reluctantly, I shook my head and set my mind to the evening's task: breaking into a top-secret research and development facility.

SEVEN

J ust before ten o'clock that evening, I approached the Blackthorn
Park access road gate and slipped through the gap once again.

The Sussex countryside had been blanketed in darkness for
hours now, but I'd still taken the time to pull on my black trousers
and black wool jumper, leaving my jewelry behind in the safety of my
room at Russet Cottage. I wore the black boots I'd broken in during
my time at Beaulieu, and a black knitted cap tugged down over my
hair hid any shine that the waxing moon might catch.

Passing the fork in the road I'd discovered that afternoon, I took
the right branch that I'd neglected earlier. Once again, I melted into
the trees but kept the road in sight until it gave way to the sort of great
expanse of lawn that one normally sees only in public parks and very
grand houses.

Edging along the tree line at the boundary of the lawn, I found what I
was looking for: two tall redbrick walls that stretched for yards in either
direction. According to the plans I'd studied, the kitchen garden was
contained by the wall to my left and on the right was what had once
been an eighteenth-century formal knot garden that had been given
over to arable land on which to grow crops at the start of the war. I also
knew from my studies that once I cleared these two walls I would come
across the veranda that stretched the entire north side of the house.

As soon as the manor house came into view, I stopped and studied the facade. As I expected, someone had drawn the blackout curtains across every window, giving me little idea of whether anyone was still working there. However, that didn't matter for my plan.

Taking a deep breath, I put my head down and sprinted out from my cover. When I reached one of the two staircases that led from the veranda down to the lawn, I dropped into a crouch and gave myself a moment to catch my breath as I looked up with satisfaction. Just as I'd expected, tucked off to the side was a door leading to the lower ground floor and what had once been the servants' areas of the grand house.

I straightened and, staying in the shadows, examined the door in the faint moonlight. I ran my fingers along the doorframe, checking for any anomalies. Satisfied that as far as I could tell I wouldn't close a circuit and set an alarm system off if I opened the door, I pulled a lock-picking kit out of my boot and set to work.

I slid the tension wrench into the lock and then inserted my hook. I moved slowly, displaying a patience I hadn't known I could possess until I'd been forced to pick locks for hours on end under the exacting eye of a gruff man from Sheffield.

After a few moments, there was a satisfying *click*.

I was in.

I depressed the door handle and waited. No alarm.

With a smile, I pushed open the door and—

A gunshot shattered the night's silence.

I froze, adrenaline rushing through my body, and then my training kicked in. Logic overruled instinct and I broke into a run, making for the servants' stairs. The shot hadn't been near me but instead sounded as though it had been discharged from in the house above. The servants' stairs would be the fastest way to traverse between the floors.

My mind did quick calculations as I climbed. While the outer walls would be thick, it was an old house made mostly of timber and plaster. Insulation between floors and walls would probably be fairly sparse. Still, the shot sounded farther away than the ground floor. I made the split-second decision to skip past the door to the ground-floor rooms and made for the bedrooms of the first floor that now served as offices.

I burst out of the servants' stairs, skidding to a stop outside of the first closed door I came across. The blueprints had listed this as Sir Nigel's office. I could see a light under the door.

I twisted the door handle, pushed, and found myself staring at a man's body splayed back against an office chair, red blood splattered across the bookcase behind him.

A wave of nausea came over me, and I swallowed hard to force it down. I had seen a dead body before—it was what had started my last case—but the violence of the gunshot wound was still a ghastly sight.

"Come on, Evelyne," I muttered under my breath. "You know what to do, now *do it*."

I went to the body. From behind the desk, I could see that the gun was hanging from the corpse's right hand, the index finger still on the trigger. Moving carefully so as not to disturb anything, I did a cursory check for a pulse, not at all surprised that there was none.

I turned my attention to the desk. I scanned for a note, but saw nothing obvious on top of the stacks of papers lining nearly every inch of the desk save for the blotter and a spot on the left.

I crouched down, looking through the legs of the desk chair, and found a fan of paperwork spread across the floor to the left of the body.

On the left . . .

I frowned.

The gun was in the dead man's right hand. If he had knocked the papers off his desk when the gun went off, wouldn't it be more likely that a stack of papers from the right would have spilled in that direction rather than to the left?

I was about to stand when I glanced up at the blotter on the desk. It wasn't lying flat. Using a handkerchief so as not to add my prints to anything in the room, I lifted the edge of the blotter and found an envelope stuffed underneath it.

I slid the envelope free and then reached over for the telephone on Sir Nigel's desk, again using my handkerchief to pick it up. The switchboard operator came on the line immediately. I asked for

Dreadnought 1804, praying that I would be connected to David before anyone else arrived.

As I listened to the line ringing, I opened the envelope I'd found under the blotter and worked the paper inside free.

"What is your message?" asked the woman who picked up before I could open the paper.

Disappointment caught in my throat. I wanted the familiar comfort of David's voice on the other end. However, I pulled myself together and said, "The apple crumble has gone cold."

"What is your exchange?" the woman asked, cool as could be.

"BEN 3746," I said, reading the exchange from where it was written on the telephone's base.

"Your message has been received," said the woman. Then she hung up.

Not knowing how much longer I might be alone, I put the telephone down and opened the paper in my hand. It was, as I suspected, a letter.

17 October 1940

Dear Sir Nigel,
    Thank you for your telephone call. Arrangements have been made for your arrival. We will expect you at 1500 Tuesday.

Sincerely,

Lieutenant Colonel Julian Gerrard

"Oh my God, Sir Nigel!"

I looked up and found a stout man in his shirtsleeves filling the doorway, his hand covering his mouth.

"What is it, Mr. Porter?" a woman's voice came from behind him.

"No, Miss Glenconner!" Mr. Porter threw an arm back to block the woman, but she ducked under it.

All of the color drained out of Miss Glenconner's face, and she began to scream.

"No! No! Oh God!"

Mr. Porter grasped her around the waist as she began to wilt. Shooting me a nasty glare, he barked, "Don't just stand there. Help me!"

I rushed forward to take one of the sobbing Miss Glenconner's arms. Almost immediately her legs gave under her.

"She needs to sit down," I said, angling my body toward a chester-field placed in front of the fireplace.

"We can't very well keep her in here. It's positively barbaric," he said, jerking his head toward Sir Nigel's body.

I was about to argue with him, but the two men I'd seen at the sheds that afternoon ran in, both balking at the sight of the corpse.

"You two, who are you?" I barked, doing my best to emulate my old headmistress from my school days.

"Tyson," said the man who'd pushed the handcart.

"Hartley," said his taller companion, who was looking decidedly green at the gills.

"Right, Mr. Hartley and Mr. Tyson, take Miss Glenconner some-place where she can lie down and compose herself," I ordered.

"The west drawing room might be most comfortable," said Mr. Tyson.

"Why are you listening to her?" Mr. Porter groused.

"Mr. Porter does have a point," said Mr. Hartley slowly. "We don't know what you're doing here."

"Hartley, she appears to know what she's doing and is taking com-mand of the situation, which is more than I can say for any of the rest of us," said Mr. Tyson.

Mr. Hartley sniffed, but didn't protest again.

"Thank you. Take Miss Glenconner to the west drawing room, will you? And is there a doctor in the village?" I asked.

"Dr. Morrison," said Mr. Tyson.

"What use will a doctor be?" hissed Mr. Porter. "Anyone can see that Sir Nigel's dead."

"Who *are* you?" I demanded.

"Bernard Porter," he said, pulling himself to his full if rather dimin-utive height. "I am the head of operations here. And I might ask you the same? I've never seen you before, and unauthorized people are not allowed on the grounds. Tell me one reason I shouldn't have you arrested."

"As Mr. Tyson said, I'm the only person who actually knows what she's doing," I fired back. "There's a proper way to do things in these situations, Mr. Porter. A coroner must be on hand to assess the body, so Mr. Tyson and Mr. Hartley are going to take Miss Glenconner downstairs and then one of them is going to call the village doctor. With any luck, he'll be properly trained as a coroner. Besides, the way that things are going, I suspect that Miss Glenconner may also need a physician's assistance soon."

Sure enough, the moment that Mr. Tyson and Mr. Hartley took Miss Glenconner under the arms, she swooned again.

"I'll place the call," Mr. Tyson promised me as he and Mr. Hartley lifted her up and carried her from the room.

"Thank you," I said. "Now, Mr. Porter, I need you to make two telephone calls. First—"

"This is a secure facility, and there are severe punishments for anyone trespassing," barked Mr. Porter.

This display of aggressive masculinity was wearing rather thin, and it was a great fight not to roll my eyes. Instead, I breathed deeply, praying for patience. "Telephone the guard at the main gate. Tell him what's happened and that no one is to enter or exit the property."

"The only people I'm telephoning are the police," said Mr. Porter, pushing me aside on his way to Sir Nigel's telephone.

At least he correctly guessed what the second telephone call I wanted him to make was.

"Mr. Porter, I think you'll find—"

"Young lady, you—someone no one knows—were the first person on the scene of a suicide. That is highly suspicious. Now give me that," he said, snatching the letter I still held in my hand.

I snatched it right back.

"You are not authorized to handle sensitive information," he thundered.

I was, actually, but I didn't think there was much point in trying to explain that to Mr. Porter. Instead, I stuffed the letter back in its envelope and placed it on a patch of desk that didn't look too blood-splattered. "Why don't we agree to leave that for the investigators?"

His eyes lingered on the envelope, but then he straightened and grabbed for the telephone, likely ruining any fingerprints in the process.

I gave an exasperated sigh.

"Hello?" Mr. Porter practically snarled down the line. "Hello? Yes. My name is Bernard Porter. I would like to report an incident. At Blackthorn Park in Benstead. Yes. Suicide and a case of trespassing. That's right. Yes, right away."

He hung up the telephone with a triumphant glare. "That was the West Sussex Constabulary. They're sending someone now."

"Excellent," I said, crossing my arms.

"Now, if you will go to the west drawing room with the others," he began to say.

"No, thank you," I said, planting my feet. "I think I'll stay right here."

I wasn't about to miss David's call, and I certainly wasn't going to leave this buffoon alone with a body.

"Right here?" asked Mr. Porter, eyeing the corpse. The man was beginning to look a little queasy.

"That's where you are. And where he is." I gestured toward the body. "It seems as though someone should guard him until the police arrive."

"I can do that," he said, doubt beginning to creep into his voice.

"You can," I conceded, "but how do I know that you won't take the chance to go through his pockets or riffle his papers? I don't know you any more than you know me."

Mr. Porter glared at me and began to drop onto one edge of the chesterfield.

"Do not sit down," I ordered, and he shot up again.

"Why not?" he demanded.

"This is a crime scene, not the waiting room of a railway station. Nothing should be touched."

He looked as though he was going to argue with me, but in the end he simply said, "Fine. Neither of us sits."

"Not until the proverbial cavalry comes," I said, praying that David would receive my message soon.

EIGHT

It was about a quarter to eleven when a young constable with his helmet lodged in the crook of his arm walked through the door of Sir Nigel's office.

"Good evening, I was told—"

The young man immediately clamped a hand to his mouth, and I thought for a moment he would be ill all over the pale blue carpet. However, he somehow managed to recover, although he was as white as a sheet when he asked, "What's happened here?"

"What does it look like? The man shot himself," Mr. Porter snarled.

The constable nodded, his wide eyes still fixed on the body.

"What's your name?" I asked the constable.

"Harold Lee," the young man gasped out.

"Constable Lee, have you been trained in what to do with a crime scene?" I asked.

The constable's nod was a little weaker this time.

"What do you know about crime scenes?" Mr. Porter asked me sourly.

"Constable," I said sharply, tearing the young man's attention from the body.

"Yes, Miss?"

"Don't listen to her. She should be arrested for trespassing," argued Mr. Porter.

"If you are not going to be helpful, I invite you to keep your thoughts to yourself," I fired back, my patience with Mr. Porter having grown very thin.

I turned back to Constable Lee. "It's very important that things be done properly here. What is the first thing you should do?"

"Secure the crime scene," he said, almost as though he was reciting from a textbook.

"Very good," I began to say, but I was interrupted by the ringing of the telephone. Both of the men stared at it until I asked, "Isn't someone going to answer that?"

Constable Lee cautiously leaned over Sir Nigel's desk. Just before he was about to pick up the receiver, he stopped himself and pulled out a handkerchief. I gave him an encouraging nod.

"Hello?" Constable Lee asked. Then he looked at me. "Are you Miss Redfern?"

"Yes," I said.

He held out the receiver. "It's for you."

Mr. Porter began to sputter when I took the telephone from the constable.

"This is Evelyne," I said with my back turned to the men.

"I received your message." David's voice filled the line, and I couldn't help but feel a flood of relief.

"We have a situation. Sir Nigel's dead."

There was a beat before he repeated, "Dead?"

"Shot."

"Suicide?" he asked.

"Possibly. The gun was in his hand, but there's no note that I can see."

"What about that letter you were holding when I came in?" Mr. Porter asked from over my shoulder.

"That wasn't a suicide note," I said, moving it out of Mr. Porter's reach before he could snatch it away.

"Have the local police been called?" asked David in my ear.

"Yes. One of them is already here," I said.

He cursed. "I'm going to need to call Mrs. White."

My heart sank. "No."

The last thing I wanted was to give Mrs. White a reason to remove me from this case because she thought I was too inexperienced.

"Can't be helped, I'm afraid," he said.

"Then I should be the one to speak to her—"

"No. Don't move. I'm on my way," said David.

"On your way?" I asked. "I don't think that's really necessary—"

"Don't move," he repeated, and then he hung up.

I hung up in a huff. So much for David trusting my training.

"What was that?" Mr. Porter demanded. "Who would call you? That is a secure line."

I ignored him and smiled at Constable Lee. "Constable, I believe that someone has already telephoned a Dr. Morrison. I would recommend that you find a key, lock the door to this office, and—once Dr. Morrison arrives and removes the body—join the witnesses downstairs."

"Yes, Miss," he said, looking a little bewildered.

"Don't worry, Constable," I said as cheerfully as a woman standing next to a dead body could. "We'll muddle through together."

———————

Mr. Porter, Constable Lee, and I trooped downstairs to join the grim crowd in the west drawing room. Mr. Tyson produced a set of keys, which he handed over to Constable Lee, who retreated back upstairs to lock the office. Miss Glenconner lay on a chaise, quietly weeping.

We spent more than an hour and a half in that room, a clock on the mantelpiece chiming the quarter hour. Other than when Mr. Tyson poked his head around the blackout curtains to announce that Dr. Morrison's car was driving up to the house, no one spoke. Instead, each person occupied their own bit of the room that still retained its character as a drawing room despite being requisitioned.

For my part, I was examining a well-thumbed copy of a Mrs. Gaskell novel I'd found on a small bookcase when I felt a presence behind me. I turned to find Constable Lee lurking in the doorway.

"Can I help you?" I asked.

"Yes—That is—" He rubbed his neck sheepishly. "You seem to know a great deal about investigations, Miss Redfern."

"Thank you," I said. At least someone appreciated my expertise.

"The truth is, I've only been a constable for about six months. I'm only in because I couldn't pass my medical for the army. This is the first crime scene I've been to . . . What should happen next?"

I smiled. I didn't need my training to answer that question; the hundreds of detective novels I'd read had been a more than adequate tutorial.

"Well, with the coroner doing his job, I think it's probably high time you collected some alibis," I said.

His face lit up. "Alibis. Yes." He fumbled with his pockets and pulled out a notebook. "Whom should I speak to first?"

"Why don't you start with her?" called Mr. Porter from the sofa where he brooded.

Really, the man's insistence on treating me like a suspect was growing tiresome.

"Yes, who is she?" asked Mr. Hartley.

"I would be happy to answer any of *your* questions, Constable Lee," I said, catching the sound of an approaching engine. "However, I believe that I'm about to be needed elsewhere."

"There's another car coming," Mr. Tyson announced, peeking around the blackout curtains again.

"I'll go see who it is. Nobody move?" The constable's instruction came out more as a question, and he scurried off.

Mr. Porter slumped back against his chair. "This is absurd. Anyone with half a brain can tell that Sir Nigel topped himself."

Miss Glenconner gave a little whimper from the chaise, and the rest of us shot him a dirty look.

"Have a little heart, Mr. Porter," said Mr. Tyson.

"I'm simply saying what everyone else is thinking," insisted Mr. Porter, even as his cheeks flushed red.

I heard the opening and closing of the front door, and moments later David strode into the room, the constable slipping in behind him.

David swept his gaze around, stopping when he landed on me.

I gave him a weary little wiggle of my fingers. "Good of you to join us, David."

Since you don't trust me to do my job.

"I came as soon as I could. Where is the body?" he asked.

"The coroner removed it about forty-five minutes ago," I said.

"Are you a detective?" asked Mr. Porter as he squared up to David.

"Who are you?" demanded David, looking him up and down.

"Bernard Porter. I am the administrative head here at Blackthorn Park," said Mr. Porter.

I noticed that despite Mr. Porter's bravado, he didn't bark at David the way he had at me, which made me scowl.

"I'm sure you are," muttered David, before he turned back to me. "Let's go."

"Wait! Go? Where is she going? Surely she's a suspect?" blustered Mr. Porter.

David sighed and turned to address everyone. "The constable will take your statements privately, one by one. After that, you may go home. Do not attempt to leave the village of Benstead tonight, or the consequences will be dire. Do not speak about what happened here with anyone, including those who are here, or the consequences will be dire. Is that clear?"

There were murmurs of assent around the room.

As we passed Constable Lee, David leaned in and said, "Take their statements and then call in to your superiors. They'll give you further instructions."

"Yes, sir. Miss," said Constable Lee.

I patted the young man on the arm. "It will be all right. Just re-member that it's the job."

Tuesday
November 5, 1940

===

TWO DAYS UNTIL CHURCHILL'S VISIT

NINE

Outside on the drive, David opened my car door, and I slid in while he rounded to the driver's side. Once he was in, he started the ignition.

"Let's go before the constable gets it into his head to ask more questions," he said.

"I don't think it's the constable we have to worry about. For a moment it looked as though Mr. Porter was of a mind to tie me up in rope and throw me in a dungeon," I said.

"Don't be silly, Evelyne. There are no dungeons in Sussex," said David.

I wasn't entirely certain that was true, but given that history had never been my strongest subject in school I let the matter drop, instead asking, "Where are we going?"

"Away," he said, angling the car to head back to the gatehouse.

"Away?"

"Yes," he replied.

"Really? That's all you're going to say?" I asked, crossing my arms over my chest.

"Don't sulk."

"I'm not sulking."

He shot me a look.

"Fine, I am sulking. You came in and that horrible man listened to you, and now you're taking charge. I will remind you that I am capable of conducting an investigation," I said.

"You've already shown me you're more than capable. However, Mrs. White still thinks you're green and if she decides that you aren't up to the job, she'll pull you out of the field. I'm here to make sure she keeps you on the case."

"Oh."

Well, I reasoned, *I suppose I could be grateful for that.*

A corner of his mouth lifted. "I also intend to return to the field."

"You were a handler for all of—what? Twenty-four hours?" I asked.

"And I hated every minute of it. I'm not suited to sitting on the sidelines. Now, we need a quiet place where we can talk, ideally with a telephone, where we can trust no one will overhear us."

"There are secure lines at Blackthorn Park," I said.

He shook his head. "It would be better if we laid low until things are sorted out. We'll find an inn and see if we can persuade the proprietor to let us use the office telephone. If there is one."

"At this time of night?" I asked skeptically.

"It's the best plan I have," he said by way of explanation.

An idea I wasn't exactly thrilled about popped into my mind, and I sighed. "Take the road to Farnham. I'll give you directions from there."

"What's in Farnham?" he asked as we approached the gatehouse.

"Not Farnham. We're heading west to Guilesgate in Hampshire."

"All right, then what's in Guilesgate?" he asked.

I twisted my lips. "Shaldeen Grange, the home of Amelia Lumley."

"Who is . . . ?"

"My aunt. She lives alone except for some staff, and I know she has an excellent telephone connection because she uses it to rule over her social circle."

There was a moment's pause before David said, "You never told me you had an aunt."

I leveled a look at him. "Because you were so forthcoming with information about your family when we met? Besides, you know I have an aunt because you read my personnel file before interrogating me in the cabinet war rooms."

"Fair point," he said.

"Aunt Amelia is my father's sister," I told him. "She's the one who took me in on school holidays." She was also, I had been surprised to learn, the one who had sometimes stepped in to pay for my school fees when Sir Reginald was short of cash or too lazy to send the money. Really, Aunt Amelia had been my one family anchor over the past few years. Not that I would ever tell her that. That would be far too sentimental for the Redferns.

When we reached the Blackthorn Park gatehouse, David slowed only to wave at the guard, who saluted him as we rolled by.

"How did you talk your way past him?" I asked. "This is supposed to be a closed facility."

"I told him that I was a detective," he said.

"And he believed you without any identification?" I asked.

Without taking his eyes off the road, David reached into his jacket pocket and pulled out a leather wallet, which he handed to me. "I have a warrant card."

I opened it up and, sure enough, there was a Scotland Yard warrant card with David's picture, information, and signature on it.

"How did you manage that?" I asked, incredulous.

"I asked Miss Summers to arrange it for me."

I decided that I would ask Miss Summers for a warrant card the first chance I got.

"Tell me what happened at Blackthorn Park," David prompted, pulling me back to the case at hand.

I told him about everything that transpired since I'd left Russet Cottage that evening.

When I finished, he asked, "When you arrived at Sir Nigel's office, was the door locked?"

"No. It was closed but not locked. Also, the light was on. I could see it coming from underneath the door."

"And did you see or hear anyone about?"

"No."

"So it looks like a suicide?" he asked.

"Well . . ."

"Yes?" he prompted.

"Something about the whole thing feels wrong. The gun was in his right hand, and he was shot from right to left as you would expect. However, a stack of papers from the left side of his desk had been knocked off."

"You're certain?" he asked.

"Positive. There was a gap on the desktop where they should have been. It looked almost as though someone brushed by them."

David grunted. "Who was the first person to arrive on the scene?"

"Mr. Porter, who was followed very swiftly by Miss Glenconner."

"The woman lying on the chaise?" he asked.

"Yes. Then Mr. Hartley and Mr. Tyson ran in. They were the ones I overheard at the equipment shed this afternoon."

"Talking about the victim, if I remember your report correctly," said David.

"Yes. I have the impression that Sir Nigel was not particularly well liked."

"But is that enough for someone to want to kill him?" David asked.

"I don't know," I admitted.

"Well, I expect we'll have the coroner's findings soon enough. In the meantime I'll telephone Mrs. White."

"I thought you'd already spoken to her," I said.

He shook his head. "I wanted to speak to you first so that I could give her the full scope of what we know."

"Remind me why I can't be the one to talk to her?" I asked.

"Because for now, I'm still the handler and you're the field agent." When I started to protest he put his hand up and said, "You've been on the ground at Blackthorn Park and from what I can see, you've already met some of the staff. You *should* be on the investigation."

"But?" I prompted.

"But Mrs. White doesn't trust you yet."

"And she does trust you?" I asked.

"As much as she trusts any agent," he said. "I've been in a situation like this before where an entire mission flies off course. Mrs. White will be locked in a tug-of-war between us, Baker Street, the West Sussex Constabulary, and who knows who else might want a part of this one. Maybe even the Corp of Military Police."

"Not them again," I groaned, remembering my nemeses Sergeant Maxwell and Corporal Plaice from my last investigation.

"Let's hope not," he said. "I'll speak to Mrs. White first and advocate for you. That's what a handler should do, isn't it?"

I begrudgingly nodded.

"Give yourself the best chance of staying on this case by trusting me. As your partner. Can you do that?" he asked.

My hesitation lasted only a second. After all, David had trusted me to design my own reconnaissance plan, and he'd come racing to Blackthorn Park without question when I needed him.

A partnership, I knew, could only work if both parties trusted one another, and I was going to have to show David I trusted him.

"I can do that," I said and settled back in the seat of the car to turn my mind to the rather daunting prospect of a surprise visit with Aunt Amelia.

TEN

We arrived at Shaldeen Grange around half past one. I should have been exhausted, but the adrenaline from finding Sir Nigel's body was still coursing through me.

David slowed the car to a stop in front of the entrance to my aunt's house and asked, "Is this it?"

I peered through the windshield at the Georgian facade that was just visible in the darkness. It seemed less imposing than it had when I had been a child sitting in the back of Aunt Amelia's huge, chauffeur-driven car, but I still couldn't look at it without a tinge of sadness. When my parents had still been married and living together in Paris, my visits to Shaldeen Grange had been an annual occurrence to be endured at Sir Reginald's insistence. He thought that summers spent with my British aunt would ward off any possibility that I might become "too French." However, after *Maman* died and my father dumped me at Ethelbrook School for Girls, I went there because, with my adventurer father always on the move, there was simply nowhere else for me to go.

"Welcome to Shaldeen Grange," I said with a sigh.

David mirrored my stoop to look up at the house. "It's . . ."

"Huge. I know. If there's one thing that can be said about Aunt Amelia, it's that she married well."

"And her husband?"

"Died decades ago," I said.

"I'm sorry to hear that," he said.

"Oh don't be. She much prefers it that way."

I forced myself to climb out of the car and march up to the front door. With my finger on the bell, I muttered, "Right. Come on, Evelyne. There's no point in stalling."

I pressed the bell and stepped back. A few moments later, the door opened to reveal a familiar figure silhouetted against the light of the hall.

"Miss Redfern, welcome back to Shaldeen Grange," said Henderson, my aunt's butler, as though it was perfectly normal for me to show up unannounced at this hour with a man in tow.

"Hello, Henderson. This is Mr. Poole," I said as I walked into the black-and-white tiled entryway.

"Good evening, sir," said Henderson with a little nod of the head as he took my knitted cap, treating it as carefully as he might a lady's hat on race day.

"Is my aunt awake?" I asked.

"I believe that Mrs. Lumley is in the music room," he said.

"The music room? I didn't even know she had one," I said while David handed Henderson his things.

"I think you'll find that Mrs. Lumley has made a number of improvements since your last visit," said the butler. "Shall I announce you?"

"No thank you, Henderson. Just point us in the right direction," I said.

"Very good, Miss. The music room is where the gold drawing room used to be."

"Well, that's good to hear," I said. "I never did like the wallpaper in that room."

I led David through the hall and down the corridor toward the back of the house. The closer that we came to the music room, the louder the squeal of a trumpet and the rumble of drums became.

"It sounds as though she has an entire band in there," said David, nearly shouting when I stopped outside of the door.

"I wouldn't put it past her," I said.

I threw open the door and planted my hands on my hips as I

surveyed the scene before me. The walls had been redecorated in indigo paper printed with a silver art deco pattern. A grand piano now stood at one end of the room, but at that moment it was the gramophone stand that caught my attention. Sound poured from it, and record sleeves were strewn on the floor around it.

And then there was Aunt Amelia.

She was dressed in an emerald and gold gown with peacock feathers in her swept-up silver hair, and she was lazing on a scarlet velvet chaise, a champagne bottle tucked between her and the back of it. In her hand was a half-empty champagne coupe. At her bare feet sat a long-haired cat wearing a collar encrusted with what looked suspiciously like sapphires. My aunt looked like the definition of decadence and I had to admit it suited her.

"Aunt Amelia!" I shouted over the blast of a trumpet from the gramophone. "Aunt Amelia!"

Aunt Amelia turned her head slightly but otherwise didn't react except to ask, "Evelyne, what are you doing here, and why on earth are you dressed like a cat burglar?"

I strode over to the gramophone and lifted the needle, bringing the music to an abrupt halt. "I know that it's your house, but I could ask you the same thing."

"I'm listening to American jazz. Wonderfully invigorating stuff," she said, hauling herself up while managing to keep both the champagne bottle and coupe steady—not a small feat.

"Louis Armstrong and His Hot Five," said David.

"'Heebie Jeebies.' Yes," said my aunt, seeming to see David for the first time. "Who are you?"

"This is my colleague, David Poole, Aunt," I said. "We have need of a telephone and a room where we won't be overheard."

"So you came here?" she asked.

"Call it the pull of familial love," I said dryly.

A smile cracked Aunt Amelia's remarkably unlined face. "Well, how could I deny a telephone to my favorite niece and a man who knows his jazz? Would you like something to eat while you make this urgent and very secret telephone call?"

My stomach growled in response.

"If it wouldn't be too much of an imposition," said David, clearly attempting to stifle a smile and failing spectacularly.

My aunt rose, the cat leaping up to follow her as she went to a velvet bellpull in the corner of the room.

"Henderson will no doubt enjoy the challenge," she said. "He's been moping about far too much recently. With this war on, it's nearly impossible to get up a party of anyone worth spending the time on. Too many evenings it's just Penelope and me."

"Who is Penelope?" I asked.

"This," said my aunt, scooping the purring cat up, "is Penelope. I forgot you wouldn't have met, because it's been—what?—five years since you've visited?"

"It has not been five years," I said a little guiltily as she deposited the cat into my arms. It had been closer to three, which, I will admit, wasn't much better.

David lost his battle, a wide grin spreading across his face, and I scowled at Penelope, who only purred louder.

Thankfully, Henderson's appearance at the door saved me from having to further defend myself from such slander.

"Ah, Henderson. Would you please show Mr. Poole to the telephone? And then I think a little late supper for my favorite niece and her guest would be welcome," said my aunt.

"Aunt Amelia, I have to be your favorite niece. I'm your *only* niece," I said.

"Don't take my affection for granted, Evelyne," warned Aunt Amelia.

Penelope leapt out of my arms in solidarity with my older relative and began to lick her paw, sending her sapphires glinting.

"If you would follow me, Mr. Poole?" said Henderson, clearly deciding it was best to remove himself from the situation.

As soon as the men had gone, Aunt Amelia said, "Good. Now we can have a little chat."

I was immediately suspicious given that I'd never heard my aunt call one of our discussions a "chat" in my entire life.

"What is it that you want to know?" I asked, sinking down onto a sofa, arms crossed.

Aunt Amelia took up her position on the chaise once more,

patting the velvet next to her. Penelope jumped up, circled three times, and curled up into a ball at her feet.

"What brings you all the way to Hampshire with a handsome stranger in tow?" she asked, her blue eyes glinting.

I stood up. "No. Favorite or not, I'm not here to provide gossip for you."

"Oh, Evelyne, take pity on a lonely old woman," she said, waving me back into my seat. "I haven't had a good bit of gossip in *months*."

"You are neither old nor lonely. I thought you had a whole gaggle of friends who were always traipsing through here," I said.

"Yes, but they're all Down right now," she said with a sniff.

I rolled my eyes. My aunt operated her own complex social ranking system by which she awarded or deducted people points that meant they were Up or Down. I suspected that even she didn't fully understand it but reveled in the fact that it allowed her to keep her various friends and enemies on their toes.

"You said that he's a colleague," Aunt Amelia prompted after a moment's silence.

"Yes," I said wearily, knowing that if I didn't give her something she would nag me relentlessly. "We are doing some work in Sussex, and we needed a private telephone."

"A secure line would probably be best, but the study should suffice given that Henderson will be occupied, you and I are here, and there's no one else in the house."

I stared at her. "What do you know about secure lines?"

A sly smile spread across her lips. "This isn't my first war, darling."

"What exactly *did* you do in the last war?" I asked, recalling that the last time I'd seen her she'd asked me to remember her to Major General Sir Vernon Kell, the former director of the Security Service, if I ever crossed his path.

"Oh, this and that," she said, waving a hand to dismiss the question.

"You know, I believe that less and less each time you say it," I said.

She grinned, her teeth flashing like a wolf's. "Just as I don't believe that you were really working as a 'typist' the last time we saw one another."

I stared at her, my lips pressed together, knowing that I couldn't say anything to confirm or deny that she was right. I hadn't just been a typist when she'd last seen me in London, just as I wasn't simply dropping in to use the telephone now.

"I suppose then that we must all have our secrets," Aunt Amelia finally said, breaking our stalemate. "Anyway, it's good you're here. It saves me a telephone call."

"Why is that?" I asked.

"I have some rather disturbing news for you," she said.

"Drop waists are coming back into fashion?" I asked.

"Oh, it's nothing like that. Besides, I looked smashing in drop waist gowns and bugle beads in 'twenty-three. No, Evelyne, I've had a telegram from your father."

I blinked. "Sir Reginald?"

"Yes, darling. Despite our best efforts to ignore the fact, he is still, unfortunately, your father."

"When was this?" I asked, ignoring her sarcasm.

She tilted her head as though thinking. "About two weeks ago. I tried to ring you, but a dopey girl picked up the telephone and claimed you were away and she didn't know when you'd be back. She took a message."

Two weeks ago I was probably on a night hike across the country-side, learning how to camouflage myself while setting dummy mines.

"I never received the message," I said.

"Clearly."

"What did he want?" I asked. "Money?"

"Surprisingly no. He was actually asking after you."

"Me? Why on earth would he do that? He's never shown one bit of interest in me," I said.

"If he were anyone else, I would say that you were being too harsh, but when it comes to my brother, I have to agree with you," she said. "He asked if you were still in London. I sent him a telegram back telling him that you were living in a boardinghouse with about a dozen other girls, and that it must be very difficult for you to have come down so far in life due to your father's own profligacy."

"But Aunt Amelia, I enjoy living at Mrs. Jenkins's. I don't feel as though I've come down in society at all," I said.

"Yes, darling, but he doesn't know that, does he? I would have thought you would enjoy taking the opportunity to guilt the man," she said.

"I don't think Sir Reginald is capable of feeling guilt."

Aunt Amelia tipped her champagne glass at me in agreement. "He did send a rather tart response back asking after your address."

"Did you give it to him?" I asked, a little aghast.

"I didn't see the harm." When she saw the horrified look on my face, she said, "Oh, darling, you're in the telephone book. If he wanted to look you up, he could."

"That would require him stepping foot in this country."

"Well, there's very little chance of that. I doubt he has the money to maintain the fiction that he is still a dashing adventurer and man-about-town. There's only so long that a gentleman can rely on credit before his tailor, haberdasher, and wine merchant begin to ask for payment in full."

"Where were the telegrams sent from?" I asked.

"Morocco," she said.

"Morocco?" I repeated with some surprise.

"Would you like to look at them?" she asked.

However, before I could decide, the music room door opened and David walked in, followed by Henderson with what looked encouragingly like a tray of drinks.

"Did you manage to get through?" I asked.

David gave me a nod, but his eyes shifted to my aunt who, incredibly, rose to her feet.

"Leave those, Henderson," she said. "I have the sneaking suspicion that these two have important things to discuss that aren't meant for our ears."

The butler set down the tray, gave a little bow, and followed Aunt Amelia and Penelope out of the room.

David watched the procession until the door shut behind them, leaving us alone in the music room.

"What an extraordinary woman," he said, looking a little dazed and a little smitten.

"Don't let her catch you saying that. She might never let you go," I said, reaching for a cocktail.

"I didn't mean—That is—"

I laughed. "Don't worry. My aunt is probably the only widow in England not looking for a new husband."

I took a sip, enjoying the sharp tang of gin against my tongue. "Gin rickey, Henderson's specialty. Cheers."

He lifted his glass to me in acknowledgment and then said, "As I expected, Mrs. White was not pleased to receive my telephone call."

"It isn't as though we killed Sir Nigel."

"I did point that out, but it didn't seem to make much difference in her eyes. Naturally the mission will have to change."

I nodded. "It's not just a case of theft now. We have the death of the senior engineer at a clandestine weapons facility, and it could turn out to be murder."

"Which is why I asked Mrs. White to persuade Baker Street to allow us full access to the investigation of the circumstances surrounding Sir Nigel's death. This is not the time for hiding behind departmental lines and bickering about jurisdiction. She's gearing up for a fight with them and the local authorities," he said.

"I would back Mrs. White in that fight." The woman had ice in her veins.

"That would be a wise bet," David agreed.

"What do we do in the meantime?" I asked, sipping my drink.

"We wait, and we think."

David sampled his drink and made a satisfied noise.

"I told you they were good," I said.

David gave a little laugh and tapped his glass gently against the rim of mine. "To Aunt Amelia's health."

———

Halfway through our gin rickeys, Aunt Amelia rejoined David and me and began regaling us with stories of her country and city friends. David and I both turned down a second cocktail, much to my aunt's disapproval and Henderson's disappointment, but David soon smoothed it all over by sitting down at the piano, picking out jazz tunes he sight-read off some sheet music he found in the piano bench.

"You didn't say that you could play," I said, turning the sheet music for "Avalon" for him.

"You never asked," he pointed out. "For all you know, I'm full of exciting hidden talents."

I snorted at that.

The telephone rang. David's fingers stilled on the keys, and all of us turned to the white Bakelite extension on a round table to the side of the sofa.

"May I?" he asked my aunt.

"Please," she said, gesturing at the telephone.

I watched him pick it up, studying his face as he greeted the caller and then listened intently, three lines forming between his brows.

"Understood," he finally said, and he replaced the receiver.

"Well?" I prompted.

"A moment of your time?" He jerked his head to the music room door. "I'd hate to disturb our gracious hostess again."

"Oh, don't mind me. Penelope and I are having a grand time," said Aunt Amelia. "You're both decidedly Up tonight."

David looked a little confused, so I said, "I'll explain later," and then steered him into the corridor.

"What did Mrs. White say?" I asked in a low voice.

"She has managed to clear the way with the West Sussex Constabulary. It turns out the police were delighted to hand things over to the Special Investigations Unit because the war means they're far too overstretched at the moment.

"As you can imagine, Baker Street was hesitant to release control of the investigation, as they are still very concerned that as few people as possible know about Blackthorn Park. However, Mrs. White convinced them that because the SIU is already familiar with the grounds and the report of possible theft, we stand a stronger chance of wrapping this up quickly."

"That's it then. We should say our goodbyes and head back," I said.

He shook his head. "We will be able to return first thing tomorrow morning when we're fresh and ready for a long day of questioning." He glanced at his watch. "It's just gone three o'clock. We can still manage a few hours of sleep if we're lucky."

"But the crime scene—"

"It is being guarded by your Constable Lee as we speak."

"He's not *my* constable," I grumbled.

"Either way, he has strict orders not to allow anyone in without our authority."

"Our authority?" I asked.

"I'm afraid you're lumped with me."

"So you're no longer my handler?" I asked.

"No."

"Then we can agree that we're equals in this investigation," I said.

He gave a little laugh and rubbed the back of his neck. "Evelyne, I learned last time that attempting to tell you what to do in a murder investigation—if murder indeed is what we're contending with—is generally a very poor idea."

I smiled. "I'm glad you agree."

He gave a long-suffering sigh that I thought was entirely uncalled for. "Shall we say that we're partners?"

I stuck out my hand to shake. "Partners it is."

"You really are the most absurd creature," he said, but he took my hand nonetheless.

"Thank you," I said, flicking my hair behind my shoulder. "Now that you've met my aunt, you'll understand that I come from a long line of absurd creatures."

ELEVEN

After managing a little sleep in a pair of Shaldeen Grange's guest bedrooms, David and I said our goodbyes to a blurry-eyed Aunt Amelia and Henderson and climbed into the car for the drive back to the village of Benstead.

When we reached the village's still-sleepy high street, the sun was just rising and only the bakery showed any signs of life.

"I'll drop you at your lodgings so you can freshen up and change. Your aunt was right, you do look like a cat burglar," said David.

"That was rather the point," I said, chewing on my lip as I pondered my limited wardrobe. I hadn't packed much, because I hadn't thought I'd be away longer than a single night. However, now that the mission had changed, I would need a few more of my things.

"What will you do in the meantime?" I asked.

"Don't worry about me," he said.

He parked in front of Russet Cottage and I hurried through the garden, opening the back door carefully to make sure it didn't squeak. From behind the boot room door, I could hear the faint sounds of Mrs. Smythe filling the teapot for breakfast. I crept up the stairs as quietly as I could.

I peeled off my all-black ensemble, splashed some water on my face, and combed through my hair. Then I pulled on the navy skirt from the suit I'd traveled in the day before, my one spare blouse, and a soft cardigan knitted in oatmeal-colored yarn. I freed *Maman*'s pearl earrings and watch from where I'd stashed them for safety the night before and then turned my attention to my hair. I did my best to tame it into a small roll at the back of my neck and tied a blue, white, and black silk scarf at my neck before dotting on some powder and a little lipstick.

It would have to do.

I grabbed my handbag, including the notebook and silver pencil Aunt Amelia replenished each year for my birthday, and fluffed out my folded navy beret before settling it on the crown of my head at an angle. With my coat and gloves on, I was ready to stave off the autumn chill.

When I reached the car, David climbed out to open the door for me. I went to slide in but realized there was a book on my seat.

"My apologies," he said, making a grab for it, but I held it away.

"What is this? Probably something hard-boiled and American," I teased. When I flipped it over, I saw the cover. "*The Postman Always Rings Twice* by James M. Cain? Another American pulp novel? You're at risk of becoming predictable, David. Is it any good?" I asked, lifting the cover with the tip of my finger.

He reached over and plucked the book out of my hands. "Enough of that."

"Can't a reader simply express an interest in another reader's book?" I asked innocently.

He studied me, as though wondering what I was about, so I smiled sweetly, knowing that part of the joy of investigating another case with David Poole would be tormenting him.

Just a little.

"It is good," he finally said. "Although I don't think Cain would be your cup of tea."

"Interesting." Naturally, being told that something wouldn't be to my taste immediately piqued my curiosity. Besides, I wanted to know what he saw in those ghastly books where every woman is a "dame" and the detectives all seemed to drink their body weight in cheap bourbon.

"Have you finished scrutinizing my reading habits?" he asked.

"For now. Is this your car?" I asked, looking about from my vantage point in the passenger seat. "It's not the one you had when you were undercover at the cabinet war rooms."

"I borrowed that one in case I needed to tail anyone. I didn't want to be recognized. This one is my car," he said.

"I like it," I decided.

"I'm glad it has your stamp of approval," he said with a small shake of his head.

"Did you change your shirt?" I asked, squinting at him.

"Yes," he said.

"Where?" I asked.

"In the car," he said. "I have a case packed with clothes in the boot at all times."

"You changed in the car where everyone can see?" I asked with mock incredulousness.

Much to my surprise, David actually blushed. "There was no one around."

"That's what you think. I guarantee that the curtain twitchers of Brook Road will be all aflutter by midday. You'll probably give me a reputation, driving off with a man who strips down to his natural state in full view of the neighbors."

His blush was fierce now, and he was beginning to sputter. "I did not strip down to my natural state, as you call it. I changed my shirt."

"And your undershirt?" I asked with a raised brow.

"I'm not discussing my undershirts with you, Evelyne," he ground out. "Besides, we need to focus on the task at hand. Mrs. White reminded me not very gently on the telephone of the prime minister's impending visit on Thursday."

That sobered me almost instantly. There might be a murderer on the loose, and Churchill was on his way. Those two facts did rather sharpen the mind.

"I thought we could start with the coroner. Do you know where the doctor's surgery is?" asked David.

"No," I said, "but I know who will. Come with me."

I popped out of the car again and ran up the path at Russet Cottage to knock on the front door, David trailing behind me. After a moment, Mrs. Smythe appeared red-cheeked, no doubt from standing over the morning's breakfast.

"Oh hello!" she exclaimed at the sight of me, wiping her hands on her apron—pink of course—and then holding it out to David. "I didn't realize Evelyne had a friend in Benstead. How do you do?"

"Cousin Caroline, this is Mr. Poole," I said by way of introductions. "We need a little information."

"How do you do, Mr. Poole? Would you like a cup of tea?"

"Unfortunately, I don't think we have the time," I said with real regret. "Would you be able to tell us how to find Dr. Morrison's surgery?"

"Yes, of course, dear," she said with a smile and proceeded to tell us the way in minute detail down to the very landmarks.

Despite the length of Mrs. Smythe's directions, the surgery turned out to be only three roads down and a right. David parked, and we both climbed out. He rang the doorbell, and a few moments later, the door swung open and we found ourselves faced with a young man.

"Hello, is Dr. Morrison in? We're here to speak to him about a body," I said cheerfully.

The youth's eyes widened. "Are you the investigators?"

"That's us," I said.

He looked from David to me. "But you're a woman."

I injected a little more sweetness into my smile. "That's what I'm told. Is the doctor here?"

"For heaven's sake, let them in, William," came a voice from inside the house.

The young man stepped back to allow us inside, where we found an older man whose impeccably maintained handlebar mustache stood in stark contrast to his rumpled suit that looked as though he'd shrugged it on the morning before. He stood in the door of what would have once been the sitting room of the house. He lifted his chin, assessed David and me, and then strode forward with his hand outstretched.

"Miss Redfern, Mr. Poole, I'm Dr. Morrison," he said. "I was told you would be coming."

"How do you do?" I asked, taking his hand. He had a firm grip without making it feel as though he was squeezing the life out of my fingers.

"Please come in," said Dr. Morrison. "Take a seat."

David and I followed him into what looked like his office and lowered ourselves into a pair of chairs facing the large oak desk.

"I'm sorry that your introduction to Benstead has been such a gruesome one," the doctor said, settling into his chair and folding his hand on top of his desk. "I'm afraid a great deal has changed since the requisitioning of Blackthorn Park, but no one would have dared guess that there would be a death on the grounds.

"It isn't very often that I'm called to a violent death, but it isn't unheard of." The doctor opened a file in front of him. "When I first examined the body at Blackthorn Park, it appeared that Sir Nigel died of a gunshot wound from a single shot fired from a .45-caliber revolver. Since he was found with a Webley Mk V in his hand, it isn't difficult to imagine that was the weapon of choice. I suspect that you'll find that it was his service revolver from the last war. We were all issued them. I still have mine rattling around in a drawer somewhere.

"Sir Nigel was right-handed, and the path of the bullet is consistent with the gun being placed to the right temple and fired. The position of the body was also consistent with suicide. However . . ."

I sat up a little bit straighter.

"Are either of you particularly squeamish?" asked the doctor.

"No," David and I said at the same time.

"Prone to fainting? Can't stand the sight of blood?" he asked.

We both shook our heads.

"Right, follow me," said Dr. Morrison, rising from his desk.

He opened a door off his office. It clearly was normally used as a storage room judging from the bookshelves neatly stacked with boxes. However, in the middle of the space was a metal table upon which a large mass was covered with a white sheet. There was a tall lamp set up next to it, along with a small cart topped with a white enameled tray holding several clean instruments.

"My grandson is rather fond of magic tricks, so I took some time last year to read a little bit about sleight of hand tricks," said Dr. Morrison. "Many of the tricks use misdirection, or drawing the audience's attention toward something irrelevant in order to keep them from discovering the true technique of the trick."

Dr. Morrison drew back the sheet, revealing a distinguished man in his late fifties. The blood had been cleaned up, making the wound at least a little bit more palatable, but the corpse's skin had a slightly waxy quality to it, giving the body an otherworldly look.

"As I said, at first it looked as though this was a clear-cut case of suicide. The man was found with a gun—likely his own service revolver—in his hand at his desk. However, I believe that was merely a clever misdirection."

Dr. Morrison pointed to a faint red pinprick on the skin right behind Sir Nigel's ear, where the hairline met the neck. "That is the mark from a hypodermic needle."

I sucked in a breath as David muttered, "Christ."

"My guess is that whoever killed Sir Nigel injected him with a sedative directly into the carotid artery. As soon as Sir Nigel lost consciousness, the murderer placed the revolver in Sir Nigel's hand, lined up the shot, and used Sir Nigel's own finger to pull the trigger. It's clever, really, because if you can hit that vein, the drug would take effect faster and cause much less fuss," said Dr. Morrison.

"However, there appears to have been one flaw in the murderer's plan. They missed on their first attempt," the doctor added.

"Missed?" I asked.

"Do you see this small scratch here?" Dr. Morrison pointed a little farther down the base of the hairline. "I think that our murderer tried to inject Sir Nigel but missed the first time."

"That might account for the stack of papers knocked off Sir Nigel's desk," I said to David.

"And the murderer didn't stop to right them," he agreed.

"If they thought someone might have overheard the struggle, time would have been even more of the essence. They would have had to stage the suicide and flee," I said before asking Dr. Morrison, "And you're certain of this?"

"I will send blood samples to a laboratory in London to be tested, but it might take some time to receive the results. I understand that they are struggling for staff due to conscription. However, I'm certain enough that this is how the murderer killed Sir Nigel that I would be happy to give evidence to as much in an inquest," said Dr. Morrison.

David blew out a long breath. "Looks as though you were right, Evelyne."

I tried not to preen, instead asking Dr. Morrison, "Is there anything else you can tell us?"

The doctor crossed his arms and gazed up at the ceiling as though pondering this.

"I suspect that you're dealing with a right-handed person who was standing behind the victim when he was attacked," Dr. Morrison finally said.

"Likely someone whom Sir Nigel would have been fairly comfortable with, given how close they must have come to him," I said.

"Also, given what is required to restrain and then inject a man in that precise part of the body, they would need considerable physical strength. Likely a man, but not necessarily. An athletic woman could have done it," said Dr. Morrison.

"Dr. Morrison, did you know the victim yourself?" I asked as the man covered Sir Nigel's corpse with the sheet.

"Only in a professional capacity. Sir Nigel came to my surgery once or twice. I also called at the Old Vicarage once to tend to Lady Balram. She suffers from migraines," said Dr. Morrison.

"Thank you, Dr. Morrison. You've been very helpful," I said.

As David and I turned to leave, I spun back around. "Dr. Morrison? Could I ask a favor?"

"Go on," he said.

"I'd like to keep the fact that Sir Nigel's death was a murder quiet for a bit longer."

I saw David jerk back a little as Dr. Morrison said, "You don't want to let the murderer know that you're wise to what he did."

"Precisely," I said.

The coroner nodded. "I can keep my own counsel until the inquest. Would that give you enough time?"

I nodded. "I suspect it will have to."

TWELVE

D avid remained silent as we left Dr. Morrison's surgery, but I could feel the tension radiating off him as we climbed back into the car.

"What's the matter?" I asked, as he slammed his door with more force than usual.

He rested his hands on the steering wheel, as though bracing himself.

"David?"

"I thought we were partners," he said slowly, as though choosing his words carefully.

"I beg your pardon?" I asked.

"You told me that you wanted to be partners in this case. That means that we both make decisions like whether or not to make it known that Sir Nigel was murdered."

Ah.

"You would be furious with me if I made a decision like that without speaking to you," he said, continuing to keep his voice calm.

He was right. In my enthusiasm for the case—and being right— I had overstepped.

"I apologize," I said immediately. "I should have discussed it with you beforehand."

"Thank you," he said.

"If you would like me to turn around and tell Dr. Morrison—"

"No." He closed his eyes. "No, it's a good idea. The murderer will no doubt be on alert because of our asking questions, but perhaps this will buy us a little time if they still think we're looking into a suicide. All I ask is that you not keep things from me, Evelyne. After all, you're the one who is always telling me how well we work together."

Sufficiently chastened, I nodded. "I'm sorry. I really am, David."

He gave me a small smile. "Shall we go solve a murder?"

"I think we'd better."

───────────

When we reached Blackthorn Park, the guard waved us through the gate and David drove up the long drive, parking in the wide courtyard created by the east and west wings of the house. It was only half past eight, but already there was smoke dancing out of several chimney pots on the vast roof.

We made our way through the heavy oak front door and up the main stairs without any incident. When we turned onto the east wing, we found a sleepy-looking Constable Lee standing outside Sir Nigel's office door.

"Good morning, Constable," I called.

He perked up immediately. "Good morning, Miss. I had a telephone call from my governor. He told me that I'm to help both of you however I can."

I had to hand it to Mrs. White, she might be a grump of the highest order but the woman was efficient.

"Well, that's certainly very kind of him," I said. "I don't think we were formally introduced yesterday. I'm Evelyne Redfern, and this is David Poole."

Constable Lee nodded in greeting and then pulled his notebook out of his left jacket pocket. "I interviewed all of the witnesses, just as you asked, Miss Redfern," he said, fumbling with the pages. "Would you like to know what they said they were doing when they heard the shot?"

"I would indeed," I said, unclasping my handbag and freeing my own notebook while David did the same from his inner jacket pocket. But when I spotted around the corner from us a flash of long black skirts like a housekeeper might wear, I stopped. "Perhaps it would be best if we go somewhere we won't be overheard."

David rounded me and tried the door next to Sir Nigel's office. He poked his head in and then said, "It looks as though this one isn't in use."

We all trooped inside, and I found myself in the middle of a bedroom that hadn't yet been converted into an office, giving me a sense of what Blackthorn Park had once been before the war. I sat down in the delicate chair of a lady's vanity while David perched on a yellow-and-white striped chaise at the foot of the bed and Constable Lee stood awkwardly by the marble fireplace.

"Now that we're alone, Mr. Poole and I should let you know that we've just come from the coroner." I glanced at David, who nodded. "It's imperative that you do not speak to anyone about this."

"I won't say a word. I swear," said Constable Lee.

"Dr. Morrison has confirmed that Sir Nigel was murdered," I said.

"Murdered, Miss?" asked the young man, his excitement clear. I couldn't blame him—not really. Finding my first body and launching into a murder investigation after reading about so many of them in novels had been a morbid little thrill. But I had quickly learned that it also was a deadly serious business.

"You can understand why it is more important than ever, Constable, that we have a clear account of everyone's movements and their relationship to the deceased," said David.

"Yes, sir," said Constable Lee.

"Now, tell us what you found out," I said.

Constable Lee looked down at his notebook, cleared his throat like a child preparing to recite a poem in school. "I spoke to Mr. Bernard Porter first. He said that he and his secretary, Miss Glenconner, were working in his office in the west wing when she went to fetch tea for them. He was waiting for her to return when he heard the shot followed by a crash and found Miss Glenconner at the top of the stairs next to broken tea things. Miss Glenconner, first name Alice, said the shot startled her and she dropped the tray she'd been carrying. After ascertaining that Miss Glenconner was unharmed, Mr. Porter offered to go investigate where the noise had come from and found you with Sir Nigel in his office." He glanced up. "He did ask me why I wasn't interviewing you, Miss."

"I'm certain he did," I said.

"After I spoke to Miss Glenconner, Mr. Frank Hartley escorted her home."

"Sensible," I said.

"Mr. Hartley said that he was working late in a workshop on the ground floor when he went outside to have a cigarette."

"It's rather a cold time of year for a nighttime smoke," I commented.

"Yes, Miss," said Constable Lee with a frown. "I didn't ask him about the weather."

I waved my hand to dismiss his concern. "Please carry on."

"Mr. Hartley said that he heard the shot and immediately thought of Sir Nigel because he knew that Sir Nigel kept a revolver in his desk. He nearly collided with Mr. Aaron Tyson on the main stair," said Constable Lee.

"Where was Mr. Tyson while this was happening?" I asked.

"He said that he'd been at the equipment sheds and had just made his way back to the house when he heard the shot," said Constable Lee.

"Was anyone else on the grounds at the time?" I asked.

He flipped another page. "A guard at the gatehouse named Peter Taylor, and a night watchman named John Finn. Neither of them report seeing anything or anyone unusual on the grounds yesterday evening. They said they saw one another at the gatehouse where Mr. Finn went for a cup of tea just before ten.

"After interviewing everyone, I told them they could go home. Then I dusted the room for fingerprints. It's the first time I used my kit," he said, sounding more than a little proud.

"That was very enterprising of you, Constable," said David, hiding a smile.

"I would expect to find Mr. Porter, Miss Glenconner, Mr. Hartley, and Mr. Tyson's prints in the room as well as Sir Nigel's. It's also possible that those of Jane Daniels, the housemaid, and Mrs. Sherman, the housekeeper, will be there," I said.

"I'll arrange to have those sent off to the expert in London," said Constable Lee, eagerly making a note.

"You've done an excellent job, Constable," I said as I started to rise.

"There is one more thing, Miss," he said. "I took up my post at the door of the crime scene around two o'clock once I had interviewed everyone. I didn't even leave to use the—" He stopped abruptly and flushed a furious red.

"I think we have a good sense of your dedication, Constable," said David.

"Around half past two in the morning, Mr. Porter came back," said the young man.

"Mr. Porter? Why?" I asked.

"He said that he needed to make sure that some documents were secured because of the sensitive nature of Sir Nigel's work. I told him that I was under strict orders not to open the door for anyone except the investigators. He argued with me for a little while, but finally he left."

I recalled the way Mr. Porter reacted when he saw the letter I'd found under Sir Nigel's blotter in my hand and wondered whether there was more to his anxiety than a concern for security.

"Thank you, Constable," I said. "You must be ready for a strong cup of tea and some rest. We'll take over from here."

"Thank you, Miss. It's been a very long night," he said gratefully, handing the key to the office over to me.

THIRTEEN

I found Sir Nigel's office much as I'd left it, save for the void where his body had once been. Now, in his place, there was a feeble attempt at a chalk line and the red-brown stain of dried blood on the floor and bookshelves. Traces of fingerprint dust were on all of the major surfaces where a killer could have conceivably left a mark.

"Poor Jane. She'll probably have to clean all of this up," I said.

"Any maid would have a challenge even without the aftermath of a murder. Sir Nigel certainly wasn't very neat, was he?" David asked, no doubt taking in all of the paperwork piled up around the office.

"Jane told me that Sir Nigel recently shouted at her for touching the papers on his desk while trying to clean it. Here." I leaned down. "I was holding this when Mr. Porter came barreling into the room and began accusing me of being a trespasser."

"Technically, you were a trespasser," David pointed out.

"David," I said, shaking the letter at him.

He smirked but took the paper nonetheless, reading out loud, "'Dear Sir Nigel, thank you for your telephone call. Arrangements have been made for your arrival. We will expect you at 1500 Tuesday. Sincerely, Lieutenant Colonel Julian Gerrard.' It's dated the seventeenth of October."

"Have you ever heard of a Lieutenant Colonel Gerrard?" I asked.

"Never. Where did you find this?" David asked.

"Under the blotter. Hidden."

"Then it sounds like the first order of business is to examine his desk and bookcase," said David.

"I'll take the drawers if you take the top," I said.

He nodded, and I gingerly pushed away the bloodied desk chair to gain access to the drawers. I was looking for something obvious—a diary containing all sorts of intimate secrets giving reasons why someone might want to kill Sir Nigel, a signed confession from the murderer—but in lieu of that I would settle for anything that looked significant. Unfortunately for me, the top drawer on the left side of the desk was packed with what looked like notes on various projects that Sir Nigel was working on. The pages bore titles such as "Waterproof Improvements upon Barnacle Bombs" and "Camouflaged Explosive Rocks." I came across one called "Shark Cutter," and immediately felt a pang of sympathy for sharks—if they were the target of such a weapon.

The next drawer was filled with technical drawings covered in red marks written in a slashing hand, including queries like "Calculations?" and "Prove efficacy."

"Anything?" David asked as I closed the second drawer on the left.

"Most of it seems to be just the sort of thing one might expect from the head of an engineering department at a weapons facility. What about yours?" I asked.

He held up what looked like more technical drawings. "I don't know what this does, but considering that this arrow is pointing to something that's labeled 'Nitroglycerine,' I think it's safe to say that it's wicked and deadly."

Shifting on my knees carefully to avoid the bloodstained patch of carpet, I moved to the right side of the desk. I gave the top drawer a tug, but it didn't budge.

"It's locked," I said.

"I wonder if the key is—" He stopped short when I pulled my lockpicks out of my handbag. "Or you could simply break in."

"It's not really breaking in if it's in service of an investigation."

"I'm not passing judgment. I'm jealous. I was never very good at lock picking in training," he said.

"Watch and learn," I said cheerfully.

I began to work the tools into the lock. After a moment, the unmistakable sensation that I was being watched settled on my shoulders. I looked up and saw David's face hovering near mine.

"Maybe not quite so close," I said.

"My apologies." He inched back.

I twisted a little bit farther and . . . the lock sprang open.

"You're quick at that, aren't you?" he said.

"Years of using hairpins to break into locked cabinets at boarding school gave me a slight advantage when learning," I said, slipping my tools back into my handbag and opening the drawer.

Unlike the desktop or the stuffed drawers on the left-hand side, this drawer was relatively neat. There was a small box of cigars, a guillotine cutter, and a half-empty box of matches. I opened a little plain cardboard box and found five bullets inside. Next to it was a crumpled handkerchief.

"David, I think this is where he kept his gun." I held up the box of bullets. "And just enough ammunition to load it."

"It certainly looks that way," he said, peering into the box.

"And I believe I've found the killer's second mistake," I announced with a grin. Mistakes were good. Mistakes meant that we were dealing with a killer who wasn't a professional. Someone who hadn't thought of everything that could go wrong during a murder.

"What's that?" he asked.

"The first was the disturbed papers, and now this. Why would a man about to kill himself lock the drawer he keeps his gun in?"

"We need to find out how many people knew about that gun and where Sir Nigel kept it," said David.

"We'll add it to our interrogation list."

The next drawer down revealed two Parker pens, a bottle of blue ink, a bottle of red ink, several pencils in need of sharpening, and a large leather book.

"Is that—?"

"A chequebook," I said, using a handkerchief to pull it free from the drawer and settling it on the blotter. I flipped the cover open and began to page through the counterfoils to look at the records of transactions. There were regular payments to several of the better London department stores, including Harrods, Fenwick, and Fortnum & Mason, as well as several sizable cheques written out to the bookshop Hatchards, the wine merchants Berry Bros. & Rudd, and what looked like a very expensive dressmaker. A few counterfoils read "Cash," usually for the value of £5 or occasionally £10.

"This looks like it was Sir Nigel's personal chequebook," I said.

"Why keep it here and not at home?" David asked.

"Perhaps he did his business at the office. Or maybe he had his secretary take care of his post so it was easier to write his cheques here." I flipped the next counterfoil and stopped. "Look at this."

David gave a low whistle. "Sir Nigel made out a £500 cheque last Thursday. That's quite the sum of money."

"And"—I flipped the counterfoil over to reveal that the following one was blank—"it looks as though it was the last one that he wrote before he died."

I flicked back through the stubs to show him some of the names on the previous entries. "There are quite a few expenses in here, but a £500 cheque for cash feels extravagant even when you compare it to these dressmaker and wine bills. We should speak to his wife. If Lady Balram doesn't know anything about it . . ."

"Then Sir Nigel must have wanted to keep it from her," he said, perfectly reading my thoughts.

"What did you find?" I asked.

"More drawings, more notes. They're all in different handwriting," he said.

"So they are likely from different engineers working at Blackthorn Park. I wonder how many of them work here."

"I don't know, but Sir Nigel's notes don't seem particularly flattering. Look at this," said David, holding up a drawing.

It showed a device at three different stages: a tightly rolled-up ball, that ball half unraveled to reveal a flat length of metal, and then that metal laid out completely with wicked-looking metal spikes protruding from it.

"'Porcupine Spikes,'" I read the label at the top of the drawing.

"Look at this." David pointed at a bit of handwriting that matched the entries in the chequebook. "'A child could tell that this alloy won't stand up to the pressure of a lorry's tires.' And here." David pointed to a place circled in red ink. "'Shoddy.' And 'a waste of time.'"

"That's not very constructive." I put my hands on my hips and looked about me. "We need to speak to the engineers."

"Among others," said David. "I'll see about securing us a room to use for interrogations."

I smiled. "Just like old times. Well, while you're doing that, I shall see if I can find our first witness."

"Who would you like to speak to first?" he asked.

"Mr. Porter," I said firmly because I couldn't think of a more pleasant way to start the day than making the pompous head of operations at Blackthorn squirm a little.

FOURTEEN

Thanks to Constable Lee's report, I knew that Mr. Porter's office was in the west wing, on the opposite side of the house from Sir Nigel's, so I left David to lock up and made my way through the Long Gallery, which connected the two wings.

As I walked along, I noticed darkened spots against the green flocked wallpaper where paintings of the Mountcastles, the family who owned the house, had likely once hung before its requisitioning. There was a sadness about this place, a sense that its glory days had been lost to time. And now a murder had been committed under its roof.

I stopped at a tidy desk topped with in and out trays tucked into the alcove where the gallery met the west wing. Steam rolled off a cup of tea that had been set to the right of a closed diary, and a woman's coat hung from a hooked hatstand next to the wall.

I heard a little whimper to my right and turned, noticing a door that had been papered and paneled so that it would blend seamlessly into the wall next to it. It was slightly ajar, and as I edged closer I could hear the gentle sound of a woman weeping.

I pushed the door open wider to reveal Miss Glenconner sitting on the floor of what was a glorified cupboard among boxes of paper, bottles of ink, and other supplies. Her light blond hair gave her an angelic look accentuated by her pale pink cardigan and the small gold cross she wore around her neck. As she looked up, I realized that she was lucky enough to be the sort of woman who was pretty even while blotched red and puffy from crying.

"Oh!" she cried, registering me in the doorway, and began to pat her pockets for a handkerchief.

"Here," I said, producing one from my pocket.

"Oh, thank you." She sniffled. Then her lip trembled, and she burst into tears once again.

"I beg your pardon," she sobbed. "I can't seem to stop crying."

"You've had a terrible shock," I said gently, kneeling on the floor next to her so that I could lay a light hand on her shoulder.

"Yes. Yes, it's been horrible. After Mr. Hartley took me home and Dr. Morrison came to give me a sedative, I still couldn't sleep. I keep . . . keep seeing his face."

She fell against me, pressing her nose into my cardigan. Living at Mrs. Jenkins's, I was well-versed in the care of crying women and had even received such care myself from time to time. I patted her on the back and made soothing noises until the sobbing subsided.

"What you must think of me . . ." She sniffed again, dabbing at her eyes with my handkerchief. "You were the one who found him."

"Were you very close to Sir Nigel?" I asked.

She looked up at me sharply. "No. Why would I be?"

"In my experience, when you work with people, you come to know them. Even more so if you're required to keep secrets about what it is you're doing," I said, recalling my time in the typing pool of the cabinet war rooms. I'd loved the company of my fellow typists, even during the tensest moments when bombs were falling on London and there was a killer among us.

Miss Glenconner gave me a tiny nod. "Blackthorn Park sometimes feels like a little bubble. The truth is that everyone here is overworked and terribly concerned about what they're doing because we all know that it could make such a difference."

"I imagine that's stressful," I said.

She sniffed. "It is, but everyone pitches in and helps where they can. I'm Mr. Porter's secretary, but I began to help Sir Nigel this summer."

"Did he not have his own secretary?" I asked, surprised. Usually a man in a role such as Sir Nigel's would have someone doing his typing, managing his diary, and taking dictation at the very least. His secretary would guard access to him fiercely, allowing him to focus on his work.

Miss Glenconner shook her head. "He didn't like the idea of keeping one. He valued his privacy. But as the demands on him grew, even he admitted that he needed someone to take dictation and do his typing. He seemed reluctant to hire from outside of Blackthorn Park, so I offered to help until he could find a girl he liked."

"Why did Sir Nigel trust you but not another secretary?" I asked.

"I suppose by that point he'd come to know me a little," she said. "The first week I was here, he noticed my accent. I've tried to lose it, but it comes back when I'm nervous and I was ever so nervous when I started at Blackthorn Park. Sir Nigel asked where in Yorkshire I was from, and it turns out that he spent time as a boy not ten miles from my father's parish church. He liked to talk to me about it. I think it was a happy time for him, and I . . ." She looked down at my handkerchief in her hands. "I think it made him trust me."

"Did you ever help him with personal matters?" I asked, thinking about the chequebook.

"No. He was very particular about his correspondence and anything related to his life with Lady Balram," she said.

"And Mr. Porter didn't mind sharing a secretary with Sir Nigel?" I asked. "I know that men can become territorial about these things."

She twisted my handkerchief in her hands. "He didn't like it, but Mr. Eccles did his best to reason with Mr. Porter."

"Who is Mr. Eccles?" I asked, remembering the name from Mrs. White's file.

"He's a go-between of sorts. I don't think Mr. Porter and Sir Nigel would have been able to work together if it hadn't been for Mr. Eccles." She clamped a hand over her mouth. "I shouldn't have said that."

"Why not?" I asked.

"Because it makes it look as though Mr. Porter might be part of the reason Sir Nigel killed himself."

"Well, is he?" I asked.

"No!" Miss Glenconner cried.

"Miss Redfern, you must understand that Sir Nigel and Mr. Porter never saw eye to eye. There was an *incident*."

"An incident?" Well, that was promising.

"It was before my time at Blackthorn so I don't know the details, but Mr. Porter claims that Sir Nigel did something that nearly killed him."

"Is that right?" I asked, storing that little piece of information away for Mr. Porter's interview.

"But that is just what I've heard," she hurried to add. "Rumors have a way of running wild here. I hate it. Really I do. People can be so cruel. The women in particular."

"I'm surprised the other women at Blackthorn haven't banded together a bit more," I said.

"Well, there aren't many of us, but we might have done it if it hadn't been for Miss Kenwood."

"Who is Miss Kenwood?"

Something flashed in Miss Glenconner's eyes. "She is the forewoman in the manufacturing barn where they make prototypes and test weapons. She only has the job because she's engaged to Mr. Hartley and he convinced Sir Nigel to bring her to the estate. What a disaster *that's* turned out to be."

"Why is that?" I asked.

"Sir Nigel had very exacting standards, and recently he'd come to the conclusion that the work being done in the manufacturing barn fell below his expectations. He believed Miss Kenwood should be replaced."

"Did Sir Nigel tell you that?" I asked.

"He didn't have to. He dictated a memo about it to me."

"When was this?" I asked.

She thought for a moment. "A few weeks ago? I think it was the middle of October."

I pulled out my notebook and made a note to ask Miss Kenwood about Sir Nigel's complaints.

"Do you remember who the memo was addressed to?" I asked.

"Several men at Baker Street, Mr. Porter, and Mr. Eccles."

"And was it ever sent?" I asked.

"I don't know," she admitted. "I suppose you think I'm terribly disloyal complaining about another woman while surrounded by all of these men. It's just that Miss Kenwood thinks she's better than all of the rest of us. Her. A glorified factory worker."

"That sounds trying," I said, doing my best to keep my tone neutral as I had once been what Miss Glenconner might call "a glorified factory worker" myself.

"My first day on the job, she was up at the big house for a meeting and Mr. Porter introduced us. She looked me up and down and then began to laugh. I immediately went bright red, and she scooped something up. It was one of my dress shields."

"Your dress shield?" I asked.

Miss Glenconner went crimson but still managed a dignified nod. "It was stitched into my dress and somehow it must have torn loose and worked its way down to the floor. She could have simply left it there or whispered to me what had happened when Mr. Porter wasn't looking. Instead, she handed it to me and said, 'I don't know how you do things in Yorkshire, but here in the south, ladies generally wear these hidden away.' In front of my superior! I nearly died of shame."

"That does seem unnecessary," I said.

"It was cruel, that's what it was." Miss Glenconner pulled her shoulders back. "I really should return to my desk. Mr. Porter will be missing me."

I had so many more questions for her, but there would be time. Instead, I said, "I've actually come to find Mr. Porter."

"As soon as he came in, he went off in search of Mr. Tyson. I believe they are expecting a large delivery of material today, which is why I really do need to return to my day," she said.

"As soon as you see him, would you please tell him that Mr. Poole and I wish to speak with him?" I asked.

She nodded, and I went off in search of my partner.

———

Well, this is a bit more aesthetically pleasing than our last interrogation room," I said as I gazed around the morning room in the west wing that David had secured for us to use. Even at this time of year, it was filled with light that caught the gilt around the massive mirror that hung above the room's mantelpiece.

Pale blue velvet curtains matched a Louis XIV sofa and chair set, and a large cabinet held an impressive array of crystal figures.

David had dragged a delicate cherry table into the center of the room and positioned two chairs on one side and another across from it. He was already sitting down in one of the pair of chairs, so I took the other.

"You took your time," he said.

"I didn't manage to find Mr. Porter. However, I did find his secretary, Miss Glenconner, crying in a cupboard," I said.

"She's not the same woman who was crying on the chaise when I arrived yesterday evening, is she?" he asked.

"The very same."

I filled him in on what I had learned about Sir Nigel's intense privacy, the "incident" between Mr. Porter and Sir Nigel, and Sir Nigel's memo recommending Miss Kenwood be replaced.

Just as I was finishing, there was a knock on the door.

"Come in!" I called.

The door opened, and Mr. Porter strode in. He looked freshly shaved, with an uncreased suit and a white shirt so crisp it looked as though it might strangle him. However, no amount of grooming could hide the deep bags under his eyes.

"My secretary said someone was looking for me—" Mr. Porter's eyes narrowed when his gaze landed on me. "You."

FIFTEEN

I didn't bother to suppress my grin as Mr. Porter turned an unappealing shade of scarlet all the way up to the shiny bald patch in the center of his head at the sight of me. "Good morning, Mr. Porter. I trust that you're well."

He turned to David and demanded, "What is she doing here?"

"Mr. Porter, why don't you take a seat?" asked David, already sounding weary.

"Not until I'm told who this woman is," demanded Mr. Porter.

"Mr. Poole and I have been put in charge of investigating the circumstances surrounding Sir Nigel's death," I said.

Mr. Porter scoffed. "You? In charge of an investigation? I don't believe it."

"It boggles the mind, but it is true," I said, my tone turning dry.

"And Baker Street knows about this?" Mr. Porter demanded.

"Mr. Porter, sit down," David barked. My brows jumped. I'd never heard him sound so exasperated, and apparently it took Mr. Porter by surprise as well, because the pugnacious little man slowly lowered himself into a chair across from us.

"I will explain how this interrogation will proceed," said David, his tone still stern. "Miss Redfern and I will ask you a series of questions, and you will answer them. Truthfully and without objection. You will address her as you will address me—with respect—or there will be consequences. Severe ones. Do you understand?"

"Yes," said Mr. Porter, even though I could tell it pained him.

"We understand that you are the head of operations at Blackthorn Park. What exactly does that entail?" I asked.

"It is exactly as it sounds." Mr. Porter crossed his arms until David glared at him, and he added, "I oversee the running of the place. Everything from finding adequate space for workshops and laboratories to making sure that we have a consistent supply of materials for the manufacture of weapons falls under my remit. At the moment, I am finishing an important project increasing the capacity of Blackthorn's manufacturing capabilities so that we are not dependent upon civilian or military facilities."

"What were you doing before the war?" I asked, picking up my pencil to begin jotting down notes.

He smoothed his tie. "I was a vice president at a steelworks company. That is where I was recruited from last November, and it's a good thing too. The place was in shambles when I arrived. Sir Nigel and Dr. Jamison had no idea how to run a facility. They were setting bombs off on the great lawn with no precautions, and running experiments wherever they saw fit. On my second day, they set the curtains in the east drawing room alight.

"One of my first tasks was designating space for everything they needed. Testing fields, workshops, laboratories. I had the access road rebuilt so that it could withstand the increased volume of traffic from lorries bringing materials onto the estate. I also worked on securing a regular supply of materials needed for experiments and prototypes."

"How would you describe your relationship with Sir Nigel?" I asked.

Mr. Porter shifted in his seat. "We had our disagreements, however, they were purely professional."

"Could you please expand on that?" I asked.

"Look, Miss—what was it?" Mr. Porter asked.

"Redfern," I said archly. I suspected that he remembered my name well enough.

"Miss Redfern, Sir Nigel was not what you would call a simple man," said Mr. Porter. "Yes, he was a talented scientist and inventor—

why else would he have been granted knighthood for his work?—however, he also had a special talent for infuriating people.

"Last December, not two weeks after I arrived, I was walking by the lake when there was a bloody great explosion. It shot water twenty feet in the air. I thought the Germans were bombing us to kingdom come. Naturally, I did what any sensible man would do and dove for cover.

"Then I heard someone laughing like a hyena. It was Sir Nigel. He'd detonated an underwater mine prototype and given no warning. It was bloody reckless if you ask me," Mr. Porter finished.

"Was he reprimanded?" David asked.

"No. Not that it would have mattered. He did exactly as he pleased, whenever he pleased." Mr. Porter leaned forward, his eyes ablaze. "But at some point, he would have pushed too hard and offended the wrong people—people we depend upon to keep Blackthorn Park operating, because even brilliant scientists need supplies. They need funds for research and materials. They need time and support to develop their inventions. They need men like me to keep the lights on. How else would he find one hundred coils of copper on short notice, or whatever else it was that he wanted? How would he find a way to source tens of thousands of boiled sweets?"

"Boiled sweets?" I asked.

"Apparently they are part of a timing device," said Mr. Porter, sitting back. "You would have to ask the engineers for more details."

"We'd like you to take us through your movements yesterday evening," said David.

"You told Constable Lee that you were working. It was ten o'clock at night. That's rather late, isn't it?" I asked.

"Not at Blackthorn Park, it's not," said Mr. Porter. "There were some reports that needed to be filed today. That's why Miss Glenconner stayed back to help."

"Where were you when you heard the shot?" I asked.

"In my office on the first floor of the west wing," he said.

"With Miss Glenconner?" David asked.

"No. She had gone to the kitchen to fetch us a pot of tea," he said.

"What did you do when you heard the gunshot?" asked David.

"The gunshot and the crash," said Mr. Porter. "Miss Glenconner dropped the tea tray when the shot startled her. When I poked my head out of my office, I saw Miss Glenconner at the top of the stairs, surrounded by broken tea things. She is skittish by nature, so I felt duty bound as her employer to first make sure she was all right," said Mr. Porter.

"I noticed that Miss Glenconner was particularly upset by Sir Nigel's death," I said.

"Yes, well, she would be. She's a very sensitive young woman who hasn't seen much of the world. I fear that what happened last night might have frightened her enough that she'll head back to Yorkshire," he said.

"What did you do next?" asked David.

"I went to investigate the shot. There are often explosions going off at Blackthorn Park, but gunshots are less common," said Mr. Porter. "I went straight to Sir Nigel's office because I happen to know that he kept his service revolver from the last war in his desk drawer."

"Would you say it was common knowledge he kept a gun there?" I asked.

"He liked to take it out and show it off. As though the rest of us didn't fight as well," Mr. Porter grumbled.

"After you gave your statement to Constable Lee, Mr. Porter, you were allowed to go home, but you didn't. Why did you try to return to Sir Nigel's office?" I asked.

The question clearly flustered the man because he flushed deep red again. "If you're implying—"

"Answer Miss Redfern's question," said David.

Mr. Porter pulled a cigar and cutter out of his jacket pocket, snipped off the end of the cigar, and stuck it into his mouth. Then he began patting down his pockets.

"Do you have a match?" he asked.

"No," David and I said in tandem.

Mr. Porter gave a grunt of frustration and had to settle for clamping his unlit cigar between his teeth.

"Over the past couple of months, Sir Nigel became even more difficult than usual," he finally said. "Every week it was something new. First, he wanted Tyson, our quartermaster, to perform an inventory on everything in the equipment sheds and to have that inventory repeated fortnightly going forward. It was a completely unreasonable request with the volume of materials we receive now that the manufacturing barn is operational, but Tyson is a good sport, so he agreed.

"Then, that same day, Sir Nigel got it into his head that he should acquaint himself with every aspect of our supply chains. He even demanded a list of the companies that we buy from so that he could telephone them himself. I put my foot down about that. Those relationships are delicate, and he was exactly the sort to go making demands or accusations and infuriating the wrong people."

It sounded as though Sir Nigel had suspicions that either supplies were not making their way to Blackthorn as they should or they were disappearing once they arrived. Almost as though someone were stealing from the site.

"When did this start?" I asked.

"The eleventh of October," said Mr. Porter.

"That's very precise," said David.

"It is my wife's birthday," said Mr. Porter.

"And how does this relate to why you returned to his office after his death?" I asked.

"In addition to the many sensitive papers that I suspected were unsecured in his office with an outsider like you around? I thought he might have written some . . . rash things down. He'd recently started borrowing Miss Glenconner in order to dictate memos complaining about someone or another," he said.

"Do you think he had written a memo about you?" I asked.

Mr. Porter leaned across the gap in the table, and I could see the light catch the growing patch of saliva on his cigar. "If someone worked at Blackthorn Park and didn't have one written about them, they probably weren't doing their job correctly."

"What about Miss Kenwood?" I asked.

He paused and then shook his head. "I don't recall him mentioning her recently."

Then either Miss Glenconner was lying about typing up a memo requesting her nemesis's replacement or Sir Nigel had never made good and sent it on.

"Did Sir Nigel ever mention that he thought someone might be stealing from Blackthorn Park?" I asked.

Mr. Porter barked a laugh. "Stealing? Not a chance. The only people who know about this place work here. It's too closely held a secret. An outsider would be spotted in an instant."

Never mind that I, an outsider, had infiltrated the grounds twice in a single day and Mr. and Mrs. Smythe in the village seemed to understand that something very secretive was going on at the manor house.

Mr. Porter rose to his feet. "If we are done, I must be going. I received a telephone call this morning to say that Eccles was due in on the 9:03 train, and I haven't seen him yet. I should find him so we can begin sorting this mess out."

I closed my notebook, and David said, "Thank you, Mr. Porter. If you would please send Mr. Eccles to us when you do find him, that would be much appreciated."

Mr. Porter looked as though he wanted to object, but then he seemed to think better of it and instead settled for huffing and shutting the door with more force than was entirely necessary.

As soon as he was gone, I turned to David. "Mr. Porter has put himself at great pains to try to paint a picture of Sir Nigel as a difficult man with very little concession to his own part in any tension between the two, don't you think?"

"I think both of them sound like a nightmare to work with," he said, dropping his pencil next to his notebook and scrubbing a hand over his face.

"I could not agree more. At least we now know that it's possible the killer knew about the gun in Sir Nigel's desk before yesterday evening," I said.

"But if it was as common knowledge as Mr. Porter says, that hardly helps us narrow the suspect list. Do you think he could have killed Sir Nigel?" he asked.

I twisted my lips, thinking.

"I believe, David, that we have only scratched the surface."

SIXTEEN

At about twenty to eleven, a man who looked like the picture of health strode into our makeshift interrogation room. His sandy hair was a little windswept, and his cheeks had a healthy pink glow. He was no doubt one of those people who think nothing of waking up early to ride or perform calisthenics or otherwise torment their bodies in the name of good health, and worse, he had the air of someone who might evangelize about such beneficial practices.

"I assume that you are Mr. Poole and Miss Redfern?" The likely athlete stopped in front of us and leaned over the table to shake David's hand. "Porter sent me through. I'm Timothy Eccles."

He shook my hand next, his grasp predictably firm and unyielding, as though he wanted to broadcast that he would show no weakness. Ever.

"Baker Street filled me in in the early hours. It was fortuitous that you were on hand yesterday evening, Miss Redfern. Although I will admit I was a little confused about why you were there in the first place until it was explained to me," he said, unbuttoning his jacket as he took a seat.

"You didn't know about the suspected thefts?" I asked.

"That's the trouble with working for a secretive bunch. They often keep secrets. And now a suicide." He shook his head. "It's a shame and a great loss to king and country. Sir Nigel was a great man."

"Mr. Eccles, as you can imagine we are trying to piece together a picture of what happened to Sir Nigel and what might have preceded it," I said.

"I'm happy to help in any way I can," said Mr. Eccles. "You see, we are anticipating a rather important visit from—"

"The prime minister," I said. "Yes, we are aware."

Mr. Eccles looked taken aback, but then smoothed his features out. "Then you can understand why it is in everyone's best interest to have this investigation wrapped up as quickly and quietly as possible."

"Why don't you start by telling us what your role at Blackthorn Park is exactly?" asked David.

"My title is government liaison, but really what I do is smooth things out between the staff at Blackthorn and Whitehall. The truth is that ninety percent of the threats to Blackthorn and the work that's being done here never come to the staff's attention because I protect them from them. Likewise, there are some things that the War Department and other ministers and undersecretary types don't need to know about what happens here. So long as we produce, I can keep the proverbial wolves at bay," he said, touching his necktie.

"What do you mean by threats to Blackthorn Park?" I asked.

"There is a great deal of infighting at the moment between the services and ourselves over materials and experts. As you can imagine, the army, Royal Navy, and RAF would all prefer that we focus on manufacturing regular weapons for them rather than those of sabotage for the SOE. The Ministry of Supply and the Ordnance Board are always nipping at our heels too. There are even some men who believe that the entire idea of 'ungentlemanly warfare' is a step too far. They think deception and sabotage is all rather un-British."

"Not quite cricket," I said.

Mr. Eccles nodded. "Exactly that. It is a high-minded and frankly naïve concern that Hitler and his high command don't have. I refuse to be a part of losing this war because we are too worried about being gentlemen to realize that our enemies have none of those qualms."

"How long have you held a position on the Blackthorn Park staff?" I asked.

For the first time since he entered the room, Mr. Eccles's smile edged over into condescending. "I would hardly call myself staff. Besides, I split my time between here and London."

"Is that unusual?" I asked.

"Everyone else who works here lives locally. It's a condition of employment at Blackthorn Park. However, splitting my time means that I can keep my finger on the pulse of what's happening in Whitehall while also ensuring that the staff here don't run amok," said Mr. Eccles. "I also have a personal reason to stay in London. My father-in-law is ailing, and about a year ago I had to step in to help run the family business. I'm not certain I would have taken the job here if I had known how demanding it would be, given everything else going on in my life, but all of us must make sacrifices in this war."

"When did you come on as government liaison?" I asked, reframing the question.

"January. I was working in Whitehall at the time, so I already had many of the connections in place that a man like Porter could never hope to possess having never worked as a civil servant. And Sir Nigel lacked the discipline and diplomacy needed to get anything done. No, it really couldn't be anyone else in this job but me."

While I didn't doubt that the man had been needed when he'd arrived on the estate, I also couldn't help but balk a bit at his arrogance.

"We understand that there was historically some tension between Sir Nigel and Mr. Porter," said David.

"Sir Nigel was not the most natural leader of men. He could grow frustrated if people were not quite so quick off the mark as he was. When I arrived, there were several members of staff who came to me and said they were ready to walk away if Sir Nigel continued to treat them as undergraduates rather than experienced chemical and mechanical engineers.

"And then there were the issues around operations. From nearly the first moment he arrived at Blackthorn Park, Sir Nigel had been making noise about building a manufacturing barn, but no one seemed particularly concerned that there was no coal for fires in the dead of winter and every time it rained the access road became a muddy pit that lorries couldn't get through," he carried on, making it sound as though, at any moment, he might take credit for conceiving of, building, and testing the devices made at Blackthorn Park too. "Sir Nigel and Porter were constantly running through the funds they were given each month. They were recruiting lower-level staff willy-nilly rather than arranging things with the Labour Board. I sorted out headaches like that. I even had a hand in choosing some of our suppliers because it was clear that some of his selections were lacking. March Chemicals, Longfellow & Son, West Sussex Electric, Kellerman Chemicals, the list does go on a bit."

"Mr. Porter didn't object to your oversight in these matters?" David asked.

Mr. Eccles laughed. "Naturally he did. He was particularly stubborn about bringing on Sheffield Steel."

"Why was that?" I asked.

"He was very stuck on the idea that we should buy from his old company, Wellington, Raleigh & Procter, but they were not able to provide a reliable supply of the materials we needed. They had to be fired. Eventually, Mr. Porter saw the light and understood that what we are creating here at Blackthorn was on a larger scope than he'd ever imagined," said Mr. Eccles.

I doubted very much that Mr. Porter had enjoyed learning that lesson.

"I'd like to turn to the events of yesterday evening," I prompted. "Were you at Blackthorn Park?"

"I was until I left for London on the 18:32 train. I always try to make it home for a late supper with my wife."

"How did you learn of Sir Nigel's death?" David asked.

"Someone from head office rang me at home to tell me about the suicide as soon as they had word," he said.

"When was this?" I asked, making notes.

"Around half past three in the morning. I caught the first train I could manage to buy a ticket for out of Waterloo this morning," he said.

"Why did you not come to Benstead sooner once you heard about Sir Nigel's death?" David asked.

"I was told it was clearly a case of suicide. Besides, I gave up my car at the start of the war. The petrol ration and all that. Walking is the best exercise by far. My wife and I are very fond of outdoor pursuits," said Mr. Eccles.

"Which train did you catch?" I asked.

"The 7:21, although it was held just outside of Woking. That seems to be happening more and more these days," he said, reaching into his jacket pocket to pull out a wallet. He produced two train tickets. "Traveling to and from Benstead, I accumulate quite a few of these. I clean my wallet out at the end of the week."

I leaned forward to examine the tickets. There was one for yesterday evening's service to London and one for this morning's return to Benstead, each with the neat punch of a ticket inspector.

"Thank you," I said, sitting back.

"Had you observed any changes in Sir Nigel's behavior recently?" asked David.

Mr. Eccles considered this for a moment. "We started to hear rumblings that the prime minister might come to Blackthorn Park last month. Sir Nigel began to become more demanding than usual, but I put this down to nerves. He knew that Blackthorn Park needed to start producing viable weapons and soon."

"Why is that?" I asked.

"According to some people in Whitehall, all we've done here is spend money with little to show for it. It doesn't help that the manufacturing barn project was completed £2,500 over budget." Mr. Eccles's expression grew serious. "I cannot stress enough how important this week's visit from the prime minister is. It is the culmination of a year's work, and if it does not go off . . . I don't know if this facility would survive such a high-profile failure.

"Sir Nigel called me into his office yesterday afternoon to tell me that he was beginning to have his doubts about the demonstration. He was worried that the barnacle bombs in particular, which we expect Baker Street to invest heavily in, would not be up to scratch. I told him that was ridiculous, that he was simply nervous." Mr. Eccles stopped abruptly. "You don't think that's why he killed himself, do you?"

"We need to explore all avenues of inquiry," I said. "Did he share what made him doubt the efficacy of the barnacle bombs?"

Mr. Eccles shook his head. "I wish he had confided in me, but he wasn't that sort of man."

"Were there ever conflicts between Sir Nigel and members of staff other than Mr. Porter?" I asked.

"I'm not certain I would call them conflicts," he said carefully. "More isolated incidents."

"What would you characterize as an 'isolated incident'?" I asked.

Mr. Eccles cleared his throat. "There was a bit of fisticuffs between Mr. Hartley and Sir Nigel."

"Sir Nigel hit Mr. Hartley?" I asked in surprise.

Mr. Eccles sighed. "I believe you'll find Mr. Hartley tried what the Americans call 'to take a swing' at Sir Nigel in the lab one day in August. You would have to ask Mr. Hartley for further details, as I was not there."

I planned to do just that.

"Were there any repercussions?" asked David.

Mr. Eccles shook his head. "From what I understand, labs can be pressure cookers, and tempers can run high. Everything blew over soon enough."

"Were you aware that Sir Nigel kept a gun in his desk drawer?" I asked.

"Yes. It was his service revolver. I think it reminded him of what it had been like in the last war and helped motivate him to continue pressing on when he found himself frustrated. He didn't want this war to be anything like the last one."

"Mr. Eccles, are you aware of any issues with security on the grounds? Unauthorized personnel or missing equipment? That sort of thing?" I asked.

He frowned. "No. Not that I can recall."

"Will you be staying in Benstead tonight if we have further questions?" I asked.

He shook his head. "I'll be on the train back to London, as usual. If you need to reach me, my office is Hunter 5547. There's an answering service if my secretary has gone home for the evening. They'll make sure a message makes its way to me, day or night."

I jotted down the exchange as he rose to leave.

Mr. Eccles had a hand on the morning room's doorknob when he turned and said, "I had a great deal of admiration for Sir Nigel. He could be a hard man to like, always complaining about something or another, but he had an incredible work ethic and he truly believed in what he was doing. I hope he didn't kill himself over the shame of any mistakes he might have made. It would be a great loss for all of us."

SEVENTEEN

After Mr. Eccles left, David said, "Well, he certainly seems to think Sir Nigel killed himself."

I stared at my notebook, tapping my pencil against the page.

"What is it?" David asked.

"Who reported the thefts at Blackthorn Park?" I asked.

"The report was anonymous," he said.

"Yes, but who is the anonymous person? Mr. Eccles appears not to know anything about it, and he's the one who has the most contact with Baker Street."

David frowned. "You think theft might be connected to Sir Nigel's death?"

"It feels like too much of a coincidence that the SIU is called upon to perform a security check at a secret government research facility and, the very same day that I arrive, the head of engineering is killed in his office in a staged suicide," I said.

"Well, when you put it like that . . ." David trailed off. "Did you manage to actually look at the inside of the equipment sheds when you had your look around yesterday?"

"Mr. Tyson and Mr. Hartley were there, so I thought I'd leave it until it was dark." A plan that had become rather derailed by murder.

"If your theory about the theft and the murder being connected is true, I think we need to see these sheds." He hauled himself up from his chair. "I'll see if I can hunt down a set of keys for us."

"And I will find some tea for us before seeking out Mr. Tyson or Mr. Hartley."

"That's right, you missed breakfast. It's a wonder you haven't faded away," David teased me.

"You laugh, but when I find us something to eat you'll thank me," I said.

He smiled. "That's probably true."

I glanced at my watch. "I'll meet you back here in a half hour."

———

I made my way down the servants' stairs to the lower ground floor and poked around until I found the kitchen. Pleased to see that someone had left a kettle waiting next to the great iron stove that dominated one wall, I opened the top to find that it was already filled. I lifted the stove's boiler plate over and set the kettle on it to heat.

After a little rummage around in the kitchen cabinets, I came up with a caddy of tea, a pot, a strainer, cups, saucers, and teaspoons— I'd learned from my time in the cabinet war rooms that one of the perks of working in a government facility is a healthy stream of tea even with rationing in place.

I was just measuring out leaves for the pot I'd found when I heard the clatter of shoes on the stones outside the kitchen, and Jane appeared in the door. Her eyes went wide at the sight of me.

"Hello," I said, setting aside the spoon.

"What are you doing here?" the maid asked.

I gave her a half smile. "I have a confession to make. I'm not Mrs. Smythe's cousin."

She sank down onto a battered wooden stool pulled up to the kitchen's huge worktable. "You're not?"

"I'm afraid not. I'm here investigating the death of Sir Nigel," I said.

Both of her hands flew over her mouth and, between her fingers, she whispered, "I hardly knew the man. I just cleaned for him. I promise I didn't have a thing to do with his death."

I raised a brow. "I never thought you did."

I had waved Jane to bed before heading up myself at half past nine o'clock the night before. Even if she had managed to traverse Russet Cottage's stairs, which I knew squeaked badly because the wall of my room butted up against the staircase, she would have had to avoid being sighted by me, the guard in the guardhouse, the night watchman, and any number of staff who were still milling around the place.

If Sir Nigel had been murdered, the murderer must have been either incredibly stealthy or someone whom no one would have batted an eye at seeing in Blackthorn Park at ten o'clock at night.

A housemaid like Jane, who was meant to leave at the end of the conventional working day, didn't fit the bill.

Jane put a hand to her chest, clearly relieved. "I just keep thinking about what I told you yesterday. That Sir Nigel yelled at me. But I swear I didn't even mind that much when he yelled at me."

"I understand, but perhaps you could still help me."

"I don't know anything," said Jane quickly.

"I don't know about that." I perched on the stool across from Jane. "I suspect you know a great many things about the people who work at Blackthorn because it helps you do your job well."

I could see the compliment working on Jane as her expression changed. "Not that any of them appreciate it. Do you know how many times I've had to try to scrub ink off the wood floor or tables in one of the workshops because one of the engineers has knocked it over? Or clean the mud out of Mr. Eccles's office carpet because he's always taking those blasted walks of his? And don't think for one moment that the ladies are any better. Miss Glenconner is always leaving cups of tea on her desk at the end of the day for someone else to clean up. She says that it was because she's so used to having help at home, but she's not at home any longer, so why she can't bother to walk her dishes downstairs is beyond me."

I leaned in and gave her a conspiratorial smile. "I've often thought that people underestimate domestics at their own peril. I'll bet you've heard all sorts of stories about Sir Nigel."

"I wouldn't like to say," said Jane, in a way that told me she very much would like to say in very great detail, "but you can hardly help overhearing things from time to time because people don't notice a maid, do they? Not that I'm listening at keyholes or anything like that."

"Did you ever overhear Sir Nigel arguing with anyone?" I asked.

Jane's eyes lit up, and I suspected that I had guessed at the right button to press.

"Well," she began, "there was one time when Mrs. Sherman—she's the housekeeper here—she told me to give Sir Nigel's office a deep clean. Apparently he'd left Blackthorn in the afternoon the day before, not telling anyone where he was going. When he hadn't shown up in the morning, she assumed he was in London or somewhere like that. But he must have come back without her realizing it because when I reached his door, I could hear him shouting at someone."

"Did you hear what he said?" I asked.

"I could hardly have not heard it," she said. "He did say something like 'Whoever is behind it deserves to be hanged for treason!'"

I held my breath, waiting for more. It certainly *could* have been a threat and motive for murder, but without any context I couldn't be sure.

When Jane failed to elaborate, I was finally forced to ask, "Is that it?"

The housemaid sat back, arms crossed, in a huff. "What do you mean, 'Is that it?'"

"Did you hear Sir Nigel say anything else?"

She lifted her chin. "I saw the office was clearly occupied, and I found something else to clean. Like I said, I don't listen at keyholes."

For someone who so clearly relished in gossip, I doubted it was quite so straightforward as that, but I held my tongue.

"Did you recognize the voice of the person he was speaking to?" I asked.

She shook her head. "Sir Nigel used to boom when he would get into a mood. That's the only reason I could hear him through the heavy door."

"Did you happen to see who left the room?" I asked, desperate for some scrap of anything.

"Like I said before, I didn't stay," she said.

"Do you remember when this was?"

She thought for a moment and then said, "Thursday a fortnight ago."

I did a quick calculation in my head. That would make it Thursday the twenty-fourth of October. Two days after Sir Nigel's planned meeting with Lieutenant Colonel Gerrard, if the letter I'd found was to be believed.

"You're very certain of that?" I asked.

"Every other Thursday, Mrs. Sherman makes me polish the paneling along the Long Gallery in the morning. It wasn't last week, so it must have been the week before," said Jane.

"That's very helpful, thank you," I said.

"Is it?" she asked, sounding pleased.

I nodded. "Now, Jane, I want you to think very carefully and tell me if you remember anything else involving Sir Nigel that might have seemed strange to you."

She gave a little laugh. "Everything is a little strange at Blackthorn. There are explosions indoors from time to time, none of the men seem at all interested in anything except science, and we can't talk to anyone about anything that happens here. I don't even know what it is that this lot is meant to be doing at Blackthorn, although I have my guesses."

"Perhaps it was something you saw in Sir Nigel's office. Something that seemed out of place?" I pushed.

"There was one thing," she began slowly. "But I would hate for anyone to think I was poking around in places that aren't my business."

"I promise, no one but my partner, Mr. Poole, and I need to know."

Jane nodded. "Normally I sweep the east wing corridor and then the next day do the west wing, alternating back and forth. Only the other day Mrs. Sherman got it into her head that the east wing needed to be swept a second day in a row because I hadn't done a good enough job. I was almost to Sir Nigel's door when I heard a woman. She was crying."

"You're certain it was a woman even though you told me you can't hear through that door easily?" I asked.

"Her tone was much higher pitched than Sir Nigel's. And she was crying. Loudly."

"When was this?" I asked.

Jane thought for a moment and then said, "It was last week."

I was about to ask her if she could remember the exact day when a sharp "Miss Daniels!" sent both Jane and me jumping.

A tall, gaunt woman with a stern expression strode into the room and stopped just in front of Jane.

"A man has died, and you're gossiping about him? Shame on you. I'd thought you'd know better than that," the woman scolded.

"I'm sorry, Mrs. Sherman," Jane mumbled, her shoulders flying up around her ears in a full-bodied wince.

"You will return to your work at once," ordered the housekeeper. Jane scrambled up from her stool, around the table, and out the door while Mrs. Sherman squared up to me, hands folded in front of her stomach like the portrait of a vengeful queen. "I take it that you are Miss Redfern."

"I am," I said, rising to my feet.

"Mr. Eccles just told me about you and that Mr. Poole." She sniffed. "Sir Nigel's body isn't even cold yet and you're poking your nose around, trying to cast aspersions on his good name."

"I'm simply trying to do the job I've been tasked with, just as your job is, no doubt, taking care of this house," I said calmly, gambling on the fact that, as one of the remaining links to the Mountcastle family left at Blackthorn Park, she would feel protective of the place.

That seemed to take the wind out of her sails a bit. "Yes, well, I should have thought it would be a straightforward matter. Sir Nigel killed himself."

"And yet we are still left with the question of why," I said as the kettle began to whistle. "Why don't you join me for a cup of tea?"

Her eyes narrowed as she spotted the pot. "That is rather presumptuous of you, helping yourself."

"I always think best with a cup of tea in hand," I said cheerfully, using a tea towel to pull the kettle off the boiler plate and pour the hot water into the teapot. Then I set the pot and both sets of china I'd liberated from the cupboard onto the table.

"I don't suppose there's anything except powdered milk in the kitchen, is there?" I asked hopefully.

Mrs. Sherman's lips thinned, but then she stiffly turned and disappeared through an open door only to reappear with a milk jug.

"There used to be a home farm at Blackthorn Park, but the Mountcastles rented it out about twenty years ago on the condition the farmer would continue to supply the house. The farmer didn't see fit to stop even after the government took over," she explained, setting the huge jug down on the table with a clunk.

"If you're going to do something, I say, do it correctly," she remarked.

"I couldn't agree more," I said, taking my seat once again. After a moment, she did the same.

"Mrs. Sherman," I said, beginning again, "I apologize for speaking to Jane before I spoke to you. I see now that I should have sought you out first."

She lifted her chin a fraction. "Jane Daniels is a silly girl who is inclined toward the dramatic."

"She could have valuable information," I said. "She mentioned that she overheard Sir Nigel and a woman arguing."

Mrs. Sherman looked away. "Well, I shouldn't like to speculate, but that's hardly a surprise. Everyone knew that Sir Nigel had a wandering eye."

"Then Sir Nigel dallied with women here at Blackthorn?" I asked casually as I poured, watching her out of the corner of my eye.

"I never said that," she snapped.

I set a cup of tea down next to Mrs. Sherman's hand. "As you can imagine, the government would be incredibly grateful to anyone who can shed light on what might have happened to Sir Nigel. No detail is too small."

I could tell that had snagged her attention when she said, "Well, if it's a patriotic duty . . ."

"It is," I reassured her.

Mrs. Sherman picked up the tea, took a sip, and then said, "Last Friday, Miss Daniels was feeling poorly. It was just a common cold, but I sent her home. I happened to cross paths with Mr. Tyson, who had just accepted a delivery of goods. He warned me that Sir Nigel was in a mood and had just demanded that they go through every box together and compare it against both the bill of sale and Mr. Tyson's own inventory sheet. I knew that could take hours, so I decided that with Sir Nigel occupied I would clean his office because it had been days since anyone had been able to dust in there.

"One of the first things I always do is clear out the grate and tidy up around the coal scuttle because the coal dust makes such a mess. However, when I looked into the grate, I saw several pieces of paper that were singed but had escaped burning."

"Was it a letter?" I asked.

She shook her head. "A cheque. One of the pieces had Sir Nigel's signature on it. I thought it was odd because who would tear up a cheque they had written and then burn it?"

"Could you see who it was made out to?" I asked.

"No, but on one of the half-burned pieces, I saw what looked like the number fifty. Now, £50 is a great deal of money, even to a man like Sir Nigel. Don't you agree?" she asked.

Yes, I did, especially when I knew that the cheque could actually have been for £500.

It would fit the timeline. The counterfoil in Sir Nigel's chequebook was dated last Thursday, and Mrs. Sherman had said she'd found the cheque the following day. And if Jane's account of hearing a woman crying last week was connected . . .

"That's very helpful, Mrs. Sherman."

"Is it?" she asked, looking rather pleased with herself. "I'm glad of that. It's a terrible thing, something like this happening at Blackthorn Park. I can assure you that no one ever died when the Mountcastles were in residence."

"I'm sure no one would have dared."

"If you ask me," she continued, "I think Sir Nigel became a little too entangled with a lady and killed himself because he knew that there was no way out. His wife is a piece of work. My husband, Captain Sherman, is the station manager in Benstead, and he tells me that there's always some parcel or another arriving on the London train for her. Their housekeeper is at the station nearly every day collecting them."

I was beginning to suspect that between Mrs. Sherman's job at the manor house and Captain Sherman's role as stationmaster, there was very little that happened in the village of Benstead that the couple wouldn't eventually make their business.

"Do you know whether Sir Nigel had any enemies here at Black-thorn? Anyone who might wish harm upon him?" I asked.

Mrs. Sherman pinched her lips together and then slid me a look. "Every single man here seems to have some sort of argument with every other one. If you ask me, if it was women who were running things, we wouldn't be in this war in the first place."

I was pleasantly surprised to find Mrs. Sherman had such an unexpectedly enlightened view of things until she added, "Of course, that's ridiculous. Can you imagine, women running the government? It's bad enough that they've let some of them become members of Parliament."

And with that, my opinion of the housekeeper came crashing down to earth.

I sighed into my cup of tea. "Thank you, Mrs. Sherman. You've been very helpful."

"It's a nasty business, and the sooner it's over, the better."

On that point I couldn't agree more.

EIGHTEEN

After our chat, Mrs. Sherman loaded up a tray with fresh tea things and a couple of rock cakes and sent me off to retrace my steps to the morning room. However, when I emerged from the servants' stairs onto the ground floor of the east wing, I could hear raised voices, one of which I was certain was my partner's.

Mindful of the tea tray, I hurried toward the argument and found David standing across from a red-faced Mr. Porter and an amused Mr. Tyson in the middle of the manor house's mahogany-paneled entryway.

"Absolutely not," said Mr. Porter fiercely.

"I understand that you are trying to protect the work that is being done here—and normally that would be commendable—however, these circumstances are far from normal. We are investigating a death," said David.

"The man bloody shot himself! What else is there you need to know?" Mr. Porter exploded.

"Hello," I said, sidling up to them. "Anything I can do to help?"

"I am trying to explain to Mr. Porter that we need keys and access to all of the spaces at Blackthorn Park and its grounds," said David with a sigh.

"And I am trying to explain that, without the appropriate clearances, I won't be able to do that," said Mr. Porter.

I glanced at Mr. Tyson, who put his hand up. "I'm only involved because I have the keys."

"Well, this is a conundrum," I said. "You see, Mr. Porter, our orders come from the very top of the government."

"As I was just saying," muttered David.

"So do mine," said Mr. Porter, squaring up to me.

"Is that right?" I asked. "Mr. Tyson, is there a telephone I could use? A secure line would be preferable."

"Right this way," said Mr. Tyson.

I followed the quartermaster across the entryway, tea things gently rattling with my every step. Mr. Tyson opened a door, and I stepped into a beautiful library lined on all sides with shelves and shelves of books and a wooden ladder that ran along a track. It was with deep regret that I set the tea tray down not to scramble up the ladder and examine the spines of every book, but to pick up the telephone that sat on a small round table next to one of the library's two tufted navy velvet sofas.

"What are you doing?" Mr. Porter demanded as I picked up the receiver.

I ignored him as the switchboard operator connected and said, "Number please."

"Miss Redfern, what are you doing?" I could hear the panic begin to creep into Mr. Porter's voice as David and Mr. Tyson, who was now munching on a rock cake, looked on with amusement.

I covered the receiver. "I'm telephoning my superior, who will telephone your superior, who—if they can't resolve the matter between themselves—will likely receive his own telephone call from the prime minister asking why you are intent on obstructing our investigation. I doubt very much that Mr. Churchill will appreciate being pulled away from the very important business of trying to win the war, but needs must."

Mr. Porter turned a rather delightful shade of puce. "You can't—"

"Is something the matter?"

We all turned and found Mr. Eccles standing in the doorway.

"Miss Redfern was just encouraging Mr. Porter to cooperate with our investigation," said David, as Mr. Tyson tried to shield what I was certain was silent laughter with his half-eaten cake.

"I don't think that will be necessary, will it, Miss Redfern?" asked Mr. Eccles, his voice calm.

"Number please?" the switchboard operator repeated.

"I'm certain we can come to a compromise," said Mr. Eccles. "Now, shall we speak about this like civilized people?"

Slowly, I replaced the telephone in its cradle.

"Good," said Mr. Eccles, closing the library door behind us and gesturing to the sofas. When we were all seated, David and me on one sofa and Mr. Porter and Mr. Tyson on the other, with Mr. Eccles occupying the sole club chair, Mr. Eccles continued. "Miss Redfern and Mr. Poole, what is it that you require?"

"Access to all areas of Blackthorn," said David, "from the offices to the equipment sheds. It is imperative to our investigation."

"I see," said Mr. Eccles.

"But their clearances—"

"I've just spoken to Baker Street. Their clearances will be more than suitable, Mr. Porter," said Mr. Eccles, efficiently cutting his colleague off. "I should not need to remind you that we will all have to adapt to some changes with Sir Nigel gone and the prime minister due in two days. I had a word with Dr. Jamison, and he has kindly agreed to step into Sir Nigel's considerable shoes and head the engineering team. Miss Kenwood will continue to supervise the women in the manufacturing barn. I will continue to work to make sure the demonstration runs smoothly. So you see, Mr. Porter, very little, if any, of this should affect you."

"As the most senior member of staff now that Sir Nigel is gone—"

"I believe you will find that *I* am the most senior person in the room now," said Mr. Eccles sharply.

Mr. Porter shrank a little bit but fought on in a manner that might have almost been admirable had I not found the man so obnoxious. "You are only at Blackthorn some days."

"Nearly every day, which has never been an issue before. I will also remind you of why I was assigned to Blackthorn in the first place," said Mr. Eccles, shooting the head of operations a warning look. "Mr. Tyson, is there a set of keys for Mr. Poole and Miss Redfern?"

"Yes," said Mr. Tyson cheerfully, clearly enjoying the spectacle.

"Is there also a current map of all the outbuildings on the estate?" I asked, remembering the lack of a manufacturing barn on the plans David and I had initially studied.

"I can find that for you," said Mr. Tyson. "I also have a map of the estate, including the woods, or at least what's left of it. Most of the Mountcastle fortune came from lumber; however, it was overlogged at the end of the last century and is not as productive as it once was."

"But it is beautiful," said Mr. Eccles. "I take a keen interest in the outdoors, and I often find the woods a pleasant place to walk when I need a moment to clear my head. I believe Dr. Jamison shares my appreciation, as do several other members of staff if you should need assistance finding your way."

"Thank you," I said, holding back the fact that I'd made my own foray into the woods twice now.

"Now, if all of that's settled"—Mr. Eccles pushed himself to standing—"I have more important things to attend to."

Mr. Porter stalked off with a last glare for David and me, but Mr. Tyson lingered. When we were alone, the quartermaster broke into a grin.

"It's good to see Mr. Porter put in his place from time to time," said Mr. Tyson.

"Miss Redfern does have a particular talent for doing that," said David, repressing a smile.

"Thank you," I said. "I shall choose to take that as a compliment from both of you."

"Oh, you should, Miss. You certainly should," said Mr. Tyson. "I have the keys in my office. If you'll both follow me."

NINETEEN

D avid and I trailed behind Mr. Tyson as he led us up the main
stairs and past Miss Glenconner, who had taken up residence
at her desk again. A little way down from what I assumed was
Mr. Porter's office due to its proximity to his secretary's desk, Mr. Tyson
paused to unlock a door using a key on a ring attached to a long chain
secured on one of his belt loops.

I suspected that, like Sir Nigel's office, Mr. Tyson's had once been a
bedroom. However, there wasn't a scrap of evidence as to the room's
former use. Instead, pegboards had been hung up on two walls, and
those boards were covered in all manner of tools. Several of the bulky
metal filing cabinets that seemed to be ubiquitous in government offices lined another wall, and a large workbench was pushed up next
to the door. In the center of the room there stood a small desk topped
with a brass and green glass lamp.

"Please come in," he said. "Now, keys. The only people that have
a master set of keys are Mr. Porter, Dr. Jamison, Sir Nigel, Miss Kenwood, and myself."

"Not Mr. Eccles?" I asked.

The quartermaster shook his head. "He never has need of the
equipment shed or places like that. If someone does need something
that's locked away, they have to speak to a key holder who is meant to
then accompany them all the way to it."

Mr. Tyson unlocked a filing cabinet and rummaged around until he came up with a key ring.

"Here we are," he said, handing it to David, who'd stuck out his hand. "This is the only spare set. These keys will let you into every door in the manor house and across the estate. They're all labeled. If there's one you can't find, just give me a shout and I'll help you."

"We'll look after them," David promised.

"You said that staff are now supposed to be accompanied by a key holder if they want access to the equipment sheds," I prompted.

"It's a new rule, and it's taken some adjustment." Mr. Tyson frowned. "Although I suppose it's really just Mr. Hartley who's been having a difficult time remembering. Just yesterday I was in the shed, and he came up without anyone else. Either he'd convinced someone like Jamison to give him a key unaccompanied, or he wanted to try his luck that I would be there."

"What prompted the new rule?" I asked.

Mr. Tyson gave me a tight smile. "Sir Nigel. One day he came storming up to my office, accusing me of being—what did he call it?—'derelict in my duty' because his engineers didn't have a certain chemical they needed. I told him that I'd ordered it, Mr. Porter had signed off on the paperwork. I even showed Sir Nigel the paid invoice made out to Collingswood Chemical Manufacturers, where we get the stuff from."

"Do you have a rough idea of when this was?" I asked, taking out my notebook for what felt like the twentieth time that day.

"I can tell you exactly when it was. Friday the eleventh of October," said Mr. Tyson.

"You're very sure of that," I said.

"Sir Nigel demanded I do an entirely new inventory. He wanted it done by the end of the month. I finished it by the following Friday," said Mr. Tyson.

"That must have been a nuisance," I said.

"On the contrary, Miss, I was happy to do it," said the quartermaster. "I don't like giving anyone reason to call my work into question. A fresh inventory meant that there would be no doubt. I showed it to Sir Nigel and told him I would be adding everything that came onto the estate so, as long as Sir Nigel did his part and gave the staff a talking to about keeping the logs up to date as they took things, it would stay accurate."

"And did he?" asked David.

"That very day. In fact, he told the engineers, Miss Kenwood, and the girls from the manufacturing hut that anyone who didn't follow procedures would be fired. I'll wager that put Dr. Jamison's nose out of joint. Mr. Hartley's too."

"What about Miss Kenwood?" asked David.

Mr. Tyson scratched his beard. "The women don't say much. Never complain. They're the easiest out of this lot."

"We understand that there has been tension between Sir Nigel and Mr. Hartley for some time," I said.

"You mean the punch?" asked Mr. Tyson. "I don't know the particulars, but it seems that Mr. Hartley, despite all of his airs and graces, has quite the right hook. It seemed as though Sir Nigel took it well, and things calmed down."

"You don't seem particularly surprised or concerned," I said.

"If you stay long at Blackthorn Park, you learn not to be surprised by much," said Mr. Tyson.

"Where were you at ten o'clock last night?" asked David.

"Here," he said.

"In this room?" asked David.

He shook his head. "I was walking back from the equipment sheds."

"Why were you working so late?" I asked.

For the first time since we'd met in the entryway, the light seemed to dim from the quartermaster's eyes, and he cleared his throat. "My wife died last year. I don't have much to go home for these days, so sometimes I work late to keep myself occupied."

"I'm very sorry for your loss," I said.

He nodded. "Thank you."

"Did you see anyone or anything unusual yesterday evening?" I asked.

"Not until I heard the shot ring out. It was a quiet night—well, you would know that, Miss, wouldn't you? I ran toward it and nearly crashed straight into Mr. Hartley at the foot of the main stairs," he said.

"Which direction did Mr. Hartley come from?" I asked.

"The east wing. I assumed he had been in the laboratory set up in the east drawing room. That's where the engineers usually are," he said.

"And which direction did you come from?" I asked.

"The west wing," said Mr. Tyson.

I frowned. "If you had just come from the equipment sheds, wouldn't it make more sense to have also been coming from the east wing? The equipment sheds lie to the east of the house."

Mr. Tyson nodded. "It would, but I stopped by the orangery first to check and see if the sealant was dry on a panel of glass I'd replaced earlier that day. Miss Daniels broke it when an explosion startled her. She put a broom straight through it."

"Mr. Tyson, would you be able to show us the procedure that the engineers are meant to use when it comes to the equipment sheds?" I asked.

"Happy to," he said.

David and I followed him downstairs and out of the house via the front door. As we walked, I asked, "How did you come to be the quartermaster at Blackthorn Park?"

"The army, Royal Navy, RAF, and Royal Marines all said that I'm no good for fighting. Apparently they only want men with two arms—damned unimaginative of them if you ask me," he said with a grin. "I was casting about, trying to figure out what to do, when my father's old captain recommended me for a job here. I didn't know the half of what I was signing myself up for."

"If you don't mind me asking, what happened to your arm?" I asked.

Mr. Tyson shrugged. "I don't mind at all. It's the ones who pretend not to see it that bother me. It was caught in a thresher when I was about fourteen years old."

"That must have been incredibly painful," said David.

"Ah, I'm just grateful my dad stopped it in time, otherwise I would have gone straight in after it," he said.

Our progress down the access road was much faster than mine had been when I'd woven through the trees. When we reached the clearing, Mr. Tyson gestured to the three sheds. "Which would you like to see first?"

"Why don't we start on the right?" I suggested for no reason other than it was the closest.

Mr. Tyson pulled out his keys, unlocked the padlock, and hauled open the door.

Metal racks lined each of the walls with some freestanding in the middle of the space. On each rack, carefully labeled, were giant spools of wire, sheets of copper, and huge bottles of chemicals all labeled with terrifying-looking warnings printed across them. On a set of racks splitting the shed into two sat boxes and boxes from Samuel & Sons Rubber. I poked my nose into one box and immediately snapped back. It was full of condoms.

"Apologies, Miss," said Mr. Tyson, taking off his hat and rubbing at the crown of his head with the heel of his hand. "They come up with some strange uses for things here. French letters for waterproofing the underwater devices. Boiled sweets as timing devices on all manner of bombs."

"Well, so long as they're effective," I said.

David, who had just looked into the box to see what all of the fuss was about, swallowed a laugh that set him into a coughing fit.

While my partner regained his composure, I asked, "What was this before Blackthorn was requisitioned?"

"It used to be a store for farm equipment," said Mr. Tyson. "I understand that about six months before the war, the farmer built his own sheds closer to the farm for the convenience. When our lot arrived, the old sheds were torn down and these ones were built."

I stamped my foot on the poured concrete. "Is the floor new as well?"

"We inherited the center one, but the right and left are new. Still, it saved me a job only having to pour two slabs myself," he said. "I'm getting ready to pour more at the manufacturing barn for their own equipment store if Mr. Eccles can manage to secure us the money."

"That was part of Sir Nigel's grand plan to make everything on-site?" I asked.

"Yes," said Mr. Tyson. "First it was the manufacturing barn for prototypes and the first stage of production. That's already up and running. In fact, the first shipment of barnacle bombs went out for practical testing at the end of September."

"Do you remember where they were sent?" I asked.

"Arisaig House, Inkerly House, and Eldermount . . . Court, I think it was? A fortnight ago I sent another lot to a railway station in Dover."

"Just a railway station?" David asked.

He shrugged. "That's what I was told to do."

"You said that the manufacturing barn was in its first stage. What is next?" I asked.

"Next stage will be new equipment stores and then a second manufacturing barn with a second team of women working under Miss Kenwood."

"That's a great deal of responsibility," I said.

"Miss Kenwood is good at what she does," said Mr. Tyson. "Sharp as a tack, that one."

"Sir Nigel must have been glad to be able to rest easy with a young woman of such talents working for him," I remarked.

Again Mr. Tyson rubbed the base of his palm against the back of his head. "I don't know that Sir Nigel ever rested easy about anything. He could be demanding, and I think he and Miss Kenwood clashed a few times, especially with Sir Nigel keeping a closer eye than ever on how much the manufacturing barn was making on account of being so close to mass production. I don't think it was serious though. That was the thing about Sir Nigel. He could blow up at a moment's notice, but if you kept your head down and did your work, eventually things would pass."

"Mr. Tyson, have you seen any loose boards in here or had to do any repairs to the walls?" asked David, looking around us.

"Sir Nigel asked me that not too long ago," the quartermaster mused. "I went over every inch of the place. The only way in or out of here is through that door. The rest of the sheds are just the same."

"Why do you think he wanted to know?" I asked.

Mr. Tyson shrugged. "I really couldn't say. Everyone's been on edge recently, imagining everything that could go wrong on Thursday. They won't say it out loud, but both Mr. Eccles and Mr. Porter have been flapping around like mother hens for weeks now, they're so worried about the demonstration going well. Their jobs are on the line."

"I imagine losing your head of engineering the same week as a visit from Churchill is not ideal," said David.

"No, Mr. Poole," said Mr. Tyson with a laugh, "but when has this war ever been concerned with anything but being a bloody nuisance?"

TWENTY

David and I left Mr. Tyson to lock up and made our way back to the main house. While we walked, I filled him in on what I'd done since we'd left the morning room following Mr. Eccles's interrogation.

"I believe I may have found a reason or two why someone might want Sir Nigel dead," I began. "I ran into Jane, the housemaid. She said that she once overheard Sir Nigel yelling."

"That seems in keeping with the man's sunny disposition," said David.

"Quite. Apparently he shouted, 'Whoever is behind it deserves to be hanged for treason!'"

"Well, that's certainly damning," he said.

"Unfortunately, on that particular day, Jane had an inconvenient moment of good conscience after hearing Sir Nigel's outburst and crept away from the door. However, last Thursday she also heard a woman sobbing in Sir Nigel's office. Before she could tell me anything further the housekeeper, Mrs. Sherman, discovered us and sent her back to work with a stern reminder not to gossip."

"That is a shame," he said.

I tilted my head. "Maybe not. For all of her professed disapproval, Mrs. Sherman does enjoy a natter."

David raised his brows in question.

"She told me that, when she was cleaning Sir Nigel's office last Friday, she found a torn-up cheque, half burned in the grate of his office fireplace," I said.

A slow smile crossed David's face. "Let me guess. It was for £500."

"The parts she could see were singed, so all she could make out was a five and a zero," I said.

"But knowing what we know . . ."

"It's not hard to imagine that that was the last cheque he wrote made out to cash," I finished.

David frowned. "That's quite the sum of money to tear up and then burn. If it was the crying woman who tore it up in the first place."

"My guess is that there aren't too many women in Sir Nigel's orbit who could afford to do that, unless they were truly furious with him. So we have a brilliant engineer murdered. He may or may not have had a credible reason to believe someone who may or may not have been working here was acting treasonously. A woman, whom we cannot identify, was crying in his office on Thursday, possibly leading her to tear up a cheque for what might have been a very large amount of money and throw it in the fire. Or maybe not."

"As clear as mud," said David. "And from Mr. Tyson, Mr. Porter, and Mr. Eccles, we know that several men working at Blackthorn Park all had recent arguments with Sir Nigel."

"And Miss Kenwood was possibly on the chopping block thanks to the memo Sir Nigel dictated to Miss Glenconner recommending Miss Kenwood be replaced," I said.

"A memo that Mr. Porter claims he never saw despite Miss Glenconner telling you that he was one of the people it was intended for," he pointed out.

"So our prime suspect is either a woman or a man who likely works at Blackthorn Park. We're making such great progress," I said gloomily as our feet crunched on the lime of the house's courtyard.

"That is the nature of investigations," said David with a shrug.

I knew he was right, but I didn't have to like it.

"There is one thing that struck me," I said, taking out my notebook.

"Tyson, Eccles, and Porter all seemed to imply that Sir Nigel was always challenging, but starting around October he'd become worse."

"All of those protocols and new systems that he put into place around the equipment sheds," said David.

"Don't forget the accusations of negligence against Mr. Porter and Mr. Tyson for not keeping tabs on the supplies. And Mr. Hartley's famous punch," I added.

"What happened in October that exacerbated Sir Nigel's natural prickliness?" asked David.

"I want to know more about Sir Nigel's life away from Blackthorn Park," I said.

"We could pay Lady Balram a visit after lunch," he suggested.

"I think that is a very good idea," I said as we stepped foot into the manor's entryway. But, before we could formulate a plan, we were met by an anxious-looking Constable Lee, who stood halfway up the stairs, clutching his ever-present notebook.

"Good morning. Again," I said.

"Miss Redfern, I . . . I've been interviewing members of staff, asking their alibis and that sort of thing. Just like you asked," said the constable, trotting down the last stairs to greet us.

I caught David's slight smile before he dipped his head.

"That's very helpful, Constable, but I thought you were going to rest," I said.

"I couldn't sleep. You said to return in the afternoon, but I thought it wouldn't hurt if I came back a little early. That is all right, isn't it?" he asked eagerly.

I pushed back my sleeve to check the time, only to find out it was high time for lunch. My stomach grumbled, reminding me of the now-cold tea and rock cakes I'd left behind in the library upon finding David squaring off with Mr. Porter.

"Goodness, the day is racing away from me. Your ambition is very appreciated, Constable," I said.

Constable Lee beamed at that while David cleared his throat and suggested we return to the morning room.

Once we were safely behind closed doors, David asked the constable, "What have you found?"

Constable Lee nearly fumbled his notebook but managed to open it and began to explain. "I assumed that you would want to speak to the main players who were present yesterday evening yourselves, so I left them off my list for now."

"Very astute, Constable Lee," I said.

He blushed. "Thank you, Miss. I took it upon myself to speak to Mrs. Sherman, the housekeeper, and the housemaid, Miss Daniels. Both said they were at home at the time of the murder. Mrs. Sherman said that she cooked dinner for her husband and then they both went to bed after listening to the wireless. Miss Daniels said that she had dinner with you, actually." He looked up. "Is that right?"

"It is," I said.

"There is also a barn where some sort of manufacturing is done? No one would really tell me more than that," he said. "It's staffed by women. With the exception of the forewoman, Miss Kenwood, those working there are all housed in the same boardinghouse. Every morning they are picked up and driven to Blackthorn Park in a coach. They arrive at eight o'clock and work until seven o'clock, when the coach returns and brings them back to their lodgings. They are not allowed in the manor house."

I glanced at David. "We can likely eliminate them, but it would still be good to make sure all of them have alibis, if you would, Constable?"

"What about Miss Kenwood's alibi?" asked David as Constable Lee scribbled a note to interview the manufacturing barn workers.

"She says she had dinner out with Mr. Hartley and then was at home for the rest of the evening," said Constable Lee. "She didn't see anyone. She said that, although no one can confirm she was there all night because she was alone, she didn't leave her flat."

"And I suppose she expects us to take her word for it?" I asked, letting a touch of sarcasm slip into my voice.

"Yes?" Constable Lee asked, clearly unsure whether I was being serious or not. "Is there something I should do next?"

"Constable, we need you to walk the perimeter of the estate. Look for any shoe prints or evidence that someone might have climbed over a fence or pushed through the hedgerow to try to avoid the gatehouse," said David.

The young man looked between us, his expression a little pained. "All of it, sir?"

"Constable Lee, do you have ambitions for yourself?" asked David.

"Yes, sir. I—I'd like to make detective one day," stammered the constable, tugging a little at the high collar of his uniform.

"Then this is your first lesson," said David. "In investigating any violent death, it pays to be thorough. No detail should be overlooked, even if it might seem tedious at the time."

That was, I thought, actually rather good advice.

Clearly Constable Lee agreed with me because he said, "I'll walk the grounds," with a renewed sense of purpose.

"As soon as you're done with confirming those alibis," I said.

"Yes, Miss," he said.

"Oh, and don't mind the woman-sized footprints a few hundred feet along from the access road gate as you head away from the village," I said.

"Yes, Miss," said Constable Lee.

"Isn't it useful then that you happen to be in exactly the right place at the right time to assist us with our investigation?" I asked cheerfully. "You'll have excellent examples of your work when you ask for a promotion."

Constable Lee broke out into a grin. "Yes, Miss."

When the constable had gone, David turned to me and said, "I think you may have a new admirer."

"I beg your pardon?" I asked.

"You didn't notice him stammering and blushing like a schoolboy? He could hardly manage the words when you first walked in."

"You're being ridiculous." Because he was. Besides, I enjoy a man's respectful attention from time to time, but I could honestly say that I had no interest in the constable. Although it's likely we weren't too far off in age, there was something youthful about his eagerness and naïveté that made me feel positively maternal toward the young man.

"I am not," David insisted, warming up to his teasing now. "I think he's quite smitten with you."

I made a little noise of frustration in the back of my throat that made him laugh, which just annoyed me even more. Poirot never had to deal with this sort of rubbish from Captain Hastings.

"Clearly you don't have enough to divert your attention if you're making up stories," I said.

"You're just tetchy because you haven't had enough to eat today," he said.

"I haven't had *anything* to eat today," I said.

"It's a wonder you haven't expired on the spot." He glanced at his watch. "It's nearly one o'clock. Would you like lunch before we go speak to Lady Balram?"

Naturally, my stomach chose that moment to gurgle with enthusiasm.

He laughed. "I don't know why I bother asking anymore. The answer is always yes."

"I managed to weasel rock cakes out of Mrs. Sherman for you, and then I had to save you from near-fisticuffs with Mr. Porter, so I never got to eat. Be kinder to me," I grumbled.

"Well, in that case, lunch is my treat."

Never a woman to turn down a good meal, I collected my handbag with as much dignity as I could muster and accepted his arm.

TWENTY-ONE

After agreeing that our chances of finding a decent lunch at Blackthorn Park on such very short notice were close to nil, David and I clambered into the car and he pointed us in the direction of the village. However, when we reached the Benstead high street, David continued on to the outskirts of Benstead.

"Where are we going?" I asked.

"I spotted a country pub called the Hand and Flower just around the bend when we were driving last night," he explained. "The sign says they do food."

Just as the houses began to thin out, the pub rose up before us on the right. David pulled the car off the road and into the yard of what must have been an old coaching inn with a wooden sign of a cavalier's gloved hand holding a rose.

"It looks as though they have rooms too," said David, pointing to another painted sign advertising rooms over the pub. "I might inquire. I need a place to stay for the foreseeable future."

Inside, we were greeted by the pleasant coziness of a wood fire burning at one end of a small dining room. I found us a table in a corner with no one nearby while David went to ask about the menu. It was limited—hardly a surprise on the ration—but there was chicken and leek pie to be had, so he placed our orders at the bar and, after returning with our drinks, settled down across from me.

"Do you know," I started, taking my lager from him, "I keep thinking about that letter hidden under Sir Nigel's blotter. Where does it fit?"

"We don't know that it does," said David. "It could be completely unrelated."

"Then why hide it?" I consulted my notebook. "The letter was dated the seventeenth of October, but Sir Nigel began to display suspicious behavior as early as the eleventh when he accused Mr. Porter and Mr. Tyson both of undermining his work."

"Maybe Sir Nigel noticed that something was amiss, but it's only after visiting Lieutenant Colonel Gerrard—whoever he is—that he realizes that someone might have been stealing from the facility," said David, sipping his ale.

"So either someone resented Sir Nigel for something and killed him—in which case we have an unrelated case of theft we also need to deal with—or Sir Nigel found out the identity of the thief and that person killed him to keep him quiet," I said.

David frowned.

"What?" I asked.

"It feels like an overreaction. Murdering a man for a few stolen spools of wire or bottles of chemicals?"

"Stealing from a"—I glanced around me and whispered—"secret government facility that Churchill himself thinks will be key to winning us the war? I suspect that the punishment for that would be very great indeed."

The waitress stopped at our table to put our pies in front of us, and we fell silent. When we were alone again, David said, "There's something that doesn't sit quite right with me. If Sir Nigel suspected that supplies were going missing, why not report it to Mr. Eccles since he's the liaison? Or directly to Baker Street?"

I picked up my knife and fork and broke through the pie's crust. It was topped only with mashed potato—no doubt a concession to the government-endorsed collective tightening of belts across the country—but there was plenty of steam rolling off the leek, chicken, and sauce inside.

"I suppose there are three possibilities. One, Sir Nigel actually did speak to Mr. Eccles, and Mr. Eccles reported it anonymously."

"That doesn't make sense. Why wouldn't he just report it as himself?" he asked.

"Mr. Eccles seems to take great pride in his role as a sort of savior and fixer at Blackthorn Park. Perhaps he worried that if he admitted to HQ that something was wrong at the facility, it would come down on his head."

"You said there were two other possibilities," said David.

"Someone we don't know yet reported the theft. Or Sir Nigel is the anonymous source," I said.

David frowned. "Why wouldn't he report Blackthorn Park to Baker Street through the normal channels?"

"We know that he'd become increasingly erratic and irritating in the last month—particularly the last two weeks. What if he believed that involving *anyone* at Blackthorn Park in his amateur inquiry risked the thief finding out?" I asked.

"But maybe the thief discovered what he was doing anyway and Sir Nigel paid the price for it," David mused. "I suppose it's plausible."

"Plausible isn't good enough. We need definitive." I chewed a bite thoughtfully, took a sip of my beer. "I think we need to find Sir Nigel's correspondence and to speak to this Lieutenant Colonel Gerrard."

David pushed away from the table and set aside his napkin. "If you'll excuse me one moment."

"Where are you going?" I asked.

"To telephone Miss Summers for Lady Balram's address and to see if she can find Gerrard."

David rejoined me to finish our lunch, but it wasn't until our drinks were nearly drained that he asked, "How did you find training?"

I looked up from my last bit of pie. "I beg your pardon?"

I noticed him shift in his seat as though uncomfortable. "I know it's been some time since I went to finishing school, but I thought I'd ask."

I carefully chewed my pie, swallowed, and then set my napkin aside. The extra time gave me a moment to compose my thoughts.

I thought of all of those men and women I'd arrived at Beaulieu with. We were all nervous, excited, glancing around at one another, wondering who would make it to the end of training and what we would all be doing for the SOE.

Seven dropped out in the first week, eleven the next. Each week we'd lose a few more, some to injury and some to the psychological stress of it all. In the end, only twenty-three of us reached our final tests.

"I made it through," I finally said. "I won't pretend that it wasn't difficult. There were times when I was so cold or so sleep-deprived that I thought I might not make it to the next day. But then I did because what else could I do?"

David gave me a small smile. "You're braver than you give yourself credit for."

My laugh sounded hollow. "I didn't make it through because I'm brave, David. I made it through because I'm pigheaded. I couldn't stand the thought of proving Mrs. White right. She doesn't like me."

"She doesn't like anyone."

"Perhaps, but at least she trusts you," I said.

"That wasn't always the case. It takes time, but once you earn her respect, you'll have it for life," he said. "Unless you betray it, of course."

I tilted the dregs of my beer toward him. "I would expect nothing less. What were you doing in the six weeks I was away? Wishing that I was there, because having me as your new partner makes your life so much easier?"

That earned me a laugh. "That's not exactly how I would put it. As you know, I spent two weeks training to become a handler for agents in the field—something Mrs. White has been pestering me about for some time."

"She won't be happy when she realizes how little you want that job," I said.

"She will not," he agreed, "but I'm not ready to leave the field. I know it's more dangerous, but it isn't as though I have anyone waiting at home for me."

I almost said, "Neither do I," but I stopped myself because that wasn't true. I had Aunt Amelia and I had Moira. Guilt made me flush as I realized that Moira's play hadn't even crossed my mind since I'd discovered Sir Nigel's body. I'd given my word to do everything I could to make it back in time to see the first performance, but I knew that a murder investigation meant I would likely be forced to break my promise.

"What did you do with the rest of your time while I was gone?" I asked, moving the subject along as much for my sake as his.

There was a long pause during which I could feel him studying me, as though weighing the prudence of telling me . . . well, anything. Finally, he said, "I was in Cornwall. Visiting family."

"I didn't know you had family in Cornwall."

"An aunt and uncle," he said.

"On your mother or father's side?" I asked, secretly delighted because David had a tendency to ration out information about himself one crumb at a time.

"My aunt Caroline is my mother's youngest sister. My parents used to send me to stay with her during the summer holidays. They would enjoy the Season until Wimbledon finished and then go off to the Riviera until September," he said.

"Without you?" I asked.

He sighed, as though resigning himself to the fact that he was not going to be able to simply brush my questions aside. "Without me. Apparently out-of-favor younger siblings are useful for taking unwanted children off your hands."

I suspected I could sympathize more than most. Even before the divorce and custody battle that had made me the focus of international press attention and earned me the absurdly inaccurate nickname "The Parisian Orphan," my father had seemed entirely uninterested in playing the role of doting father. He had, after all, only fought *Maman* for custody because he knew how much she loved me. Her untimely death had been the only thing that had quashed his cruel desire to separate us out of spite.

"Why was your aunt Caroline out of favor with her family?" I asked.

"She married my uncle Rupert. My mother is a bit Victorian and a terrible snob, and she thought that the son of a Cornish dairy farmer was a poor match for any sister of hers. When Uncle Rupert's father died and he gained control of the dairy, he finally had a chance to act on his ambition. He grew Hodge Farm Dairy into what it is today."

I sat back, impressed. Hodge Farm Dairy had a reputation for excellent butters, creams, and cheeses, and had a royal warrant to prove it.

Before I could ask any more, David stood for the second time during our meal.

"If you'll excuse me again, I'll just be a moment," he said.

He strode toward the back of the dining room and disappeared through a door that I assume led to the loo just as our waitress returned.

"There's a telephone call for a Mr. Poole," she said.

"He's just stepped away. Did the caller say who they are?" I asked.

"A Miss Summers," said the waitress.

"I can take it," I said.

"It's just at the bar," said the woman, looking a little uncertain about the idea of me coming through to the bar when women were meant to stay in the lounge or dining room.

I shot her a conspiratorial grin. "I promise not to tell if you won't."

She smiled and then led me through to the telephone.

I picked up the receiver off the bar and said, "Hello?"

"Miss Redfern?" came Miss Summers's voice over the receiver.

"Hello, Miss Summers. Mr. Poole is temporarily indisposed, so I'm afraid that you'll have to settle for me."

"Very good." I could almost hear the smile in the young woman's voice. "I've found that address for you."

I shifted the receiver to cradle it so that I could unclasp my handbag and pull out my notebook. Taking the silver pencil out of its loop, I said, "I'm ready."

"Lady Balram is at the Old Vicarage, Morton Lane, Benstead," she said.

"Thank you, Miss Summers." As I scribbled, an idea struck me. "Is there any chance you might also be able to send over the personnel files for all of the employees at Blackthorn Park?"

"Of course." I could practically hear her sharpening her pencil as we spoke. "It might take a couple of days to make the appropriate requests."

"That's fine," I said.

"As soon as I have them, I'll send them down," she said.

"There is also a man we're trying to find. A Lieutenant Colonel Julian Gerrard. You wouldn't happen to know who he is, would you?" I asked hopefully.

"Mr. Poole mentioned him, but I don't believe I've heard that name before," she said. "Do you have any more information? Perhaps where he's serving?"

The letter I'd found under the blotter had given almost no clues as to the man's identity. "I'm afraid not."

"Never mind. Leave it with me. Is there anything else?"

"Not that I can think of," I said. "Oh yes! My things. Would you telephone my boardinghouse and ask my friend Moira to pack me some things? I didn't bring much with me, as I didn't think I'd be here long."

"Of course," said Miss Summers.

"If she could include a pair of trousers, that would be a great help," I said.

I spotted David rounding the corner of the bar and glancing around.

"And if she can find a copy of *The Postman Always Rings Twice* by James M. Cain on short notice, I would appreciate it," I added quietly.

"The novel?" asked Miss Summers.

"That's right."

"Consider it done. I will make sure it's on the mail train tomorrow morning," she said, and rang off.

"I thought ladies weren't allowed in here," David said, glancing around at the empty space.

"Well, you know me. I never met a rule I wasn't tempted to break," I said as I hung up the telephone.

He raised a brow. "No, I imagine you haven't."

"Miss Summers gave us that address, and she's going to see if she can locate the lieutenant colonel as well as the personnel files for all of the members of staff."

"More personnel files," he grumbled, no doubt remembering the hours we pored over the files of my colleagues in the cabinet war rooms.

"I'm afraid it can't be helped," I said with a shrug.

"I've had a word with the innkeeper and booked myself a room," said David.

"Well, if that's all sorted, shall we pay a visit to Lady Balram?" I asked.

David gave a nod. "I think we should."

TWENTY-TWO

Outside the pub, David and I clambered back into the car and, a few minutes later, pulled up in front of a large redbrick house just a stone's throw from a church of an older vintage. As a house, the Old Vicarage wasn't exactly elegant—and it certainly wasn't beautiful—but it had a solid sense of permanence that seemed to command the road on which it stood.

At the door, we asked for Lady Balram, and a housekeeper showed David and me through to an expensively appointed drawing room to wait. I expected that, less than twenty-four hours after her husband's death, Lady Balram might wish for a moment to compose herself before greeting visitors. However, when the door opened moments later, the woman who glided in on a cloud of perfume—Guerlain Shalimar if I wasn't mistaken—was far from what I'd expected.

Lady Balram was encased in a fine emerald wool dress that clung to her body with such precision that the garment could only have been crafted by the most skillful of dressmakers. At her throat, she wore a triple strand of pearls that shone with the rich creaminess of age, and on her ears she wore a pair of impressive baroque pearl drops topped by gold fans. Her black hair was piled high on top of her head, and her lips were painted vermilion red. There was not an inch of her that looked as though she intended to wear mourning for her husband today, tomorrow, or any day in the future.

"My housekeeper tells me that you're here to ask about Nigel," she said, her tone clipped and polished.

"Yes, Lady Balram," said David, rising from the pale-yellow shot silk sofa on which he'd perched uncomfortably. "I'm David Poole, and this is my associate, Miss Redfern."

Lady Balram reached for a large gold cigarette box on the coffee table between us and extracted one. Then, as though only just remembering her manners, she turned the box to us. "There are American on the right and French on the left, although who knows how much longer I'll be able to find those."

David and I both declined her offer and she shrugged, reaching for a heavy gold lighter. She drew on the cigarette and then fixed us with a look. "Well, ask your questions. I haven't all day."

A little taken aback, I said slowly, "We want to offer our condolences on the death of your husband. I'm certain that this must be a difficult time for you."

"Difficult?" She laughed. "Yes. Let's call it that."

"As you can imagine," I pressed on because what else was I supposed to do, "the sudden death of a man of your husband's importance is great cause for concern, and we've been asked to review some of the facts of his life these last few months."

"You mean you want to know why Nigel decided to off himself?" she asked.

I met her gaze. "That is a rather blunt way of putting it, but yes. That would be helpful."

If Lady Balram wasn't going to pretend that she cared one bit about the death of her husband, I wasn't going to tie myself up in knots worrying about offending her.

She settled back in her seat and studied me as though she was seeing me for the first time. Finally, she said, "I really couldn't say. For the most part, Nigel and I lived separate lives. I hardly saw him."

"Why is that?" asked David.

"Our parents wanted us to marry, so we did. You did that sort of thing thirty years ago," said Lady Balram before taking another drag on her cigarette and blowing it out in a long stream toward the ceiling. "The man was obsessed with his work. From the very first day of our marriage he cared about little else. He even spent our honeymoon on his little drawings. He never really had any time for or interest in me.

"After a number of years, I learned to stop trying. I had my own life, my own friends. Besides, I was the only reason that Nigel had anything resembling a social life. I introduced him to everyone who was worth knowing. I put him in front of the right people who could secure him his knighthood. Not that he was grateful."

"That sounds . . . rather lonely," I said.

"Miss Redfern, I can assure you that the one thing I have not been is lonely," she said with a wry smile. "After our son Charles was born, I had the freedom to do what I wished with very few questions asked. Even more so after Charles went off to Cambridge, and Nigel began to earn something for his patents. I was *very* happy, not that it mattered in the end," she finished.

"Why is that?" I asked.

"At the start of this bloody war, some very somber men came to the London house one day and sat with Nigel in his study for hours. As soon as they left, he announced that he had been hired to run an engineering facility, and we had to move to this godforsaken place," she said.

"Why didn't you stay in London?" I asked.

Lady Balram sniffed. "Nigel decided that, given that his work would require him to move to Sussex, we should give up the lease on our house in London. I fought him tooth and nail, but once he had decided something it was final. Without a by your leave, he moved me away from all of my friends, my club, any semblance of a civilized life."

"And have your feelings on your situation improved since moving to Benstead?" David asked.

"It's ghastly," she said, extinguishing the rapidly approaching end of her cigarette and plucking another out of the box to light. "There's nothing to do except ride, and there is no one worth knowing socially outside of the riding club. I can assure you that even that pales in comparison to what I'm used to in London. No, Nigel seemed content to let me rot away in this miserable house while he played around with his gadgets or whatever it is that he does in that horrible country pile on the edge of the village."

I glanced around, silently deciding that if all of the beautiful furniture and window dressings and books and paintings were nothing, I could be very content with living such a modest life.

"We've seen Sir Nigel's chequebook," David started.

Lady Balram sat straight up. "Where is it?"

"His desk in his office at Blackthorn Park," I said.

She dropped back against the sofa with a huff. "Of course it is. I thought perhaps he locked it in the safe in his study here, but that would be just like Nigel to keep it at work instead. He never trusted me with it.

"I'll be needing it now that he's gone. You can drop it around later. My housekeeper will be in if I am not," she said.

"I'm afraid that won't be possible until after our investigation is complete," I said.

"And how do you expect me to pay for things?" she challenged.

"If you write to your husband's banker, I'm certain he would be happy to make a provision for you until his solicitor sorts out his estate," said David.

Lady Balram scowled at that and brought her cigarette to her lips again.

"We found a number of cheques written out to various London shops on a fairly regular basis. Places like Harrods. Do you know about those purchases?" I asked.

"I have all of our food sent down weekly from Harrods," she said with a sniff. "I tried the local butcher, but the quality was simply unacceptable. The greengrocer too."

Well, that sounded very nice indeed.

"We also saw counterfoils for cheques written out to what looks like a dressmaker," I prompted.

"And a tailor. Don't forget about that. He might have fancied himself above it all, but it wasn't as though Nigel was willing to live without his beautiful suits," she grumbled.

"Lady Balram, were you aware of your husband ever writing cheques for cash?" I asked.

"From time to time," she said, leaning forward to ash her cigarette.

"Are you aware of him ever writing these cheques for large sums of money?" I asked.

She shook her head. "Nigel did everything through shop accounts, so he only withdrew £10 or £20 every once in a while."

"The last counterfoil in your husband's bank book was written out last week for the amount of £500," I said.

Lady Balram's jaw dropped. "What?"

"Yes, we were struck by the amount as well," I said.

The fingers of Lady Balram's free hand dug into the cushion of the sofa, and she hissed out, "That cad! Only last month I asked him for £100, and he insisted that he couldn't spare it. He claimed that our expenses were too high as it was, and he was threatening to start refusing to pay my bills. Have you ever heard of anything so ridiculous?" She stopped herself. "Was the cheque ever cashed? Do you know if the money is still in his account?"

"We really couldn't say," I said.

"Unbelievable," she muttered again, looking away to stare out of the window.

"Lady Balram, do you know whether your husband had any enemies? Perhaps someone he worked with?" asked David.

She cast me an exasperated look. "I've never met the people in his employ. It would hardly be the thing for me to entertain them here. As for other people who might have called him an enemy, I'm sure he had a few. Nigel could frustrate a saint."

"Do you recall any names?" he asked.

"As I said before, my husband and I lived largely separate lives," she said.

"Lady Balram, where were you yesterday evening around ten o'clock?" I asked.

She let a little smile lift her lips. "I was here, entertaining a friend from the local riding club," she said.

"Could we ask the name of your friend, please?" I asked.

"Captain Martin Harrison," she said.

"Is there anyone who can verify this?" David asked.

"Other than Martin? No," she said. "It was an intimate sort of evening. I'm sure you understand."

"Ah," said David, looking away.

I bit my lip in amusement. The man was actually blushing.

"When did the captain leave?" I asked.

"About eleven o'clock. As soon as Martin was gone, I took off my face and went to bed right away," she said.

"Didn't you worry that your husband might come home during this . . . intimate evening?" I asked.

"Nigel would often keep late hours. Sometimes he wouldn't come home at night at all. He claimed he was at work and would sleep on the sofa in his office," she said.

"Claimed?" I asked.

She fixed me with a look. "My husband had affairs, Miss Redfern. He knew I knew, just as he was aware of my friends like Martin."

"Do you know if Sir Nigel was involved with anyone at Blackthorn Park?" I asked.

She took another drag on her cigarette. "There was a girl he worked with."

"Do you recall her name?" I asked.

"Clarissa Kenwood," she said in such a matter-of-fact manner that it almost startled me.

David seemed to choke and begin to cough, and I could certainly understand why. Clarissa Kenwood was the forewoman of the manufacturing hut, who, if I was not mistaken, was currently engaged to Mr. Hartley.

"How did you find out?" I asked, doing my best to school the shock from my face to regain some semblance of professionalism.

"Nigel told me." Lady Balram leaned forward to ash her cigarette with three sharp taps. "He was the sort of man who could stomach three whiskeys and then would suffer from a precipitous drop in judgment while drinking the fourth. He confessed it all one night after five. Apparently the affair had just ended, and he was looking for sympathy. Not that he found it in me."

There was a bitterness lacing her voice that made me wonder if she was quite as unbothered about her husband's affairs as she was making out to be.

"When was this?" I asked.

"At the end of the summer, I think. I didn't really pay attention."

"How did you learn about your husband's death?" asked David.

"A telephone call woke me up. It was sometime after one o'clock. The man on the line said he was from Nigel's work and he was very sorry to tell me, but my husband was dead." She drew on her cigarette. "I thanked him for letting me know and then poured myself a drink and went back to bed sometime later.

"I suppose I shall have to make arrangements for a funeral. It's all rather a lot of bother."

"Lady Balram, we would like to take a look at your husband's study," I said.

She sighed and reached for a small bell on the coffee table. She gave it a ring, and a moment later the housekeeper appeared.

"Show Miss Redfern and Mr. Poole to Sir Nigel's study," ordered Lady Balram.

I stood and was gratified to find David shooting up right after me. "Thank you, Lady Balram," I said.

"When you're done, you can see yourselves out," she said, clearly already bored with us.

We followed the stone-faced housekeeper out of the room and down a hall until she stopped at a door.

"This is Sir Nigel's study," said the woman.

"Thank you," I said.

However, the housekeeper didn't move immediately. "Is it true that he's dead?"

I looked at David with some alarm. Lady Balram hadn't even bothered to tell her staff that her husband was dead.

"Yes, I'm afraid so," I said softly.

The housekeeper lifted her chin as though steeling herself and then nodded. "If there is anything else you require, simply ring the bell."

As she walked away, I glanced at David.

"Can you imagine a marriage like that?" I asked quietly.

"No, I can't. Do you think she could have killed Sir Nigel?" he asked.

"No. Not if her alibi stands up to scrutiny. Besides, she strikes me as the kind of woman who would take a particular pleasure in poisoning her victim and sitting back to watch him die, rather than shooting and running."

TWENTY-THREE

As soon as Sir Nigel's study door closed behind us, I put my hands on my hips and peered around. The study was much as I expected, all dark wood paneling and hunter-green walls with a massive wood desk piled high with books sitting in the middle of it. I could imagine that, with the fire lit, it might be a cozy room, but that afternoon the grate was empty and the air held a distinct chill.

"Lady Balram mentioned a safe," I said.

David strode around the desk, pulled out the chair, and stooped to look under it. "Not here. Do you want to ask her where it is?"

"Not a chance," I said.

Against one wall there was a pair of handsome bookcases framing either side of a cabinet. I opened the cabinet door and found a box containing a chess board and pieces, an *ABC Railway Guide*, and a few other oddities.

"Nothing," I said.

"We could start with the desk," said David.

I was about to join him when something caught my eye. The large gold-framed landscape painting hanging on the wall to the right of the desk was hanging ever so slightly askew. Now, having spent summers at an old house like Shaldeen Grange, where there isn't a straight wall in the place, I knew that it wasn't usual for pictures to be slightly off. However, every other painting in the room was perfectly straight.

"Help me lift that up," I said, pointing to the landscape.

With both of us grasping the frame, David and I lifted the painting off the wall and set it aside, revealing the heavy iron door of a safe embedded into the wall.

"Excellent," I said as we set the painting aside. "Now it's a question of the combination."

"It doesn't sound as though he trusted Lady Balram with it, so I doubt we'll have any joy asking her," said David.

"Would you like to try to crack the safe or shall I?" I asked.

"Unlike lock picking, this is one area of training I excelled at," said David, shooting me a smile and then dragging a chair in front of the safe so that he could stand on it.

Left with little else to do, I rounded Sir Nigel's desk, sat down in his chair, and began to look through the books stacked there. However, as I leafed through them, all I could find was jargon.

"If only Ethelbrook School for Girls had seen fit to teach us chemistry or engineering," I muttered, unable to make hide nor hair of what I was looking at.

"Strangely enough, Harrow didn't place a great deal of focus on the subjects either," said David with his ear pressed against the safe door.

"You went to Harrow?" I asked, glancing up from my work.

"That is the family school. My grandfather's grandfather went there, and so on."

"You never stood a chance of going anywhere else, did you?" I asked.

"None," he said.

For a few more minutes, we worked in companionable silence until I heard the clunk of a handle being depressed and I turned to see David opening the safe's heavy door.

"Full marks on safecracking, Mr. Poole," I said, putting down the book I had been leafing through to join him.

"Thank you," he said, reaching into the safe and beginning to pull things out. I set them on Sir Nigel's desk, and when the safe was empty, David came to join me.

I picked up the notebook first and paged through. It appeared to be some sort of record of his work at Blackthorn Park, including notes on improvements and calculations. A few of the pages were dated, but not all.

I flipped through the book until I began to see blank pages and then skipped back a way until I found a date in July. I began to read, doing my best to decipher the technical jargon.

A few pages in, I found an entry that deviated from the usual scientific notes.

"David, look at this," I said.

"What is it?"

"A list of some sort. 'Jamison—competent but works too slowly; delusions of his own importance and efficacy,'" I read out. "'Hartley—waste of space; more worried about London parties than dedicating himself to the job; sloppy in his note-taking and drawings and requires constant review and revision; watch carefully.'"

"Aren't Jamison and Hartley the engineers who worked under Sir Nigel?" asked David.

I nodded. "And it looks from this as though Sir Nigel was unhappy with their work."

While David went back to the safe, I flipped a little farther forward and found a sheet of paper stuck in between some pages toward the back of the journal. When I unfolded it, I saw it was a typed document. I gave it a quick skim.

"Here's a memo asking Baker Street to add more engineers to Blackthorn Park's staff," I said.

"Is there anything about removing Miss Kenwood?" asked David over his shoulder.

"Not in this one," I said, extracting the next loose page and opening it. "This one complains about Mr. Porter and recommends his removal from Blackthorn Park's staff effective immediately." I opened the next one I found and gave it a quick read. "And this one criticizes nearly everyone at Blackthorn Park. Porter, Tyson, Hartley, and Miss Kenwood."

"It sounds like Sir Nigel's reputation was well earned," said David.

"Ah, here's the memo about Miss Kenwood that Miss Glenconner mentioned," I said, opening the last inserted paper. I spread it open and began to read, "'Dear Sirs, I am writing to you about a matter of grave importance. It has recently come to my attention that Black-thorn Park's forewoman Miss Clarissa Kenwood is not suitable for the expanded nature of her role here, and I implore you to begin to imme-diately search for her replacement.' Then it looks as though it goes on to list the requirements for the job."

"Does he say why Miss Kenwood should be removed?" he asked.

"No, but I doubt that he was keen to keep her around after their af-fair ended," I said, holding up the paper. "This is dated the fourteenth of October. It's addressed to Mr. Porter, Mr. Eccles, and several names I don't recognize. I assume those are men working at the Baker Street HQ." I flipped the page over to see if there was anything further, but it was blank. "Mr. Porter said that he'd never seen a memo about Miss Kenwood, so I think it's safe to assume this was never sent."

"But it does give Miss Kenwood a neat little motive for murder, not to mention the possibility that she was angry about the end of their affair," said David before holding up an envelope and a sheet of writing paper. "You'll want to read this."

I took the letter from him.

10 October 1940

Dear Sir Nigel,

I am writing to you as a courtesy and in deference to our families' very long friendship. We have known each other for many years thanks to the affectionate bond between our parents, and I have long held your work in great esteem. However, I must inform you of an issue with one of the barnacle bombs issued to this training facility and to urge you to investigate the cause of the irregularities we experienced.

So that you understand the gravity of the situation, Arisaig House serves a vital purpose as a training facility for commandos tasked with some of the most dangerous work undertaken behind enemy lines in this war. It is because of this that it is imperative that all of the equipment and weap-onry that we train with is reliable and accurately reflects what our men will be using in the field.

Earlier today, a group of a dozen men were undertaking a training mission, simulating a very real opportunity to assassinate a high-ranking member of the enemy in an occupied country of great importance to the outcome of this war. (You will understand that necessary discretion cannot allow me to name that country or the target.) An instructor secured one of two barnacle bombs to the underside of the vehicle and triggered the timing device, which should have given him five minutes before detonation.

The instructor has told me that he intended to walk around the vehicle and affix the second device to it; however, there was a question from a commando that required him to step away. It is fortunate that he did because not a minute and a half after setting the device, it exploded.

It is also fortunate that, due to a trick of fate, none of the men were injured, including the instructor who subsequently removed the fuse from the remaining bomb. However, you can imagine the grave concerns that all of the instructors at Arisaig House and I now have over handling any devices produced by Blackthorn Park.

I am writing to urge you to review everything from the conception to the manufacture of the barnacle bomb before it is approved for usage in the field. I'm certain that you can understand why, if you do not take the necessary steps, I shall be forced to report this incident and my own observations to our head office.

Sincerely,

Major Bartholomew Richards

"Didn't Mr. Tyson say that he sent out a shipment of barnacle bombs over a month ago?" I asked.

David nodded. "At the end of September. There's no postmark on the envelope, which means that it was likely sent via dispatch rider."

I opened my notebook and checked my notes before saying, "Mr. Tyson told us that on the eleventh, Sir Nigel demanded that a complete inventory be done at Blackthorn Park. He also said that the new rules about keys came in around the same time. I think this letter from Major Richards set off Sir Nigel's suspicions that something was afoot at Blackthorn Park."

"When was the letter you found under Sir Nigel's blotter written?" asked David.

"The seventeenth of October," I said.

"Is there anything in Sir Nigel's notebook?" David asked with a nod.

I quickly paged through, my shoulders slumping. "Nothing on the tenth or the following few days after it. Nothing for the seventeenth either."

"Do you mind?" asked David, gesturing to Lieutenant Colonel Gerrard's letter. He skimmed it quickly and then asked, "What date would the Tuesday after the seventeenth have been?"

I quickly counted in my head. "The twenty-second."

I flipped pages, my excitement beginning to grow when I saw a date scrawled across the page. "Here it is. It just says 'Burtlesby.'" I deflated a bit. "Who is Burtlesby?"

"Are there any entries beyond that?" he asked.

I sighed. "They're all formulas and calculations. I can't make hide nor hair of them."

"It's not exactly helpful, is it?" asked David.

"No, it's not." I sighed. "I've already asked Miss Summers to track down Lieutenant Colonel Gerrard for me. Let's see if she can find Major Bartholomew Richards too."

"We can take these things with us and telephone from Blackthorn."

"You don't think Lady Balram will mind?"

David snorted. "If it doesn't have to do with Sir Nigel's bank account, I don't think she cares one bit."

"Right," I said, gathering up the letter, Sir Nigel's notebook, and my own. "Before we do any of that, I think we should pay Miss Kenwood a call."

TWENTY-FOUR

When we returned to Blackthorn Park, twilight was already beginning to dip even though it was hardly a quarter to four. David parked the car, and we immediately struck out in the direction of the manufacturing barn.

Our path took us across the lawn and by the outer edge of the walled garden, and when we rounded the corner we found Constable Lee hovering near a gardener in a worn cloth jacket and wellies as the gardener spread mulch from a battered old wheelbarrow.

"Hello, Miss Redfern," said Constable Lee, snapping to attention as David and I approached.

"Good afternoon, Constable," I said.

"I was just speaking to Mr. Parker about the woods. He has been the head gardener here for—"

"Nearly thirty-five years," said the gardener, doffing his battered tweed flat cap and leaning on his gardening fork.

"That's impressive," I said.

"I told the old mistress that I couldn't countenance the thought of the gardens going to ruin, even if most of them have been dug over to make room for growing food," said Mr. Parker.

"I imagine that means you know the Blackthorn Park estate better than anyone," said David.

"I was just asking Mr. Parker if he's seen anything suspicious on the grounds recently," said Constable Lee quickly.

"The constable tells me that you have him wandering the woods looking for footprints and such," said Mr. Parker. "We have a fair few poachers around the woods, especially with meat on the ration. Used to be that Blackthorn had a game warden, but he retired a few years back and the family decided not to replace him. They aren't so keen on it, the new Mr. and Mrs. Mountcastle.

"I'd do my best to chase off any trespassers if I ever came across any, mind you, but mostly what I see are tracks and the occasional cold campsite."

"Campsite?" I asked.

"I used to come across them from time to time. Mostly they were men who couldn't find work and took to sleeping rough, but there's been less of that since the war started," said Mr. Parker.

"Have you come across anyone camping recently?" I asked.

"No, I haven't seen anyone, but I've spent most of this week digging up potatoes and transplanting cabbage seedlings. I report it to one of them up at the big house every time I see one, though," the gardener said.

"Where were these old campsites? I can go check them," said Constable Lee eagerly.

Mr. Parker gave him some directions that seemed mostly to consist of walking to certain trees that I doubted Constable Lee would find as easily as the gardener of thirty-five years. However, I kept my countenance, huddling a little deeper into my coat as rain began to fall on us.

"Right," said Constable Lee, looking more than a little overwhelmed.

"Thank you, Mr. Parker," I said.

The gardener tugged on the brim of his hat and went back to spreading mulch.

By the time we reached the manufacturing barn, the heavens had properly opened and I sprinted to the covered porch at the entrance of the building. A guard who hadn't been there the day before nodded to me.

"Rotten weather, Miss," he said, shouting over the unholy racket of machines coming from inside the building.

"It is indeed," I shouted back as I shook the rain off my coattails as best I could. "Are you new?"

"Just arrived around lunchtime. New security measures."

"I see," I said, turning to watch David trudge the last few feet to join me.

"Lovely day," he shouted over the racket of machines filling the air around us, tipping off his hat to let a stream of water drip off when he reached the porch. "It wasn't this loud when we walked by with Mr. Tyson earlier."

"We weren't that close."

After we properly identified ourselves to the guard, he opened the door to us and pointed us to an office down a corridor constructed out of temporary walls that had been thrown up to split up the barn into useable space. Just as we arrived at an office door, the clanging of metal ceased. The air around me seemed to continue to ring even in the relative silence.

"Thank God for that," David muttered, and I really couldn't agree more.

He knocked on the door, and a few seconds later we found ourselves face-to-face with a statuesque woman who, despite her boiler suit, managed to exude glamour from her silk headscarf to her lacquered red nails that matched her lipstick. I recognized her as the woman who had emerged from the barn and called the smokers in to work when I had been doing my snooping the day before.

"Miss Kenwood?" I asked.

"Yes?" she said, not bothering to pretend to be even the littlest bit curious about who we were.

"I'm Miss Redfern, and this is Mr. Poole," I said.

"The investigators," she said. "Yes, I know."

"Did Mr. Hartley, your fiancé, tell you?" I asked.

"I haven't seen Frank all day. No, I heard from Mr. Tyson when he stopped by with a shipment just after lunch. Apparently you're asking all sorts of questions and setting everyone on edge," she said.

"I'm glad our reputation precedes us," I said. I wanted people on edge but uncertain about what exactly we had learned, especially the murderer. It was more likely they would make a mistake that way.

"As much as I would love to stand around chatting, I have things to do," she said, placing her hands on her hips.

"This won't take a minute," I said with a tight smile, dropping my shoulder to edge past her and through to the office.

Behind me, I heard Miss Kenwood huff, but when I turned around I saw her step back to let David through.

I watched her manage the incredible feat of slinking back to her desk in work boots. She arranged herself on her chair, pushing up her sleeves to reveal strong wrists and elegant hands. I glanced at David, who wore a bored expression. Miss Kenwood seemed to realize this too and lifted one shoulder.

She did not, I noticed, invite us to sit in the two spare chairs facing her, so I firmly planted myself in one of them and twisted to look out of the window that sat perpendicular to her desk. It gave a good view of the factory floor, and I could see the quick, efficient movements of the women as they worked.

"We're behind on our quotas because we've been understaffed for what feels like ages, and the new girls are only due to start tomorrow. Add to that all of the faff around the prime minister's visit on Thursday, and I'm beginning to wonder whether I'll be able to make it home before eleven o'clock tonight," said Miss Kenwood. "And now there's you two."

"What do you do at Blackthorn Park exactly?" asked David.

She gestured to the window behind us. "I manage all of this. Everything that is made in this facility, from the very first prototypes of whatever the engineers have dreamed up to the devices now being tested in the field."

"Is it correct that you joined when Mr. Hartley suggested you for the job?" asked David.

"He put my name forward, but I can assure you that I have kept the job on my own merits," she said.

"What was your working relationship with Sir Nigel like?" I asked.

"Good at first. Then more difficult," she said. "He had always been demanding, but at least he was realistic about what the output of this facility could be. However, a couple of weeks ago he disappeared for the better part of two days. He didn't tell anyone where he'd gone, but when he returned he demanded that I figure out who had worked on a series of weapons that were sent for testing off-site. I told him that every woman who works under me would have touched those bombs."

"Who arranges shipments off the property?" I asked.

She shrugged. "I don't really know. Mr. Tyson or Mr. Porter, probably. You have to understand, everything is new here. We're all working at breakneck speed, and no one stopped to think that we should track lots. Sir Nigel went ballistic when I told him that. He immediately demanded that Mr. Porter put a system into place, and we've only just used it for the first time on a lot of underwater mines and remote bombs we sent up to Scotland for testing last week."

"Miss Kenwood, did you have a personal relationship with Sir Nigel?" I asked.

"No," said Miss Kenwood.

"Then you never had an affair?" I asked.

If I hadn't been watching her so closely, I might never have seen the tiny jerk of her shoulders and then the slight roll of them downward as she corrected herself.

"A personal relationship? No. An affair? Yes," she answered. "Who told you?"

"Lady Balram," I said.

She gave a little sniff. "He always swore he would never tell her. I suppose I shouldn't be surprised to find he was lying."

"When did the affair start?" I asked.

"April, and it was over by August, so it was hardly going to set the world alight."

"How did it begin?" I asked

"How do these things ever begin?" she asked with a raised brow. "I was working late to resolve an issue with one of the devices that the girls were meant to be manufacturing. They were only working on prototypes at the time, so we had a smaller staff then, but the pressure was no less great and I worried about missing Sir Nigel's testing deadline. He came to the manufacturing barn to check on my progress. I knew that he sometimes worked late, but I suppose I was in a mood and rather bored myself, so I asked if his wife would be fretting that he had missed supper. He said that his wife didn't really care when he went home—if he went home at all. Then I felt like kissing him, so I did.

"He was a very dynamic man. Fiercely clever and a little bit fearsome too. It gave him a certain degree of appeal. He was also uninterested in pretending that he would one day leave his wife and make a good woman out of me, and I was entirely uninterested in pretending that I wanted anything more from him but . . . well, you know."

I rather thought I was beginning to see the picture.

"You weren't concerned about the small matter of having a fiancé?" asked David.

"Mr. Poole, are you worried about my honor as an engaged woman? How provincial of you." Out of one of her desk drawers she produced her handbag and drew out a ring. She held it up for me, and I took it, admiring the sparkling ruby set on a thin band of yellow gold worked in a filigree.

"This is the ring Frank gave me," she said. "I can't wear it at work, of course, because of the machinery, but I keep it with me nonetheless—not because I'm a sentimental woman. I am pragmatic through and through, and an engagement to Frank suits me just fine."

"Why is that?" I asked.

She stared at the ring for a moment, twisting it between her fingers so that the ruby caught the light. "Frank's father is a cobbler. However, he knew enough to realize that he had a very bright boy on his hands, and he pushed Frank to win a scholarship to Eton, where he met my brother.

"When you become engaged to someone you've known for so many years, you have the advantage of understanding one another." Miss Kenwood stopped. "Miss Redfern, do you plan to marry?"

"Maybe one day," I said, feeling acutely David's curious gaze on me. "If the right sort of man asks me."

"Be careful of the right sort of man," she said with a rueful smile. "Frank is the right sort of man in character but he has the misfortune of being from the wrong sort of family. We are not from the same world. During all of the summers and holidays he would come home with my brother, I think he fell in love with the country estate and the house in Mayfair."

"Not with you?" I asked.

"Maybe a little. For a little while," she said.

"Then why become engaged at all?" asked David.

Miss Kenwood looked up sharply. "Did you know, Mr. Poole, that before this war I was a champion swimmer and runner? I'm a crack shot, and I can ride to hounds with the very best of them. I have no intention of giving it all up after I marry, no matter what my mother, grandmother, and aunts think. With Frank, I won't have to."

"He'll have entry into your world and, I assume, some of your family's money to go along with it, and you'll have freedom," I said, understanding Miss Kenwood a little better.

"Precisely, Miss Redfern," she said. "I will be able to continue with my athletic pursuits, and he can go up to London to see his various girlfriends every weekend." A sly smile spread over her lips. "Does that shock you, Mr. Poole?"

"It takes a great deal more than that to shock me, Miss Kenwood," said David sternly. "How would you characterize your relationship with Sir Nigel after your affair ended?"

"It was completely professional, as it had been before. I take my work very seriously, not that it's always appreciated," she said.

"What do you mean?" I asked.

"Dr. Jamison seems to think that all the engineers have to do is snap their fingers and my girls should be able to produce their designs to their exacting specifications at double speed. I have frequently reminded Dr. Jamison and Sir Nigel that if they push us, mistakes will be made, and when you are creating ammunition and weaponry, mistakes can be lethal," she said.

"Did you and Sir Nigel ever argue about your work?" I asked.

"Frequently," she said.

"Do you recall whether you argued with him last Thursday?" I asked.

"That's a rather specific question," she said. She opened her drawer and pulled out a diary, flipping it open to consult it before closing it. "No. I was on-site in this barn the entire time. I keep a log of what I do throughout the day because I find that the days are long enough that they often blend into one another. Why do you ask?"

"Someone overheard Sir Nigel in his office with a woman last Thursday. She was crying," I said.

She pursed her lips but shook her head. "That could have been any woman on the estate. Nigel often picked on people he thought less intelligent than him, and he considered every woman to be intellectually inferior, ergo . . ." She trailed off. "Anyway, I haven't been in that man's office since August. I preferred to conduct my business dealings with Nigel out in the open, either in the engineers' laboratory or here. It was cleaner that way."

"We understand that no one can verify your alibi that you were at home in bed yesterday evening at ten o'clock," I said.

"That's right. Frank dropped me home around half past eight because he said he wanted to go back to work. I have a separate entrance to what amounts to my own self-contained flat, so I let myself in and listened to the radio before bed." Miss Kenwood rose. "If that's all, it's high time I walk the floor."

"Thank you, Miss Kenwood. If you think of anything else, please do let us know," said David.

TWENTY-FIVE

David and I slogged back to the house along now rain-sodden paths, the lime churning up into a pale-yellow muck that clung to my shoes and weighed them down. By the time we reached the manor house's front door, the rain was coming down in sheets and we both tumbled through the door in search of the dry warmth of indoors.

As soon as Mrs. Sherman, who stood near the grand entryway's stairs with a bucket and mop in hand, saw us, she cried, "Oh! Look at what you've done to the floors! We've only just finished cleaning them."

Sheepishly, David and I both edged toward the door as Jane tried not to laugh.

"Oh, do stop cowering. The damage is done," grumbled Mrs. Sherman. "I suppose Miss Daniels and I will have to mop everything again, and Mr. Porter will be expecting his tea now that Miss Glenconner has gone home."

"We are sorry," I said.

"I'll do the floors, Mrs. Sherman," Jane piped up. "I don't mind."

"Well, all right then," Mrs. Sherman huffed. "See that you don't take too long."

We all watched Mrs. Sherman go, and Jane turned to me. "She's been in such a mood all day because she saw the state of Sir Nigel's office. Apparently there's black dust everywhere."

"That would be the fingerprint dust. I'm afraid it can't be helped," I said.

Before Jane could say another thing, an explosion shook the entryway. David and I both ducked, but when I looked up I found Jane still standing but a few shades paler than she had been a moment before.

"I *hate* when they do that!" she cried. "Everyone claims that you become used to bangs and crashes working here, but I don't see how. At least that one was outside."

"How can you tell?" I asked.

"If it's inside, the glass in the windows usually shakes harder. Sometimes plaster falls from the ceiling too," she said.

David cleared his throat as he straightened. "What happened to Miss Glenconner? Mrs. Sherman said she left."

Jane shrugged. "She claims she had a headache. She's been crying all morning, so it's hardly a surprise."

I nodded slowly.

"If you ask me," said Jane, leaning in, "she'll leave within the month. She never was well suited to what goes on here, claiming everyone's unkind to her. And now Sir Nigel's only gone and killed himself, hasn't he?"

Jane rocked back on her heels with a satisfied look, as though that told me everything I needed to know.

"Jane, do you happen to know where the engineers are at the moment?" I asked.

"Are you going to interrogate them?" she asked a little too enthusiastically.

"We just need to ask them a few questions," said David.

"East drawing room. That's where their main workshop is. First door on the right," said Jane, pointing to a door leading off the entryway.

"Thank you. You've been a great help," I said.

As soon as David and I were out of earshot, he whispered, "A great help?"

I shrugged. "You never know."

W hen David and I walked into the east drawing room, two
heads immediately popped up.

"Who are you? You can't be in here!" shouted a short
bald man wearing a white coat over his tweed jacket and waistcoat. I
recognized him as the man I'd accidentally bumped into after speaking to David the night I'd arrived in Benstead.

"It's all right, Dr. Jamison," said Mr. Hartley from a scarred
wooden table set up in front of a marble fireplace at the end of the
vast drawing room. "They're the ones I was telling you about. She
found the body and ordered Porter around as though it was nothing.
It was quite the show."

David pulled out that damned warrant card again. "I'm David
Poole and this is Miss Redfern. We'd like to ask you both a few questions about the death of Sir Nigel."

Dr. Jamison, who had stopped in front of us, took off his thick
glasses and rubbed the bridge of his nose. "Horrible business. Just
horrible. Sir Nigel was a great man."

Out of the corner of my eye, I noticed Mr. Hartley raise a brow.

"We've already told the constable where we were," he said.

"If you could please let us have the room so we might speak with
Dr. Jamison?" I asked in a way that was more demand than question.

"Don't go far," said David.

I thought Miss Kenwood's fiancé might object, but instead he
shrugged off his lab coat, revealing a beautifully cut gray suit that
would have been more at home in a city bank than a country manor
house's makeshift laboratory. Then he rounded his table and walked
out of the room without another word.

As soon as David and I were alone with Dr. Jamison, I put my hand
on my hips and looked around. "This is quite the laboratory you have
here."

The drawing room had been stripped bare of its niceties, and now
only practical furniture remained. There were four pine tables, three
of which were covered with all manner of wires and equipment along
with notebooks and plans. The fourth was empty.

"Dr. Jamison, how long have you worked at Blackthorn Park?" I asked.

"Since September of last year, right after Chamberlain announced we were at war. I was the first person Sir Nigel contacted when he was establishing a laboratory," he said, crossing his arms over his chest.

"Did you know Sir Nigel before then?" I asked.

That earned me a guarded nod. "We were at Cambridge together. I toyed with the idea of studying medicine like my father had done before I found a love for engineering. Sir Nigel was just plain Nigel Balram then. We became colleagues, and I would like to think that we developed a congenial relationship because of our fellow devotion to the discipline."

"You'd characterize yourself as colleagues rather than friends?" I asked.

Dr. Jamison cleared his throat. "Yes, well, I'm not certain that Sir Nigel ever really had friends. However, he was more than capable of showing his respect for a fellow scientist. After receiving our degrees, I stayed on to pursue an academic career, but he left to work in industry."

"It sounds as though he was very successful," said David.

"Yes. The king generally only grants knighthoods to those who are," said Dr. Jamison.

"What was Sir Nigel like when you were students together?" I asked.

"Brilliant," said Dr. Jamison. "He had the sort of mind that could piece together things before anyone else. He seemed to have a particular knack for mechanical engineering that our old tutor said he's never seen before."

"How is it that you came to work together again?" I asked.

"He was given *carte blanche* to create a facility at Blackthorn Park. He wrote to me just after war was declared saying that he had need of someone with my expertise and would I come along to help him."

"What is your expertise?" asked David.

"Chemical engineering, but I have a particular focus on explosives." Dr. Jamison touched his bow tie. "I am well-known for it in my field."

"How did you find working with Sir Nigel this time?" I asked.

"He demanded a great deal from everyone at Blackthorn. Hard

work, long hours, and exacting standards. However, that was nothing that Sir Nigel didn't also demand of himself. Every man working for him admired him, not to mention those in his wider field," said Dr. Jamison. His body language was so stiff, it almost felt as though I were watching a marionette parrot the words that a puppeteer wanted him to say.

"Mr. Porter doesn't seem to have felt the same admiration for Sir Nigel," I said archly.

"That is because Porter is a bore who is more concerned with lording what little power he has over those around him than the greater good," said Dr. Jamison with the most vehemence he'd shown since he'd shouted at us for intruding.

"Then things were tense?" I prompted.

"Miss Redfern—"

"Perhaps you could tell us what you did yesterday evening," said David, cutting off Dr. Jamison as his voice began to rise again.

Dr. Jamison sighed. "I left Blackthorn Park around half past seven."

"Did you see Sir Nigel before you left?" I asked.

"I said goodbye to him. He was in his office, as usual. He often works late. We spoke for a few moments about things related to the laboratory, and then I took my leave and walked home as I always do," said Dr. Jamison.

"Did anyone see you?" David asked.

The scientist darted a look in my direction. "Miss Redfern. She walked right into me and made me drop my things."

"It was an accident," I said, not entirely certain why I should shoulder the blame. If he'd been looking, he would have seen me.

"When was this?" David asked me.

"Right after our call. Around eight o'clock," I said.

David nodded. "What happened then?"

"I went straight home," the engineer said. "My wife, Margaret, was in bed with a migraine. She told me that she'd left supper for me in the oven. I ate alone," said the engineer.

"And did you leave the house after that?" I asked.

"No," he said.

"When did you learn of Sir Nigel's death?" I asked.

"This morning, when I arrived at half past eight. Mr. Hartley told me." He sighed. "It's a great loss."

"No one telephoned you?" David asked.

"I don't know. I always take the telephone off the hook when Margaret has a migraine. Loud noises can worsen the pain," he said.

"What was Sir Nigel's mood like recently?" I asked.

Dr. Jamison shrugged. "He was worried about the state of the world, as we all are."

"Did he seem unusually worried?" I pressed.

"He was eager to make sure that the prime minister's visit went well. He had us reviewing and retesting every device that we would be demonstrating and making minor tweaks," said Dr. Jamison.

"Did that strike you as strange?" I asked.

The engineer shook his head. "The war means that we must move quickly. It's perfectly natural to continue to improve upon a device and make sure that future versions are even more effective."

"Did these tweaks ever bring about any tension between Sir Nigel and the staff?" I asked.

"Miss Redfern, you must understand that each of us brings his own expertise to the job. We all work on different devices. I will often manage the explosive compounds. Mr. Hartley excels at chemistry and is a dab hand with mechanical engineering too. However, that doesn't mean we always agree on the manner in which to go about things. Ultimately it was Sir Nigel who had the final say because lives depend on these devices working. Everyone at Blackthorn Park knew that," said Dr. Jamison.

"We understand Mr. Hartley and Sir Nigel didn't necessarily see eye to eye," I said.

Dr. Jamison looked at me sharply. "Who told you that?"

"Is it true that Mr. Hartley punched Sir Nigel?" I continued, ignoring his demanding question.

"There was a scuffle," said Dr. Jamison, weighing his words carefully, "but it was nothing more serious than that."

"Why did it happen?" I asked.

"Miss Redfern, you must understand that this work is fast-paced, and mistakes can be critical. Sir Nigel felt that the quality of Hartley's work had been slipping recently. Hartley took objection to that. He might pretend to be blasé and uncaring, but Hartley is supremely talented and it matters to him that he performs well. You do not achieve a first in my laboratory at Cambridge if you don't."

"You were his professor?" asked David.

Dr. Jamison nodded. "Before the war. I personally recommended him to Sir Nigel because of his skill across multiple disciplines. That is unusual and invaluable."

"And what about yourself?" I asked. "Did you ever have any altercations with Sir Nigel?"

"I do not have 'altercations,' Miss Redfern," said Dr. Jamison.

"Then you were completely happy at Blackthorn Park, working under Sir Nigel?" I asked.

"Yes."

I narrowed my eyes, recalling the letter I'd seen spill out of Dr. Jamison's bag when we'd collided. "If that is the case, why did you seek employment elsewhere?"

Dr. Jamison's eyes bulged. "I—Who told you that?"

"Please answer the question, Dr. Jamison," said David.

The man took off his glasses, wiping them on a handkerchief, and then replaced them. Finally, he said, "I've been thinking for some time that perhaps my skills would be of better use outside of Blackthorn Park. As I mentioned, I ran my own labs before the war, and I am more than capable of doing so again. I thought that I might be of more use to the army or one of the other branches of the military if I was developing weapons for them."

"Why? You said yourself that the work you are doing at Blackthorn Park is important," I said.

"There's a need for experts in explosives across the services. Sir Nigel and Mr. Hartley had enough combined experience here to make up for the loss of me if I went somewhere else. Even more so if Sir Nigel had received permission to recruit more engineers as he wanted to do," said Dr. Jamison.

"Did you apply to a specific job?" asked David.

Dr. Jamison's eyes skirted to me, and I raised a brow, challenging him to lie when I knew what I'd seen fall out of his briefcase.

"I wrote to a friend who had told me about a vacancy leading one of the army's weapons research teams," the engineer finally said. "I spoke to the head of their program. However, as I began to explore the opportunity further, I came to understand that I was needed here."

"Did you withdraw your application?" I asked.

Dr. Jamison looked down. "No, not in so many words."

"Then you are still being considered for the vacancy?" I asked, continuing to press him.

"No, I am not."

"What happened?" asked David.

"Sir Nigel found out when the head of the program contacted him for a reference. These sorts of positions are all vetted, of course. Apparently Sir Nigel indicated that I was needed here, and my application was withdrawn on my behalf."

So Sir Nigel had torpedoed Dr. Jamison's chances at running his own team, forcing him to stay at Blackthorn Park.

"When did you find this out?" asked David.

"Monday. The letter came to Blackthorn by dispatch rider," said Dr. Jamison shortly.

"That must have frustrated you. You said yourself that you came up together at Cambridge and now you were working for Sir Nigel," I said.

Dr. Jamison looked up sharply. "You are sorely mistaken. I understand my value here. Sir Nigel made a point of telling me in great detail about his plans for Blackthorn Park. He had incredible ambitions, and I was a key part of that," said Dr. Jamison.

"When did he lay out this plan for you?" I asked.

"Monday evening, after the letter came," he ground out.

"And now you're the head engineer at Blackthorn Park," I said.

"Miss Redfern, if you're implying—"

I held my hands up. "I'm simply stating a fact, Dr. Jamison."

"I do not appreciate what you are implying. Sir Nigel killed himself," said Dr. Jamison. "If you knew him as I did, you would realize that I could have no more influenced him toward that decision than I could change the weather."

"You must understand, we have to ask the question," said David.

"Well, then ask someone else. Sir Nigel was my superior and I greatly admired him," he said fiercely. "Now, I must return to my work."

"Just one last question, Dr. Jamison," I said. "Did Sir Nigel ever complain to you about missing supplies?"

The man took a deep, steadying breath and said through gritted teeth, "We had an issue with some sloppiness across the staff. That has since been rectified."

"So you don't think there was any merit in Sir Nigel's complaints?" I asked.

"No, I don't," said Dr. Jamison.

He turned away, giving us his back. However, that didn't matter because, with his crushed ambitions, Dr. Jamison had just put himself firmly on my list of suspects.

TWENTY-SIX

fter our interview with Dr. Jamison, David and I found Mr. Hartley on the edge of what had once been the walled formal garden near the east wing of the house, walking in circles and puffing away furiously on a cigarette.

As soon as he saw us, he stopped and called out, "I suppose you'd like to talk to me."

"We would rather," I said.

"We're not allowed to smoke in the laboratory," he said, holding up his cigarette by way of explanation. Then he reached over the flower bed and ground it out on the brick wall.

"Is that why you were outside yesterday evening when you heard the gunshot?" I asked.

He nodded. "I had been at my lab table for hours working on the armadillo device I've been trying to perfect for months now. When the numbers started dancing in front of my eyes, I knew I needed a break. I came out here, heard a shot, and ran in the general direction of it. I found Sir Nigel dead at his desk."

"Why run toward the sound of shooting rather than away from it?" I asked.

Mr. Hartley raised a brow. "Miss Redfern, I knew that a shot fired anywhere on Blackthorn Park's grounds could not have been good.

I'm not on the front lines in this war, but that doesn't mean that I'm a coward."

"Why aren't you on the front lines?" I asked.

"Other than the fact that my knowledge is far more valuable here? I have asthma. Couldn't get the medical clearance," he said.

"How did you come to work at Blackthorn Park?" asked David.

"I was a doctoral candidate at Cambridge. One of Dr. Jamison's students, actually. About four months after he left, he wrote to me and asked me if I would care to join him at a lab he was working at. I said yes, although I realize now that it wasn't a request so much as a demand."

"How did you find working under Sir Nigel?" I asked.

"I suppose this is where I say that Sir Nigel did his very best to make my life a living Hell—but that doesn't mean I killed him," said Mr. Hartley, reaching into his jacket pocket to extract a silver cigarette case.

I stilled. "No one said that anyone killed Sir Nigel."

Mr. Hartley snorted. "No, but you're asking questions that make it sound as though this is a murder investigation. Ergo, he must have been killed. Oh, don't worry about me spilling your little secret."

"What secret?" I asked.

"From what I can tell, you've been letting everyone believe that it's a suicide because that is what it looked like," he said with a shrug.

I met David's gaze. "We are still waiting for confirmation from the coroner."

Whether Mr. Hartley knew it was a lie or not, he shrugged. "If you ask me, whoever did it did the people here a favor. Sir Nigel might have been a genius, and losing him might set our efforts back, but he was a nightmare to work with."

"Of all of the people we've spoken to, you seem to have the dimmest view of Sir Nigel," I said.

"Yes, well, Sir Nigel seemed mostly uninterested in me during my first months at Blackthorn Park until I improved upon one of his precious inventions," he said, crossing his arms over his chest.

"What did you do?" I asked.

"He left out some plans for one of his prototypes. I knew that he'd been having some difficulties with the anti-handling device that prevents bombs and mines from being removed once the fuse is set, so I thought I'd take a look and see if I could help. And I could," said Mr. Hartley.

"And he took exception to that?" I asked.

Mr. Hartley laughed. "That is one way of putting it. He *hated* what I'd done because I improved on his work. The great man of science knighted for his brilliance bested by a scientist barely out of Cambridge."

"What exactly did you do?" asked David.

"Sir Nigel had built the anti-handling device so that the last thing that the person setting it would do was remove a metal plate protecting a thinner glass one. If anyone attempted to tamper with the device, the glass would break and it would detonate. The problem was the glass was far too sturdy and it wouldn't always break reliably. I figured out that if you made it out of sugar, it was strong enough to transport with the metal plate in place but delicate enough, once the device was set and the metal removed, to shatter if someone tried to disarm it."

"What happened when he found out?" I asked.

"He ripped me to shreds in front of Dr. Jamison and Mr. Porter. He spent most of August doing his best to try to find fault with the sugar plate in testing, but even he had to admit that the improvements were actually improvements. By the middle of September, he finally begrudgingly ordered that the new sugar plates should be included in the batch of bombs the manufacturing barn produced for testing off-site.

"You might think that Sir Nigel would be grateful that I found a way to fix his mistake before the prime minister's visit, but instead he started to blame me for everything that went wrong in the lab. He sent back every single one of my plans with the sorts of critiques that one might write to a first-year undergraduate," said Mr. Hartley.

"Is that when you hit him?" I asked.

Annoyance flickered across Mr. Hartley's face. "Yes. Sir Nigel had the audacity to accuse me of trying to ruin Thursday's demonstration. In his rage, he went too far. I hit him, and that seemed to stun him into sense. I suspect Eccles may have had a word with him because he began to steer clear of me again."

"You said this was a couple weeks ago?" I asked. The letter I'd found under Sir Nigel's desk blotter was from around that time.

"I don't remember the exact date, but Sir Nigel had just done his vanishing act," he said.

"Vanishing act?" I repeated.

"Yes. One afternoon he just disappeared. None of us could find him. He resurfaced the following afternoon and shut himself up in his office. He wouldn't even speak to Jamison." Mr. Hartley snorted. "It's pathetic, really, how Dr. Jamison would run around after Sir Nigel picking up his scraps. Of course, he didn't count on Sir Nigel torpedoing his prospects when an opportunity finally came up."

"Dr. Jamison told you about his job offer?" I asked, surprised.

"I overheard them talking about it. Well, shouting about it is more like it," he said.

"When was this?" I asked.

"Yesterday evening. I needed a notebook from the store cupboard near Miss Glenconner's desk, and the quickest way is up the servants' stairs by Sir Nigel's office. As soon as I reached the landing, I heard Dr. Jamison bellowing about a letter and Sir Nigel blocking him from a job."

That was hardly the calm conversation that Dr. Jamison had led us to believe had happened between himself and his employer.

"What time was this?" I asked.

Mr. Hartley rolled his eyes but then said, "Just before seven. I remember because I was late to see Clarissa."

"Your fiancée," I said.

"Yes. Her brother and I went to Eton together. Old Surrey family, the Kenwoods. Clarissa is a cracking girl. You'll never meet a better seat, shot, or swimmer. She had her sights on this year's Summer Olympics before they were called off because of the war."

"Which event?" I asked.

"Running and swimming, although if women competed in the modern pentathlon, she would have had gold." There was a begrudging admiration in his tone that almost made this blasé man sound romantic.

"It must be a great luxury to work at the same facility with your fiancée," said David.

"One not many couples have. We go to dinner on Mondays because it is her day off. Afterward, I dropped her home and returned to Blackthorn Park to continue my work on the armadillo," he said.

"Mr. Hartley, I'm curious about this disappearance you mentioned. Do you have any guesses as to where Sir Nigel went a couple of weeks ago?" I asked.

The scientist shrugged. "I assumed he went down to London for meetings and he got a talking to about expense. Eccles usually takes care of that sort of thing, but every once in a while there's something even Eccles couldn't shield Sir Nigel from.

"If you ask me, that's why Sir Nigel was so wound up about this week's visit. It wasn't just that everything needs to go well. It needs to be perfect."

"Why is that?" I asked.

"Sir Nigel had ambitions for Blackthorn Park that far outstripped reality. He wanted underwater, desert, and cold-weather testing facilities. He wanted a second manufacturing barn dedicated solely to making approved weapons so that Clarissa and her girls can focus on prototypes, and he wanted vast equipment sheds built to stockpile all of the materials needed to achieve those ends. Essentially, Miss Redfern, he wanted to turn Blackthorn Park into a weapons factory, testing site, and research and development facility in one.

"All of that sounds well and good on paper, but someone has to be willing to pay for it. Tyson let it slip that Eccles was trying to do damage control because the manufacturing barn had cost far more to build than expected."

"Thank you. We'll let you know if we have further questions," said David.

"Oh, Mr. Hartley," I called out to stop him as he turned. "One more thing. You mentioned that your improved anti-handling device was a part of several devices. Which ones were they?"

"The armadillo, the submersible bomb, and the barnacle bomb so far," he said.

"And which of those is being demonstrated for the prime minister on Thursday?" I asked.

"The submersible and the barnacle bombs. The armadillo still needs some work," he said.

"Why is it called a barnacle bomb?" I asked.

Mr. Hartley grinned. "Because it affixes to whatever surface it is applied to and won't let go."

"Like a barnacle," I said, returning the smile.

"It's an extraordinary device, Miss Redfern. Compact, but highly effective. We should all pray that the demonstration goes off without a hitch," he said.

"Why is that?" I asked.

"Because if Sir Nigel was right, it could change the course of the war."

TWENTY-SEVEN

By the time we'd finished with Mr. Hartley, Dr. Jamison had left
for the day, so David and I agreed that we would resume our
investigation the following morning. He dropped me at Russet
Cottage on his way back to the Hand and Flower. He also promised
to check in with Miss Summers about whether she'd had any success
tracking down Lieutenant Colonel Gerrard and to also ask whether
she could add his fellow letter writer Major Bartholomew Richards to
the list.

As David drove off, I paused at the garden gate, watching until he
swung the car around the corner and out of sight. Then I turned on
my heel and made for Benstead's high street telephone booth.

It was, thankfully, empty when I arrived so I pushed into the booth,
picked up the receiver, and gave the switchboard the exchange for
Mrs. Jenkins's. *Maman*'s watch told me that Moira would likely be at
rehearsals, but I waited on the line anyway because there was nothing I wanted more than to hear my friend's voice.

The adrenaline that had carried me through the day was beginning to wane, and the sick reality of the case weighed on me. Not only
had a man lost his life by the hand of someone clever enough to try to
make it look like a suicide, it had happened on the grounds of a vital
wartime facility. It was unsettling at best and terrifying at worst and

I wanted nothing more than to unburden myself to my friend. However, knowing that I'd vowed not to speak of my work, I would have to simply settle for a chat about everything except what I was doing in Sussex.

The line connected and I heard my landlady give her familiar greeting, "Jenkins's residence; lady of the house speaking."

"Mrs. Jenkins, it's Evelyne," I said.

"Oh, Evelyne! It is good to hear your voice. How are you?" asked my landlady.

"As well as I can hope to be," I said.

"Do you know, a young lady came along this afternoon and said she was meant to be collecting something for you. I told her I didn't know what on earth that might be, but then Moira came downstairs with a case of your things all packed for her," said Mrs. Jenkins.

That, no doubt, would be the industrious Miss Summers. "Thank you, Mrs. Jenkins. I'm afraid the trip that's taken me out of London has been unexpectedly extended."

"When will you be back? I only ask because—my goodness, I hate to be so crass as to mention it, but you didn't make any provisions for your rent this week."

I smiled despite myself. That was Mrs. Jenkins through and through, a sort of surrogate aunt who would make sure all of her residents had a solid breakfast in the morning and a place to shelter from air raids at night while also maintaining a firm grip on her business.

"I will speak to Moira about making sure that my rent is paid on time," I said.

"Thank you, dear."

"Mrs. Jenkins, I'm sorry to be unsociable, but I don't suppose Moira is home. I was hoping I might catch her before she went for rehearsals this evening."

"Oh." Mrs. Jenkins sucked in a breath. "Then you haven't heard?"

"Heard what?" I asked.

"One moment. I'll go find her for you."

I heard the clatter of the receiver being placed down on the telephone table and the retreating thud of Mrs. Jenkins's heels against the corridor carpet.

A few minutes later, I heard Moira's voice fill the line. "Evie?"

I smiled. "Hello, darling, how are you?"

Moira sighed. "Absolutely wretched, actually."

"What's happened?" I asked, immediately on alert even though I was miles away.

"You don't need to worry about making it back to London by Friday. The play's off."

"What do you mean it's off?" I asked, guilt and relief warring in me as I realized that I wouldn't have to make an excuse if I hadn't wrapped the case in time to return to London for Moira's first performance.

"We all showed up for rehearsals at the theater today and the doors were padlocked," she said. "Apparently the investor, Mr. St. George, had been borrowing money all over town from anyone who would give it to him all while neglecting to pay back his loans. Some bank or another decided that it had had enough. They've foreclosed on the theater, and Mr. St. George is nowhere to be found."

"But why would he do that?" I asked.

"We've all been asking ourselves the same thing. He's produced plays before and he owned the theater, so none of us expected anything like this, but the stage manager says that Mr. St. George's father died last year and the death duties have been absolutely ruinous. The stage manager's theory is that Mr. St. George thought that if he had a hit he would be able to float along for a little while longer."

"But the banks called in their loans and that was that," I finished.

"Precisely."

"Oh, Moira. I'm so sorry. You must be so disappointed."

I knew how hard my friend had fought to make her way out of bit parts in Ministry of Information films reminding women not to gossip about war secrets and modeling jobs where she was little more than a glorified hanger.

Moira's laugh filled the line, but it didn't sound particularly joyful. "I *am* disappointed."

"What will you do now?" I asked.

Moira sighed deeply. "Honestly, I don't know how much more of this I can stand. Maybe I should pack it all in."

188 JULIA KELLY

"But you love acting," I insisted.

"It doesn't seem to love me back at the moment though, does it?"

Moira had given up a life of rarified luxury to pursue her passion for the stage and screen. Her father had cut her off without a cent, but he liked to dangle cash in front of her from time to time to try to tempt her back into the familial fold. It usually happened at the family dinners that her mother begged her to join every six months or so. Moira would inevitably drag me along for moral support, and I would do my best to chatter away about anything other than the awkwardness hanging heavily around the dinner table. Then, after the cheese course, Mr. Mangan would usher his daughter into his study. Ten minutes later, she would storm out, demanding that we leave because her father, yet again, had tried to lure her back into the fold with money.

"You can't give up, Moira. You just can't," I said.

I could practically hear her smile on the other end when she said, "Don't worry, I'm simply being dramatic. An actress's prerogative."

"You frightened me there for a minute," I said.

"I'm giving myself tonight to lick my wounds, and then I'll dust myself off, don my makeup, and haul myself off to the auditions again. Something will break my way," she said. "It has to, because if I don't land something soon, I'll be asking you for a loan against my share of the rent."

"About that, I'm afraid I'm going to be gone a little longer than expected. I don't suppose that you could dip into my bedside table drawer and pull out the money to pay Mrs. Jenkins on Friday, could you?" I asked.

Moira drew in a sharp breath. "Well, that explains why a Miss Summers telephoned and asked me to pack up more of your things today."

I waited for her to mention the fact that I'd promised to do my best to make it back for Friday, but instead she simply sighed and said, "Yes, of course I'll do it."

"Thank you."

"I don't suppose you can tell me where you are or what you're doing," she said.

My stomach twisted. Given that I'd spent a great deal of my

childhood under the spotlight of the international press due to my parents' vicious custody battle in the twenties, it might make sense for me to have become an intensely private person. Instead, I'd gone in the other direction, sharing openly with a small circle of close friends.

However, this was one part of me that I couldn't share. Not with Moira. Not with my aunt. Not with anyone.

The only person I had who could understand this part of my life was David.

I shook my head and shoved that thought aside. David was my partner, not my friend. Not yet at least.

"I'm very sorry, Moira, but I really can't say anything else," I said.

There was a pause on the line.

"I wish I was there with you," I added.

"I wish you were too, darling."

"When I'm back in London, I will treat you out to a night on the town, just you and me. You just pick the time and the place," I said.

"Really?" she asked, her tone brightening a little.

"Really. Now, tell me who is taking you out right now? Can he step in until I come home?" I asked. Moira was utterly unapologetic about the fact that she changed boyfriends like some women change dresses, and I loved her for it.

"Douglas," said Moira.

"Tell me about him," I said.

"He's an army officer. He can dance, he has good manners, and he's devastatingly handsome."

"He sounds perfect," I said.

"I'm thinking of calling things off," she said.

"Why?"

"He is as boring as he is handsome, and I don't think I can stand another conversation about Napoleon."

"Napoleon?" I asked with a laugh.

"That's all the man talks about. He's mad for him. I think I'm going to have to let him down gently and soon."

"That sounds wise, but in the meantime, ask him to push you around a dance floor or two until I'm back," I said.

"Only if there's champagne involved," she said.

I grinned. "Naturally. We do have our standards, darling. Listen, I will do my best to ring tomorrow."

"Only if you can," said Moira, a concession despite how wretched I'd been at keeping in touch while away at Beaulieu.

"I will do my best. Besides, I want a full report on auditions and Douglas the Bore. Now, drink a bathtub of champagne for me tonight."

"Oh, Evie," she laughed. "You know I will."

Wednesday
November 6, 1940

ONE DAY UNTIL CHURCHILL'S VISIT

TWENTY-EIGHT

I awoke the next morning feeling refreshed and optimistic because, although David and I had a murder on our hands and no real leads, I knew that the things Moira had packed for Miss Summers should have arrived on the early train. Soon I would have my most comfortable cardigans and trousers in hand. In the meantime, I pulled on the navy suit, coat, and beret I was wearing when I'd arrived in Benstead. With my armor on, I waved goodbye to Mrs. Smythe, who was hovering over the hob as she cooked breakfast, and let myself out of the back door of Russet Cottage.

It was about twenty to eight when I passed through the open door of the railway station's tiny ticket hall and spotted Captain Sherman's back as he paced the empty platform, hands encased in white gloves folded behind him. I waited until the stationmaster turned sharply on his heel and began his slow march over to me.

"Good morning, Captain Sherman," I called, waving.

Even from a distance, I could see his eyes narrow before he continued his journey toward me.

"Are you Miss Redfern?" he asked.

"I am."

"A case addressed to you arrived this morning." He reached into his heavy navy overcoat and produced a set of keys. "If you'll follow me."

I trailed down the platform after him to a small door, which he unlocked. He opened the door and stepped inside, giving me just enough of a view to see that it was a parcel room.

"Here we are," he said, producing the familiar sight of my second-best suitcase. My heart warmed at the thought of Moira packing it for me.

Captain Sherman removed the tag with my name and address tied to the handle with twine and handed the case to me.

"Thank you very much," I said.

"Are you planning on staying longer with us in Benstead?" he asked.

"Yes, I imagine I am. I believe I met your wife yesterday. I'm surprised she didn't mention me," I said, wondering if I'd misjudged the housekeeper, who seemed to relish the gathering and dissemination of information that was gossip.

"Mrs. Sherman takes her work at Blackthorn Park very seriously. She would never betray her oath," he said before looking from side to side and then leaning across the gap between us. "However, she was very distressed to learn of Sir Nigel's suicide. Naturally, she needed to tell me so that I could console her as a husband should console his wife."

"Naturally," I said, glad that my suspicion about the nosy nature of both of the Shermans had been accurate. "Perhaps, in her distress, she disclosed that my partner, Mr. Poole, and I are currently investigating the circumstances behind Sir Nigel's death, what with him being such a prominent man."

"She might have mentioned something of the sort," he said stiffly. "Terrible business."

A thought struck me. "Captain Sherman, I'm certain that a man of your experience in the army and the Home Guard will understand that it's very important that my partner and I understand Sir Nigel's comings and goings before his untimely death. Would you happen to recall whether he took a train on the twenty-second of October?"

"What day of the week would that have been?" he asked.

"A Tuesday, I believe."

Mr. Hartley had mentioned Sir Nigel's disappearance a couple of weeks ago, a rough time frame that coincided nicely with the twenty-second of October, the date that Lieutenant Colonel Gerrard had high-lighted in the letter I'd found under Sir Nigel's blotter. Perhaps . . .

Captain Sherman frowned and then gestured for me to follow him once again. This time he led me through to the ticket hall. He rounded the wooden ticket counter, giving the older man who sold tickets a nod, and retrieved what looked like an old ledger from beneath the counter.

Captain Sherman joined me again on the customer's side of the counter and laid the ledger out, flipping pages until he stopped on one marked for the twenty-second.

"I take notes on who comes and goes from the station," he said by way of explanation. "Only the unusual arrivals and departures, mind you. The regulars I can remember easily enough."

"Why?" I asked before I could stop myself for fear he might take offense to the question.

Fortunately, Captain Sherman seemed to take pride in his ledger and said, "It is a matter of security. As the head of Benstead's Home Guard, it's my duty to understand who is in our community, espe-cially with everything going on"—he lowered his voice—"up at the big house.

"Now, on that day, Sir Nigel caught the 12:46 train to Waterloo. I remember it because it was unusual to see him board a train during the week—even more so during the working day. However, I wanted to be sure, given the sad state of affairs," he said.

"Did you speak to Sir Nigel?" I asked.

"We said good afternoon, as I recall," said Captain Sherman.

"Then you wouldn't know if London was his final destination?" I asked hopefully.

Captain Sherman paused and then shook his head. "His ticket took him to London, but there was nothing to say he didn't buy an-other ticket for an onward journey once he was there."

"Sir Nigel didn't happen to mention what his business was, did he?" I asked.

"He did not," said Captain Sherman.

"Did he return that same day?" I asked.

"He did not," said Captain Sherman without referring to his book.

"He returned the following afternoon on the 15:53 train from London," said the stationmaster.

"Did you see him arrive?" I asked.

"I did." Captain Sherman frowned. "I remember he walked straight by me without a word. It was rude, but hardly remarkable from what my wife tells me."

Why had Sir Nigel, a man who seemed singularly driven by his work at Blackthorn Park, made arrangements via a letter to a lieutenant colonel and then, on the appointed day, written "Burtlesby" in his diary? Where had he gone for a little more than twenty-four hours, and did it have anything to do with why, less than two weeks later, he'd been murdered?

As I turned over those questions in my mind, another one surfaced.

"Captain Sherman, you wouldn't happen to remember whether anyone unexpected arrived in Benstead on Monday, would you?"

"Monday? Well, there was you on the delayed 10:23 train. Then Mrs. Hester left on the 10:43 to Portsmouth to visit her daughter. She returned on the 20:04 train. Normally she's on the 19:02, but she said that she was running a little bit late on account of her shopping. I had to have a chat with the ticket inspector about her."

"Why?" I asked.

"She'd accidentally handed the inspector both of her tickets on her journey to Portsmouth in the morning and he punched them together. She didn't realize until she boarded the train back to Benstead that evening, and when she disembarked I had to account for her character. The inspector was going to fine her for a mistake she didn't make," he said.

"Was there anyone else?" I asked, desperate for something other than village gossip.

"I do recall Mr. Eccles came up from London on the 7:21 as he usually does in the morning."

"Do you remember the train he left on?" I asked, resisting the urge to pull out my notebook and cross-reference Mr. Eccles's return train time.

"It was the 18:32, same as always. He's like clockwork," said Captain Sherman. "Then there was the doctor—what's his name?"

"Dr. Morrison?" I asked, surprised that the stationmaster would have forgotten the name of the only doctor in the village.

"No, no, not Morrison," he mused. "Jamison! He left on the 20:43 train Monday."

"Dr. Jamison? Are you certain?"

It was a direct contradiction to the story Dr. Jamison had told David and me of arriving home to a solitary supper because Mrs. Jamison was ill in bed. Ill in bed and unable to truly confirm that he was at home all evening as her husband had told us.

"I am positive," said the stationmaster sternly.

"Did you see him return?" I asked, my interest piqued.

He shook his head.

"Is there any way that he could have slipped off a returning train without you noticing?" I asked.

"That would be impossible. I greeted the last train of the evening and then went to bed."

"And did you see him return the following day?" I asked.

"No," he said.

"But I've seen him at Blackthorn. In fact, I spoke to him myself yesterday afternoon," I said.

"Well, I can't account for that, All I can say is that he didn't return by a train that arrived at this station," said Captain Sherman definitively.

How intriguing.

"Was there anything else unusual? Anything at all?" I asked.

"Mr. Tyson came to accept a shipment yesterday afternoon. He looked rather shaken up, which makes sense now that Mrs. Sherman told me what had happened." He thought for a moment. "Mr. Kilburn went to London yesterday."

"Who is Mr. Kilburn?" I asked.

"He's the village butcher. I don't know what business a butcher has in London during a working day, but I suppose it isn't my place to say," said Captain Sherman, sounding very much like he wished to make it his place, but Mr. Kilburn wasn't keen to share.

I doubted very much that Mr. Kilburn was a suspect given that the village butcher was sure to be well-known and his presence on the Blackthorn Park grounds would raise more than a few questions.

No, the murderer was one of the current Blackthorn Park staff. I was as certain of it as Hercule Poirot was confident in his "little gray cells."

There was a whistle in the distance, and Captain Sherman twisted to look at the station clock. "That will be the 7:50, right on time. Excuse me, Miss Redfern."

I chewed on my lip as I watched Captain Sherman retreat. There was something I was missing. Something right on the tip of my tongue that I couldn't quite grasp.

With a sigh, I picked up my case and made my way out of the ticket hall. I was a few steps down the road when a shout stopped me.

"Evelyne!"

I turned on my heel to find David driving up in his black car, the window rolled down.

"Good morning, fancy meeting you here," I said.

"Mrs. Smythe told me that you ran out of the house without breakfast because you had to catch a train. I thought that couldn't be right, so I came to see for myself," he said.

"Miss Summers sent provisions," I said, lifting my case.

He jerked his head back. "Put it in the back."

I didn't have to ask twice. I dumped my case on the back seat and slid into the passenger seat.

"How are you this morning?" David asked.

"I just had a rather enlightening conversation with Captain Sherman, the Benstead stationmaster. He told me that on Monday evening, he saw Dr. Jamison board the 20:43 train to London Waterloo."

David looked over at me sharply. "He's certain?"

"Completely."

"Then Dr. Jamison lied to us," said David. "What are the chances that he might have picked up the knowledge of sedatives somewhere along the way?"

"I'd say they're strong. Don't forget that he told us that he'd originally thought to study medicine like his father," I said.

"And if they'd known each other for so long, it wouldn't be surprising to learn that Dr. Jamison knew that Sir Nigel kept his old service revolver in his desk. That gives him means and opportunity for the murder," said David.

"And Sir Nigel intervening and denying Dr. Jamison the opportunity to run his own laboratory would provide him with plenty of motive," I said. "I think that, before we do anything else this morning, we should pay Dr. Jamison a little call to see if he would like to revise his alibi."

TWENTY-NINE

David and I might have had every intention of marching up to the engineers' workshop and demanding to know why Dr. Jamison had lied to us about his whereabouts on Monday evening, but as soon as we entered the main house we found ourselves faced with a wall of men and women standing shoulder to shoulder while, above them on the first floor balcony, Mr. Eccles gazed down at the crowd.

With his hands braced on the banister, Mr. Eccles said in a somber voice, "I'm afraid that I have had some disturbing news from Baker Street. Early yesterday morning, a mission to disable a major target behind enemy lines in occupied France failed."

The crowd groaned.

"This was the first time that commandos were sent into the field with our new barnacle bombs, and Baker Street has reason to believe that this was not the failure of the brave men who volunteered for this mission, but rather the equipment they were sent, which included devices produced at this facility," Mr. Eccles continued.

All at once, we were surrounded by murmurs of "What?" "That's not possible," and "But they've been tested."

"The investigation into the failure of the mission is still in its infancy, but I can tell you there are major concerns about our weapons," Mr. Eccles continued. "As you can imagine, this is especially distressing

news considering the loss of Sir Nigel two nights ago. There is also the
pressure added by the impending visit of the prime minister tomorrow because Mr. Churchill will expect a demonstration of the barnacle
bombs as well as our other devices, and I can tell you that he is not
easily put off.

"I should not have to remind you how important it is to the future
of the work that we do here that all of this goes off without a hitch.
Dr. Jamison, who has graciously stepped into Sir Nigel's shoes as the
head of engineering, will be scrutinizing every detail of the barnacle
bomb designs." Mr. Eccles gestured to a point across the entryway
from David and me, and I spotted Dr. Jamison in the crowd.

I nudged David with my elbow and he nodded.

"Dr. Jamison and his team will try to pinpoint what might have
gone wrong in the field and if it had to do with the design of the device," Mr. Eccles continued. "In the meantime, Miss Kenwood will be
reviewing all of our manufacturing processes.

"We *must* make sure this does not happen again. If you have any
knowledge of anything that might have contributed to the weapons
failure—even a suspicion—I encourage you to come speak to me directly. Thank you," he finished.

David leaned over as the murmuring crowd of employees began
to disperse. "What do you make of that?"

"I think the consequences of what's happening here are becoming
more deadly by the day," I murmured. "Let's catch Dr. Jamison before
he has the chance to slip out."

We wove through the dispersing crowd until we reached the new
head of engineering. He was speaking rather animatedly to Miss Kenwood. The manufacturing barn's forewoman towered over the little
man, wearing a distinctly irritated expression that stood in stark contrast to the ennui she'd greeted us with the day before.

David and I were a foot away when Dr. Jamison caught sight of us
and flinched away from Miss Kenwood.

"Miss Redfern. Mr. Poole," said Dr. Jamison, fussing with his red
bow tie.

"We're sorry to interrupt," I said.

"Isn't that precisely what you're here to do?" asked Miss Kenwood sharply. "I imagine that Mr. Eccles's announcement has made it even more important to figure out why Sir Nigel killed himself."

"You think Sir Nigel might have had something to do with the bombs failing?" I asked.

Miss Kenwood lifted an elegant shoulder, but Dr. Jamison balked. "Surely you cannot be suggesting that Sir Nigel sabotaged his own equipment, Miss Kenwood."

"You can't deny that the timing is curious," she said.

"Miss Kenwood," said Dr. Jamison, his tone unmistakably censorious, "I know you had your disagreements with Sir Nigel, but—"

"I do not have time for this," said Miss Kenwood, cutting the scientist off. "I have new girls starting this morning, and all of this faff means that I wasn't there to greet them. It'll be a wonder if they haven't burned the place down by now."

"The processes, Miss Kenwood," Dr. Jamison interjected.

She rolled her eyes and muttered, "As though I don't have enough to deal with today."

I watched Miss Kenwood slink away before turning to Dr. Jamison. "Processes?"

He sighed and pushed his glasses up so that he could pinch the bridge of his nose. "I have ordered a check of every aspect of the devices sent with the commandos to try to ascertain what went wrong. Mr. Hartley is reviewing the schematics. Again. Miss Kenwood will look at the manufacturing processes to see if there is a flaw in our construction. I believe Mr. Eccles is making an inquiry into what exactly happened to the weapons after they left Blackthorn Park in case they were tampered with. I've suggested to Mr. Porter that he and Mr. Tyson perform a check of their own supply chains, although suggesting anything to Mr. Porter is a dicey business."

"Miss Kenwood seemed offended by the implication that her employees might be the root of the problem," said David.

"Miss Kenwood could find offense at anything," said Dr. Jamison.

"Is that where her disagreements with Sir Nigel stemmed from?" I asked.

Dr. Jamison cleared his throat. "I shouldn't like to say . . ."

"Please do," I said, my invitation wry.

He seemed to consider his words for a moment and then said, "When Miss Kenwood first arrived at Blackthorn Park, Sir Nigel was eager to involve her in all manner of conversation about his future plans for manufacturing. However, at the end of the summer, his enthusiasm seemed to cool."

A cooling off that lined up nicely with the end of Miss Kenwood and Sir Nigel's affair.

"He never said as much to me, but he was growing frustrated with the output of the manufacturing barn, and he laid that squarely at her feet," he said. "The girls on the line are her responsibility, after all. Then in September there were some issues with consistent failures on the timing device of a prototype he was making. She insisted that her girls were making the device exactly to his specifications, but he couldn't reliably reproduce his results in any of the prototypes the manufacturing barn made. There were words, and he even threatened to have Eccles find a replacement for her. However, that all seemed to go away."

"Do you know if Mr. Hartley was aware of Sir Nigel's frustrations with his fiancée?" asked David.

Dr. Jamison shook his head. "No, and it's a good thing he wasn't. I suspect if he was, we might have had another kerfuffle."

I leaned back a little, considering this. What if the end of Miss Kenwood's affair with Sir Nigel hadn't been quite as amicable as she'd made it out to be? What if he had wanted her gone from Blackthorn Park, so he'd concocted a reason to blame her for the failure of the prototypes? If Sir Nigel had become frustrated enough, he might even have threatened to expose their affair, and she would have been forced to protect herself. Wouldn't she?

That line of inquiry, however, would have to wait, because there was another consideration at hand.

"Dr. Jamison, we have some further questions about your movements Monday evening," I said.

"I told you, I walked back from work, went home, ate my supper, and went to bed," he said.

"Then you didn't go home, see that your wife had taken to bed with a migraine, and then decide to leave Benstead on the 20:43 train to London?" I asked.

Dr. Jamison's mouth fell open.

"Just a few minutes ago, I spoke to the Benstead stationmaster, who clearly recalls you boarding that train," I said.

"Why did you lie to us?" asked David.

"It was a personal matter," said Dr. Jamison in a small voice. "And not one I wish to share with anyone."

"We are not just anyone, Dr. Jamison," I reminded him.

Dr. Jamison swallowed and then glanced from side to side. "It's a matter of great discretion."

"It's our job to be discreet," I said.

He closed his eyes as though steeling himself and then gave a single nod. "From time to time, I go up to London to relieve some of the pressure of working here."

"What do you do? Drink?" I asked.

He shifted from foot to foot. "Sometimes."

"Where?" I asked.

"Here and there," he waffled.

"I'm afraid that you'll have to be more specific than that," I said.

Dr. Jamison looked as though he wished for nothing more than the floor to swallow him whole. "A place called the Windmill."

"Where is the Windmill located?" I asked, reaching for my notebook.

David cleared his throat and said, "I think you'll find that it is on Great Windmill Street."

"You know it?" I asked.

"It has quite the reputation," said David. "Their slogan is 'We Never Closed.' They're very proud of it."

"Have you been to this pub?" I asked.

David half choked on a laugh. "It's not a pub exactly."

I looked between the two blushing men, but when neither elaborated, I put my hands on my hips. "Would someone please explain to me—"

"Showgirls, Evelyne. The Windmill is known for its nude *tableaux vivants*," said David.

"Really?" I hadn't thought Dr. Jamison had it in him to visit somewhere quite so scandalous.

"It's just a bit of fun," Dr. Jamison hurried to reassure us, his cheeks flaming red now. "It's harmless, really. I don't even participate in the Windmill Steeplechase."

I looked to David, who stared resolutely at the ceiling as he explained, "All of the men in the back wait until the show ends and clamber over the rows to find seats in the front for the next show."

"How many shows are there?" I asked in fascination.

"Five shows a day, six days a week," said Dr. Jamison before clearing his throat, perhaps realizing that some might find it unbecoming that Blackthorn's new head of engineering was able to provide this level of information about an adult establishment. "I was at the theater until rather late, and then I took a cab to my club before catching the first train in the morning."

"Did you see anyone who would be able to verify this?" I asked.

"I exchanged a few words with the porter at my club when I was securing a room," he said.

"When was this?" I asked.

"About two o'clock in the morning," he said.

I shook my head. There was a gap in his alibi between a quarter to nine and two o'clock. He was going to have to do better than that.

"What about at the Windmill?" asked David, reading my mind. "Perhaps you spoke to a dancer."

Dr. Jamison frowned.

"Or bought cigarettes?" I asked.

The head of engineering's face brightened. "Yes! There is a girl I always see when I go. Her name is Ellie, I think. I took my seat around ten o'clock and bought cigarettes from her."

I looked forward to explaining to Constable Lee his new task of verifying Dr. Jamison's new alibi.

"When did you return from London?" I asked. "Captain Sherman doesn't recall seeing you disembark from a train Tuesday morning."

Dr. Jamison cleared his throat. "That's because I got off one up the line and walked. I . . . I didn't want to risk anyone seeing me in case it made it back to my wife that I was not home. You know how villages are. As soon as I reached my home, I went straight upstairs to kiss my wife good morning and was halfway through dressing when the telephone rang with the news of Sir Nigel's death," said Dr. Jamison.

"Why did you tell us we could verify your alibi with your wife?" I asked.

"I didn't see the harm in it, really."

The man was a fool but, if the cigarette girl and the club porter would confirm what Dr. Jamison had told us, it also eliminated him from our inquiries because he could not physically be in London buying cigarettes and shooting Sir Nigel at Blackthorn Park at the same time.

"Would you also like to tell us anything about your conversation with Sir Nigel about your job prospects?" I asked.

"What do you mean?" asked Dr. Jamison, immediately guarded.

"A witness tells us that around seven o'clock in the evening on Monday, they overheard a loud argument between you two in Sir Nigel's office," said David.

"I . . . I . . . I don't know what to say," said the engineer.

"The truth would be a good place to start," I said.

"I was angry on Monday when I received the letter telling me that Sir Nigel had ruined my chances for that job. I confronted him about it in his office, but then he told me *why* he did it. His ideas for how Blackthorn Park could grow vastly outstripped anything Porter or Eccles or even I had dared to imagine." Dr. Jamison swallowed. "I believed him when he said that he needed me here at Blackthorn Park, but I won't pretend that I wasn't disappointed. *That* is why I went to London Monday evening. I promise."

Clearly Dr. Jamison's promises weren't worth very much, but lying about where he'd been Monday evening didn't make him a murderer.

"Thank you, Dr. Jamison. We will let you know if we have further questions," I said.

As the man scurried off, I turned to David with a raised brow and asked, "*Tableaux vivants?*"

"It's how they manage to skirt the censorship laws. If the naked woman doesn't move, it isn't rude."

I snorted. "How inventive."

"If you think that's inventive, you should see what they do with fans and a spinning rope," said David, twirling his index finger around quickly in demonstration.

"Not at the same time, surely," I said, horrified and fascinated at the same time. "How would the performer hold on?"

"They're separate acts," he reassured me.

"Oh, well, that's all right then."

"Much as I would love to discuss the intricacies of Soho clubs all morning, shall we see if we can find out more from Mr. Eccles about what happened in France?" asked David, gesturing to a spot over my shoulder.

I looked up at the balcony where Mr. Porter, red-faced at the best of times, appeared to have turned the shade of a very ripe tomato. The head of operations gestured wildly with both hands as he spoke, sending ribbons of smoke from his cigar dancing around his face. Mr. Eccles, for his part, wore a pained expression, as though he was barely tolerating his companion.

"Let's," I said. "Something tells me that Mr. Eccles will welcome the intervention."

THIRTY

"Y ou cannot tell me that they intend to place the blame on us,"
Mr. Porter hissed at Mr. Eccles as David and I approached.

"They are looking at every possibility, as you can imagine,"
said Mr. Eccles, sounding much calmer than his counterpart.

"But we already have investigators on-site, poking their noses
into—"

"And here are those investigators now," Mr. Eccles cut into Mr.
Porter's rant as his eyes lit on David and me.

"A difficult morning," said David, nodding to the now nearly empty
entryway.

Mr. Porter grunted.

"What exactly happened?" I asked.

Mr. Eccles lowered his voice. "The commandos who parachuted
into occupied France were tasked with destroying a power station.
It looks as though they set their barnacle bombs, but one of them
must have been faulty. It went off unexpectedly, causing a chain
reaction and detonating all of the bombs. All but one of them appear to have been killed when the building collapsed. We only know
about it because Baker Street received a coded message from the
one man who managed to make it to a resistance bolt-hole that had
a wireless operator. He died within the hour."

I shuddered with the horror of it. I knew that some of the people I had trained with were destined for dangerous fieldwork. They would be sent wherever the Special Operations Executive thought they might be useful in tearing apart the infrastructure that kept the German military in power. France, Denmark, the Netherlands, Norway. All of those occupied countries had been whispered at my training camp as we all played the same game of speculation that soldiers on the eve of receiving their orders play.

"This could not have happened at a worse time with the prime minister's visit tomorrow . . ." Mr. Eccles trailed off, his shoulders slumped as he let exhaustion slip through for the first time since I'd met him the day before.

"Did anyone here have any suspicion that the bombs might not behave as expected in the field?" David asked.

I knew what he was thinking. Thanks to Major Richards's letter about the failure of the barnacle bomb in a training exercise that we'd found in Sir Nigel's home safe, we knew that the engineer would have had good reason to be suspicious of the efficacy of his own invention. However, what we didn't know was whether anyone here at Blackthorn Park harbored similar concerns.

It also meant that if Sir Nigel had done nothing to stop those faulty bombs from making their way into the field, there was blood on his hands.

"No," said Mr. Eccles.

"Did Sir Nigel ever express concern about the stability of the weapons to either of you?" I asked.

"Of course not," Mr. Porter nearly spat. "Otherwise why would we have shipped them to Dover?"

"I believe what Mr. Porter is trying to say," said Mr. Eccles with an edge of annoyance in his voice, "is that there was nothing to indicate that something like this might happen." But then he jerked back as though hit with a disturbing realization. "You don't think Sir Nigel killed himself because he knew that the bombs would fail, do you?"

"We must explore all theories," I said.

"Theories," scoffed Mr. Porter. "Some of us don't have time for theories that won't amount to anything that really matters."

"Mr. Porter, perhaps it's time for you to return to your desk," said Mr. Eccles.

"Don't worry, Eccles," said Mr. Porter with a sneer. "I plan to review every bit of wire and every chemical that went into those bombs from supplier to storage, starting with the order sheets. No one will be able to pin this on me. Good day."

As soon as he was gone, Mr. Eccles sighed. "I apologize for Porter. As you can imagine, tensions are high at the moment."

"I'm beginning to see why he and Sir Nigel might have clashed," I said.

"They were, in many ways, cut from the same cloth. Proud men who hated being challenged," said Mr. Eccles.

"It must have been difficult managing them when you first arrived," said David.

"Yes, well, I've always found that money is a great motivator. Once I showed I was effective at keeping the funds flowing in, we learned to live with one another. Now, how has your investigation progressed since we last spoke? You're certainly going above and beyond for a suicide," said Mr. Eccles with a frown.

"I imagine that, after France, it's more important than ever to find out the reason behind Sir Nigel's death," said David.

"About that." Mr. Eccles hesitated. "I've been racking my brain trying to think of why Sir Nigel might have been desperate enough to—" He cleared his throat. "About a month ago, he asked for an advance on his salary."

"Did that strike you as unusual?" I asked.

"Well, yes," said Mr. Eccles, rubbing his chin. "Sir Nigel was a gentleman of another era, and I suspect it pained him to have to ask for a favor about something as base as money."

"Did he say why he needed the advance?" I asked.

"I gather that Lady Balram has expensive taste, and he was short of cash," said Mr. Eccles.

Having seen the Balram family chequebook, I could understand why.

"Did Sir Nigel name an amount?" David asked.

Mr. Eccles shook his head. "I think natural embarrassment took over and he said he'd been mistaken to ask and left my office in a hurry. I will admit, I'm not certain I would have done it even if he'd persisted. Advancing anyone their salary isn't something I encourage."

Mr. Eccles glanced at his wristwatch. "I don't mean to be rude, but I will have to hurry to catch the 9:02 train. I have a noon meeting in Whitehall I cannot miss."

"Didn't you just arrive?" I asked.

He touched his tie. "I had a rare night at the Hand and Flower yesterday evening. I felt it was my duty to stay with all of the work ahead of tomorrow's visit."

"All of this back and forth must be tiring. It's a wonder you can find any time at all to help your father-in-law," I said, recalling what he'd told us about his ailing family.

He gave me a tight smile. "I'm afraid that it's necessary. Fortunately, my wife does an exemplary job caring for him. However, I will be happy to be on the other side of Mr. Churchill's visit *and* this awful matter with Sir Nigel."

"On that we all agree," David said.

Mr. Eccles checked his watch again. "I really must go."

As we watched the government liaison walk away, David leaned over and asked, "What do you make of that? Sir Nigel is desperate enough for cash that he asks for an advance but then rescinds his request."

"I think that a man who is short of funds doesn't write a cheque for £500 on a whim," I said.

"What if Sir Nigel, looking to make money quickly, begins to steal and sell equipment and supplies from Blackthorn Park on the black market? His work before the war would put him in contact with plenty of companies desperate for supplies during rationing."

"Then why would someone kill him?" I asked.

"What if he had a business partner?"

"And his partner turned on him and killed him?"

David shrugged. "Or Sir Nigel had a moment of conscience and threatened to report his collaborator to save himself."

"From what we know of Sir Nigel, it feels more likely that he exposed the thief and they shot him for it," I said.

"This bloody case. There are still too many loose ends and not enough leads," he grumbled.

I sighed. "David, I don't think you've ever said anything truer."

THIRTY-ONE

I've often found that, when confounded with a particularly troubling dilemma, it is helpful to go back to the very beginning and review the facts as I know them. And that is precisely what David and I decided to do in order to try to unpick the tangled web of our case.

We left the house, the fresh but damp morning air filling my lungs, and made a beeline straight for the estate's access road. There, I took David through a tour of the events of the evening as I knew them. I showed him how I ran across the great lawn and to the walled garden—just as he and I had planned back in the SIU's Gosfield Street office. I crept around the wall, much to the gardener Mr. Parker's amusement as he stopped raking leaves to watch us reenact the night. I even showed David how I checked the door for alarms and let myself in, although this time I could simply twist the doorknob rather than pick the lock.

"So from here you heard the shot?" he asked, looking around as somewhere above us I could hear the sound of someone's shoes clattering on wood stairs.

"Yes," I said. "It was quieter then."

"And then you ran up the servants' stairs?" he asked.

"Indeed."

He gestured to the corridor leading through the lower ground-floor rooms. "Lead the way."

We climbed the servants' stairs and emerged onto the first-floor landing. As soon as the door shut behind us, David looked around the corridor. "It's about ten feet to Sir Nigel's office door from here. Why did you go there and not run down to the west wing?"

"I assumed that for me to hear the shot, it must have been on the east side of the house. Sir Nigel's office was the closest to the stairs, and I saw a light under the door. That's why I went to it first," I explained.

"How long do you think it was between hearing the shot and arriving in Sir Nigel's office?" he asked.

"Less than a minute."

He nodded, continuing to look around. "The murderer would have had to be fast."

"First, they would have to inject him," I said, miming a stabbing motion. "They miss, and scratch Sir Nigel's neck. They inject him again"—another stab at the air—"and this time they hit their target. During the scuffle, Sir Nigel or the killer knocks over a pile of papers."

"There would have been noise even before the shot. Anyone could come in at any time," said David.

"The murderer must have had a plan. I think they removed Sir Nigel's service revolver—which was widely known to be stored in his desk drawer—and then they shot him."

"How do they get access to the drawer?" David asked.

"They take the key off Sir Nigel's person," I said.

"When you tried the desk drawer, it was locked," David pointed out.

"Perhaps instinct took over and they panicked, locking the drawer without thinking that a man about to commit suicide likely wouldn't care to lock his desk drawer. They could easily pocket the key by mistake, which would explain why we didn't find it among Sir Nigel's things," I said. "Now, once that gun goes off, the killer is on borrowed time. They must flee, but to be seen running away from what is meant to look like a suicide would defeat the whole purpose of staging the scene. They must have hidden until they were certain they wouldn't be caught. Then they slipped away. Which begs the question: where?"

"One of the bedrooms?" suggested David.

I considered this. "It's possible. We know that the ones that hadn't been converted into offices yet weren't kept locked, because we let ourselves into one to speak to Constable Lee yesterday, but there are no servants' stairs on the far end of each of the wings. The lower ground floor only stretches the length of the Long Gallery. If the murderer hid in one of the bedrooms, they would have had to risk sneaking past all of the people who ran up after the shot was fired."

"They could have stayed hidden in the bedroom until everyone left," he said.

I shook my head. "Again, it's too risky. If Mr. Porter hadn't been so focused on me, he or anyone else in that room might have had the idea to search the house."

As my eyes swept over the Long Gallery, taking in the uninterrupted wood paneling topped with green wallpaper that made up the side of the corridor, a thought struck me. The previous year, I'd read a short story called "The Horror at Staveley Grange" by Sapper while in an air-raid shelter during what thankfully turned out to be a false alarm. It featured a country house and, more importantly for my purposes, a red herring in the form of a hidden room. What if . . .

I began to press on the panels of the wall next to the servants' stairs.

"What are you doing?" asked David.

"On the other side of the building, there's at least one storage cupboard built into the wall. It probably was a linen cupboard at some point, but it's been fitted out with filing cabinets. It's where I found Miss Glenconner crying—" The wood gave under my hand and sprang back. "Here we are."

I opened the cabinet door and David reached around me to pull on a cord, flooding the space with light. It was cold and bare, but it was a space big enough for a man to hide.

"Well done, Evelyne," said David with a grin.

"Thank you," I said, dipping into a wobbly curtsey that probably would have made Aunt Amelia groan with despair. "I would like to try something. Will you please step out into the hall?"

David took a step back and I turned, pulling the door to. Then I reached up to pull the cord and plunge myself into darkness.

"Can you tell the door is open?" I shouted.

"No!" David called back.

I pushed the door open again and stepped out.

"The paneling is almost perfect when it's pulled to like that," he said.

"If the murderer waited in here—"

"They could have slipped out and gone into Sir Nigel's office as soon as people had run past. They would have had a clear shot at the servants' stairs and an escape," David finished for me.

"Miss Redfern!"

I looked to my right and found Miss Glenconner striding toward me, a frown deeply etched on her pretty face.

"I have a message for you," she called.

I turned to David. "Why don't we discuss this further in the morning room?"

He gave me a nod, and I strode down the Long Gallery to meet Miss Glenconner where she stood at the top of the stairs, a fresh cup of tea in her hand.

"Good morning, Miss Glenconner. I hope you're feeling better," I said.

"Better?" she asked.

"Mrs. Sherman mentioned that you'd gone home early yesterday because you were unwell," I said.

"Oh, yes." She pressed her free hand to her stomach as though steadying herself. "It's all been so much, but I am trying my best to carry on."

"I'm certain Mr. Porter appreciates it," I said.

She scoffed at that as she began to lead me back toward the east wing. "I don't know about that. He's on a tear this morning."

"A tear?" I asked. "Is something the matter?"

She stopped in front of a half-open door next to the one I'd found her inside the day before. I could see a half dozen of the ugly beige filing cabinets I'd come to associate with government facilities, one of which had a drawer open exposing the dozens of neat files. The floor was littered with small stacks of files in a semicircle with a void in the middle from where, I imagined, Miss Glenconner had just stood up.

"Mr. Porter has gotten it into his head that he needs every contract that we hold with suppliers of materials used in the barnacle bombs by noon so that he can review them," she said, setting down her cup on a small wooden table. "I had to have Dr. Jamison and Mr. Hartley give me a list of materials, but now finding the company that we actually work with . . . Do you know how many companies have supplied us with materials since the requisitioning?"

"Many?" I guessed.

"That would be an understatement. For a time we had four different companies delivering us shipments of copper wire alone because none of them could manage the volume that Sir Nigel and the engineers demanded. And that was before they began this ludicrous plan to manufacture on-site." She pushed her blond hair off her forehead, her expression turning from annoyed to desperate.

"And now I come in here this morning and find that nothing is in the right place. I found a 'C' file stuck in 'L,'" she complained.

"Has someone been in here?" I asked.

Her lips thinned. "No one is supposed to come in here except for me."

"But . . ." I prompted her.

"Last Tuesday, when I returned from my tea break, I found Sir Nigel standing in the middle of the room, four different drawers open and files all over the floor."

"What was he looking for?" I asked.

"He didn't say," said Miss Glenconner shortly. "All I know is that he created an entire afternoon's work for me, putting things to rights, and apparently it still isn't correct."

This, I was fascinated to hear, was not the rosy picture of Sir Nigel that Miss Glenconner had painted for me when she had been weeping to me just the day before.

"This is entirely unreasonable," Miss Glenconner grumbled as she peered around the filing cabinets. "I'm only one woman."

"Where is Mr. Porter?" I asked. "Shouldn't he be helping you if he wants those files by noon?"

"Help?" she snorted. "He wouldn't condescend to do a secretary's work. Besides, he took a telephone call from an outside line, and then he raced off somewhere just before half past nine."

"In that case, if you'd like to give me the message you took down for me, I can leave you in peace," I said with a smile.

She led me to her desk where she picked up a piece of paper and handed it to me. "There. The woman on the line said you were looking for this and you would understand."

I read the note quickly because there wasn't much to it, just the letters "BR," a telephone exchange, and the words "Secure line."

My heart rate ticked up. "Thank you, Miss Glenconner."

I left her staring at her desk, tears rising in her eyes. The poor young woman was clearly at her wits' end, but I had other concerns.

I hurried downstairs to the morning room. David looked up as I walked in, holding up the message.

"It looks as though Miss Summers has tracked down Major Richards. She reminds us that we'll want a secure line," I said.

"There's one in the library," said David, rising from the table.

In the library where, just the day before, we'd argued with Mr. Porter about gaining access to the grounds, I picked up the telephone and gave the exchange to the switchboard as David picked up the extension. A young woman answered the telephone.

"Major Bartholomew Richards, please," I said.

"May I ask who is calling?" she asked politely.

"Miss Evelyne Redfern. I'm from—"

"One moment, Miss Redfern. The Major has been expecting your call," said the young woman.

David caught my eye and raised a brow, but before I could say anything a deep voice filled the line.

"Miss Redfern."

"Major Richards?" I asked.

"I heard that you were looking for me. Given that we work for the same master—in a sense—I thought it would be best to be ready for you. How can I help?" he asked.

"I don't know if you're aware, Major, but my partner David Poole and I have been asked to investigate the death of Sir Nigel Balram."

I could hear the major suck in a breath on the other end. "I'm very sorry to hear that. How did he die?"

"He was shot, and it was staged to look like a suicide," I said.

"Murdered?" asked Major Richards.

"I'm afraid so," I said.

"That's a bloody shame. Sir Nigel was at my parents' wedding. They'll be sorry to hear it," he said.

"My partner and I found a letter that you sent Sir Nigel recently," I prompted.

"About the failure of some of the devices he sent up north to us for testing. Yes. Almost blew a dozen commandos to high heaven," said Major Richards.

"What happened?" I asked.

"An instructor here at Arisaig House armed a device as part of a demonstration. It was stuck to the underside of a motorcar, simulating a mission that the commandos were set to embark upon. We'd specifically modified the original plans to include this barnacle device at Sir Nigel's request because he wanted to see more 'real world' applications of it before it was released in the field.

"The timing fuse should have given them a good five minutes before it detonated. Instead, it was more like ninety seconds. Fortunately the instructor had just moved away to answer a question about the route that the car would likely take in the proposed scenario when the thing exploded. Everyone escaped with only cuts and bruises. I wrote to Sir Nigel warning him and received a shirty telephone call in return telling me that I must have been mistaken because his devices had all been tested extensively at Blackthorn Park. I asked him what the point of shipping them up to my men was then."

"What did he say to that?" I asked.

"Not much at first, but he finally promised he would personally see to it that no faulty devices were issued out of Blackthorn. He even told me that he was going to track down a friend to help him look into it further," he said.

"Do you know that friend's name?" I asked.

"He's a chap named Gerrard," said Major Richards.

"Lieutenant Colonel Julian Gerrard?" I asked. It was the name of the man who had written the letter to arrange for Sir Nigel's mysterious visit on the twenty-second of October.

"That's the one. He's a rugby man like I am. Good sort from what I remember of our school days, but mad as a box of frogs. He runs things over at Burtlesby," said Major Richards cheerfully.

Out of the corner of my eye, I saw David work free Sir Nigel's scientific journal and open it. He stuck it in front of me and tapped the page where "Burtlesby" had been written.

Burtlesby wasn't a person. It was a place.

"This has been very helpful, Major. Thank you," I said.

"I hope you catch the bastard who did it, Miss Redfern," said the major before signing off.

David and I put down our receivers at the same time.

"Well," I said, my voice trailing off.

"So Sir Nigel received a complaint from Major Richards and arranged a trip to another training camp run by Lieutenant Colonel Gerrard because he believed that he could figure out why the barnacle bomb malfunctioned at Arisaig House," said David.

"Almost as though he didn't trust the staff here," I said. "We need to speak to Lieutenant Colonel Gerrard and find out what Sir Nigel discovered at Burtlesby."

David reached for the telephone. "I'll telephone Miss Summers and let her know that Gerrard runs this Burtlesby place. That should help her track him down."

But before he could even pick up the receiver, Constable Lee burst through the door, wide-eyed and red-faced.

"Mr. Poole, Miss Redfern, come quickly!" he gasped out.

"Why?" David asked at the same time I demanded, "What's happened?"

"It's Mr. Porter. He's—" The young man swallowed. "He's dead!"

THIRTY-TWO

I f the future competence of a police officer could be judged purely on athletic ability, Constable Lee would have been the cream of the crop.

David and I raced out of the house after the young man, hot on his heels, but by the time we saw he was heading for the service road, the distance between us was lengthening and I was already out of breath—and that was with the benefit of six weeks of intensive training for the SOE's best instructors. However, I put my head down, legs burning, until David and I broke free of the tree line into the clearing where the equipment sheds stood.

The door of the farthest shed from the path stood open, and Mr. Tyson was hovering half inside of it. Constable Lee, who had come to a halt next to the quartermaster, was doubled over, sucking in deep breaths.

"Mr. Tyson, are you all right?" David called, huffing and puffing next to me in a manner that made me feel at least a little bit better about my own condition.

Mr. Tyson didn't say anything; however, as soon as we took a few steps closer, we understood why.

Hanging from one of the crossbeams of the equipment shed was the body of Mr. Porter.

"Dear God," David whispered.

I swallowed hard. We hadn't been fast enough, and now I feared the killer had struck again.

"I didn't know if I should try to cut him down or not," said Mr. Tyson, not taking his eyes off the body.

"You did the right thing," I said, stepping forward to place a hand on Mr. Tyson's arm. "Constable Lee is going to take you back to the house so that we can speak to you in a few minutes."

That seemed like an appropriate plan until I saw just how pale Constable Lee now looked.

"On second thought, David, you'd better go with them both."

David nodded. "I'll telephone the doctor."

"We have to let Baker Street know," said Mr. Tyson. "Or maybe Mr. Eccles should do that. No—he's already gone back to London to prepare for tomorrow." Mr. Tyson took off his hat and rubbed his head with the heel of his hand. "Tomorrow. The entire bloody world is showing up here tomorrow. What are we going to do?"

"David," I prompted with some urgency.

"Come with me," said David, placing a hand on the quartermaster's shoulder and directing him away. Constable Lee followed limply behind.

As soon as they were out of sight, I took a deep breath and turned to face the body. To see a man who had loomed large in life with a blustery, almost bullying personality in such a state—all I could do was shake my head.

I made a quick examination of the exterior of the shed, finding nothing. Then I stepped inside, giving the body a wide berth. There would be plenty of questions to ask Dr. Morrison when he arrived, but for now all I wanted to do was take everything in and do my best to commit it to memory.

There was an overturned stool a few feet away from Mr. Porter's feet that gave me a good idea of how the hanging was meant to have happened. However, what I was looking for was a mistake. Something the killer might have left behind. Any clue as to their identity.

I searched the area around the body first, then moved to the shelves. Nothing jumped out at me until I turned back to the door and saw a streak of fresh, dark mud on the wooden threshold to the shed. I went to look at Mr. Porter's shoes. Nothing but the road's crushed lime dust turned into a yellow mud from the morning's rain.

"So how did you get there?" I murmured, looking back at the mud.

I straightened and, using my handkerchief to protect any fingerprints, began to work my way through the contents of the shelves and the various boxes on the floor, but I wasn't surprised when I found nothing out of the ordinary. I was just picking through a box of bolts when David jogged back up to the shed.

"The doctor's on his way," he called.

"Stop there!" I shouted before he could walk into the shed. He froze, his hands in the air. I pointed down to the threshold. "Look at that."

He crouched down. "It's mud."

"Mud, which looks as though it was tracked in. It could be from the murderer's shoes."

"Or from Porter when he walked in here," he said, carefully stepping over the threshold. "It's been raining for long enough that we've all picked some up," he said, showing me his shoe.

"But look," I said, pointing to his shoe and the mud on the threshold. "That's different from the sort you picked up running on crushed lime."

Understanding dawned on David's face. "The stuff on the threshold looks as though it's from dirt."

"When did it start raining this morning?" I asked, already beginning to form a picture of a timeline in my head.

"Just before ten. I'll check Mr. Tyson's and Constable Lee's shoes when we return to the house," he said.

"Where are they?"

"I stashed Mr. Tyson in the morning room and told Constable Lee to find a glass of water and have a sit-down outside the door to make sure Mr. Tyson doesn't move," he said.

"Good. What about the doctor?"

"He and his assistant are coming over now. I also called HQ and let Mrs. White know what's happened. She asked what the Hell is going on out here."

"Her exact words?" I asked.

"Yes." David peered up at the body. "What do you think?"

"At first glance, it looks to be a suicide," I said.

"Just like Sir Nigel's death. It could be that Mr. Porter killed Sir Nigel and then killed himself," said David.

"Why?" I asked.

"Guilt? Fear of being caught?"

I shook my head. "Just this morning Mr. Porter asked Miss Glenconner to go through every single one of their orders related to the materials used for the barnacle bombs that failed. I think he was looking for something that someone didn't want him to find."

"If the murderer realized Mr. Porter was close to figuring out what's really happened to the bombs, he could have killed him to keep the secret."

I nodded. "So the murderer kills Mr. Porter and hangs him, making it look like another suicide. That would be convenient, wouldn't it? The case wraps itself up just in time for Mr. Churchill and other dignitaries to come on-site."

"Or just in time to torpedo everything." David squinted up at the body, and his frown deepened. "Do you see that?"

I moved to his side. "See what?"

He pointed up at the body. "Right there. On his neck just above the rope. Is that a pinprick?"

"The angle's all wrong for me. I'm too short," I said.

David looked at me, rolled his eyes, and then crouched down, showing me his back.

"What exactly are you expecting me to do?" I asked.

"Hop on and I'll lift you up," he said.

"I don't think so," I said.

"You didn't hesitate to stand on my shoulders when you were trying to see into a murderer's flat a couple of months ago," he said.

That, I supposed, was true, so with a grumble I hiked up my skirt and hopped on his back.

"Oof!" David staggered, nearly dropping me.

"I knew this was a bad idea."

"Let me just find my balance," he said. After a moment, he straightened, lifting me a bit higher.

I squinted at the body. Boosted well above my usual height, I could more clearly see above the line of the rope. Sure enough, there was a red mark, almost like a small red freckle, on Mr. Porter's neck.

"What is that?" I asked.

David put me down as the sound of a car's crunching tires came into earshot, and we turned to find a large black car pulling up to the equipment shed. A grim-faced Dr. Morrison and his assistant climbed out.

"Good afternoon, Miss Redfern and Mr. Poole. I'm sorry that we meet again under such difficult circumstances," said the doctor by way of greeting. "Mr. Poole informed me that we have another death on our hands."

I nodded to the shed. "He's in there."

"Has anyone touched the body?" Dr. Morrison asked, peering inside the shed.

"No. Not that we're aware of," I said. "An employee found it. He stayed here while Constable Lee went to fetch us. I've been here ever since."

"Good," said Dr. Morrison before sighing. "Right, William. Let's cut him down."

We stood back and watched as the doctor and his assistant worked as a team to maneuver Mr. Porter's corpse to the ground as carefully as they could. Once the body was laid out on a sheet William had spread, Dr. Morrison crouched down and began to do an initial physical examination.

"Will you be able to tell how long he's been dead?" I asked.

"Patience, Miss Redfern. Patience," murmured Dr. Morrison.

I watched with morbid fascination as the doctor worked, taking the temperature of the body and then calling out the number to William, who jotted it down in a notebook he produced from the inner pocket of his dark gray wool jacket.

Dr. Morrison then looked at the rope around the neck and sat back on his heels. "There's another one."

"A pinprick. David thought so," I said.

"William, note down that lividity clearly has begun to take hold, and there is a mark on the right side of the neck, just a few millimeters from the jugular," said Dr. Morrison.

Dr. Morrison then proceeded to go through Mr. Porter's pockets, handing us his wallet, keys, cigar case, cigar cutter, matches, and a pair of spectacles I hadn't seen Mr. Porter wear.

"Given his age, I'd say they're likely for reading," said Dr. Morrison, noting my curiosity at the glasses. Then the doctor straightened. "Right, we'll have to take him back to my surgery before I can give you anything definitive, but I feel fairly confident in saying that you have another murder on your hands."

A double murder.

"Are you certain, Dr. Morrison?" I asked.

"I would stake my career on it," said Dr. Morrison. "It appears to have been done the same way as Sir Nigel's murder. A hypodermic needle delivered a dose of sedative and gave the killer the opportunity to kill the victim and stage a suicide."

Theft, a staged suicide, faulty weapons, and now another murder dressed up to look like suicide. This case was becoming ever more expansive, and I could feel my grasp on it beginning to slip.

"Any ideas as to who might have done it?" asked David.

Dr. Morrison looked up at the crossbeam of the shed. "Someone who was strong enough to hang him. Other than that, I couldn't say."

"Could you please telephone us if you find out anything different during your examination?" I asked.

"I will," said the doctor.

We watched Dr. Morrison and William move the body to the car and then drive off. As soon as they were gone, I let out a deep breath.

"Well."

"Two bodies," said David. "I don't think we're going to be able to hide the fact that this is a murder investigation for much longer."

I nodded. It was time to apply a new kind of pressure, to let the murderer know that we were onto them.

"We need to reinterview everyone and find out what they've been doing since Mr. Eccles's speech this morning," I said.

"We should see if Constable Lee has recovered his composure. He can establish alibis and see if he can help us figure out who was the last person to see Mr. Porter."

I nodded. "We should start with Mr. Tyson and then speak to Miss

Glenconner. And I want to see if we can reach Mr. Eccles in London," I said.

"To check out his alibi or to inform him of the murder?"

"Both."

David turned to look at the equipment shed, hands on his hips. "It always feels like such a waste, all of this death."

I came to stand next to him, a quiet moment amid the hectic nature of our investigation. "It's terrible the things we do to one another. Simply terrible."

THIRTY-THREE

Constable Lee greeted us outside the door of the morning room, his helmet in his hand.

"Miss, sir. I apologize for—Well, I wanted to say—"

David held up a hand to stop him. "Understood, Constable."

Constable Lee swallowed but then gave a firm nod as though bolstering himself. "How can I be useful?"

"We need you to speak to everyone on the estate. Find out where they were from half past eight this morning until Mr. Tyson discovered the body. When was that exactly?" I asked.

"A few minutes before half past eleven," said Constable Lee.

"Good," I said. "I also need you to check their shoes for dark brown mud. Can you do that?"

He nodded rapidly, jotting things down in his notebook. "Right you are. I'll do that straight away."

"Good man," said David.

"And Constable? This is now officially a murder investigation. I want you to pay attention to how people react when you tell them that," I said.

His eyes grew wide. "Two murders, Miss?"

My lips settled into a grim line. "Two."

I could see his Adam's apple bob as he swallowed. "Right, Miss."

As the constable scrambled down the corridor, I said to David, "I'll certainly give him credit for enthusiasm."

When we opened the morning room door, Mr. Tyson looked up and rose from his seat.

"Is there any news?" he asked urgently.

"The doctor has taken Mr. Porter's body away to examine it," said David.

"So he was—There's no doubt that he's—"

"Dead?" I finished for him as gently as I could. "Yes, I'm afraid so."

Mr. Tyson dropped into his chair, raking his hand through his hair. Then he gave a grim laugh. "I know that it was silly, really, to think that he could be anything but dead, but I'd hoped . . . I just cannot believe that Porter would kill himself."

"That's because he didn't," I said. "We have reason to believe he was sedated and then someone took great pains to make it look as though he hanged himself. Much like Sir Nigel was made to look as though he shot himself."

"Someone murdered them?" Mr. Tyson asked, looking more than a little sick.

"Mr. Tyson, we need you to tell us everything you can remember about finding Mr. Porter's body," I said.

He straightened in his seat. "Where would you like me to start?"

"Why don't you tell us what you were doing in the sheds?" I asked.

"I was working on the weekly inventory and making sure that we had enough space for a delivery of copper wire that we're expecting today," he said.

"You'd been there since Mr. Eccles's speech this morning?" David asked.

Mr. Tyson shook his head. "I went up to my office in the house to catch up on some paperwork ahead of that delivery. Mr. Porter stuck his head in. I thought he'd finally have news about the assistant I've been asking for for some time. It's too much managing and maintaining all of the equipment on the property by myself. I need help. Instead, he wanted to know whether I had spoken to the two of you that morning."

"What did you tell him?" David asked.

"That you'd interviewed me yesterday. He asked what you asked

about. I told him that most of the questions were about Sir Nigel's relationship with the Blackthorn staff. I also said you were curious about
who had access to the equipment sheds and the recent changes such
as the new inventory I'd conducted," he said.

"What did Mr. Porter seem to make of this?" I asked.

"I don't know. He nodded, thanked me, and disappeared again,"
said Mr. Tyson.

"What time was this?" David asked.

"Just before nine? He wasn't there for very long," said Mr. Tyson.

"And what did you do after that?" I asked.

"The post had come, so I sorted through that. Then I had a telephone call saying that something we're expecting Friday won't be
arriving until Monday. I knocked off for a cup of tea at twenty to
eleven. Miss Glenconner came down when I was just finishing, looking
a little peaky. I told her that some fresh air might do her good. Then I
went to the equipment sheds," he said.

"When was this?" I asked.

"Just after eleven? I didn't look at my watch, so I can't be certain
of the exact time," he said.

"Did you see anyone on your way?" I asked.

"No," he said.

"And did you notice anything unusual when you arrived at the
equipment sheds?" I asked.

"No, everything was locked up, just as I left it," said Mr. Tyson.

"Did you find the body immediately?" David asked.

"No, no. I was due to pick up where I left off cataloguing the contents in the middle shed, but after a few minutes I broke my pencil.
I keep a sharpener in the far right shed, so I went to open it up, and
that's when I saw Mr. Porter's body." He shuddered. "It was a terrible
shock."

"I'm certain it was," I said. "Why did Constable Lee come to fetch
us rather than you?"

"I . . . I don't really know. I suppose I must have shouted when I
found the body, and a few moments later, the constable came running
up. He told me to stay where I was and not to let anyone touch anything. I'm ashamed to say I don't think I could have moved from the
spot if I tried."

"Do you remember the direction that Constable Lee ran from?" David asked.

"He came crashing through the trees. I could hear him before I saw him," said Mr. Tyson.

"Do you keep a penknife on your person while you are working?" I asked.

"Yes." He dug into his trouser pocket and produced the small knife. "It comes in handy for small jobs. Cutting bits of wire or twine. Even tightening a screw in a pinch."

"If you keep a penknife on you, why did you need a pencil sharpener? Why not simply sharpen the pencil with your penknife?" I asked.

Mr. Tyson looked taken aback. "I—I don't really know."

"Mr. Tyson, can we please see the bottom of your shoes?" I asked.

With a frown, the quartermaster lifted his shoes. David crouched down and peered at each. Finally he said, "Thank you."

When he straightened and resumed his seat, he shook his head. No dark mud like that I'd found on the threshold. That, it would seem, had been left by our killer.

"Mr. Tyson, can you think of any reason that someone might have wanted to hurt Mr. Porter?" I asked.

Mr. Tyson shook his head, looking somewhat haunted by the question. "He could be a hard boss—he had a temper—but that didn't make him a bad person."

"And can you think of any reason someone might have wanted to kill Sir Nigel?" I asked.

He shook his head. "He might not have had many friends, but everyone here was willing to put up with that because we all knew that Sir Nigel was brilliant, and we all believe that what we're doing at Blackthorn will help us win the war."

"Thank you, Mr. Tyson. You can go, but we need to remind you not to speak to anyone about what you've seen," said David.

"Would you also let Miss Glenconner know that we need to see her? If she could also bring Mr. Porter's diary, that would be greatly appreciated," I said.

Mr. Tyson murmured his agreement as he left the room.

"Do you think that he had anything to do with it?" David asked as soon as the door shut.

I shook my head. "Restraining two different men and sedating them at the same time seems like a tall order with one arm, especially since it's unlikely Mr. Porter would have been sitting like Sir Nigel was."

David nodded. "It's not out of the realm of possibility, but I suspect that there would have been evidence of a scuffle about Mr. Tyson if he was behind it. Or he could have had an accomplice."

"Who?" I asked. "Which two people would have the means, motive, and opportunity to kill two men in the space of three days?"

"Perhaps the murders aren't connected," suggested David.

I pursed my lips and then shook my head. "It's all connected. The deaths, the thefts, the weapons failures. It *must* be."

David sighed. "Let's hope Miss Glenconner can shed some light on everything for us."

THIRTY-FOUR

Miss Glenconner entered the morning room on a wave of tears. "I can't stand it!" she cried as she slumped into a chair across the table from David and me. "I simply can't stand it!"

"Miss Glenconner, please," David tried.

"And he was murdered? And Sir Nigel too?" she cried. "Oh, I never should have left home!"

I sighed and rolled my head from side to side, trying to ease the tension that was rapidly building in my neck. "I understand that this is very distressing news, but we really must ask you some questions."

Miss Glenconner pulled out a handkerchief and blew her nose soundly. "I don't know what I can tell you."

"You were Mr. Porter's secretary. It's important that we talk to you so that we understand where he was and who he was supposed to meet with today," I said.

She sniffed, beginning to regain some of her composure. "I suppose that makes sense."

"Can you please walk me through Mr. Porter's diary for today?" I asked, gesturing to the appointment book that she held in her lap.

She hesitated but then flipped it open and, in a wavering voice, read out, "After Mr. Eccles spoke to all of us, Mr. Porter asked me to pull all of the files we have related to materials used in the barnacle bombs, as I told you. Then he had a call to London to speak with a Mr. Kendricks in the War Department at nine o'clock. He didn't have any further meetings until he was supposed to ring a Mr. Davidson at four o'clock today." She whimpered. "I suppose I should telephone Mr. Davidson and tell him that won't be possible."

"Don't worry about that right now," I said. "Did Mr. Porter place any other telephone calls today?"

"No, but he took a call from an outside line around twenty past nine," she said.

"Do you know who was on the line?" I asked.

She shook her head. "All the switchboard operator said was that the call was for Mr. Porter, so I put it through."

"What happened then?" I asked.

"He left," she said.

"Did he say where he was going?" I asked.

She frowned. "No."

"Was that unusual?" asked David.

"Yes, it was. Normally he was very strict about not missing calls, so he always let me know where he was so that I could find him rather than taking a message," she said.

"What did you do after Mr. Porter left?" I asked.

"I worked on the files for a little bit longer, then the telephone rang and I took the message for you, Miss Redfern. After that, I got up to make myself a cup of tea just before eleven," she said.

I checked my notes. The time matched up with when Mr. Tyson remembered seeing her there.

"Was anyone in the kitchen?" I asked.

"Mr. Tyson. He was nearly done with his cup of tea. He said that I looked a bit pale, and it was true. I felt queasy, so I thought a cup of tea would settle my stomach. After he left, I took my tea upstairs where I saw you, Miss Redfern. After I gave you your message, I saw Mr. Porter's door was still closed, so I assumed that he was still out and went back to my work."

"But you can't be certain?" I asked.

She hesitated and then shook her head. "I suppose he could have slipped by me while I was in the filing room that morning."

"Was there any sound from his office? Typing perhaps?" asked David.

Both Miss Glenconner and I stared at him for a moment before Miss Glenconner said, "I don't think Mr. Porter knew the first thing about using a typewriter. He left that sort of thing to me. I was happy to do it, you understand. It's my job."

"Miss Glenconner, could you please lift your shoes for a moment?" I asked.

I crouched down just as David had with Mr. Tyson. The shoes were brown leather, not exactly fashionable but a good solid style. They had obviously been reheeled a few times, and when I touched the leather on the heel, I could feel a faint dampness there.

"Have you been outside today?" I asked.

She blinked as though surprised. "Oh, yes. After I had my cup of tea, I took a turn around the kitchen garden for a bit of fresh air. Mr. Tyson suggested it on account of me being so pale, and I didn't think it could hurt."

"You went outside even though it was raining?" asked David.

"It was only misting at the time. Mrs. Sherman keeps an old mac by the door to accept deliveries. I used it to cover my hair," she explained.

"Did you wipe your shoes with a cloth when you returned?" I asked.

"I always do," she said. "My mother always says that if you take care of your shoes, they'll take care of you."

While that might have been sound advice, it had the unfortunate effect of making it impossible to eliminate Miss Glenconner from our list of suspects. I didn't think that this slight young woman—so very different from the statuesque, athletic Miss Kenwood—could likely restrain, sedate, and hang Mr. Porter all by herself, but she could have had help. The gap of time between when she'd last seen Mr. Porter and when she'd met Mr. Tyson in the kitchen also gave her the opportunity to go to the equipment sheds and return to the house.

Things were only more complicated by the fact that, now that we'd found the cupboard next to Sir Nigel's office, we also knew that on the night of Sir Nigel's murder she could have left Mr. Porter's office, gone to the kitchen to fetch the tea things, left them in the cupboard, killed Sir Nigel, and then rushed to the head of the stairs to drop the tray in time for Mr. Porter to find her distressed and shocked.

"Miss Glenconner, do you know why anyone would want to kill Mr. Porter?" I asked.

"No," she said plainly.

"What about Sir Nigel?" I asked.

She looked up, her pale blue eyes filled with a fierceness that I hadn't expected. "No, but I hope you find the person who did this."

"We will," I promised.

"All right, Miss Glenconner. You can return to your work," said David. "We will let you know if we have any other questions."

She rose to leave, but just before she reached the door, I stopped her. "Miss Glenconner, could you please find us Mr. Porter's home telephone exchange?"

We would need to inform the man's wife of what had happened— a task I was dreading but knew would have to be done nonetheless.

"Also," I added quickly, "we'd like to see those files that Mr. Porter asked you to pull for him."

She nodded, then closed the door behind her.

———

A little while later, I hung up the morning room telephone, deflated. If Mrs. Porter had been distraught, breaking into hysterics when I told her about her husband's death, that might have been one thing. Instead, she was controlled, a faint waver in her voice the only hint that she had taken in my news at all.

I closed my eyes, remembering the awful moment I'd learned *Maman* had died. There had been no telephone call. No warning. I'd knocked on the door of her bedroom in the hotel suite we'd called home since her separation from my father and, like I did every morning, waltzed in so that we could start our day. But she hadn't moved from under the rumpled satin quilt, and I knew, even as a child, that she was gone.

I felt a hand fall lightly on my shoulder, and David said, "The first one is always the worst."

When I looked up at him, I could see the sympathy softening his dark brown eyes.

"Is that really true, or are you simply trying to make me feel better?" I asked.

He sighed. "I don't know."

"Well, thank you for trying."

He frowned. "Are you sure that you're all right?"

"I keep thinking of my mother," I said.

"She died when you were very young?" he asked.

I knew that he'd seen my personnel file and I doubted very much that David would have forgotten that detail. However, I appreciated the opening to allow me to speak if I wanted to.

"I was thirteen years old. The police sent a detective who made a few inquiries—whether it was because she was a well-known socialite with connected friends or because the press coverage was inevitable due to my parents' custody battle, I don't know. The detective asked a few questions, poked around a bit, and closed the case as quick as could be. Accidental overdose," I said.

"You don't sound entirely convinced," said David.

I sighed. "It's mad, I know, but it's never made sense. *Maman* suffered from insomnia, but she was so careful with the laudanum she used to help her sleep. She had to be because I was all she had. She didn't trust my father to take care of me."

It was an instinct that had proven to be true. After her death, I had waited for Sir Reginald, the man who had fought my mother so hard to keep me, to arrive and finally be the steady, loving father he'd promised the French courts that he could be. Instead, Aunt Amelia had appeared a few weeks later, telling me that she was there to take me from Paris to London and then on to an English boarding school, because "Your father thinks it best for you."

Imagine, the man who had hardly seen me since I was eight having the audacity to believe he knew anything about me.

I straightened and shook out my hands, trying to cast off the pall of my sadness.

"What will help?" David asked.

"Work," I said.

He nodded. "Then we'll work."

I picked up the telephone receiver again. "We should inform Mr. Eccles of what's happened."

When the switchboard operator came on the line, I asked for the exchange Mr. Eccles had given us in case we needed to reach him. To his credit, David stepped back to give me space.

The line connected, and I heard a soft woman's voice say, "Hello?"

"Hello, is this Hunter 5547?" I asked.

"It is," said the woman blessed with beautiful enunciation.

"I'd like to speak to Mr. Timothy Eccles, please," I said.

"May I ask who's calling?" the woman asked.

"My name is Evelyne Redfern."

"I'm sorry, Miss Redfern, but Mr. Eccles is currently in a meeting and will be for some time."

"I'm afraid that this can't wait," I insisted.

The woman made a *hmmm* sound in the back of her throat, and I could hear her turning the pages of what I imagined was a diary. "Mr. Eccles's schedule is rather full."

"This is important. I really must speak with him."

My imploring had no effect on the secretary, who said, "I'm not certain when Mr. Eccles will be able to return your call, but I can tell him that you telephoned."

I sighed. "Thank you. Again, please tell him that it is urgent that we speak as soon as possible," I said before giving her instructions for Mr. Eccles to ring us back on Miss Glenconner's telephone.

As soon as I set the receiver down, David asked, "Anything?"

"Apparently he's in a meeting and can't come to the telephone right now."

"We should verify that he actually caught the train this morning," David said, glancing at his watch.

"Captain Sherman at the station would know," I said. "We should also tell Miss Summers about Lieutenant Colonel Gerrard's connection to Burtlesby. Hopefully that will make it easier to find him."

"If you ring Miss Summers, I'll try the station," said David.

I nodded. "I'll make the call in Mr. Porter's office and search his desk to see if anything jumps out at me."

David tossed me the spare keys Mr. Tyson had given us and wished me good luck.

THIRTY-FIVE

There was no sign of Miss Glenconner at her desk or in the file room, but I spotted a stack of files with a note on top of it that read:

Miss Redfern and Mr. Poole,

I am going home, as I am feeling unwell. These are the files Mr. Porter asked me to collect this morning.

Sincerely,
Alice Glenconner

I discarded the note in the bin and scooped up the files in one arm. With my free hand, I tried the keys on the ring David had given me until I found the right one for Mr. Porter's office.

The room was cool and, even with the electric light on, dim because of the drawn curtains. Mr. Porter's office had an impersonal feeling to it, which was brought into even sharper relief by the green and gold wallpaper and complementary window treatments that harkened to the room's former status as a guest bedroom. By contrast, the office furniture that had been brought in for him was spartan with only a desk, leather chair, and set of filing cabinets. A single lamp supplemented the overhead light and a crystal ashtray half-full of the remnants of one of Mr. Porter's cigars was the only hint as to the nature of the man who had once worked here.

I set my handbag down on Mr. Porter's desk in order to make a cursory check of it, but found little in the drawers. The blotter was neat save for a fountain pen lined up perfectly parallel with the leather edge and a pad of notepaper within reach of the right-hand side. For a man who dealt with the operations at a facility such as Blackthorn Park, he seemed to have an aversion to keeping paperwork to hand, although I supposed he probably felt that fell to Miss Glenconner.

I sat down behind the desk in Mr. Porter's large chair, the leather seat creaking in protest as I leaned back. I didn't exactly know what I was looking for, but I felt that there must be something—anything—about the man's last hours that would point to what had happened to him.

I began to open drawers and found little of note other than a few sharpened pencils, a cigar, cutter, and lighter, and several blank, unsealed envelopes. With a sigh, I picked up the telephone.

A few moments later, I heard Miss Summers's usual cheerful "Hello."

"Miss Summers, it's Miss Redfern."

"Oh, hello, Miss Redfern. I was just about to ring you."

"Were you? That's quite the coincidence," I said.

"It's about two matters. Firstly, the personnel files you've requested. I'm afraid it hasn't been a straightforward process trying to secure them. As you can imagine, it isn't as easy as typing up a request and sending it to a department," she said.

"I imagine not."

"There are always competing interests in these sorts of matters, and it does take rather a lot of soothing hurt feelings because people seem to think you're implying that they don't know how to hire their own staff," she elaborated. "In the end though, Mr. Fletcher was able to have a few words with the gentlemen at Baker Street, and it's all being sorted. I hope to have everything to you tomorrow morning."

"That's excellent news because I'm afraid another person has died," I said. "Murder again."

"Oh dear, that is rather inconvenient," said Miss Summers with surprising good humor.

"Indeed," I agreed. "David and I wanted to ask if you've had any luck with that lieutenant colonel we asked you to track down."

"Yes, Lieutenant Colonel Gerrard of Burtlesby Abbey. That was the second piece of news I had for you," said Miss Summers.

"You found him?" I asked, the chair creaking under me as I sat straight up.

"Yes, and it took some doing."

"Who is he exactly?" I asked.

"He's in charge of an army explosives training group at Burtlesby Abbey. It's a lovely country house just outside of Basingstoke, only hardly anyone knows about it. The army have been keeping it a secret for months. Even Mr. Fletcher hadn't heard of it, which he was not terribly pleased about."

"Miss Summers, you are a gem. You don't happen to have a telephone number for Lieutenant Colonel Gerrard, do you?" I asked.

"Burtlesby is on a special line, so I'll need to put your call through via our switchboard here. If you would wait for a moment."

"Of course," I said. "Thank you, Miss Summers."

"I'm glad I could help. I'll have you connected with Burtlesby in two ticks."

I waited a few moments before I heard a ringing on the line.

"Hello?" answered a man in a gruff voice.

"Hello, I'm looking for Lieutenant Colonel Gerrard," I said.

"What?" barked the man. "Who are you?"

"My name is Evelyne Redfern," I said.

"How were you connected to this exchange?" he asked. "You shouldn't be able to call this telephone at all."

"A colleague connected me," I said.

"You must hang up," the man ordered.

"I know Major Bartholomew Richards!" I blurted out.

The man, who at this point I suspected was Lieutenant Colonel Gerrard himself, went quiet for a beat. If I hadn't heard the occasional crackle and pop on the line, I might have thought that it had gone dead.

"It is imperative that I speak to the lieutenant colonel. I believe that a Sir Nigel Balram made a visit to Burtlesby Abbey on the twenty-second of October. I need to know why and what the lieutenant colonel spoke to him about," I pushed.

"Why?" asked the man.

"Because on Monday, Sir Nigel was murdered."

The man sucked in a breath. "I can't speak over the telephone about this."

"I'm in Sussex right now, sir. My colleague and I can drive to you this afternoon."

The man grunted. "Fine. Four o'clock. Give your name to the guard at the gatehouse."

Then he hung up the telephone.

I was just replacing the receiver when David stuck his head through the door.

"I made it through to the station. Captain Sherman said that he remembers Mr. Eccles departing on the 9:02 this morning. He says he remarked upon it to himself because of how unusual it is to see Mr. Eccles going up to London in the morning rather than the early evening," said David.

"So that's Mr. Eccles accounted for. I've found Gerrard," I replied. "Or rather Miss Summers has. Have you ever heard of Burtlesby Abbey?"

David frowned. "I don't think so."

"It's outside Basingstoke, apparently. We have a four o'clock appointment with the lieutenant colonel."

"He wouldn't speak on the telephone?" he asked.

"I suspect it's a miracle he spoke to me at all," I said.

David pushed up the sleeve of his gray jacket. "We should go if we're going to make it in time."

I nodded and made to stand.

"Did you write down the address?" he asked, gesturing to the desk.

I glanced down at Mr. Porter's notepad next to my hand. "No, I . . ."

I trailed off as I picked up the notepad, turned on the desk lamp, and tilted the paper a bit under the light.

Then I put it down and ran my fingers over the surface of it. It was bumpy.

"What are you doing?" David asked as I plucked one of Mr. Porter's pencils out of his desk drawer.

I held up one finger to silence David and then tilted my pencil to begin lightly shading over the top page. When I finished, I held it up to show him.

"Is that . . . ?" David stopped himself.

"The last thing Mr. Porter wrote on this notebook, yes," I said, reading out the faint letters that had appeared in relief. "West Sussex Electrical, Moreland Mining, Sheffield Steel, Longfellow & Son, Samuel & Sons Rubber, Collingswood Chemical Manufacturers, March Chemicals. The list goes on and on."

I tapped the files I'd retrieved from Miss Glenconner's desk. "I would hazard a guess that if we look we'll find that all of these names are in the supplier files that Mr. Porter asked Miss Glenconner to pull for him."

"Why?" asked David.

"I don't know, but I suspect that whatever the reason is was enough to get Mr. Porter killed."

David's lips formed a grim line. "Can you read in a moving car?"

"Yes."

"Good, because I can't," he said. "Bring them along, and let's see if we can't figure out what Mr. Porter was looking for."

THIRTY-SIX

True to my word, I read in the passenger seat of the car as David drove us along the country roads toward Hampshire for the second time that week.

"Anything?" he asked after I closed the fourth file of the trip.

"I don't know. The names on the list from the notepad all correspond to the files Mr. Porter asked Miss Glenconner to pull this morning before he was killed, but not every file is on Mr. Porter's list. That has to be significant," I said.

"Which company's file is that?" asked David, nodding to the one I'd just closed.

"Moreland Mining," I said, flicking through the collected papers. "From what I can tell, all it has in it are invoices, bills of sale, the original contract, and a few handwritten notes—maybe from a telephone call?"

"Who signed off on the invoices?" David asked.

"It looks like Mr. Porter did."

"And the contract?"

"Porter," I said again. "Maybe we can cross-reference the orders against Mr. Tyson's inventories and essentially re-create the investigation that we suspected Sir Nigel was trying to conduct when he died."

He groaned. "That could take hours."

"Or days depending on how many orders he placed," I said in grim agreement. "Speaking of paperwork, Miss Summers is still on the case about the personnel files."

David grimaced. "I hate it when a case becomes about slogging through paper."

I stared down at the files on my lap. "At this point, it feels like the only real place to look for a lead that we have left."

Out of the corner of my eye, I could see David glance over at me before saying, "Then let's hope that this lieutenant colonel of yours can help."

I sighed. "Can we at least find lunch? I've hardly eaten all day, and I'm not certain I have the fortitude to go toe to toe with a lieutenant colonel who appears so paranoid about security that he would not speak on a secure line."

I caught David's smile. "We'll stop somewhere near Basingstoke. I promise."

After a rather unsatisfying lunch of sandwiches in an underwhelming café, we found Burtlesby Abbey not long before four o'clock. We had a brief negotiation with a suspicious-looking guard at a gatehouse set at the top of a long drive that reminded me a great deal of Blackthorn Park, and then David drove us to the house. Made of stone, it looked as though it had been built by the most sinister of monks in the Middle Ages, although in reality it probably had been constructed by some fabulously wealthy but eccentric Victorian who loved *The Castle of Otranto* a little too much.

At the oak and iron front door, we were greeted by a slight second lieutenant with glasses and a pinched expression and led to an office door.

"Enter!" came a shout from inside after the second lieutenant knocked.

Inside, we were greeted by a broad-shouldered man with a short army haircut who seemed to unfurl from his desk he was so tall.

"Miss Redfern and Mr. Poole here to see you, Lieutenant Colonel," said the aide.

"Thank you, Kipen," barked Lieutenant Colonel Gerrard at the second lieutenant. "Miss Redfern, Mr. Poole, sit down."

I scooted forward a little faster than I normally would, spurred on by the sense that if I didn't, this man might make me go peel potatoes in the mess.

"Now, what's this about Sir Nigel being dead?" the lieutenant colonel fired the words at us like bullets as he settled down in his office chair.

"Shot on Monday, sir," I said, dispensing with any pleasantries. "This morning the head of operations at Blackthorn Park was found hanging. Both were staged suicides."

"That's damned inconvenient," muttered Lieutenant Colonel Gerrard.

"We found a letter from you to Sir Nigel in his personal effects. We were hoping you could shed some light as to why he visited you two weeks ago," I said.

Lieutenant Colonel Gerrard folded his hands on his desk and leaned in. "I understand that you both work for Lionel Fletcher at the Special Investigations Unit. Don't look so surprised I've been checking up on you."

"That's right," said David.

"Never met him, but I've heard he's a good man. Helped a fellow I know out with a little problem up in Scotland earlier this year." The lieutenant colonel looked between the two of us and then nodded. "What do you two know about Burtlesby Abbey?"

"Virtually nothing," I said honestly.

"Good. That is what we like to hear. We are a facility that was set up for the testing and training of munitions for use for the army," he explained. "We also support specialized missions, but the bulk of what we do is confirm that weapons do what they're meant to do and recommend the best ways for them to be deployed. Sir Nigel wanted to test some of the weapons he'd developed at Blackthorn Park."

"Did he say why he wanted to come here when Blackthorn Park has its own testing facilities?" I asked.

"I've never been to Blackthorn Park, so I can't attest to the quality of the facilities; however, Sir Nigel had another reason for wanting to test here," said Lieutenant Colonel Gerrard. "He was convinced there was a saboteur working at Blackthorn Park."

David and I both sucked in a breath as Lieutenant Colonel Gerrard's words hung in the air. It was the confirmation that David and I had been looking for. The reason Sir Nigel had gone off on his wild chase, making demands of his engineers and the rest of the Blackthorn staff. He thought someone was tampering with his bombs.

"Did he say why he thought that?" I asked.

The lieutenant colonel shook his head. "All I know is that he didn't trust the staff any longer. He wrote to me and asked that I take receipt of a lot of weapons called barnacle bombs that had been shipped from Blackthorn to various sites around the country for training."

"Why?" I asked.

"As I said, he was suspicious of everyone. He also didn't seem to know what exactly he was looking for," said the lieutenant colonel.

"What did you do when the weapons were assembled here?" I asked.

"I sent him a letter by special courier to let him know that they were ready and I would expect him in two days' time," said Lieutenant Colonel Gerrard.

"What happened when Sir Nigel arrived?" asked David.

"He began detonating devices around half past three in the afternoon and only stopped when it became too dark to see. He tested everything. He was systematic about it, making sure he noted down what the device was and where it had come from. The following morning he requested that I provide him with sheltered space where he could dismantle some of the different versions of that weapon.

"When he emerged in the afternoon, I thought it would be to arrange for lunch, but instead he declared that he was done. He thanked me for the use of the facilities and asked for a lift to the railway station. Then he was gone."

"Did he say what he'd found?" I asked.

"No," said Lieutenant Colonel Gerrard.

"Are you saying that Sir Nigel told you he believed someone was sabotaging his work so he asked you if he could spend almost twenty-four hours here, and then when he left you didn't ask what he'd discovered?" asked David.

"I had other things on my mind," said Lieutenant Colonel Gerrard, the strident tone coming back into his voice. "It is a mistake you lot make far too often thinking that you're going to save all of us in this war. The army is a giant compared to the SOE."

As SIU agents, David and I weren't, strictly speaking, the SOE, but I doubted very much that the lieutenant colonel would take kindly to me pointing that out. Besides, we had what we'd come for: confirmation that Sir Nigel had found what he'd been looking for and given the killer a very good reason to silence him for good.

━━━━━

D avid and I said a stiff goodbye to the lieutenant colonel a moment later and then were escorted out by his aide.

Once we were in the car, I hauled the stack of files I'd been reading back onto my lap and leaned back against the passenger seat, suddenly weary. The sun had already gone down, and the air in the car settled around me, chilling me to the bone.

"Well," said David as he closed his door. "That wasn't entirely fruitful."

"But it wasn't a waste either." I held up my fingers and began to count off. "One. We now know that, before he died, Sir Nigel believed that something was the matter with the barnacle bombs. Two. We know that he believed there was a saboteur working at Blackthorn Park. And three. We know that after taking the barnacle bombs apart, Sir Nigel thought he'd discovered whatever was the matter with the devices."

"But we still don't know what that was," said David.

I thought for a moment. "Neither you nor I can make heads or tails out of most of what is written on the schematics that we found among Sir Nigel's papers. We don't understand anything beyond the fundamentals of how these devices work."

"We don't really know anything except how to set them off," David muttered.

"Precisely. Because we're trained to use devices like that, not to build them. Major Richards told us what he knew from the instructor and the commandos who witnessed the barnacle bomb explosion. They believed it was a timing device issue because no one touched the mine again in a way that would have triggered the anti-handling device. Naturally, they thought that the issue must have been with the fuse. But what if they were wrong?"

"Because they don't understand how a device works. They only really care that it does," said David, almost as though he were reading my mind.

"I want to go back to Blackthorn Park and speak to one of the engineers about how someone might tamper with a barnacle bomb."

David shifted gears, our speed increasing. "Then that's exactly what we'll do."

THIRTY-SEVEN

An hour later, David and I walked through Blackthorn Park's front door and, for the second time that day, we were confronted with the backs of the facility's employees.

I nudged my way into the crowd until I could see that they were once again staring at an exhausted-looking Mr. Eccles, who stood in the middle of the entryway floor. When he held his hands up in front of him, all of the murmuring among the staff stopped, and silence echoed about the room.

"I did not expect to see all of you again today, and I'm very sorry it has to be under such distressing circumstances," he began. "I came back to Blackthorn Park because I learned of the sudden death of our esteemed colleague Bernard Porter."

No one gasped in surprise, and I suspected that Constable Lee had been thorough in his work that afternoon. I scanned the faces around me. The engineers looked stoic, and Mr. Tyson held his hat in his hand, his head bowed. A few of the women who worked in the manufacturing barn looked pale, and one of them even dabbed at her eye with a handkerchief. Miss Kenwood stood straight, her hands behind her back as she listened.

"I can imagine that many of you will want to take a private moment to reflect on the loss of Mr. Porter," Mr. Eccles continued. "Please take that time, but I urge you to continue the very good work that is being done here at Blackthorn Park as Mr. Porter no doubt would have wanted."

Everyone except for Mr. Hartley, Jane, and Mrs. Sherman had at least an inch of water staining their leather shoes and the yellow residue of crushed lime turned to a sort of pale mud caked around the soles. Only Dr. Jamison, Mr. Parker, and Mr. Eccles also had the same sort of dark mud that I'd found on the threshold of the equipment shed.

"Look at their shoes," I whispered to David. "Look at the mud."

"Parker's is probably from the garden," whispered David as he squinted.

"What about Dr. Jamison and Mr. Eccles?"

"We'll ask," he reassured me as, out of the corner of my eye, I saw Jane's hand shoot up on the edge of the crowd.

Mr. Eccles frowned. "Yes, Miss Daniels?"

"Will there be a funeral?"

"I suppose that will be the choice of Mrs. Porter. She may choose to handle the arrangements with discretion given the circumstances," he said.

"What do you mean by 'the circumstances'?" called out Mr. Hartley. "He was killed, wasn't he?"

Mr. Eccles looked shocked. "Well, that is—I hadn't yet—"

"The constable's interviewed all of us. He told us that Mr. Porter was murdered, and so was Sir Nigel," said Miss Kenwood.

"Are we safe?" asked Jane in a tremulous voice.

"Ladies and gentlemen," Mr. Eccles called out over the growing din, his hands spread wide, "it is very important that we all remain calm."

"Calm?" Mr. Hartley gave a half laugh.

Mr. Eccles found David and me in the crowd. "Here are the investigators."

I had the disconcerting experience of feeling every single pair of eyes fix on me at once, everyone looking expectant.

Delightful.

I cleared my throat. "Mr. Poole and I are continuing our investigation. If you know anything that could be a help to us, anything at all, please do not hesitate to speak to us. You might not think that a detail is important, but it could prove vital in both of these cases."

There were murmurs, and I heard someone who sounded suspiciously like Jane ask a neighbor, "How many people will die before they catch the killer?"

My eyes narrowed. I was determined that no one else would lose their lives at Blackthorn Park.

"Will tomorrow's visit be rescheduled?" Mr. Hartley asked, swinging attention back to Mr. Eccles.

"Why would it be rescheduled?" asked Mr. Eccles.

"Two people have lost their lives," said Miss Kenwood.

"And many more people will lose their lives if we do not keep our attention on the job at hand. The tragedies of this week do not change the importance of what you are creating here. It is vital that tomorrow's visit is a success or Blackthorn Park could cease to exist," he finished with a flourish.

That sent new murmurs through the staff.

"Everyone here has a role to play," Mr. Eccles continued. "I am relying on Dr. Jamison and his engineers to carry off a satisfactory display of the armadillo, the anti-tank spikes, the barnacle bomb, and the new heat-resistant battle armor on the demonstration fields. I expect that Miss Kenwood and the ladies in the barn will be at their most efficient, and Mrs. Sherman will ensure that the house is looking its best. Even Mr. Parker will be on hand in case there is a matter that needs to be attended to with regards to the grounds," said Mr. Eccles with a nod toward the gardener, who was standing with his hands in his pockets.

"Now, if there are no more questions, you may return to your work," Mr. Eccles finished.

The crowd began to dissipate, and David and I walked straight to Mr. Eccles, who, up close, looked rumpled, wan, and far from the confident, ruddy-cheeked walker we'd met Tuesday morning.

"Miss Redfern, Mr. Poole," he said. "A terrible tragedy."

"Did you not know that Mr. Porter and Sir Nigel were murdered?" I asked.

He shook his head, looking more than a little stunned. "Mr. Tyson

told me that he'd found Porter at the end of a rope in one of the equipment sheds. I assumed . . ."

"Yes, well, the killer did rather count on that assumption," I said.

"You're certain?" he asked. "About Sir Nigel too?"

"Completely," I said. "The coroner found clear evidence of foul
play. In both cases the men were sedated before they were killed."

"How long have you known?" asked Mr. Eccles.

"Since Tuesday morning," said David.

"But you didn't say. I'm meant to be running this facility now—"
Mr. Eccles started but then stopped himself. "Why? Why would someone kill the pair of them?"

"We believe Sir Nigel had discovered something about a fault
in some of his barnacle bombs that were sent out for testing," I explained, holding back the sabotage detail for now.

Mr. Eccles blanched. "France."

I gave him a grim nod.

"And Porter?" he asked.

"We are still looking into the connection between the two murders, but we are certain that there is a connection," said David.

Mr. Eccles blew out a long breath. "I still should have been told.
I stood up in front of all of those people with the wrong information.
They are looking to me now for guidance."

"We tried to contact you this afternoon to let you know what had
happened," I said.

"I was in Whitehall from noon in meetings. When I telephoned my
secretary to check my messages, she told me that you'd rung asking to
speak on an urgent matter. When I tried to reach you, I got through to
Tyson instead. I jumped straight on the first train out of Waterloo." He
sighed and added, "I even left without a change of shirt for tomorrow's
visit, but I imagine the enterprising Miss Glenconner or Mrs. Sherman
might be able to find me something suitable. A shoe brush too."

"That's quite a bit of mud," I said as he lifted the sole of his right
shoe.

"Yes, I walked from the railway station," he said.

"I thought that the road was paved," I said.

"It is, but there was a convoy of army vehicles that went by. I was nearly forced into the hedgerow and stepped straight into the mud," he said. "Again, Miss Glenconner—"

"Miss Glenconner left early," I said.

"I wondered why I hadn't seen her assembled," said Mr. Eccles. "No doubt the shock of two deaths in a matter of days was too much for her."

"Are you really going forward with the demonstration knowing that you have two murders on your hands?" asked David, clearly incredulous.

"We *must*." Mr. Eccles glanced around before lowering his voice to say, "In one of my meetings today, someone with a great deal of influence in the government suggested that if Blackthorn is not able to show its progress, the entire thing should be shut down and resources reallocated to the military branches where they believe the need is greater. It is produce or die."

"But for Churchill to visit with a killer on the loose . . ." I trailed off when Mr. Eccles dropped his gaze. "You're not going to tell them, are you?"

"I told my superiors at Baker Street that we had another suicide as soon as I found out about Porter. The decision has been made that it should not become more widely known until after the prime minister has left to ensure that there are no distractions tomorrow."

"But these are murders you're dealing with," I pressed.

"I don't see why that should matter," said Mr. Eccles.

Of course it mattered, but before I could say anything, David asked, "Doesn't that rather risk the prime minister's displeasure if he finds out?"

David and I knew more than Mr. Eccles probably could guess how the people who worked around him could sometimes feel the need to tiptoe around Mr. Churchill, but I also doubted that the prime minister would appreciate being lied to, especially about a pair of murders at a facility he'd personally backed.

Mr. Eccles wearily rubbed his forehead. "Mr. Poole, I have a job to do, and that is to deliver a display of working, viable devices tomorrow. I can't begin to think about anything else until that is done."

"Mr. Eccles, you must pull the barnacle bombs from tomorrow's demonstration," I said.

"Pull them? But that's ridiculous. The entire reason the prime minister is coming tomorrow is because of those bombs," he protested.

"But what about the other things you mentioned? The armadillo and the anti-tank device?" I asked.

"The barnacle bomb will stick onto a surface—nearly any surface—and explode on a timing device. Nothing else has such a wide application or is more desperately needed in this war, Miss Redfern. Nothing. The entire basis of what we're doing here is predicated on the barnacle bombs working. I am not going to remove them from the demonstration."

"Sir . . ."

However, before I could say anything further, I heard Constable Lee shout, "Miss Redfern! Mr. Poole!"

We all spun around. The constable was soaked through, a combination of mud and wet lime climbing four inches up his trousers, but there was a bright-eyed look about him.

"What is it?" I asked hurriedly.

Constable Lee grinned, his eyes bright with excitement. "I think I may have found something."

―――――――

We left Mr. Eccles in the entryway and followed Constable Lee out of the house. A misty rain had begun to fall since we'd gone inside, and again I sighed as I tried to tuck my hair up under my beret to keep the wet off it.

"I don't know why I bother," I muttered. "It's a losing battle."

In the light of the rising moon, I could just make out David's smile, but then his expression fell back into seriousness when he asked, "Constable Lee, where are you taking us?"

"It's in the woods, sir. It's best to show you," the young man insisted.

"Constable, I appreciate the need for suspense, but perhaps you could tell us what else you discovered this afternoon," I said.

"Yes, Miss," said the constable as he switched on a torch and cast the beam over the sodden drive. "I started at the house. Mr. Hartley was working in the east wing's dining room. He said that he needed quiet for some calculations that he was doing."

"How long was he working by himself?" I asked.

"From nine o'clock in the morning until one in the afternoon when he broke for lunch, which he used to go and say hello to Miss Kenwood at the manufacturing barn," said Constable Lee.

"Did anyone see him that time?" David asked.

"Yes, sir," said Constable Lee. "He said that Miss Daniels, the housemaid, came in around ten o'clock to empty the bins and do a little dusting. I checked with her, and she remembers seeing him as she cleaned the ground-floor rooms this morning."

"That still leaves quite a bit of time for Mr. Hartley to slip out of the house and kill Mr. Porter," I said.

Constable Lee swallowed. "Yes, Miss."

"Go on," I said.

"The housekeeper, Mrs. Sherman, confirmed that she and Miss Daniels worked to split up the ground-floor rooms, each taking one before meeting up to move on to the next section. Apparently they worked until one o'clock when they broke for lunch in the kitchen.

"Dr. Jamison was working in the engineers' workshop on the ground floor all morning. Apparently Miss Daniels and Mrs. Sherman didn't clean in that room in order to avoid disturbing him. Dr. Jamison then went for a walk around the lake on the eastern side of the estate around half past ten and then ate an early lunch at his desk."

"Did Dr. Jamison say that he saw anyone on his walk?" I asked.

"No," said Constable Lee. "He said he walked around the lake once, and that he was gone about three-quarters of an hour."

"That's a big lake," I commented, but my mind was already on something else. Dr. Jamison's walk might explain how he had mud on his shoes, but an unaccounted-for three-quarters of an hour was plenty of time to slip off to the equipment sheds, kill Mr. Porter, and then make his way back.

"What about the women in the manufacturing barn?" asked David.

"There are seven in total," said Constable Lee, gesturing for us to follow him off the path when we reached the fork in the service road. "Miss Kenwood said that the women were working on a timing device? I didn't really understand that part."

"Don't trouble yourself with that," I said, ducking under a tree branch just in time after the torch beam sliced across it.

Constable Lee nodded. "The ladies arrived on the estate via coach as usual at eight o'clock. Apparently Miss Kenwood greeted two women whose first day it was—what a day to start a job—and then she immediately brought them to some sort of meeting at the main house.

"They returned by half past eight and then they worked from nine until eleven, when they had their normal break. Because they're not allowed up to the manor house, they mostly mill around outside. Work resumed again from half past eleven until one o'clock, when they stopped for lunch," Constable Lee finished.

"Where do they have their lunches?" David asked.

"There's a small tea room attached to the barn," said Constable Lee. "They're allowed outside to smoke, but again, they must stay within sight of the building at all times."

"Did any of them leave their workbenches outside of their tea and lunch breaks?" I asked.

"No," he said. "I think Miss Kenwood runs a strict shop."

"And did any of them remember seeing Miss Kenwood in her office this morning?" I asked.

"All of them said that they saw her because there's a window that makes up one of her office walls." He continued as we hurried along. "The daytime gatehouse guard, a Mr. Winchester, said that he didn't see anything suspicious and he didn't leave his post. He takes his lunch sitting in the gatehouse. Oh, and the gardener, Mr. Parker, was spreading mulch over the vegetable beds most of the morning."

With our telephone call to Mr. Eccles and our conversations with Mr. Tyson and Miss Glenconner, that would cover all of the staff who were meant to be on the Blackthorn grounds that morning.

"Someone's lying to us, David," I said.

He nodded.

"Here it is," said Constable Lee, stopping just ahead of us.

At first, I didn't see what it was that he was referring to, but as I cleared the constable's back, he shone his torch on the ground ahead of us and I understood.

Next to me, David stopped. "Is that . . ."

"A campsite," I said with a grim nod at the long-dead campfire, small stack of wood, oilcloth slung up over the branch of a tree, and abandoned sleeping bag under it.

"And then there's this," said Constable Lee, lifting up a rock to show us the shattered remains of a glass, two metal hypodermic needles, and a key that looked as though it might be the perfect size to fit a desk drawer.

"Constable Lee," I said, sucking in a breath, "I do believe you've found our killer's camp."

THIRTY-EIGHT

David, Constable Lee, and I worked methodically, combing over the campsite to see if there was anything else to be found. While the men traded holding the torch aloft, I went through every inch of the sleeping bag and oilcloth, looking for an identifiable marking that might give us a clue as to who had used it. I found nothing.

Neither was there anything in the ashes. Unlike Sir Nigel's half-burned cheque, if the killer had thrown anything on the fire, it had long since been destroyed.

Finally, with an aching back, wet knees, and stockings likely ruined from crouching down on the ground, I declared that we had probably discovered as much as we were going to that evening.

"Collect the needles, key, and what you can of the glass for evidence and see if you can lift any fingerprints off them, Constable," I said. "Once you dust it for prints, you might as well try the key in Sir Nigel's desk drawer as well. I'm certain it will fit."

"Yes, Miss," said Constable Lee.

"Did anything come back on the fingerprints from Sir Nigel's office?" asked David.

"Nothing yet, sir. The laboratory is understaffed. It's the war," said Constable Lee.

"We'll come back here tomorrow morning and see if anything else comes to light," I said with a heavy sigh.

We said goodbye to Constable Lee at the front of the house, and then David and I climbed into the car.

"Supper?" David asked.

"Supper," I agreed.

Delighted at the prospect of a hot meal, my stomach rumbled periodically all the way to the Hand and Flower. It was easy to imagine a time before the war when the pub's windows might have glowed with warm light, welcoming weary travelers looking for a comfortable place to rest. Now, however, with the regulation blackout pulled tight over all windows, it wasn't until we were inside that I felt the warm welcome of the pub.

I knew I looked like a mess with dirty knees and hair that was probably going every which way, but I hardly cared. There were more people in the dining room than during our lunch visit, but I managed to secure us the same table we'd eaten at the previous day, which was well away from other diners, while David went to investigate the evening's offerings. When he returned a few minutes later, he was bearing two pints of a dark beer.

"It looks as though the best we can expect tonight is Woolton pie," he said.

I shrugged. "It might lack meat, but the chance of finding good vegetables seems stronger in the countryside than it does in town. What is this?" I asked as he set the beer in front of me.

"Bitter," he said.

I tilted my head. I'd never had a pint of bitter before. I'd had lager, on occasion. However, ale was usually the purview of men.

"I think you'll like it," he said.

I reached for my pint and took a sip. It was, as its name would indicate, quite a bit more bitter than the drinks I was used to. "It's different."

"If you're being too polite to say you dislike it, don't. I can fetch you something else," he offered.

Cautiously, I took another sip. With my taste buds prepared this time, I found myself welcoming the bitterness. I shook my head. "It's good."

"Excellent," he said, taking a sip of his own pint.

"Shall we talk about the case?" I leaned an elbow on the table, resting my head in my hand and lowering my voice as a precaution, and asked, "Why, after more than a year of working together, are two men whose dislike for one another was well-known murdered in the space of three days?"

"We don't know," said David.

"So what do we know?" I asked.

"They were killed in the same manner," he said.

I nodded. "Sedated and then dispatched in such a way that it would look as though they had taken their own lives. The only variation is in the weapons they supposedly used. Sir Nigel died from a gunshot from a service revolver and Mr. Porter was hanged."

"In both cases, the murderer could be certain that the bodies would be found—quickly in the case of Sir Nigel's murder. A bullet from a gun makes a racket. The murderer must have known that it would attract attention. Which, we can assume, is why the murderer shot him late at night," said David.

"But not while the house was completely empty," I mused.

"They took a risk."

I nodded. "Which makes me think that something drove the murderer to kill them now."

"Sir Nigel's investigation," said David.

"I think so. But we were sent here originally to investigate theft." I sat back. "Do you know, I thought that perhaps Sir Nigel was behind the anonymous report, but if he told Lieutenant Colonel Gerrard he believed that there might be a saboteur in the staff's midst, why not report it as sabotage?"

"It would have attracted too much attention on the program at Blackthorn Park and jeopardized his work," said David.

I frowned. "Maybe. Either way, I think the killer is someone who thought that Sir Nigel was too close to putting all the pieces together and uncovering what was actually happening at the facility."

"And Mr. Porter?" he asked.

I thought for a moment. "Mr. Porter asked Miss Glenconner to find all of the files related to suppliers whose materials go into the barnacle bombs the morning he was murdered. He also wrote a secondary list on his office notepad with only some of those names. What if he picked up the thread of Sir Nigel's investigation and inadvertently made the murderer feel threatened enough that they believed they had to kill again?"

David sat back in his chair, looking contemplative. "Put it all together for me."

I took a deep breath, ordering my thoughts before launching in.

"Last month, Sir Nigel receives a letter from Major Richards complaining about the quality of a product predominantly of his design and that was produced on his watch. The major believes that a timing device malfunctioned and nearly killed an instructor."

"But we aren't certain that it actually was the timing device that was the problem," David reminded me.

"Correct. Let's just say *something* was wrong. Sir Nigel is tempted to dismiss this because he believes that the work that his team is doing is good—excellent, even. Why wouldn't it be? He is the one leading them, and he was brilliant enough to be knighted. He is also arrogant enough to conduct an affair right under the noses of his wife and his colleagues," I said.

"Charming man," muttered David.

"I couldn't agree more. The one thing that holds Sir Nigel back from dismissing Major Richards's warning outright is that he knows the man socially. Or at least his family does. This prompts him to telephone Major Richards.

"On that telephone call, Major Richards manages to extract a promise from Sir Nigel that he will personally investigate what might be the matter with that shipment of barnacle bombs. Sir Nigel begins to look into matters at Blackthorn Park and becomes suspicious that all is not well. He goes on a tirade, making everyone's life difficult as he puts new demands on Mr. Tyson, the engineers, Miss Kenwood. Somewhere along the way, he becomes convinced that there may be a saboteur in their midst at Blackthorn Park."

A breaking glass shattered the quiet of the dining room. I was half under the table before I realized that no one else had moved except for my partner.

Both David and I straightened, exchanging sheepish looks at our swift reactions.

"If there was any question that we're the Londoners in the room . . ." I said, trailing off.

David huffed out a laugh. "I doubt the village of Benstead is a likely target for a Luftwaffe air raid."

"Not if you ask Captain Sherman, the stationmaster," I said, clasping my trembling hands in my lap to hide them. "I would wager his branch of the Home Guard is ready for an invasion by air, sea, or land."

David gave me a smile. "You were saying?"

"Right. Sir Nigel writes to Lieutenant Colonel Julian Gerrard to ask to use Burtlesby Abbey's testing grounds to see if he can pinpoint the problem with the barnacle bombs. He does this because he doesn't trust anyone he works with any longer. There, his worst fears are confirmed: there is a problem with the barnacle bombs. Sir Nigel must have begun to panic."

"Worried that his funding might be pulled," said David.

"Or worse, the entire operation shut down. Remember how dicey Mr. Eccles said things are in London? I think all of that spurred Sir Nigel on to launch his own investigation. Remember, Jane said that she heard him shouting that someone should be hanged for treason two weeks before he died."

"What about France?" asked David.

I held up a finger and consulted my notebook. "Mr. Tyson told us that he received orders to send a shipment of barnacle bombs to a Devon railway station the same day that Sir Nigel left for Burtlesby. It is possible that Sir Nigel didn't know that the bombs had left Blackthorn Park for use in an active mission. I don't know if we'll ever know whether he had the power to stop them and save those commandos."

"Poor sods," David muttered.

David sat back in his chair as the waitress approached. She slid our plates down in front of us, the scent of potato crust and cheese wafting up to me.

As soon as she was gone, David asked, "What about Porter?"

I picked up my fork and broke into the crust, sampling the hot pie. "This is better than I thought it would be."

"I'm suspicious of anything that the government tries to encourage us to eat," said David.

"Rightly so. I think that much the same thing happened to Mr. Porter. He became suspicious of something going on at Blackthorn Park and started to investigate."

"And the killer thought he was getting too close to finding out the truth, so they killed him."

I nodded. "Miss Glenconner said that he took an outside call, and then he left. I think that telephone call was meant to draw Mr. Porter out to the equipment sheds. Only he had no idea he was walking to his death. The next time anyone sees him, it's poor Mr. Tyson who discovers his body."

"What does everyone have to gain from Sir Nigel's and Mr. Porter's deaths?" asked David before taking another bite.

"When Sir Nigel died, Dr. Jamison became the de facto head of department," I said. "Plus, he had the motivation of revenge. Sir Nigel interfered and blocked his application to head up another facility."

"Mr. Hartley might want to rid himself of a demanding boss who questioned his work ethic and his pride—not to mention the affair between Miss Kenwood and Sir Nigel," said David.

"If he knew about it," I pointed out. "Which leads us to Miss Kenwood, the jilted lover who had plenty of motive herself to kill Sir Nigel."

"And we know that she spends time at the manor house, so there's no reason for her presence to raise alarm bells. Plus she admitted herself that no one can verify her alibi as to where she was at the time Sir Nigel was killed because she was alone."

"True," I said, "but we have multiple witnesses who placed her in the manufacturing barn for the duration of this morning."

He rubbed a hand over his chin, the stubble making a rasping noise. "Unless she has an accomplice. Her fiancé."

I frowned, mulling this over. "Mr. Hartley could have used the time when Dr. Jamison was walking today to kill Mr. Porter, but what about Sir Nigel? He and Mr. Tyson's stories about seeing each other at the foot of the stairs just after hearing the shot match. It doesn't give him enough time to have killed him and doubled back down the stairs without being seen by Miss Glenconner or Mr. Tyson."

"What about this? Miss Kenwood kills Sir Nigel and hides in the cabinet you found in the east wing. Then Mr. Hartley kills Mr. Porter today," said David.

"And how do the barnacle bomb, sabotage, and thefts fit?" I asked.

He made a frustrated noise low in his throat. "Who else does that leave us with?"

I pulled out my notebook. "Jane and Mrs. Sherman were at home for Sir Nigel's death and spotted cleaning the main house during Mr. Porter's window. Mr. Eccles was in London both times—once at home and once in meetings. I suppose there's Mr. Parker or the guards at the gatehouse to consider."

"Constable Lee says the alibis check out for all of them," David said. "Besides, what would their motive be?"

"Covering up the thefts—or the sabotage?"

"Which is it?" asked David.

"I don't know," I admitted, growing frustrated with all of the holes that still remained in this case.

"What motive would someone have to tamper with the bombs?" asked David.

"They didn't want the demonstration to go forward," I said.

"And what about the thefts?"

"The black market?" But even as I suggested it I knew it sounded like I was taking shots in the dark, and we both fell silent.

"There's something we're missing," I finally said. "Something that's right in front of us."

"You sound like a detective in one of your novels," he said.

"If only it were that easy. Nothing about this case feels neat. There are too many things that don't add up," I said. "I think we need to go back to basics. I want to take a proper look at the files we took from Miss Glenconner's desk, Mr. Tyson's inventory, and that list of names I found on Mr. Porter's notepad."

"Why?" he asked.

"I want to do a comparison. Maybe we can find a pattern to the supplies that went missing and how they relate to the barnacle bomb. Maybe the sabotage and the thefts are somehow one and the same."

"Right," said David, standing up and adjusting the cuffs of his shirt.

"Right what?" I asked, looking up at him.

He stuck his hand in his pocket and turned his back to the room so that I was shielded from view. "Hold out your hand."

I did as I was told, and he deposited a key into the middle of my palm. My fingers closed around it before I fully understood what it was: his room key.

"Go up as discreetly as you can and wait for me," he said.

I raised a brow. "Wait for you? In your room? I had no idea you became so forward after a single pint."

"Evelyne, if I ever decide to become forward with you, I promise you'll know."

My eyes widened a little at that, but then David added, "I'll drive back to the estate and pick up Mr. Tyson's inventory and ask one of the engineers for a schematic of the barnacle bomb. It shouldn't take me more than half an hour. If we go up together, I'll no doubt have the manager banging on my door complaining that I'm bringing ill repute upon the place, or something along those lines."

As though anyone would ever accuse David Poole of being anything but honorable.

———

If anyone could have seen David and me that evening, they would have been left with no illusions about how very unscandalous our situation was.

I sat on the bed with my muddy shoes off and stockings drying over the radiator, surrounded by papers, while he occupied the one chair in the room with the inventory open on his lap. I did my best to decipher handwriting and notes while he did the tiring work of cross-checking Mr. Tyson's records.

Around midnight, David nodded off as I sorted through a particularly thick file related to March Chemicals. The inventory began to slip down his leg, and I scooted forward to catch it before it fell to the floor and woke him up. Carefully, I lifted the quilt off the end of the bed and covered him with it before returning to the pages.

With the inventory next to me, I continued to plow on, looking for inconsistencies. Only I couldn't find them.

With a frown, I flipped back to the month of August and began to go through the files again. Around half past one, August became July.

About an hour later, it hit me, and I sat straight up, the file I'd been reading sliding off my lap. I couldn't find inconsistencies between the order amounts on the invoices and Mr. Tyson's inventory because there were none.

Nothing was missing from Blackthorn Park because no one had stolen anything. There was no thief.

I opened my mouth to tell David, but then I saw how content he looked asleep in his chair. I would tell him the following day when we could do something with that piece of information. Then we would figure out what had actually happened at Blackthorn Park.

Thursday
November 7, 1940

THE DAY OF CHURCHILL'S VISIT

THIRTY-NINE

I awoke the next morning, blurry-eyed and immediately grumpy because someone had the gall to gently shake me by the shoulder.

"Evelyne, Evelyne, you need to wake up."

"Where am I?" I muttered, lifting my head from the duvet. Seeing David looking down at me, his expression a mixture of amusement and embarrassment, brought it all swiftly back.

The inventory, the contracts, and the realization that nothing at Blackthorn Park was what it seemed, not even the case we'd initially been sent to investigate.

"What time is it?" I croaked.

"Seven o'clock," he said.

"You fell asleep," I said, pushing myself up to sitting.

"So did you," he pointed out.

I shook my head. "You fell asleep, and I found something."

"You did?"

"The numbers all add up," I said, grabbing the inventory and the closest file to show him.

"Yes, because Mr. Tyson has been keeping a closer eye on the inventory," he said.

"No, the numbers all add up for months." I flipped back in the book to show him. "I looked all the way back to May. I can't find anything. Not even a clerical error."

"Not even with Mr. Hartley complaining about being blamed for sloppy administrative work?" he asked with disbelief.

I shook my head emphatically.

"But the thefts . . ."

"Never happened," I finished for him.

He let out a long breath. "I don't understand."

I swung my legs over the edge of the bed and grabbed my stockings. "I don't understand either, but I think we're close to figuring this all out."

W hen we arrived at Blackthorn Park—David in a new shirt and me in the same mucky stockings from the day before—we went straight up to see Miss Glenconner, only she was not at her desk.

"No coat," said David, looking around.

I began to open her desk drawers—an invasion of privacy, yes, but given that we had two murders on our hands, I thought that there was an exception to be made.

"No handbag either," I said, straightening. "I don't think she's been in today."

Jane rounded the corner, red-faced and huffing as she hauled a pail and mop. "Oh!" She stopped when she saw me. "I didn't see you at Russet Cottage this morning, so I thought you'd gone, Miss Redfern."

"Good morning, Jane. Have you seen Miss Glenconner yet?" I asked.

"She's downstairs in the kitchen," said Jane with a sniff.

"In the kitchen?" I asked as the telephone on Miss Glenconner's desk began to ring.

David picked up the receiver as Jane said, "Miss Glenconner came in the front door and claimed she was going to faint, so Mrs. Sherman took her downstairs for a cup of tea. I can't imagine Mrs. Sherman ever doing anything so kind to me—and for the second day in a row.

"She's a misery guts, that one. Always walking around with her face pinched in like she's bitten into a lemon just because she doesn't like it in the south."

"I think she's found it hard to adjust," I said, remembering that

Miss Glenconner had said it was what had endeared Sir Nigel to her, his connection to her part of Yorkshire, born out of childhood visits. It was what had prompted her to help him, to act as his secretary . . .

Something in my brain fired, and all at once, I realized that I had been so stupidly trusting that I'd missed what had been right in front of me all along.

"You said Miss Glenconner is downstairs in the kitchen?" I asked.

"That's right. Sitting around while the rest of us are working, which is what I should be doing before Mrs. Sherman sees me," grumbled Jane as she wielded her cleaning things once again and walked off.

David hung up and turned to me to say, "That was Miss Summers. She said that the personnel files will be arriving on the 8:24 train." He glanced at his watch. "Do you want to come collect them?"

"I need to speak to Miss Glenconner," I said. "And I want to try to reason with Mr. Eccles again. Hopefully the bright light of morning has knocked some sense into him and he's realized that demonstrating the barnacle bomb isn't worth the risk of accidentally blowing up the prime minister."

I knew I was exaggerating for dramatic effect, but only a little. I had a healthy respect for weaponry that worked, and a real fear of it if there was any chance that something might go wrong.

"Right, you take Miss Glenconner and Mr. Eccles, and I'll meet you back here," he said.

He strode off in the direction of the main stairs while I let myself into the servants' stairs and followed the winding staircase down to the lower ground floor. My heels clicked on the smooth floor, echoing off the empty corridor that must have once been a hive of activity when the house had been in its full glory.

I rounded the kitchen door and found Miss Glenconner, pale and wan, staring at a nearly full cup of tea in front of her on the wooden kitchen table. A sour smell hung about the place.

"Good morning," I said softly. "I was looking for you upstairs, but Jane said you'd nearly had a spell and come down here."

Miss Glenconner nodded miserably.

I slid onto a stool across from her and folded my hands on the scarred wood surface.

"I can understand being lonely, you know," I said softly. She looked up sharply, but I continued, "There have been times in my life when I've thought that no one else could understand, and then someone came along and I was so grateful.

"For me it was my best friend, Moira." I hesitated. "For you, I think it was Sir Nigel."

"I don't know what you're talking about," she whispered, her voice hoarse.

"I imagine it was particularly flattering when Sir Nigel began to pay you special attention. It wasn't just that he needed a secretary. He made you feel as though someone wanted you around. He talked to you about Yorkshire—perhaps he even told you some stories about his childhood—and at some point it became more than talking, didn't it?" I asked.

I thought she would protest, but instead she burst into tears and buried her face in her hands.

"You think I'm stupid!" she wailed.

"I don't think that at all," I said. Instead, I thought she was a frightened young woman who had probably believed that a man who made her feel special and loved would never hurt her.

"I'm a good girl. I promise I am," she insisted through her tears.

"We all make mistakes," I said. "Why don't you tell me what happened? You don't have to carry this secret around with you any longer."

I thought she'd deny it again, but then she sniffled.

"I know how I seem, the naïve vicar's daughter who manages to become mixed up with a married man less than a year after leaving home. I promise that it wasn't like that at all," she said.

"Why don't you tell me?" I asked gently.

"Coming south and joining a place like Blackthorn Park made me feel important. I was excited to be working somewhere that was doing such worthy work.

"At first, being Mr. Porter's secretary was fine. He could be brusque, but he was an important man in an important job. But then, he began to stand a little too close to me. He began to ask personal questions. He started bringing me little presents and leaving them in my desk," she said.

"What kinds of things?" I asked.

"A new pen because I complained that mine had leaked. A record that I had been humming. Pairs of silk stockings. At first I thought he was simply being nice, but then he tried to kiss me." She shuddered. "I was shocked. I suppose I knew that some men do this, but I thought that Mr. Porter was happily married. He spoke to me about his wife all of the time. He had me telephone to say when he would be home for supper.

"I told him that trying to kiss me was wrong. That wasn't how my parents raised me, and I wasn't that sort of girl. He seemed to understand that, but I still didn't trust him."

"So you began to work for Sir Nigel to try to get away," I said.

She nodded. "I offered to type his correspondence because it was no great hardship to add it to what Mr. Porter asked me to do and it meant that I could spend more time on the other side of the house. However, at some point I began to do more and more work for Sir Nigel." She looked down at her hands folded in her lap. "I liked him. He made me feel special."

"And that's why you said yes to him after you said no to Mr. Porter," I said.

She nodded. "I knew that Sir Nigel had a wife too, but he told me that anything romantic had been over between them for years. He told me that Lady Balram has affairs. That she neglected him. That made it easy for me to think that it would be different, because Lady Balram wasn't like Mrs. Porter since she didn't care."

"I think that was likely the truth," I said, considering what I knew of Lady Balram.

She gave a wobbly laugh. "Well, at least there's that. I believed Sir Nigel when he told me that this was the first time he'd ever felt this way. That I was worth risking everything for."

"Did you know that Sir Nigel had had an affair with Miss Kenwood?" I asked.

She winced, but nodded. "I found out later. I was so angry that he'd lied to me. He told me that he'd broken things off with Miss Kenwood because he couldn't stop thinking about me. He said she wasn't important. Not the way I was.

"You must believe me, Miss Redfern, I never set out to do anything so *bad*," she said, whispering the word. "It's just that Nigel made me feel special. He made me feel safe. He told me that he loved me, and I truly believe he did until things became too difficult."

I had my doubts about whether Sir Nigel really did have the capacity to love in the way she believed given that he bounced from Miss Kenwood to her, but I kept my own counsel on that.

"When did the affair start?" I asked.

"August," she said.

"When did it end?"

She traced her finger over the handle of her tea mug. "A couple of weeks ago. I told him that I didn't think that it was wise for us to see one another any longer."

"Why?" I asked.

"I knew that he wasn't going to leave his wife. I told him that he should hire another secretary—his own—because I didn't want to work for him any longer."

"Where was this?" I asked.

She shot me a tormented look. "In his office."

"And you said this was a couple of weeks ago?" I asked, frowning.

"Yes," she said.

"Did you ever speak to him privately again?" I asked. When she didn't respond, I pressed her, asking, "Did you and Sir Nigel have an argument in his office last Thursday?"

Miss Glenconner pressed her lips together, as though not speaking would somehow render the truth invalid.

"On Thursday the twenty-fourth of October, a witness remembers hearing an argument between Sir Nigel and a woman, but they couldn't be certain of the woman's voice. The following day, Mrs. Sherman found the remains of a torn-up and half-burned cheque. She thought it was for £50, but I've seen Sir Nigel's chequebook. It was made out for £500.

"That's a substantial amount of money for most people, even Sir Nigel. I think that he wrote you that cheque to try to make sure you did something for him. And I think you tore that cheque up because what he was asking you made you really and truly angry."

"You don't understand—"

But before she could finish the sentence, Miss Glenconner pushed off her stool and lunged for the deep kitchen sink, holding on to the edge as she vomited. Her head hung down as she groaned miserably.

"Miss Glenconner, how long have you known that you're pregnant?" I asked.

With a trembling hand, she pulled a handkerchief out of her pocket and dabbed at her lips. Then she turned the tap on the faucet to wash away the sick, although the water didn't completely remove the smell from the air.

"Long enough," she croaked, turning back to me with real fear in her eyes.

"Did you tell Sir Nigel you were pregnant, and is that why he ended things?" I asked as gently as I could.

She sank onto her stool again.

"Did he offer you money to buy your silence?" I asked.

Tears began rolling down her face. "He told me that I could take care of it. He would give me the money to arrange it, and enough to do as I pleased afterward. He was so cold about it. I thought, perhaps . . . I thought . . ."

"You thought that maybe he would leave his wife?" I asked, reaching out to place a hand on hers.

"I was such a fool," she whispered. "When I realized that I was late, I didn't know what to do. I went to Dr. Morrison in the village because I thought maybe I was wrong . . ."

"But you weren't wrong. You know exactly what is happening to you," I said.

"I didn't kill him. I *swear* that I didn't, but I wanted him to know that this wasn't something he could simply buy his way out of or pay to disappear. I wanted him to admit that what he'd done was wrong. That he was responsible too.

"Do you know what happens to unmarried girls who get into trouble where I'm from?" she asked, her tone somewhere between fiery and desperate. "They go away and we all pretend that it's not strange that they had an illness that lasted six months and required them to leave home. When they come back, they walk around like ghosts. They hardly smile anymore. Everyone knows why. I—I don't want that."

Her shoulders slumped. "I can't go home, Miss Redfern, but I can't have a child either."

"What will you do?" I asked.

"I have an aunt who lives in Plymouth. She knows someone who can . . . help."

I nodded, understanding her meaning perfectly.

"I suppose you think I'm stupid for ripping up the cheque and then going to do the exact thing that Sir Nigel was trying to give me money for," she said.

"I think that you're doing what you need to in order to survive," I said. "I'm very sorry, Miss Glenconner."

"I can't stay here," she said. "I can barely make it through a day's work without being ill, and it won't be that many weeks before I begin to show. And now with two murders—I'm terrified."

I sighed, knowing I was about to do something very stupid myself. "I really shouldn't let you leave. Not while there's an active investigation underway."

She grabbed my hands. "Please, Miss Redfern. Please, I'm begging you. I can't stand the thought of staying here any longer. I need to go before it's too late for me."

I sighed and reached across the table to where a stack of scrap paper and a pencil lay. I scribbled down the post office box in London that I was meant to use for work. It was unconnected to my home address or the address of the Special Investigations Unit's offices, but Miss Summers had assured me that anything sent there would make its way to me swiftly.

I handed Miss Glenconner the paper and placed another blank one in front of her.

"Give me your aunt's address in Plymouth," I said. "I want you to write to me the moment you arrive. A postcard with something from Plymouth on the front of it."

"Thank you," she whispered as she wrote. "It's not fair, you know."

"No. No, it's not."

"I really was good at my job, Miss Redfern."

"I believe it."

I rose, feeling a thousand years old, and left her staring into her now-cool tea.

FORTY

I went in search of Mr. Eccles, climbing the stairs to knock on his office door. When I received no answer, I went downstairs to check in the engineers' workshop. Dr. Jamison looked up when I walked in.

"Dr. Jamison, have you seen Mr. Eccles this morning?" I asked.

"No."

"Did he speak to you last night about checking over the barnacle bombs?" I asked.

"No," he said. "I went straight home after his announcement yesterday."

"Damn," I swore quietly. "I need you to look over all of the barnacle bombs that will be used for the demonstration."

"Why?"

"Because I think Sir Nigel discovered that someone had tampered with the ones sent out for testing last month, and if one of them malfunctions today . . ."

I saw the engineer's eyes go wide. "I will find Hartley and start checking them now. We'll look at everything that will be demonstrated today."

I nodded and resumed my search for Blackthorn Park's government liaison.

I was just poking my head into the library when I saw Mr. Tyson.

"Good morning," he said.

"Mr. Tyson, have you seen Mr. Eccles this morning?" I asked.

"No, but I know he stayed over at the Hand and Flower yesterday night. He could be going straight to the railway station to meet the dignitaries," said the quartermaster.

"When are they due in?"

"I believe they're due in a special train getting in at nineteen minutes past the hour. They're supposed to arrive here at half past nine," he said.

I glanced at my watch. That gave me about an hour until the prime minister arrived at Blackthorn Park. If Mr. Eccles was one of their party, it was likely I would be able to pull him aside for a quiet word to try again to dissuade him.

"Are you setting up the demonstration today?" I asked.

He nodded.

"The engineers are checking all of the barnacle bombs for faults. I want you to promise me that you will not set a single one off without their reassurance that they are all safe to use. Can you do that?" I asked.

He nodded. "Yes, Miss. I keep them under lock and key. They won't make it out to the testing field until Dr. Jamison says so."

"Good."

When I crossed the entryway again, I spotted David nudging the manor house's front door open with his shoulder, a large box in his arms.

"Let me get that for you," I said, running up to take the weight of the door.

"Thanks," he said. "Did you manage to speak to Mr. Eccles?"

"I couldn't find him. Mr. Tyson said he's likely meeting the London train later."

"Did he speak to the engineers last night?" asked David.

I shook my head. "Dr. Jamison said he didn't see him after the announcement. I gave Dr. Jamison the message though. Are those all of the personnel files?" I asked.

"All ready and waiting as Miss Summers promised. I put the files from yesterday in there too," he said. "What about Miss Glenconner?"

"I'll tell you when we're alone," I said.

When we got to the morning room, I held the door open for him.

"Thanks," he said.

I shut the door. "Miss Glenconner was the woman Jane overheard arguing with Sir Nigel in his office. She was the one he tried to give the cheque to. They had an affair."

"He tried to buy her silence?" David asked.

"She's pregnant."

"Bloody Hell," David muttered.

"She's pregnant, and she's terrified, and the man who got her into trouble was trying to buy her off with £500."

"And now he's dead," he said.

"I don't think she did it. The timeline *might* work in either murder, but I don't think she's capable of killing either man, no matter how angry and hurt she was by Sir Nigel or how much she disliked and disapproved of Mr. Porter."

I expected him to object. However, David simply nodded and said, "I trust your judgment."

I can't deny that I wasn't relieved to hear it.

I watched him move to the morning room table, drop the file box onto it, and tip off the top.

"Where do you want to start?" he asked.

"Why don't you give me Sir Nigel?" It couldn't hurt to review our first victim's file to see if there was anything that we'd overlooked.

I settled down across from David, opened the file, and began to read. It was much as I had expected. He was fifty-seven when he died. He had been born in Surrey, educated at Cambridge. His London home address had been crossed out and replaced by the Old Vicarage. The same with his telephone exchange.

There were small notes that filled out some of the details that I hadn't known about, such as the fact that his knighthood had come in recognition of his work in explosives meant for use in mining. Apparently he had been personally recruited by Brigadier Colin Gibbons, who himself had been appointed to lead the SOE this past July.

David closed his file, and I looked up. "Anything?"

"I have Mr. Hartley's file. It's relatively short. He was born in Buckinghamshire. His father is a cobbler. He went to Eton on scholarship, like Miss Kenwood said, before attending Cambridge. He was made Reserved Occupation on account of his work, but there's a note here about the asthma he told us about too. What about you?" he asked.

"Nothing jumps out at me," I said with a sigh. "Obviously we know the more salacious details of Sir Nigel's life. His affairs."

"His wife's affair," said David.

"Again, that should be affairs too, if she's to be believed," I corrected.

"Next file?" David asked.

I stuck my hand out.

"Jane Daniels," I read out from the tab. "It always feels strange reading the file of someone I know."

"It's an odd profession," he agreed.

"Don't think for one moment that I think it's fair you've seen my file," I warned.

"No one ever said that it was," he said, pulling out a file for himself, "although I believe that most of what's in your file could be found by some enterprising library patron, so long as the library holds news-paper records."

That, I had to admit, was a good point.

"Besides, most of what is in there is about your parents, not you."

I jerked my chin at his file. "Who do you have?"

He held it up to show me the tab. "Timothy Eccles."

"Right, I'll see you on the other side," I said.

Jane's file, I was not terribly surprised to find out, was short. She was twenty, had been born in a neighboring village, and had never married. Her only work had been as a domestic.

"That must be convenient," David muttered from across the table.

I lifted my head. "What's that?"

"Mr. Eccles lives on York Terrace West. That's just a couple of roads away from the SOE HQ on Baker Street. I'll wager he walks to work," said David.

I raised a brow. "The money must come from his wife's side. I doubt a civil servant affords an address in that part of London on his salary alone." I paused. "Can I see that?"

David handed it to me.

I scanned the typed sheet, my eyes darting over the information.

```
Surname, Forename: Eccles, Timothy
Title: Mr.
Date of birth: 12 February 1899
Place of birth: Chelsea, London
Place of residence: 5 York Terrace West, London
Telephone exchange: HUN 5547
Spouse: Mrs. Joan Eccles (née Longfellow)
```

"David, give me my handbag," I said, eyes fixed on the page.

He shoved it across the table to me, and I fumbled with the catch.

"What is it?" he asked.

I ignored him, wrenching free my notebook and flipping through the pages until I found what I was looking for. I checked the file, and then I checked the notebook again, hardly believing what I was seeing.

"Look at this," I said. "Mr. Eccles gave me the exchange Hunter 5547 to telephone him at work. But that's also the exchange listed for his home."

David squinted at the page. "That can't be right."

"There. And look at this," I said, poking the file again. "Mrs. Eccles's maiden name is Longfellow."

"And?" David prompted.

"Where are the files Mr. Porter asked Miss Glenconner to find?" I asked.

He gestured to a stack on the table. I began to flick through the tabs until I found what I was looking for.

"Here," I said, stabbing a finger at the page. "Longfellow & Son. The company name is the same as Mrs. Eccles's maiden name, and we know that Mr. Eccles has been helping her father run the family business."

When I looked up, I realized David was holding a sheet of paper in his hand. "Longfellow & Son is on the list you retrieved from Mr. Porter's desk yesterday. Can I have the file Miss Glenconner pulled?"

I handed it to him, and he splayed it open on the table between us before beginning to riffle through. After a moment, he stopped and pointed at the page in front of him. "Look."

"It's a contract," I said, reading it over quickly.

"It's a contract signed April of this year," he clarified. "After Mr. Eccles began working at Blackthorn Park. When did the rest of these companies on Mr. Porter's list come in?"

We set the list between us and began pulling more files and contracts.

"May," I read out.

"April again," said David.

We continued down the list until the last file sat open in front of us.

"Every single one of them was signed to a contract after Mr. Eccles became government liaison," I said.

"You think he arranged for a contract with his father-in-law's company?" asked David.

"The same father-in-law who he said is ailing? Whose business Mr. Eccles is helping? Yes."

I strode over to the telephone and picked it up for an internal call, clutching at the receiver so hard it was a wonder it didn't crack in my hands. After three rings, Mr. Tyson picked up with a "Hello?"

"Mr. Tyson, Evelyne Redfern."

"All of those bombs are secured, Miss. The engineers are reviewing them now," said Mr. Tyson with obvious relief.

"That's very good news, but listen. I have a quick question about something else entirely. What does the company Longfellow & Son supply to Blackthorn Park?"

Mr. Tyson gave a little laugh. "You'll love this one, Miss. You'd never guess."

"I'm certain I wouldn't," I said, my gaze flashing to David, who was pacing back and forth on his side of the table.

"They make boiled sweets. It's brilliant stuff really. The engineers tested all sorts of different things to try to make sure the timing devices worked correctly, but the one thing that seemed to be most reliable was a boiled sweet allowed to dissolve," he said with a chuckle.

"And you get your sweets from Longfellow & Son? No one else?" I asked.

Something about the tone of my voice must have told him that this was a very serious matter indeed, because there was no more jocularity in his tone. "I believe they used to source them from a number of sweet companies, but in the spring Mr. Eccles suggested consolidating the orders into one contract. He argued that we would have better consistency that way. You need consistency so that the things detonate reliably."

"Does Longfellow & Son produce any other parts of the weapons at Blackthorn Park?"

"Well, yes. Mr. Hartley figured out that using a small sheet of sugar rather than glass could nicely trigger an anti-handling device if it wasn't correctly disarmed. From what I understand, it's worked beautifully," said Mr. Tyson.

"When was the last time you received shipments of boiled sweets and sugar sheets from Longfellow & Son?" I asked.

"The sugar sheets came in around August." I could hear the sound of pages turning. "It looks as though we received a small shipment of the boiled sweets we use for timing devices in September to tide us over because we ran out before our regular shipment arrived in October. We'll need many more than that soon, though, because they go into every bomb we make," said Mr. Tyson.

I stilled. Dr. Jamison had said that in September there had been issues with some of the timing devices coming out of the manufacturing barn, but then the issue resolved itself. It just went away—almost like the sweets in that shipment had all been used up.

"Mr. Tyson, did the sugar sheets in the August shipment go into the barnacle bombs built and shipped out for external testing at the end of September?" I asked.

"Well, yes. It was only a small order, you see, because the improvement was so new and—"

"Were the same sugar sheets used in the lot of devices that went to Dover and then were used in France?"

"Well yes, they were all the same . . ." I could hear his voice get weaker.

"Thank you, Mr. Tyson," I said, dropping the telephone back into its cradle even as I could hear him protesting on the line.

I quickly related to David what I'd just learned.

"So Mr. Eccles secured a contract for Longfellow & Son to Blackthorn Park—"

"Which would provide a steady stream of income to the business," I jumped in, growing more excited by the minute.

"And all is going well—and then, what? Suddenly the sugar doesn't . . . work as well?" he asked.

"Think about it, David. For something to act predictably, it needs to be consistent. Timing devices made from boiled sweets must dissolve at a reliable rate. Sugar sheets that are only meant to break when someone who doesn't know how to defuse a device need to be reliably strong once a metal plate protecting them is removed.

"I think something went wrong with the consistency in quality of the Longfellow & Son sugar products that suddenly rendered Mr. Hartley's improved sugar sheets in the barnacle bomb's anti-handling device unpredictable. What if Sir Nigel went looking into Longfellow & Son and traced the contract—and the company—back to Mr. Eccles?" I asked.

"Why would Mr. Eccles need to kill Sir Nigel?" asked David, a little skeptical.

"Because if someone at Baker Street found out Mr. Eccles has used his position to secure a lucrative contract for his wife's family's company that he has a hand in, he could be accused of profiteering. If he knowingly gave Blackthorn Park faulty supplies, the charges could be far worse. His credibility within Baker Street would be shot. His career would be over. It isn't unreasonable to think that he could be facing the gallows on charges of treason. If that isn't a motive to kill Sir Nigel, I don't know what is," I finished with a flourish.

"And Mr. Porter?" asked David.

"You heard how angry Mr. Porter was about France after Mr. Eccles's announcement. He was determined that no one should pin anything on him. In his anger, he told Mr. Eccles and us that he planned to go through all of Blackthorn Park's contracts related to the barnacle bombs. He even went so far as to write down a list of all of the companies sourced by someone other than him: Mr. Eccles. Mr. Porter was connecting the dots, and Mr. Eccles realized it would only be a matter of time before Mr. Porter would make the Longfellow & Son connection."

David inclined his head as though he was about to agree, but then he said, "You're forgetting something important."

"What?" I asked.

"Mr. Eccles was in London at the time of both murders. We saw his train tickets. They were punched and everything."

I looked up sharply. "David, you genius."

I dove for the telephone again, waiting impatiently to be connected to Benstead Station. The line rang, and rang, and rang.

Finally, the switchboard operator came back on the line. "Would you like me to try again?"

"No, thank you." I put the telephone down and turned to my partner. "David, we need to drive to the station. I must speak to Captain Sherman. Now."

FORTY-ONE

I explained to David as he drove at double speed, and by the time he screeched to a halt in front of Benstead Station entrance, he said, "Go find Captain Sherman. I'll keep the engine running."

I jumped out of the car and ran into the ticket hall. Captain Sherman was nowhere to be seen, so I rushed to the platform door. Sure enough, at the end of the platform stood the stationmaster, shining a button on the front of his dark uniform coat with the edge of his handkerchief.

"Captain Sherman!" I called out. He looked up, squinting as I hailed him. "Captain Sherman, I must speak to you urgently."

"I'm afraid that won't be possible, Miss Redfern. A special train is due in at any minute—"

"This cannot wait. You once told me that you see everyone who comes in and out of this station. You never forget a train or a face."

"Yes, well, it's all part of the job," he said, puffing up his chest. Only I didn't mind. Captain Sherman's high opinion of himself and his value to the Benstead community was what was going to crack the last little bit of this case for me.

"You told me that you remember seeing Mr. Eccles leaving on the train on Monday evening?" I asked.

"Yes," he said.

"Did he return to Benstead on Tuesday morning?" I asked.

"He did."

I nodded. "Now, this is very important. Do you remember Mr. Eccles leaving Benstead yesterday morning?"

"Yes," he said. "On the 9:02 London train."

"And when did he return?" I asked.

Captain Sherman frowned. "I beg your pardon, Miss?"

"What train did Mr. Eccles return to Benstead Station on? Because yesterday evening, I saw him at Blackthorn Park, speaking to the staff."

"I . . . I don't understand." He sounded confused, as though he was trying to work out a puzzle that wouldn't quite fit.

"Captain Sherman, this is very important. Was it possible that Mr. Eccles could have arrived on a train from London any time yesterday without your knowledge after he departed on the 9:02 to Waterloo?" I asked.

A distant whistle sounded and, after a moment, Captain Sherman said quietly, "No, I don't think so."

"You don't think so, or you know so?" I asked.

He straightened his shoulders. "I know so."

"You didn't leave your post for lunch or anything else?" I asked.

"Mrs. Sherman packs a lunch for me every morning, and I eat it behind the ticket hall desk between trains. The first time I left the station would have been for supper after seven o'clock," he said.

Well after Mr. Eccles made his second speech of the day to the Blackthorn Park staff.

"Thank you, Captain Sherman," I breathed. "Thank you."

He frowned. "What does it mean?"

"That Mr. Eccles, who was supposed to have been in meetings in London all day, no longer has an alibi. I just have to figure out how he managed it."

"Managed what exactly?" the stationmaster asked sternly.

"To appear to take the train from Benstead to London on Monday evening but actually stay in Benstead the entire night."

I heard the low chug of a train approaching as Captain Sherman said, "That's easy enough, Miss. The 18:32 is a stopping service, and it always goes through Houghton Station. That's not three miles' walk from here, which isn't too much bother for a man in good health, is it? He could have gotten off and retraced his steps. Here, come with me."

With a glance at the billowing plume from the approaching train, he dipped into the ticket hall, went behind the counter, and picked up the telephone.

"Houghton Station, please," he said, his eyes cutting over to the platform and then to me. After a moment, he straightened. "Mr. Guthrie? It's Captain Sherman from Benstead Station. Yes, I did see the special train coming through. Yes, it is about to pull in.

"Mr. Guthrie, please," said Captain Sherman, letting his exasperation show. "Did anyone alight at Houghton Station from your 18:45 train to London on Monday? No, I don't need to know who boarded. Did anyone alight?" He listened carefully and then nodded. "What did he look like? Did he? And did you happen to see him again yesterday on your 9:15 train to London? You did? Did he now? Thank you, Mr. Guthrie. You are a credit to the profession."

Captain Sherman turned to me. "The stationmaster for Houghton says that appparently only one person left the London train there on Monday night. A tall, barrel-chested man with very red cheeks and blond hair."

"Mr. Eccles," I said.

Captain Sherman nodded. "Mr. Guthrie says that a man of that description also boarded the train to Benstead on Tuesday morning. Mr. Guthrie might not have remembered it except that apparently this was the same man who left the London train yesterday morning. Only this time he stopped to use the station's telephone for some time. Mr. Guthrie then saw him return to the station to use the telephone again around half past three before walking out of the station again and turning in the direction of Blackthorn Park."

So that was how he'd done it. Just like Dr. Jamison alighting a station before Benstead and walking home to avoid being seen after his visit to the fleshpots of London, Mr. Eccles had boarded the London train at Benstead Station the previous morning to make it look as though he'd left the village. However, he'd disembarked one station up the line and set about his plan to kill Mr. Porter on foot before placing a telephone call to learn from Mr. Tyson of Mr. Porter's death that afternoon. After that, all that was left was for him to wait the duration of a train journey before returning to Blackthorn Park and maintaining the fiction that he'd only just arrived from London.

The sound of a train pulling into the platform pulled Captain Sherman's attention away. "I really must go," he said, edging toward the door of the ticket hall.

"Evelyne?"

Over my shoulder, I saw David had come into the station.

"You were gone so long, I parked the—"

"I've figured out how Eccles did it," I cut him off. "He must have realized that Sir Nigel was onto him and so, on Monday evening, he left Blackthorn Park and boarded his usual train to London from Benstead Station. I think he handed both his ticket to London and his ticket back to Benstead Station to the inspector so that man accidentally punched them both. Then he alighted at Houghton Station, one up the line from here. He doubled back to Blackthorn Park and made camp to wait until he thought it was quiet enough to subdue and shoot Sir Nigel. Then he returned to his camp, waited until the next morning, and reboarded the train at Houghton Station. He told us that he keeps a change of clothes in his office, so he could have made it look like he had arrived like usual, fresh from a night in London."

"What about Mr. Porter?" asked David.

"He repeats his trick," I said. "Mr. Porter makes the mistake of telling Mr. Eccles without realizing it that he plans to expose Mr. Eccles, so Mr. Eccles tells us that he has to catch a train to return to London for meetings in Whitehall. Who better to vouch for you and your alibi than the investigators working on the case?"

"Good point," said David.

"This time, Mr. Eccles boards the 9:02 train and disembarks at Houghton Station at 9:15. The stationmaster there said he used the telephone. Mr. Eccles gave us his home telephone exchange, Hunter 5547, but told us that it was his office."

David lifted his chin, understanding clearly dawning on him. "His wife. She's been playing at being his secretary."

"Which would allow him to string us along this entire time," I said, speaking faster. Everything was clicking into place now, and I could see the whole nasty plot before me. "After he warns his wife, he telephones Mr. Porter and arranges a meeting at the equipment sheds to talk. Mr. Porter was just arrogant enough to think that he could handle this on his own."

"And he didn't know at the time that Eccles was a killer," David pointed out.

"Precisely. So Mr. Eccles crosses the countryside to Blackthorn Park and waits at his camp again because he doesn't hold keys to the equipment shed. At the appointed time, he persuades Mr. Porter to unlock the shed and kills him. Then he retreats to the woods until something—perhaps Constable Lee searching the woods—startles him into action. He smashes the hypodermic needles, leaves the key to Sir Nigel's desk, and flees the campsite. However, he also knows that he can't pretend that he had no knowledge of Mr. Porter's death because I left a message for him. He decides to return to Houghton Station and telephone Mr. Tyson in order to receive news of the death and give him a reason to pretend as though he's just rushed down from London on the first train he could catch.

"His story that he was pushed off the road by a convoy of vehicles after leaving the station neatly accounts for all of the mud he must have picked up crossing the countryside," said David.

"I think you're right," I agreed, but I'd lost my partner's attention as his eyes drifted to something over my shoulder. I turned as a group of men in dark gray suits walked into the ticket hall from the platform. In the center of them stood Mr. Fletcher, and next to him was Winston Churchill.

Of course my first official arrest as an SIU agent would be in front of the prime minister and my boss.

However, as I turned back to my partner, I spotted something else. Mr. Eccles, striding into the ticket hall.

FORTY-TWO

Mr. Eccles," I said, calm as I could. The last thing I wanted to do was scare the man into running.

There was a hitch in the murderer's step as he looked over at me.

"Miss Redfern, what are you doing here?" he asked. "You're not authorized to be here."

"Mr. Eccles," I repeated, "we must speak with you."

Something in the man's face shifted, and he whipped around, seeking the door. However, David was now standing in front of it, blocking his way.

"If you will just come with us," I started.

"Not a chance in Hell," the murderer ground out.

David lunged, his fingers brushing the fabric of Mr. Eccles's suit, but Mr. Eccles was just far enough away that he slipped from David's grasp and broke into a sprint through the ticket hall. The men who had just entered from the platform, including—Lord help me—the prime minister, dove away as Mr. Eccles plowed through them, cleared the platform door, and disappeared out of view.

"David!" I shouted, breaking into a sprint of my own.

David made a low sound in the back of his throat and took off after me.

I pushed past the dignitaries, praying I hadn't just knocked Mr. Churchill or Mr. Fletcher to the ground, but I couldn't stop to apologize. Instead, I focused on the pounding of my shoes against the concrete of the platform, Mr. Eccles in my sights.

I could not lose him.

"Stop!" I shouted as I ran.

"Stop, Eccles!" David called out.

Mr. Eccles did not stop. Instead, he reached the end of the platform and hopped over the little gate there, dropping onto the soft grass next to the train tracks.

"Bloody Hell," David ground out.

"Why do they always try to run?" I gasped.

David reached the end of the platform first and made his jump, followed by me. My feet hit the ground hard but true, and in a split second I was running again.

Ahead of us, Mr. Eccles angled himself so that he ran down the verge and onto the train tracks. I thought he might continue on in that manner, but after a moment he again cut across to the tree line of the woods.

"We're going to lose him," I shouted.

"You keep going, I'll go in behind him and try to cut him off," said David.

I pumped my arms harder, leaping over the rails and diving into the trees. The change from light to dark pulled me up and set me blinking for a moment, and as my eyes adjusted, I did my best to listen. I could hear David moving through the brush behind me . . .

I heard the whistle of foliage being whipped through the air ahead, and I set off again. I was slower now, needing to duck and dodge around the trees, but I thought from the sounds ahead I was closing in.

That is, until a shot rang out through the woods.

I dove behind a tree as birds exploded into the sky.

Another shot hit a tree about three feet away from where I was hiding, sending a shower of bark splinters raining down on me.

"Don't move!" Mr. Eccles shouted.

"We know what you did," I called back. "Killing me won't make any difference. If we figured it out, someone else can too."

"I don't know what you're talking about," he shouted.

I had to scoff at that. "If that was really true, you wouldn't be trying to shoot a hole in my best suit. Why did you do it, Eccles?"

An uneasy silence settled over the woods.

"Do you want to know what I think?" I shouted. "I think that it was all about money. I think you found yourself in a unique position. Your father-in-law owns a business that made something Blackthorn Park needed a great deal of. Boiled sweets used as timing devices? Think of all of the bombs that the SOE might need in this war. And so you put together the contract. Your father-in-law probably arranged for you to receive a nice little payment for that."

"You don't know what you're talking about," he bit out.

I shrugged, even though he couldn't see me. "A big government contract like that, anyone might be tempted to cut themselves in. It seems as though it worked for a little while too. For months, Longfellow & Son managed to supply Blackthorn Park with the boiled sweets it needed for its various devices. They worked so well, Mr. Hartley even figured out a way to work a sugar plate into the anti-handling device on the barnacle bombs."

I edged a little bit along the tree, fighting to keep my voice steady as I shouted, "But then something changed, didn't it? Suddenly, the sugar plates weren't breaking predictably any longer. Even the small-batch shipment of boiled sweets sent on in September didn't dissolve at a consistent rate."

I held my breath and took another step, exhaling only when I didn't find myself with a bullet through me.

"No one noticed at first," I continued. "The Longfellow & Son products must have visually looked the same as what had been sent previously or the women in the manufacturing barn would have raised the alarm. But something was wrong with the sweets.

"Maybe you didn't even know what had happened until you saw Sir Nigel behaving suspiciously. He'd heard that one of the barnacle bombs had spontaneously exploded during a test. He didn't believe it at first because the devices had been rigorously tested at Blackthorn Park before the batch was made for external testing, but Sir Nigel was, if nothing else, a man of science. He had to verify what was going on, and the more he dug the more suspicious he became that the problem originated at Blackthorn Park. Two weeks ago, he went to another facility to figure out what was the matter."

Out of the corner of my eye, I saw a flash of light gray. David was trying to creep up and around where Mr. Eccles was shooting at me. I knew I had to keep Mr. Eccles occupied and distracted to give my partner any chance.

"I think Sir Nigel discovered that the sugar sheets were the culprits during that round of testing he did off-site. He must have remembered the issues with the boiled sweets in the timing devices made by the manufacturing barn in September. He thought that someone was sabotaging his work. He didn't trust his staff any longer, but you told me yourself that you aren't staff. You spend half of your time in London. You don't even live in the village of Benstead.

"I think Sir Nigel confided in you that someone was tampering with his inventions. You reassured him that you would look into it quietly so that it didn't jeopardize the upcoming demonstration. You thought that your promises would satisfy him, but he kept digging behind your back."

"He wouldn't leave well enough alone," snarled Mr. Eccles. "He still wanted to make a report to Baker Street directly even though I told him it could cost Blackthorn Park *everything*."

I stiffened. It was the first time that he'd said anything of significance, and I hoped it would prove to be the crack that might just let me in.

"What did you do?" I called out.

"I made an anonymous report last Thursday that there might be small-scale thefts going on at Blackthorn Park," he said. "Something that could be brushed off, or, if Baker Street did send someone around to look, dismissed as recklessness by the staff because there was nothing to find. It should have been enough, but then on Monday Sir Nigel called me into his office. He said he'd been looking at all of the companies that supply materials for the barnacle bombs. Going through the files with a fine-tooth comb."

"And you knew that if he began asking Mr. Porter where he'd found these companies, Mr. Porter would tell Sir Nigel that some of them were your suggestions," I said. "Sir Nigel was too close to figuring out your connection to Longfellow & Son, so you decided to return that night and kill him."

My accusation was met with silence.

"Knowing that he often worked late, you arrived at Blackthorn Park with two train tickets from London Waterloo to Benstead Station in your pocket, one for your journey here and one for a return journey Tuesday morning. Then you went about your usual day on Monday, including leaving on your usual train. Only instead of going all the way home, you doubled back on yourself to a camp you'd set up during one of your walks," I said.

I risked peeking a little around the tree, but I couldn't see anything. Where was David?

"You waited until it was dark and things seemed quiet on the grounds, and then you went to Sir Nigel's office," I said. "You probably thought that if it looked like a suicide, no one would think to ask questions about what Sir Nigel had been looking into before he died. You restrained him, sedated him, and put his service revolver into his hand."

At that moment, another bird flew through the trees, and another deafening shot rang out, sending adrenaline surging through me.

Calm, I told myself. *Calm.*

"You pulled the trigger, and then you hid in the cupboard next to the east wing's servants' stairs. While everyone was gathered around the body in Sir Nigel's office, you slipped down the stairs and fled the house, camping in the woods until the next morning when you could slip into your office to change so you could reappear as though you'd just arrived. You thought you'd figured it all out."

He had been so smug, offering to help David and me in our investigation. Saying all of the right things.

"You have it all wrong. I was at home," Mr. Eccles insisted. "Baker Street rang me to tell me about Sir Nigel's death. You can ask them."

"I think they did, but I don't think that it was you who picked up. Your wife took the call. I will admit, it was clever to make your wife pose as your secretary and your answering service as you needed it. A harried secretary placing a call for her boss would hardly notice that your office and your home share a Hunter telephone exchange. It would be easy enough to give out one exchange in place of the other.

"You went on with your normal life, thinking it was all over until, unfortunately for you, Sir Nigel's death prompted Mr. Porter to go down the same route as Sir Nigel," I continued, wondering where David was. "That Longfellow & Son file is your connection to everything. And Mr. Porter, a proud man, would have remembered how hard you fought him to bring Longfellow & Son on in the spring. Did he threaten to expose you?"

"He wanted me gone!" shouted Mr. Eccles, breaking once again. "The imbecile actually thought he could run the place himself when he'd failed so miserably before I arrived!"

"And so you repeated your railway station trick, arranged to meet Mr. Porter, and killed him in the one place on the property that was isolated enough that you could have the time you needed, because you'd learned your lesson," I said.

"Porter was in my way," Mr. Eccles snarled.

"He has a wife and children. He didn't deserve to be killed—for what? Money?" I asked in disgust.

"It wasn't about money," Mr. Eccles spat. "It was about legacy. All my married life, Joan's family has looked down on me because I had to work—I had to *strive*—while they lived off the profits of a candy business built two generations ago. Her father would sit in his office and play at being a businessman, making deals that amounted to nothing and running Longfellow & Son into the ground. And I had to sit there and pretend that I didn't see it all happening, because the business paid for everything.

"But then the war happened, and my father-in-law's supply chains began to fail. He couldn't source vital ingredients as easily any longer. His profits were slumping, and all of his recklessness was beginning to catch up with him, just as his health failed him too.

"When I came to Blackthorn and learned about the need for unconventional materials, I put Longfellow & Son forward. I told my father-in-law that I would take care of everything. I stepped into the role of 'Son' in the company name as he once had, but I did it better. I was managing the company and working for Baker Street. I was doing everything, but I didn't mind because for the first time it didn't matter that Longfellow & Son supplemented my entire life. It was my effort and my money."

"What happened?" I asked.

"My father-in-law couldn't let things be," said Mr. Eccles, the bitterness clear in his voice. "He had to meddle. He began to order the factory to substitute things into the products to stretch our raw ingredients further. As he experimented, the consistency suffered, and the idiot didn't bother to separate out those trials. He shipped everything to Blackthorn as though nothing had happened.

"If it had just been candy we were making, it might not have been too bad, but in weapons, subtle changes can be deadly."

"France," I said.

"I didn't know that the sugar plates were now too delicate to use. There was no margin for error. The moment a commando extracted the metal plate, if he didn't do it perfectly, the casing would immediately crack and the device would explode," he said.

"And knowing that, you didn't warn anyone, even with the demonstration today." Just as Sir Nigel hadn't raised the alarm as soon as he'd received Major Richards's letter and made sure that all of the barnacle bombs were destroyed before they could have been used in the field. The arrogance of these men . . .

"It would have worked today. The engineers have been over everything," he insisted.

"The engineers wouldn't have known what to look for if I hadn't told them. What if someone had died today?"

"I couldn't say anything. You *must* see that," he said, his anger becoming something pathetic. "I would have lost my job. Longfellow & Son would have lost the contract. I couldn't let that happen."

"Your greed and your pride cost those men in France their lives, and it does not justify killing Sir Nigel and Mr. Porter," I said.

"They were in my way. I don't like things that are in my way."

There was a crash, then a shout from David as another shot rang out. I pushed off the tree and raced through the undergrowth in the direction of the sound. I saw Mr. Eccles and David locked in a tangle as they both wrestled for the gun. I rounded the two of them and when Mr. Eccles reared back, I leapt onto him. I managed to lock my arms around Mr. Eccles's neck, squeezing tight as he bucked.

The gun went off again, but I hung on as David untangled his limbs from the other man's.

"Evelyne, lean back!" he shouted.

I did, and David pulled back his fist and punched Mr. Eccles clean across the jaw. The man's body went limp, and his weight crashed painfully on top of me.

"Get him off!" I shoved at Mr. Eccles.

David looped an arm under Mr. Eccles's shoulder and hauled him to the side before dumping him in a heap. When he glanced back at me, his expression fell into a hard line. "He hit you."

I looked down. Sure enough, blood was trailing down my left calf.

The pain crashed down on me all at once, and I gritted my teeth. "It stings."

He crouched and pulled up the hem of my skirt a little to look at the wound.

"How bad is it?" I asked.

He began to shake his head. "Do you want the good news or the bad news?"

"The good news. Why would anyone want the bad news first?"

"You'll live. It looks like it grazed you," he said.

"It doesn't feel like it grazed me," I grumbled, the pain beginning to dull to a throb.

"What does it feel like?" he asked.

"It feels like I've been bloody shot! What's the bad news?"

"There is going to be an absolute mountain of paperwork for you to do when we return to London because Mrs. White is going to want to know why one of her newest agents is already out of commission."

I dropped my head back and groaned. "You're right. That is very bad news indeed."

FORTY-THREE

David used his and Mr. Eccles's neckties to bind the man's arms and legs and hauled Mr. Eccles, still unconscious, over his shoulder to carry him back to Benstead Station. I grumpily followed slowly behind, limping my way out of the woods.

When we arrived at the station, there was no sign of any dignitaries, only Captain Sherman, looking more than a little stunned, and Constable Lee, who seemed genuinely disappointed to have missed the action.

"I telephoned the police when you two went racing off," explained Captain Sherman.

"So it was Mr. Eccles this entire time?" asked Constable Lee.

"Who did you want it to be?" I asked, grimacing.

"I thought that it might be some sort of German spy," Constable Lee admitted.

"Only in radio dramas, Constable. This was a case of old-fashioned greed. Now, will you please telephone Dr. Morrison and tell him that I'm in desperate need of medical attention?"

David dumped Mr. Eccles's body onto a bench and shot me a look that told me he believed I was being dramatic. Not that I cared what he thought. He wasn't the one who had just been shot.

Things moved rather quickly after that. Constable Lee handcuffed

Mr. Eccles, which gave him no end of pleasure, and helped David bundle him into the car while Dr. Morrison took one look at me and insisted I return to his surgery.

"You seem to be taking being shot rather well, all things considered," said Dr. Morrison while he swabbed my wound as I sat on his examination table.

"It's a hazard of the job, I suppose," I said, clutching at the edge of the table.

"Does this happen to you on a regular basis?" he asked.

"I don't know. This is only my second go-round with solving a murder," I said.

"How is your solve rate?" he asked, threading a wicked-looking needle.

"Two for two," I said.

"Impressive," he said. "Perhaps you'll make it three for three at some point."

"Perhaps," I gritted out.

"It's going to be very quiet around Benstead without you and Mr. Poole. Now, hold still, Miss Redfern. This is going to hurt."

And hurt it bloody well did.

———————————

Dr. Morrison showed me a great deal of grace considering the various names I called him as he stitched up my wound. Then he gave me some painkillers, which helped take the edge off. I asked him whether there was any chance he could give me something stronger like whiskey or morphine, but he simply laughed and said that medical practice had come a long way since those days.

I told him he was no fun, and he merely nodded in acceptance.

He drove me back to Blackthorn Park and dropped me at the front door. Then he reached into the back of the car and pulled out a walking stick.

"It's only temporary, but it will help keep you from hurting yourself by putting too much weight on it," Dr. Morrison explained.

I nodded, and he went around to open the passenger door for me.

Somewhere in the direction of the demonstration fields, a blast went off.

"I hope that was intentional," he said.

"From what I understand, it usually is," I said, hoping very much that whoever had set that device off had carefully checked to ensure that none of Longfellow & Son's faulty parts were in it.

The front door opened, and Jane stuck her head out. "Miss Redfern—" She stopped when she saw my walking stick. "What happened?"

"Nothing," I said, grimacing as I put my weight on my injured leg.

Jane swallowed. "It doesn't look like nothing."

"Have you seen my partner, by any chance?" I asked. "Tall, brown hair, probably looking rather guilty at the moment because I'm the one who was shot in the leg?"

"Actually, Mr. Poole asked me to keep an eye out for you. He and another man are waiting for you in the library," she said.

I nodded and slowly made my way into the house.

"That's right, take it steady," said Dr. Morrison from behind me.

"Don't worry, I won't be entering any footraces anytime soon," I grumbled.

At the library door, I paused to knock. There was a slight shuffling around and David opened the door.

"You're alive," he said, but I could tell from the way he stared at my leg that he really was relieved to see me.

"Just," I said. "I currently have more stitches in my leg than it will take to patch the bullet hole in my skirt."

"And you have a new accessory," he said, nodding to my stick, before addressing Dr. Morrison. "Thank you for running her back."

"It's my pleasure. If you two ever find yourselves in this part of the world again, I hope you'll call in on me."

"Perhaps without a double murder next time," I said.

"One can only hope." Dr. Morrison smiled, tipped his hat, and left.

"How are you really?" asked David in a low voice.

"I'm fine," I said. "Really, I am. Mostly, I'm annoyed that Mr. Eccles managed to hit me at all. It's a good thing he's a rotten shot."

He nodded as though he understood this sentiment perfectly. "I'm glad of it."

There was a softness in his voice that told me that for all of the joking and teasing, he meant it, and I believed him.

"Are you going to invite me in?" I asked, lifting my chin a little.

David raised his brows and then stepped back.

As I hobbled into the room, I was not entirely surprised to see Mr. Fletcher sitting on one of the sofas.

"Miss Redfern," he said, standing. "It is a pleasure to see you, as always."

"Good morning," I said, easing myself down onto the sofa.

"I hardly recognized you as you raced by me in the railway station. Mr. Poole has been filling me in on your dramatic chase with admirable detail," he said.

"Where is the prime minister?" I asked quickly.

"He is on the testing field right now. And before you ask, all of the devices being shown today passed the necessary checks," said Mr. Fletcher.

I exhaled in relief. "Then there is no chance that anyone might be harmed?"

"Your concern is admirable. Mr. Churchill and the other visitors are at a safe distance and behind a blast screen as well," he said.

"What does Mr. Churchill think of all of this?" I said.

Mr. Fletcher took a moment to pluck a bit of fluff off his gray-striped trousers. "He does not know, and he won't be made aware of it. At least not directly."

"Then he doesn't know why a mad woman nearly knocked him over in a small village railway station?" I asked.

"I told him you are one of mine, so I suspect he knows you have your reasons," said Mr. Fletcher with a laugh. "There will be a report written, but I would not be surprised if it becomes distilled into a memo that's placed toward the bottom of the pile of many documents Mr. Churchill receives every day."

"What will happen to Mr. Eccles?" asked David.

"I think it is safe to say that he'll pay dearly for his treason," said Mr. Fletcher.

"Mr. Fletcher, did you know that something more nefarious was happening at Blackthorn Park when I was first sent out here undercover?" I asked.

"No, Miss Redfern," he said with a little smile, "although I can understand, given the way you were recruited, why you might not take my word at face value. Mrs. White and I really did agree that investigating a simple case of theft might be the best way for you to cut your teeth in the field, and for Mr. Poole to have his first experience as a handler."

David rubbed the back of his neck the way he did whenever he was feeling sheepish. "I didn't do a particularly good job with the remote part of that assignment."

"No, you didn't," said Mr. Fletcher with some amusement. "I suspect that your heart is still in the field, Mr. Poole."

David inclined his head.

"Good, I'm glad you agree, because we would like you two to continue working together. If you have no objections," said Mr. Fletcher.

I looked at David, wondering if he would say anything as he had the last time this conversation had come up. Instead, he kept his lips resolutely sealed.

"We will, naturally, need some time for Miss Redfern to heal. Miss Redfern, you will join us on Gosfield Street during your convalescence. Mr. Poole, I expect there is some small job Mrs. White may be able to find for you in the meantime," said Mr. Fletcher.

"Thank you," David and I said in unison.

Mr. Fletcher rose and smiled. "Now, I should return to my party. The next time Mrs. White tells me that there is something vital that our agents must have in the field, I want to know what it is that I'm buying."

David and I watched Mr. Fletcher until the door shut.

"Well," I said, breaking the silence left by his absence. "It looks like we'll be seeing a great deal more of one another."

"So it would seem," said David with a little smile, his hands folded behind his back.

I looked down, a sudden awkwardness overcoming me.

"Will you go back to Cornwall to visit your aunt and uncle before your next mission?" I asked rather gloomily. I found that I didn't *like* the idea of parting ways and not seeing one another for what could be weeks while my damned leg healed.

"I might. It depends on Mrs. White," he said.

"Of course," I said. "I suppose we'll need to make our report in London as well."

He nodded. "That is usually the way of it."

"And we'll have to drive back," I said.

"Unless you want to take the train," he said.

"I think I've had rather enough of Benstead Station for one day. Besides," I said, glancing down at my leg, "I'm not certain I'm fit to be seen at the moment."

"I think your case is still on the back seat of the car."

"Goodness! I completely forgot about the things Miss Summers sent me. I haven't even had the chance to open them up."

He laughed. "Come on then. Let's get your things so you can change. Then, after I settle my bill at the Hand and Flower, I'll run you home."

"Thank you," I said, already looking forward to seeing Moira, Mrs. Jenkins, and the rest of the ragtag little family we'd made at Bina Gardens.

"If you're nice to me, I might even let you try to convince me to read a Margery Allingham novel," said David.

I straightened my shoulders, on surer ground now. "I will have you know, David Poole, that Albert Campion is a fine detective . . ."

FORTY-FOUR

In the end, I didn't end up changing, because I didn't want to ruin any more clothing until my wound stopped seeping blood.

That is why, when I arrived back in London, I put my much-neglected case down in my room and promptly neglected it for another week. Instead of unpacking, I settled into a routine of sorts. I would wake up, dress my wound, dress myself, and then make my way to the Special Investigations Unit's HQ on Gosfield Street. There, I would sit at a desk and pore over agent reports, learning a great deal about what was expected from SIU agents and consulting on anything related to French missions due to my knowledge from a childhood spent there. Occasionally, Miss Summers would drop a cup of tea and a biscuit at my right hand, and at one o'clock the two of us would go for lunch. By five o'clock, I would pack up my handbag and leave for home.

There was something satisfying about the dullness of the routine, broken up only by little things like the arrival of a postcard from Plymouth that read "I am here. —A. G." The predictability was precisely what I needed while I was healing. However, I was disappointed not to see David. Right after we told a stone-faced Mrs. White about our adventures in Sussex, she sent him off somewhere and he had yet to resurface. I kept an eye out for any correspondence or reports from him, but nothing crossed my desk.

I distracted myself by spending all of my free time with Moira. She didn't ask any questions about where I'd been or why I'd returned with what was clearly a bullet wound that I tried to pass off as a cycling injury.

"You will tell me when you are ready," was all that she said, which managed to make me feel immensely grateful and deeply guilty at the same time.

For the first time in our friendship, we were talking about everything but what really mattered, and I hated it. However, I did my best to be the bright and engaging friend I knew I could be on my very best days. She went back to auditioning with a new vigor, and when she soon landed a role in a proper feature-length film, I insisted on celebrating.

"It's just a small role," she told Jocelyn, our journalist friend who lived in the room opposite ours in Mrs. Jenkins's, and me one night as we all drank whiskey to celebrate Jocelyn's return.

"It's a film role," I said firmly.

"A feature," said Jocelyn.

"It's what you've always wanted," I said, lifting my glass to her.

It was gratifying to see Moira, unflappable in many things, blush.

"Thank you," she said. "It's good to have you home, Evie."

And I could tell she really meant it.

———

Moira was out of our room at a meeting with her agent when I returned home from work one evening and decided that I finally needed to unpack. Careful of my leg, I lifted my neglected suitcase onto my bed and undid the clasps. It fell open, my clothes threatening to spill out. On top of my things was a copy of James M. Cain's *The Postman Always Rings Twice*. I blushed a little, remembering my impulsive request to Miss Summers for a copy of the book David had recommended to me.

I lifted it to look at the cover and saw that there was something sticking out of it. I opened the book and found an envelope inside and a note written in Moira's handwriting.

This came for you while you were away.

—M

I looked at the envelope. The address was typewritten to "Miss Evelyne Redfern"—all normal there—but what wasn't normal were the stamps. They were Portuguese.

I couldn't think of a single person I knew in Portugal. The country had remained neutral during the war and had thus already become one of the last escape routes from Europe for people trying to flee from the swift progress of the German military across Europe. The newspapers said that Lisbon had become something of a way station for people desperately using every connection they had to leave for Britain, America, or anywhere they thought they might finally be safe.

I worked my index finger under the flap of the envelope and tore open the top. When I pulled out a piece of paper, a key fell out onto the desk. I picked it up and turned it back and forth. There was nothing particularly unusual about it—it was just a little silver key after all— but why would anyone send me a key?

I unfolded the paper and was further confounded when I found myself staring at a blank page.

"Positively vexing," I muttered to myself.

I squinted at the paper, then turned it over.

Nothing.

I held it up to the light.

Nothing.

I stuck it under my nose. It had the distinct smell of . . . ordinary writing paper.

Growing increasingly irritated, I stared at the blasted thing. There had to be some reason that someone posted me a letter with nothing written on it.

I frowned, an idea forming. One of my first classes at Beaulieu had been about sending messages. Ones that were hidden in plain sight.

I rummaged around in my handbag and pulled out the silver lighter I had taken to carrying with me since embarking on training.

I didn't smoke, much to the amusement of my many instructors who often resembled chimneys in the height of winter, but I had learned just how useful a reliable flame could be for an agent.

I sparked the lighter and, careful not to singe or ignite the paper, held it close enough that the heat thrown off by the flame would . . .

There it was.

I could see the faint lines of invisible ink begin to develop in the heat.

London Safe Deposit Company
Lower Regent Street
Box 5297

I stared at the handwriting for a moment. It had been a long time since I'd seen it, but I knew it instantly. It belonged to a man I'd heard neither hide nor hair from in years.

Sir Reginald Redfern.

My father.

ACKNOWLEDGMENTS

It has been such a joy revisiting the adventures of Evelyne Redfern—and David too! Although Evelyne and her cases are complete fiction, I enjoyed drawing on real aspects of history for inspiration. In the case of *Betrayal at Blackthorn Park*, this was The Firs, a requisitioned manor house in Buckinghamshire that was used by the Special Operations Executive for the development and testing of weapons. Although The Firs was never the site of a double murder (that I'm aware of), the house's fascinating and important history prompted me to play a game of "What if . . . ?," which is often the starting point for my books. The barnacle bombs central to this mystery too were pure fiction but based on a real-life device called a limpet mine. Although the sugar plates used in the anti-handling devices were also figments of my imagination, boiled sweets were used as timing devices in SOE-developed bombs because of how reliably they dissolved. (Naturally, any errors in engineering or chemistry are all mine.) If you would like to read more about The Firs, clandestine weapons, or the SOE, I highly recommend *Churchill's Ministry of Ungentlemanly Warfare: The Mavericks Who Plotted Hitler's Defeat* by Giles Milton, which is a good overview and a cracking read.

In terms of thanks, I must begin as always with my wonderful agent, Emily Sylvan Kim. I am forever amazed by how far we've come every time I write one of these acknowledgments. Thank you also to Ellen Brescia for always keeping the show on the road.

Thank you to my friends Alexis Anne, Lindsay Emory, Mary Chris Escobar, Alexandra Haughton, Laura von Holt, and Madeline Martin for their digital encouragement, and thank you to Mary Shannon for being my "colleague" during weekly writing sessions at the London Library.

Thank you to my editor, Madeline Houpt, and the rest of the team at Minotaur Books, including Kelley Ragland, Kayla Janas, Allison Zeigler, Gabriel Guma, David Rotstein, Alisa Trager, Susannah Noel, Diane Dilluvio, Carla Benton, Rachael Clements, Katy Robitzski, Isabella Narvaez, Maria Snelling, Emma Paige West, and Drew Kilman.

I am deeply grateful for my family. Justine, Mark, Mum, and Dad, your encouragement and enthusiasm over the years have meant the world to me. Thank you also to Diana for your unfailing kindness and support. I love you all.

And last but certainly not least, thank you to my wonderful husband (!) Arthur, who is always quick with a cup of tea and is never too busy to stop and work through a tricky plot hole. I cannot believe the years we've had, my love, and I cannot wait for the years to come.

ABOUT THE AUTHOR

Scott Bottles

Julia Kelly is the international bestselling author of historical novels about the extraordinary stories of the past. Her books have been translated into fourteen languages. She has also written historical romance. In addition to writing, she's been an Emmy-nominated producer, a journalist, a marketing professional, and (for one summer) a tea waitress. Julia called Los Angeles, Iowa, and New York City home before settling in London.